Tree-
House
Comix
Proudly
Presents

DOG MAN

WRITTEN AND ILLUSTRATED BY **DAV PILKEY**

AS GEORGE BEARD AND HAROLD HUTCHINS

WITH COLOR BY JOSE GARIBALDI

graphix

AN IMPRINT OF

SCHOLASTIC

FOR DAN, LEAH, ALEK, AND KYLE SANTAT

Library of Congress Control Number 2016932063

978-1-338-74103-2 (POB)
978-1-338-61194-6 (Library)

10 9 8 7 6 5 4   21 22 23 24 25

Printed in China   62
This edition first printing, August 2021

Edited by Anamika Bhatnagar
Book design by Dav Pilkey and Phil Falco
Color by Jose Garibaldi
Creative Director: Phil Falco
Publisher: David Saylor

DOG MAN

~~The~~ Behind the Scenes

One Time, George met Harold in kindergarten.

They became best friends and started making comics.

Their very first comic was a epic novella called:

Over the years, they made **Tons** of DOG Man comic books.

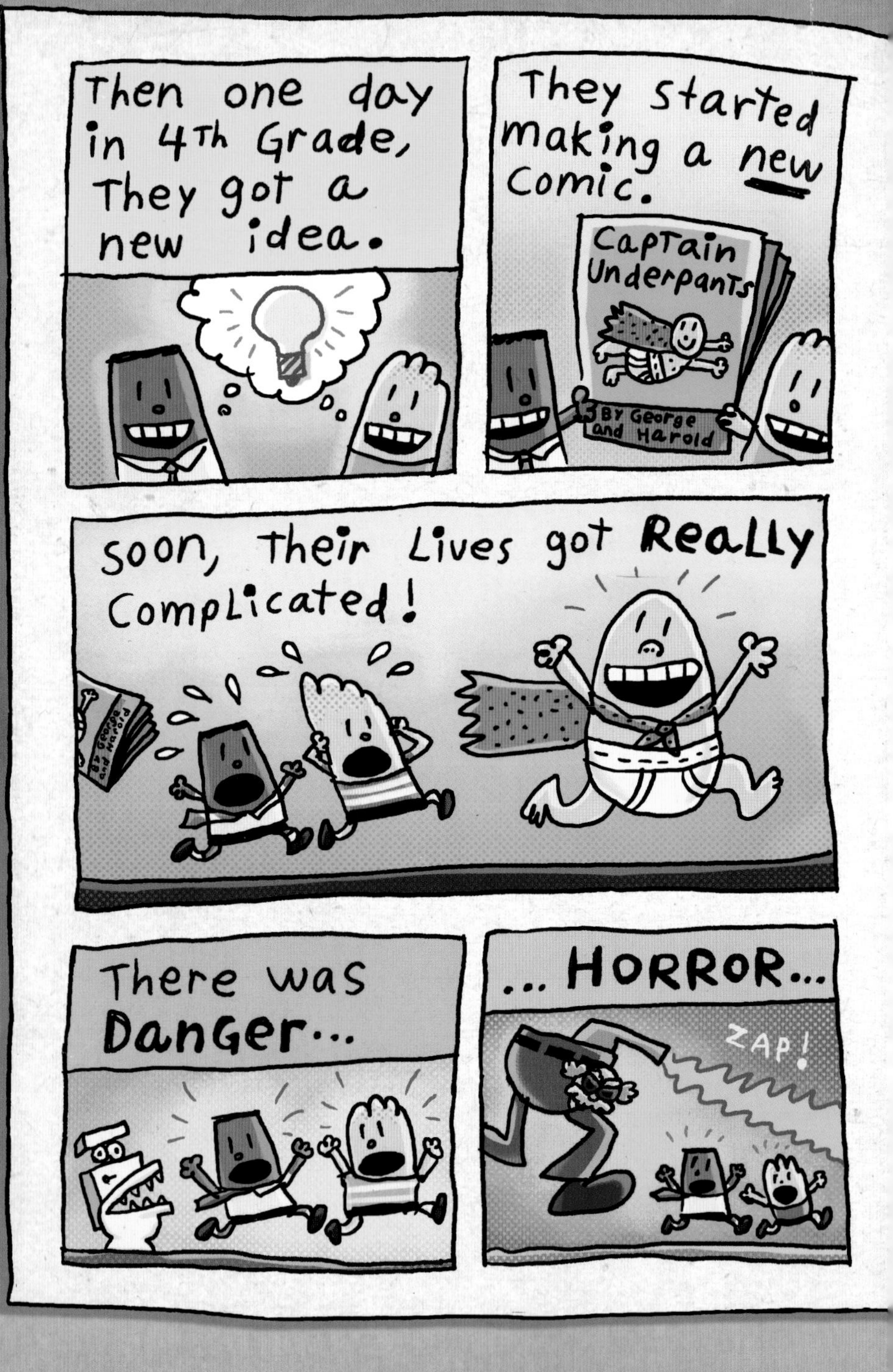
Then one day in 4Th Grade, They got a new idea.
They started making a new Comic.
Captain Underpants
By George and Harold
Soon, their Lives got ReaLLy CompLicated!
By George and Harold
There was DanGer...
... HORROR...
ZAP!

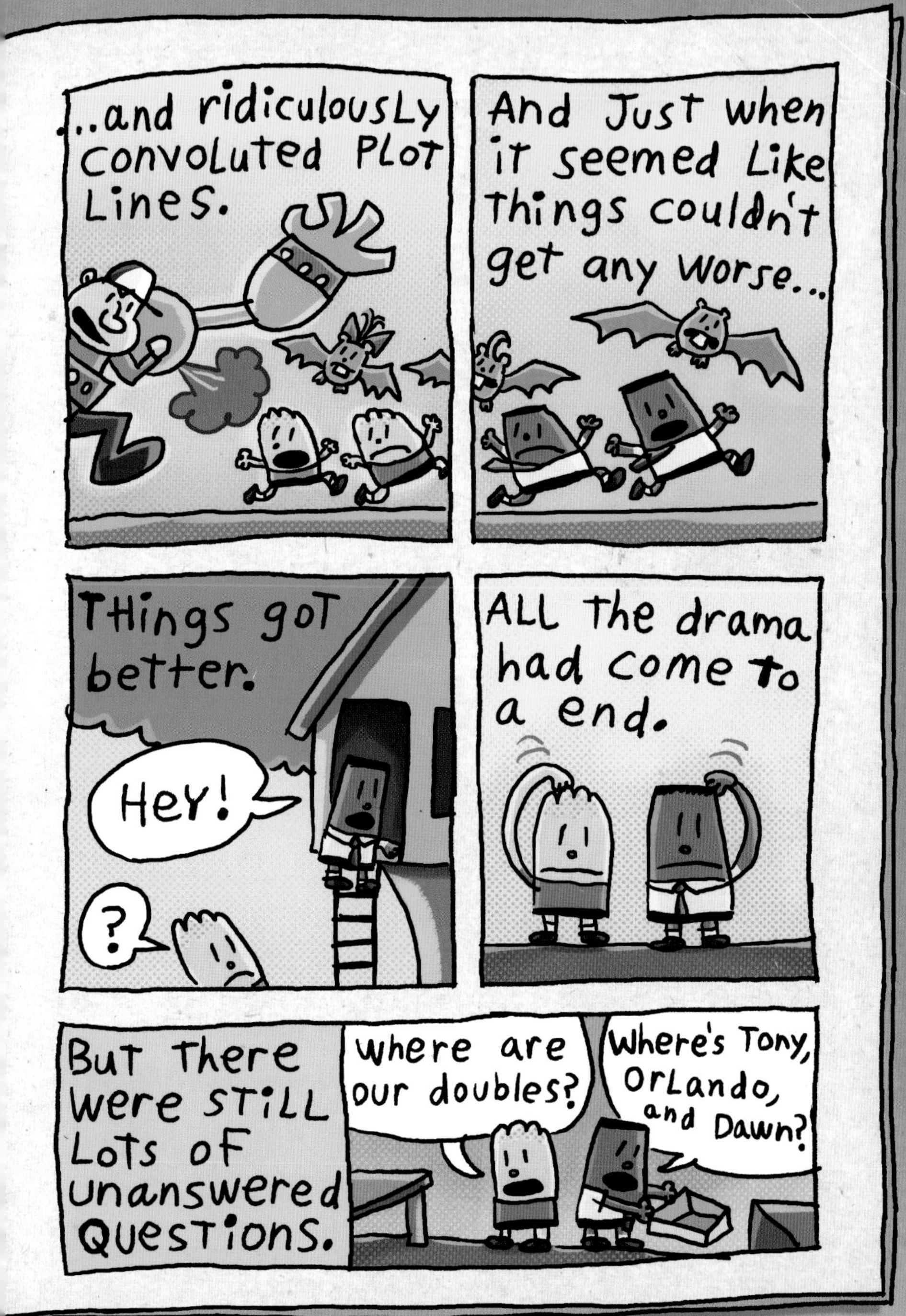
...and ridiculously convoluted plot lines.
And just when it seemed like things couldn't get any worse...
Things got better.
Hey!
?
All the drama had come to a end.
But there were still lots of unanswered questions.
Where are our doubles?
Where's Tony, Orlando, and Dawn?

George and Harold searched their tree house for clues...

...but soon, they got distracted.

Hey, Look!

aw, cool!

DOG MAN vs. Mecha-Flippy
George ~ Harold

It's a box full of ~~the~~ old Dog Man comics we made when we were kids.

Hey, I forgot all about these!!!

DOG MAN BIG Fight
rge and Harold

They read for hours

Ha Ha Ha Ha

I crack me up!

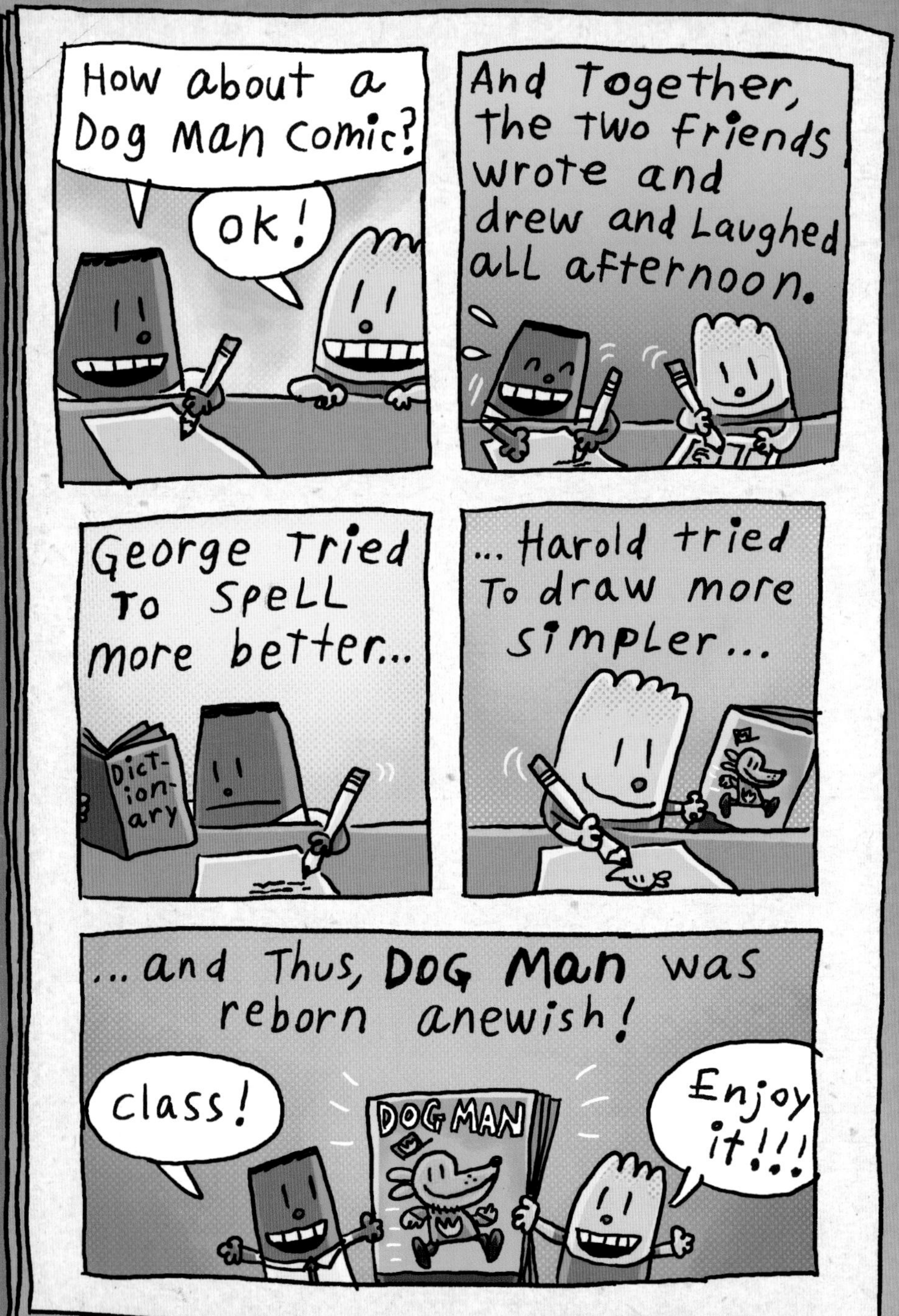
How about a Dog Man Comic?
ok!
And Together, the two friends wrote and drew and Laughed all afternoon.
George Tried To SpeLL more better...
Dict-ion-ary
... Harold tried To draw more simpLer...
... and Thus, DOG Man was reborn anewish!
Class!
DOG MAN
Enjoy it!!!

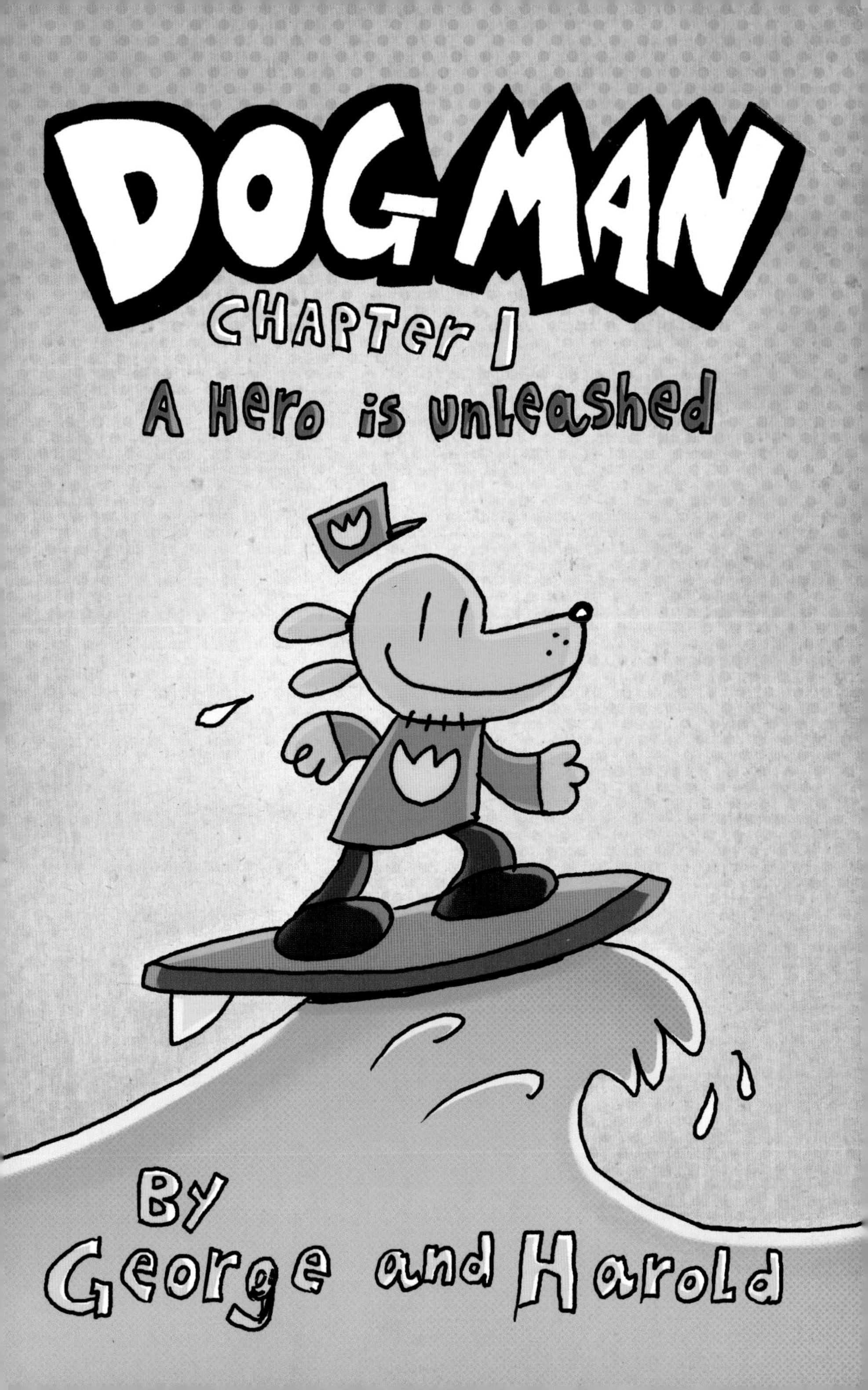
DOG-MAN
CHAPTER 1
A Hero is unleashed
By
George and Harold

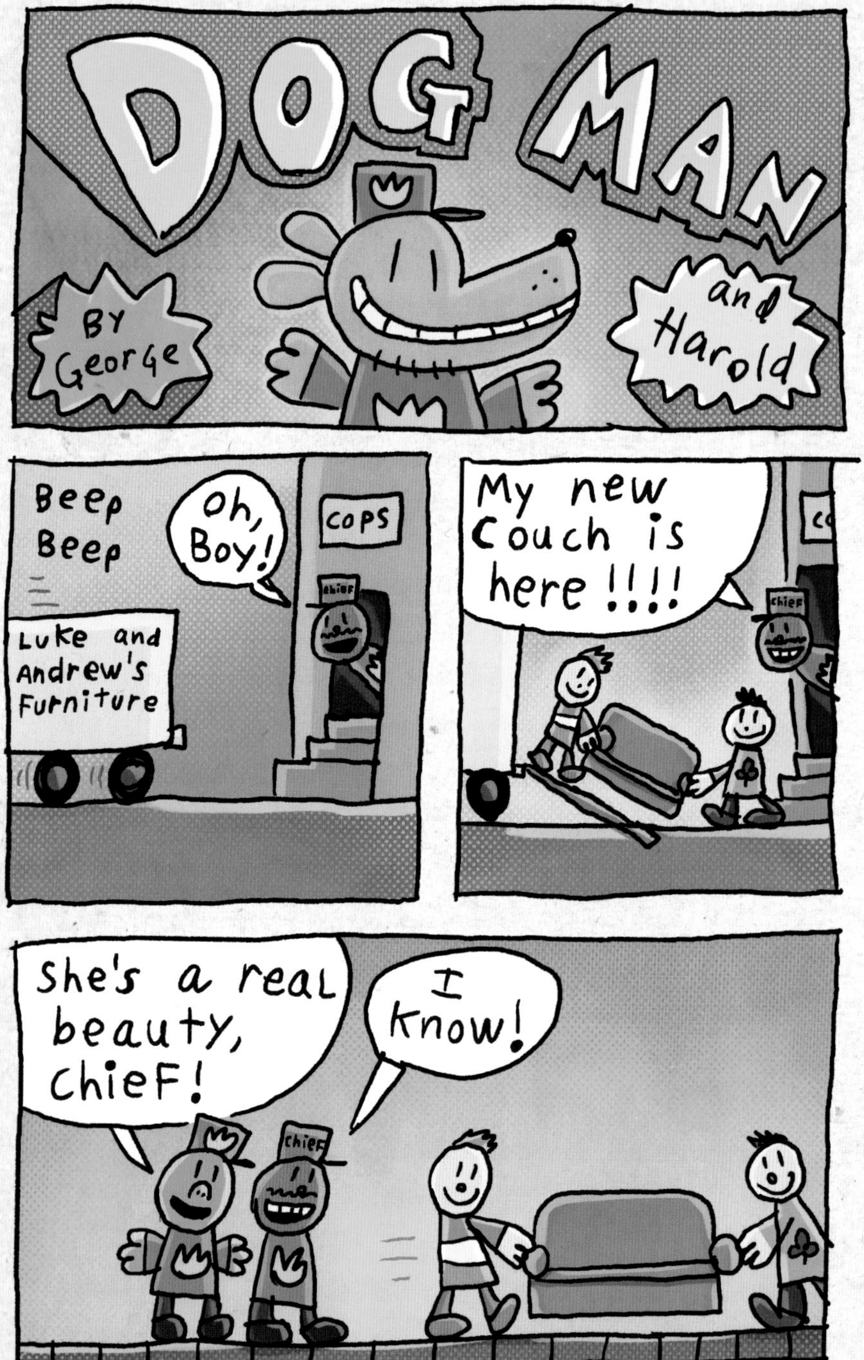

DOG MAN
BY George
and Harold
Beep Beep
Oh, Boy!
COPS
chief
Luke and Andrew's Furniture
My new Couch is here!!!!
chief
She's a real beauty, Chief!
I know!
chief

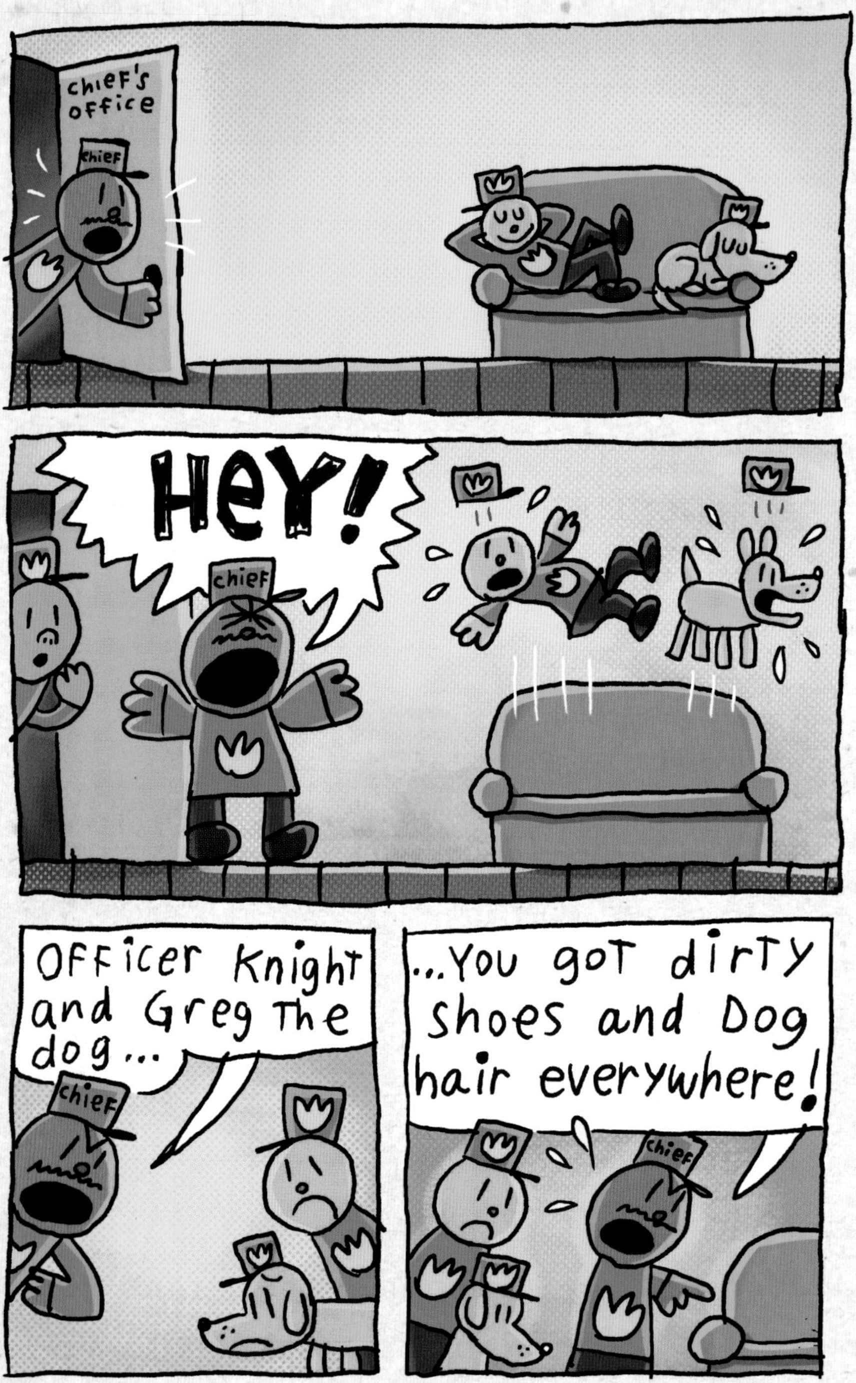
Chief's office
Chief
HEY!
chief
Officer Knight and Greg the dog...
chief
...You got dirty shoes and Dog hair everywhere!
chief

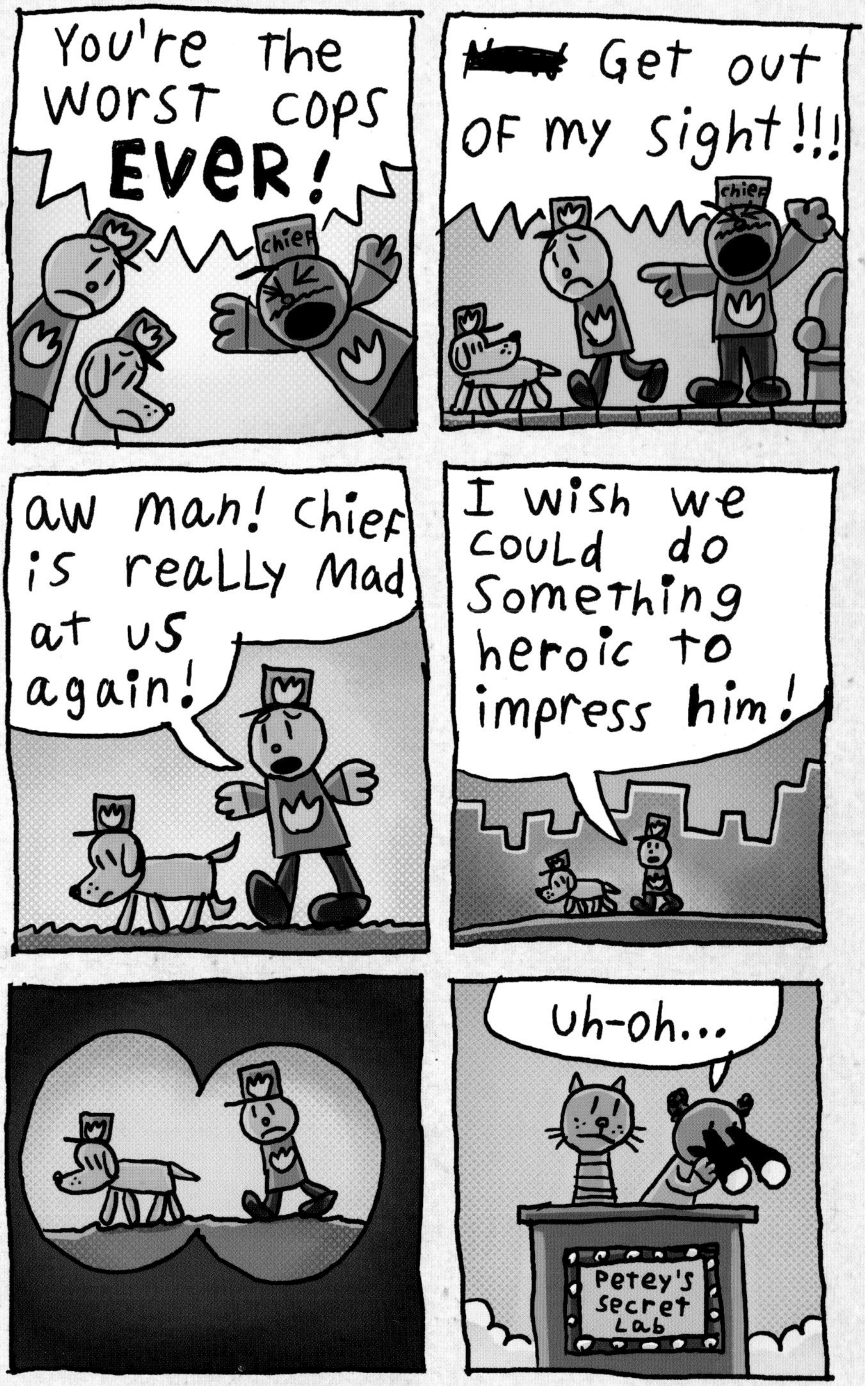
You're the worst cops EVER!
[redacted] Get out of my sight!!!
chief
aw man! chief is really Mad at us again!
I wish we could do Something heroic to impress him!
Uh-oh...
Petey's secret Lab

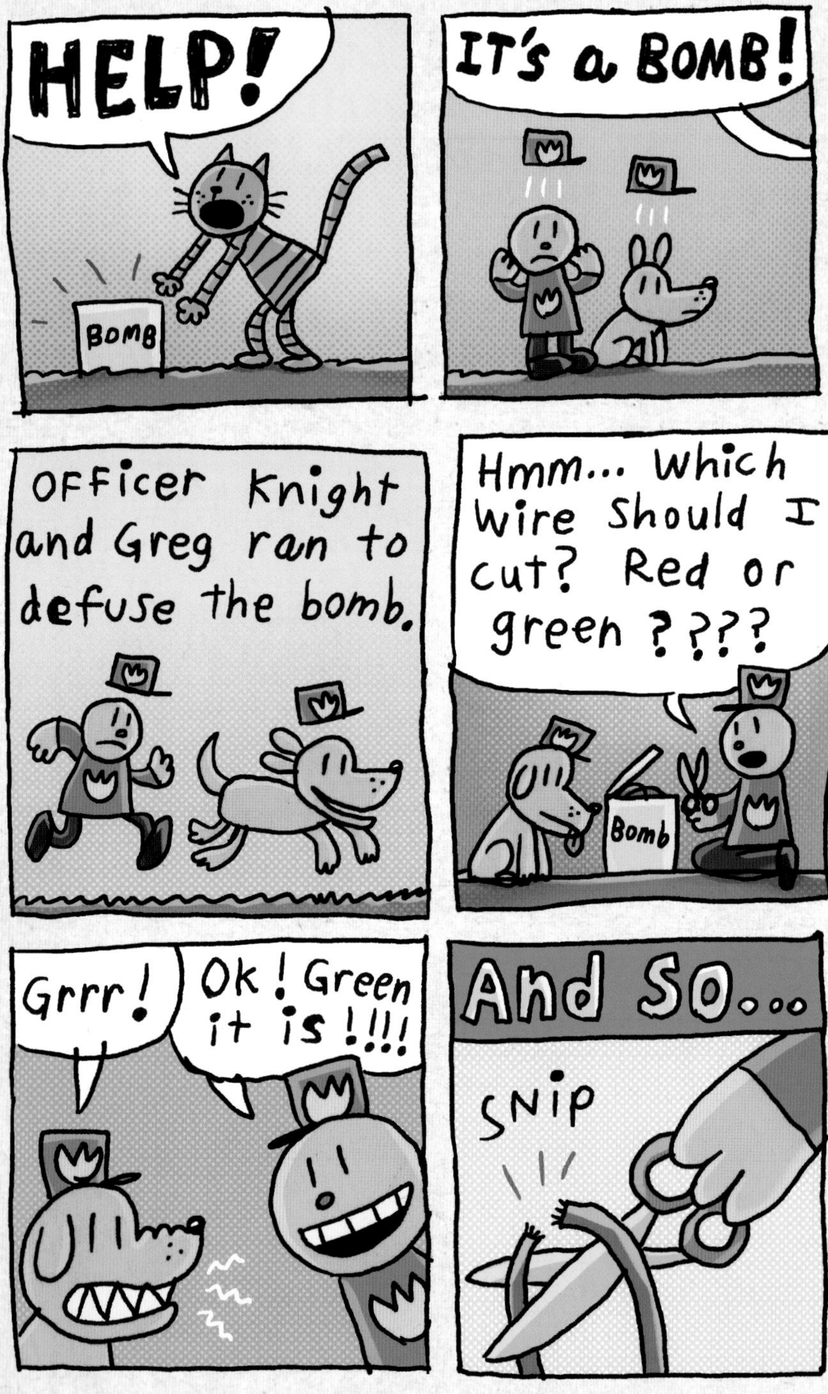
HELP!
BOMB
IT'S a BOMB!
Officer Knight and Greg ran to defuse the bomb.
Hmm... Which wire Should I cut? Red or green ????
Bomb
Grrr!
Ok! Green it is!!!!
And So...
SNIP

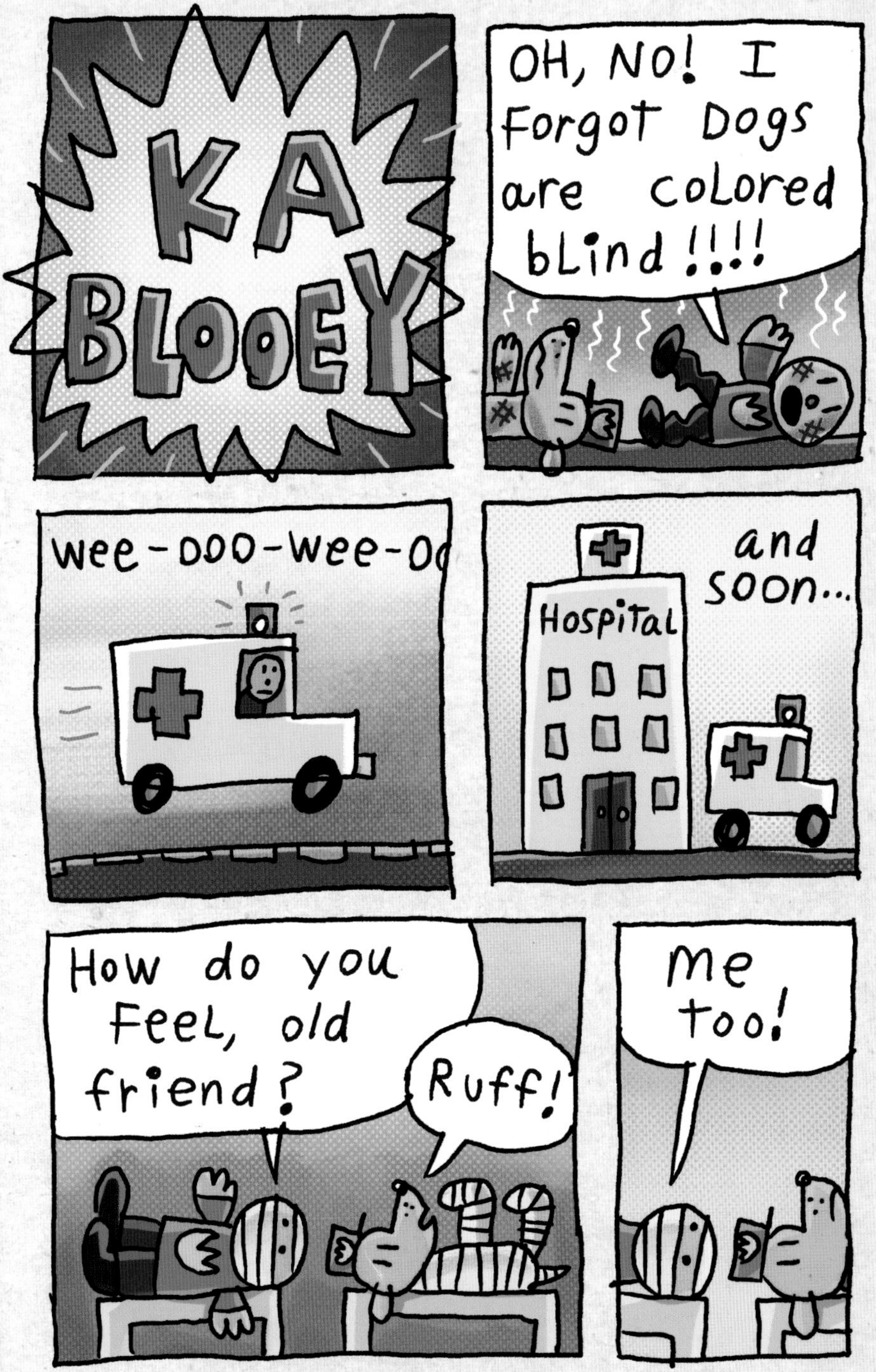
KA BLOOEY
OH, NO! I Forgot Dogs are colored bLind!!!!
wee-DOO-wee-Oo
and soon...
Hospital
How do you FeeL, old friend?
Ruff!
me too!

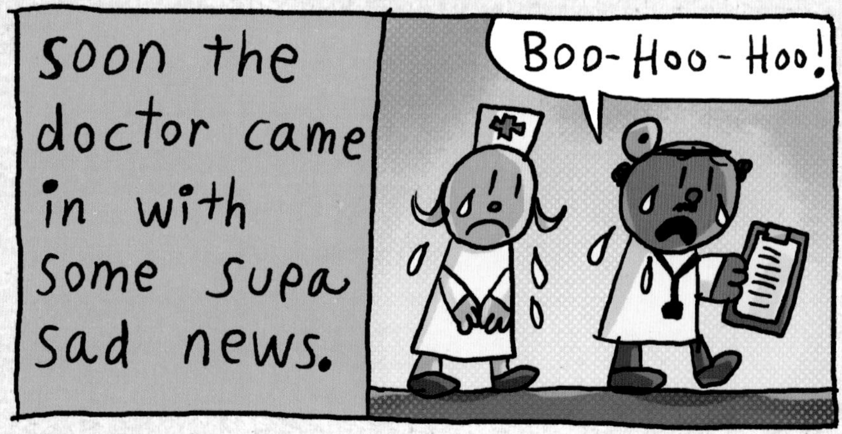
Soon the doctor came in with some supa sad news.
BOO-HOO-HOO!

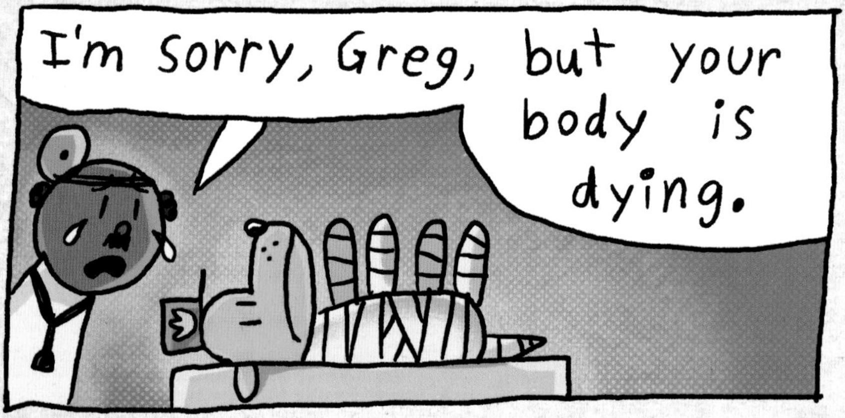
I'm sorry, Greg, but your body is dying.

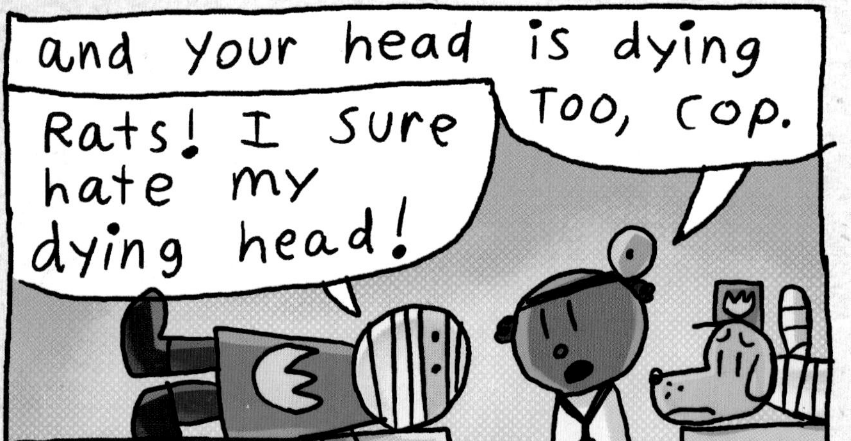
and your head is dying too, cop.
Rats! I sure hate my dying head!

But just when all seemed lost...

HEY!

← nurse Lady

why don't we sew Greg's head onto cop's body?

Good idea, nurse Lady! You're a genius!!!

Hooray!

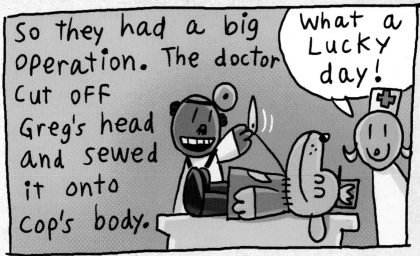

So they had a big operation. The doctor cut off Greg's head and sewed it onto cop's body.

What a Lucky day!

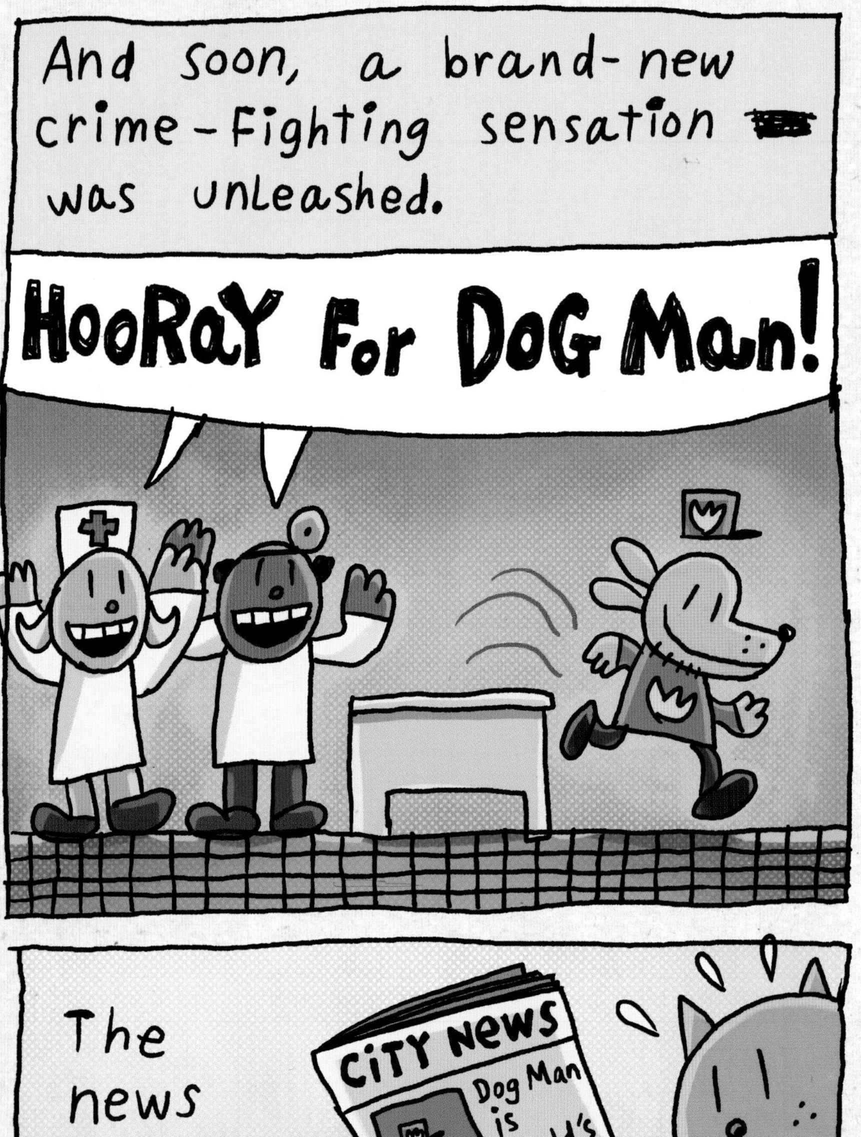
And soon, a brand-new crime-fighting sensation was unleashed.
HOORAY FOR DOG MAN!
The news spread quickly!
CITY NEWS
Dog Man is world's greatest cop!!!!!

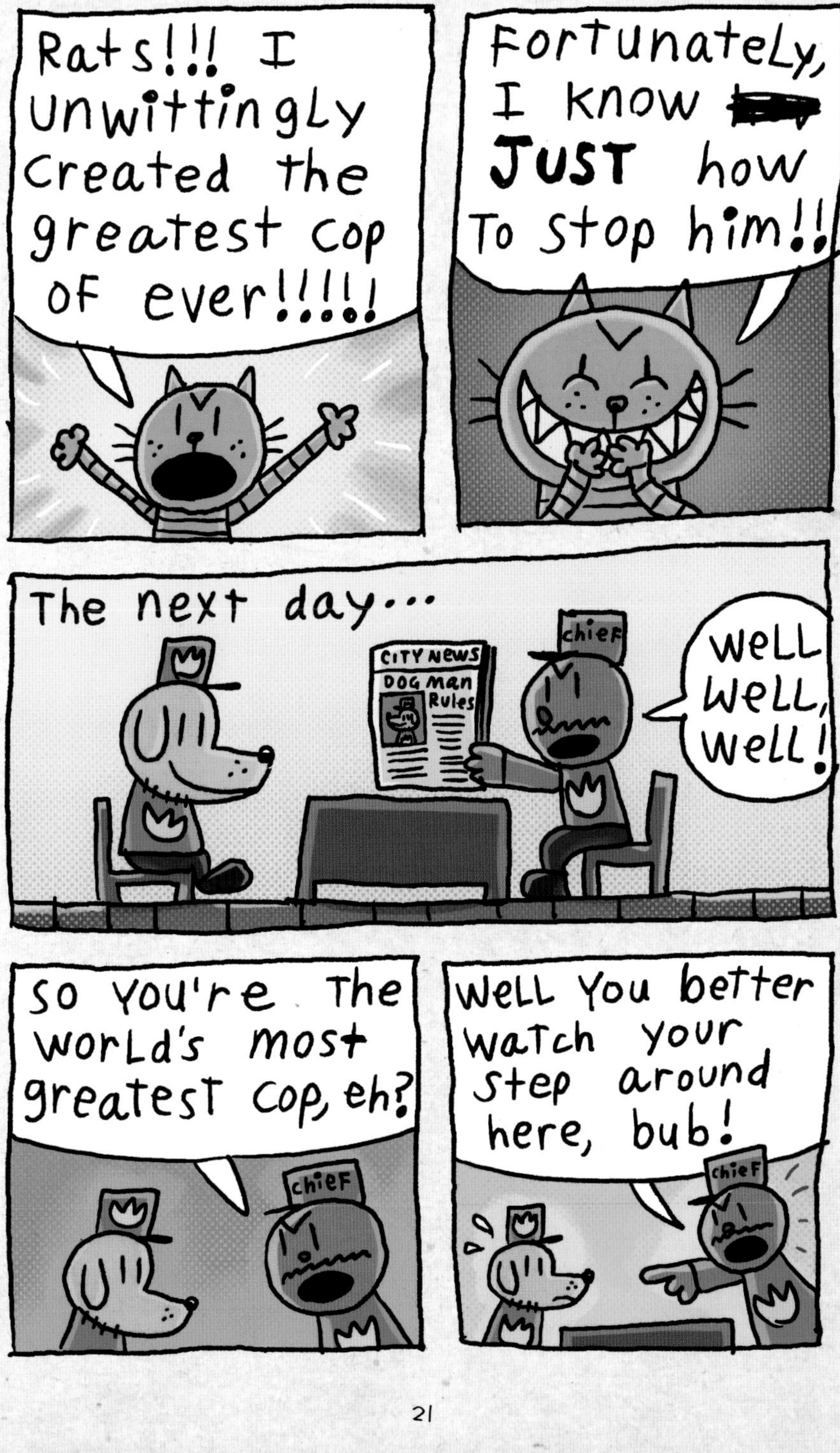
Rats!!! I unwittingly created the greatest cop of ever!!!!!
Fortunately, I know JUST how to stop him!!
The next day...
CITY NEWS
DOG Man Rules
chief
Well well, well!
So you're the world's most greatest cop, eh?
Well you better watch your step around here, bub!

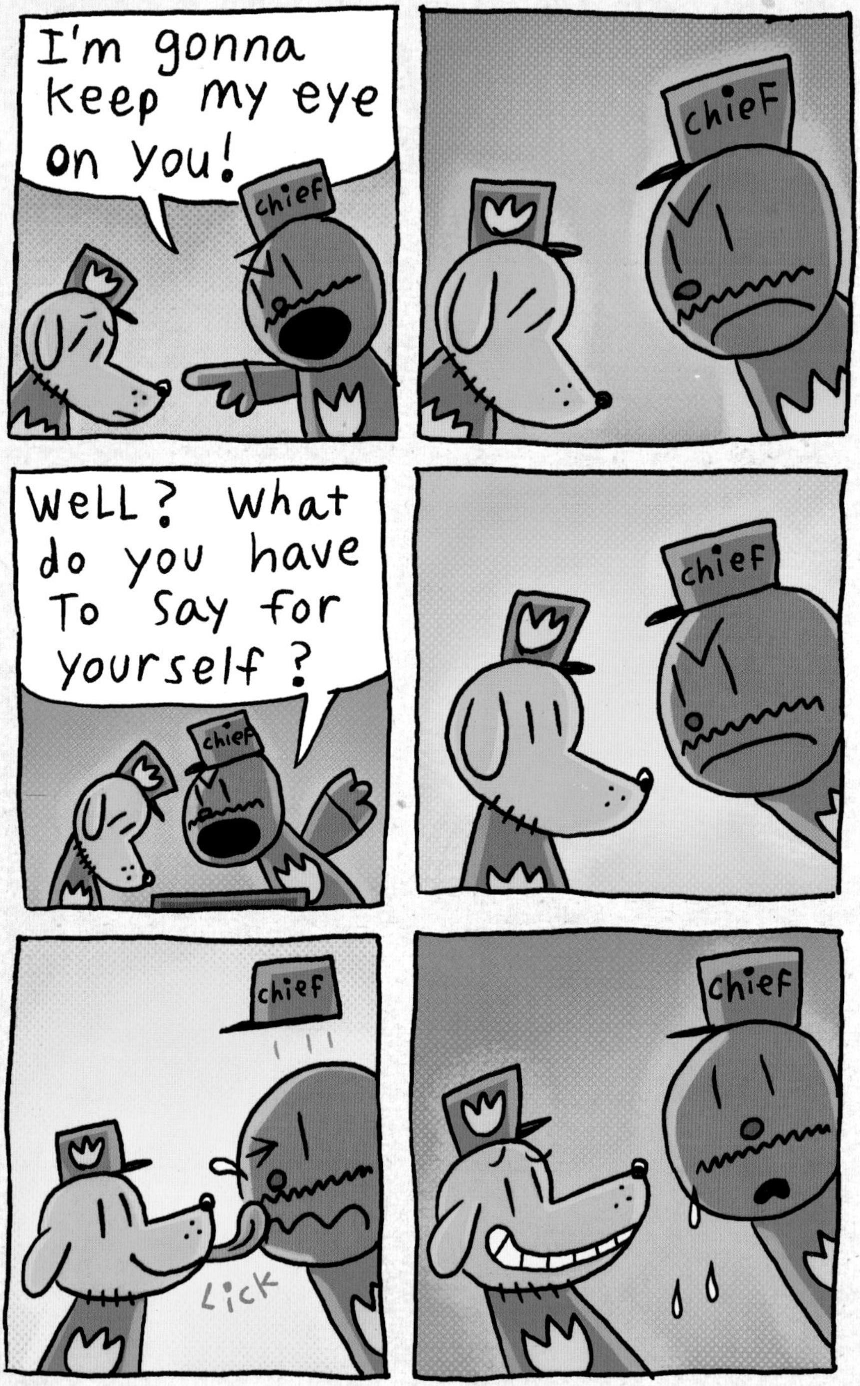
I'm gonna keep my eye on you!
chief
chief
WELL? What do you have To say for yourself?
chief
chief
chief
Lick
chief

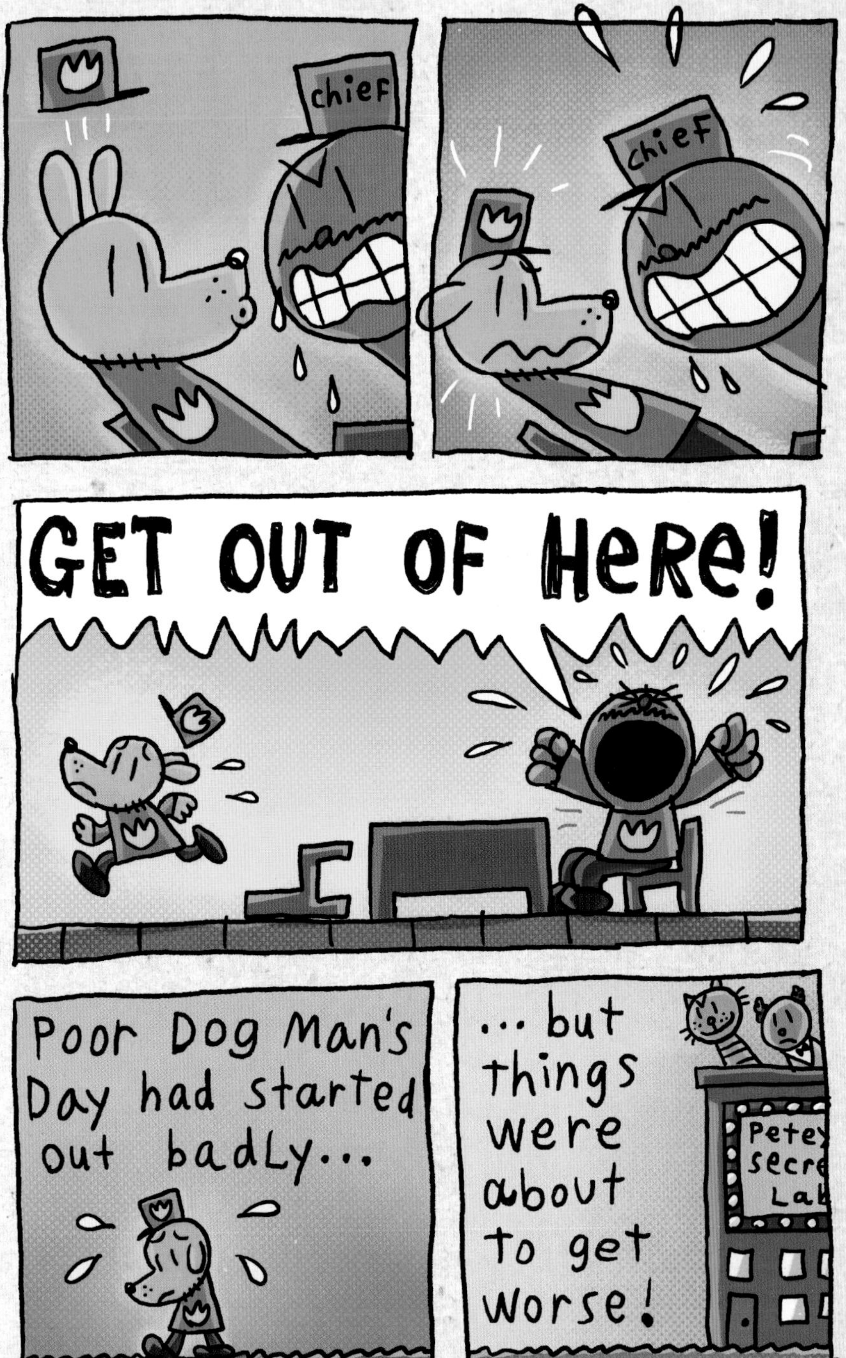
chief
chief
GET OUT OF HeRe!
Poor Dog Man's Day had started out badLy...
... but things were about to get worse!
Petey
secre
Lab

24

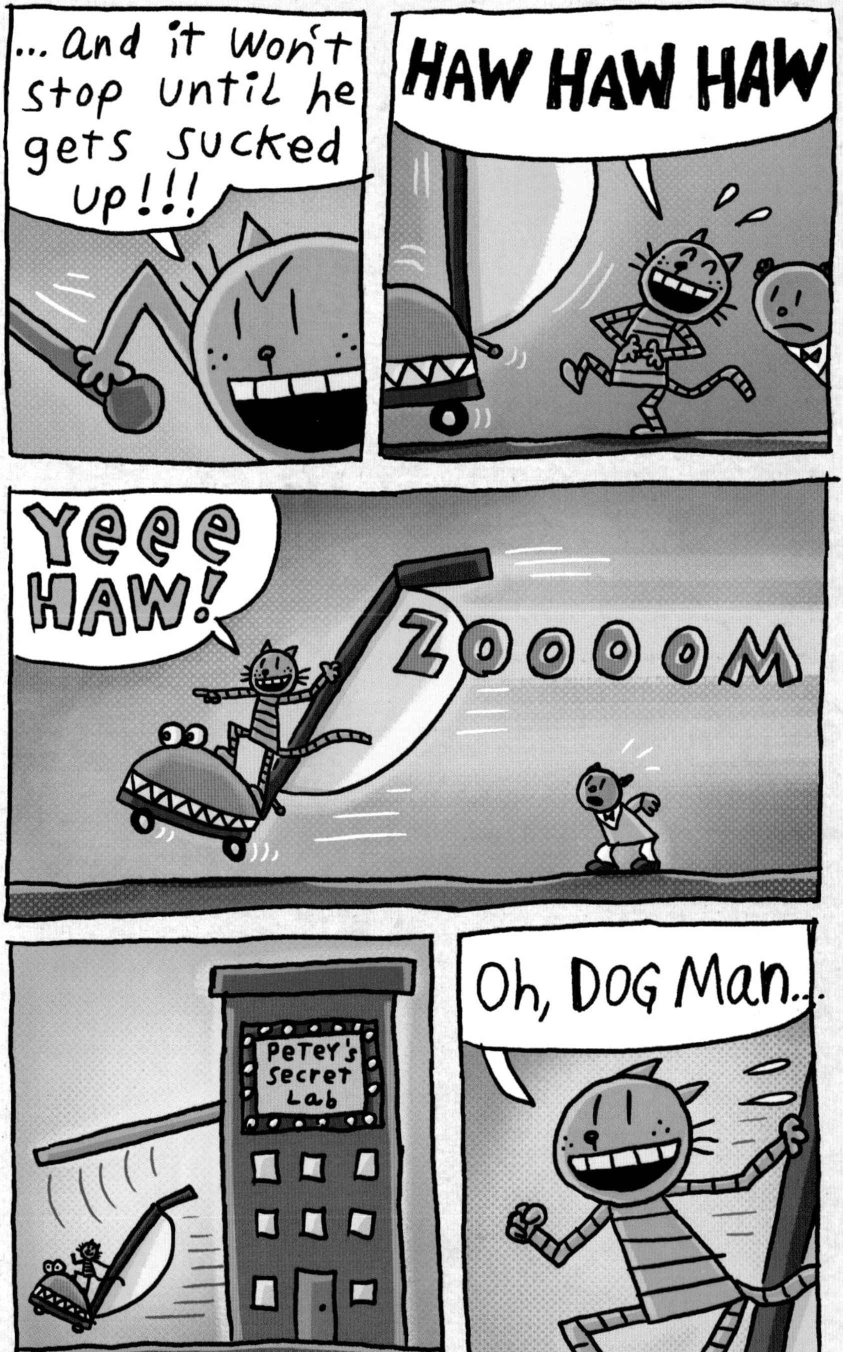
...and it won't stop until he gets sucked up!!!
HAW HAW HAW
Yeee HAW!
ZOOOOM
Petey's Secret Lab
Oh, DOG Man...

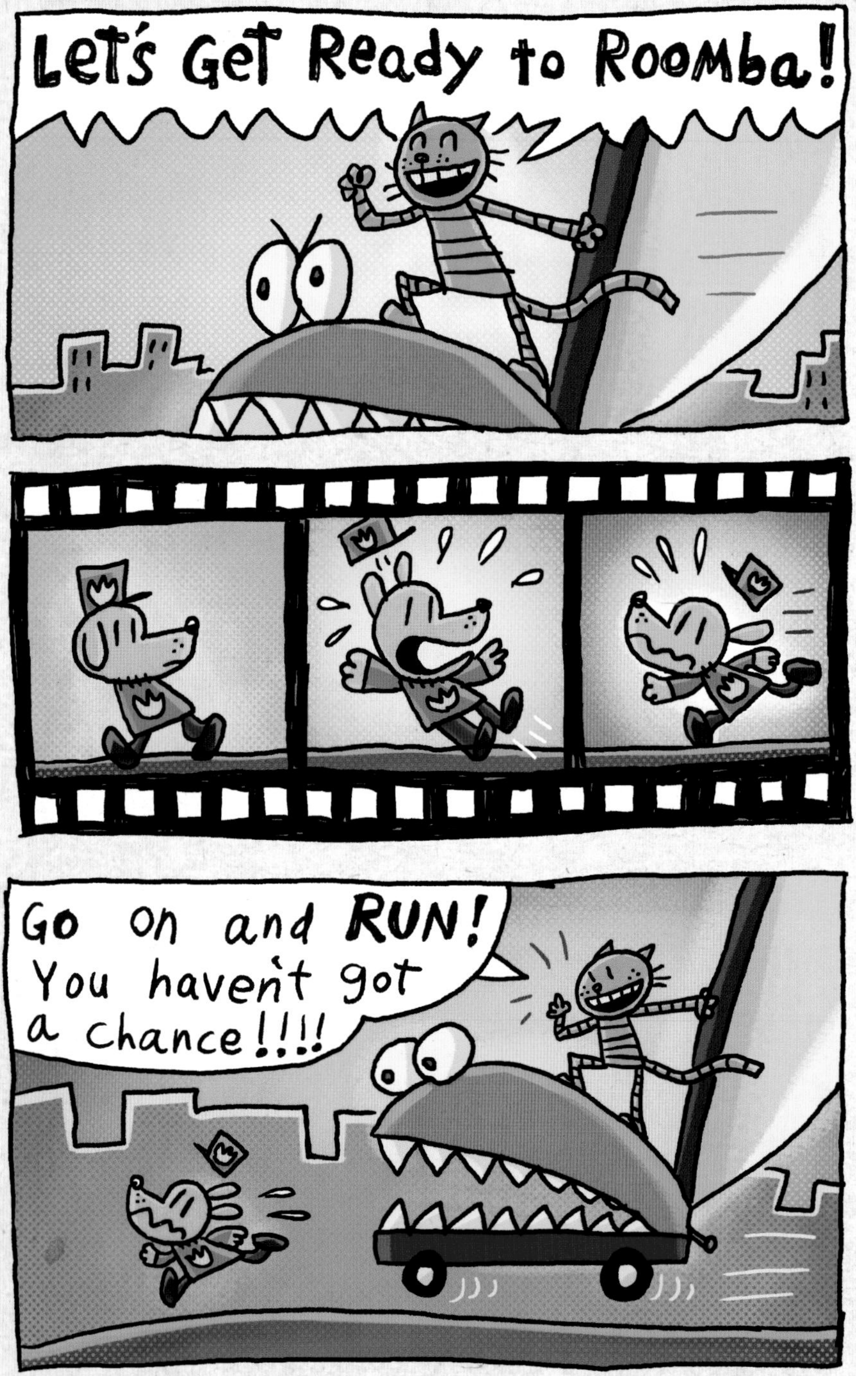
Let's Get Ready to Roomba!
Go on and RUN! You haven't got a chance!!!!

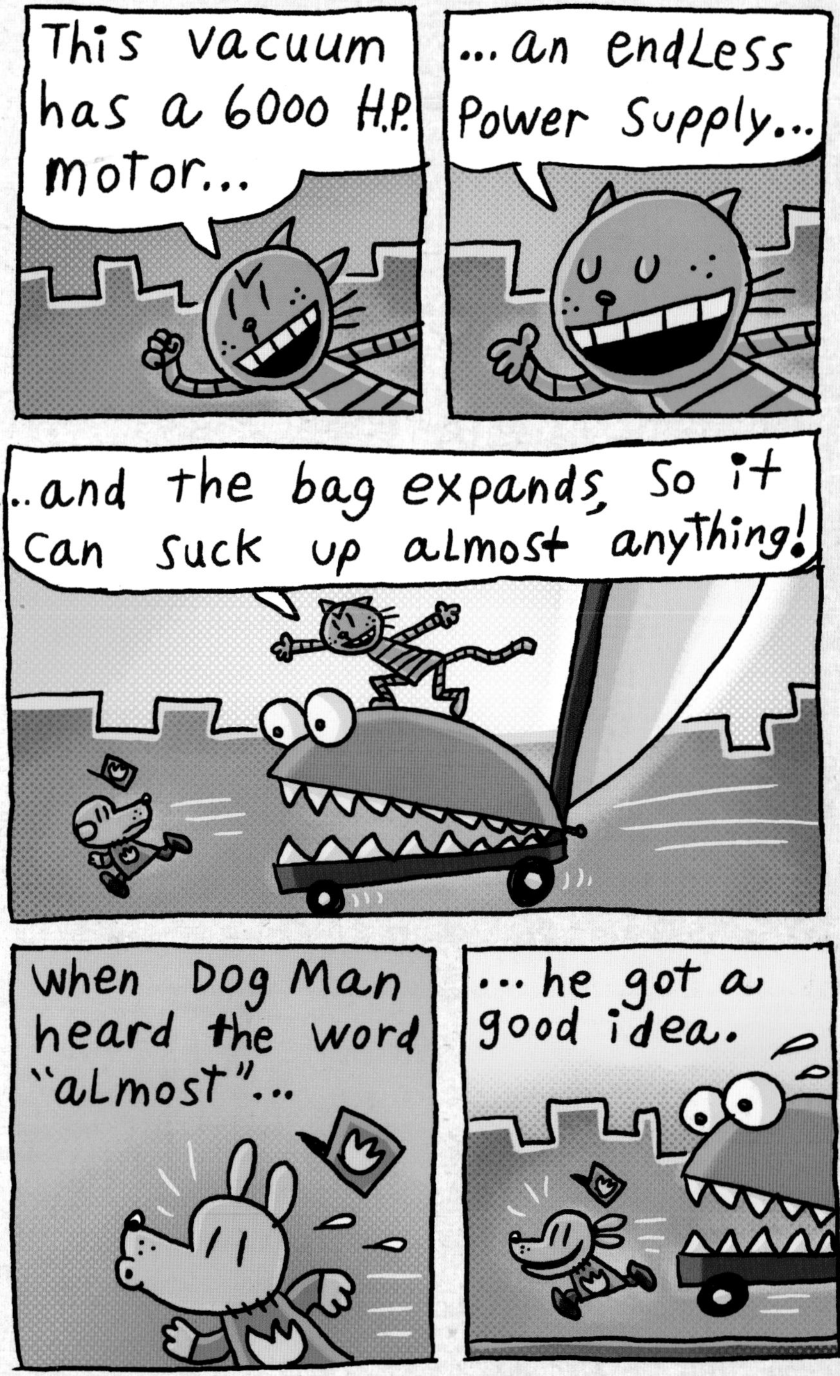
This vacuum has a 6000 H.P. motor...
...an endless power supply...
...and the bag expands, so it can suck up almost anything!
When Dog Man heard the word "almost"...
...he got a good idea.

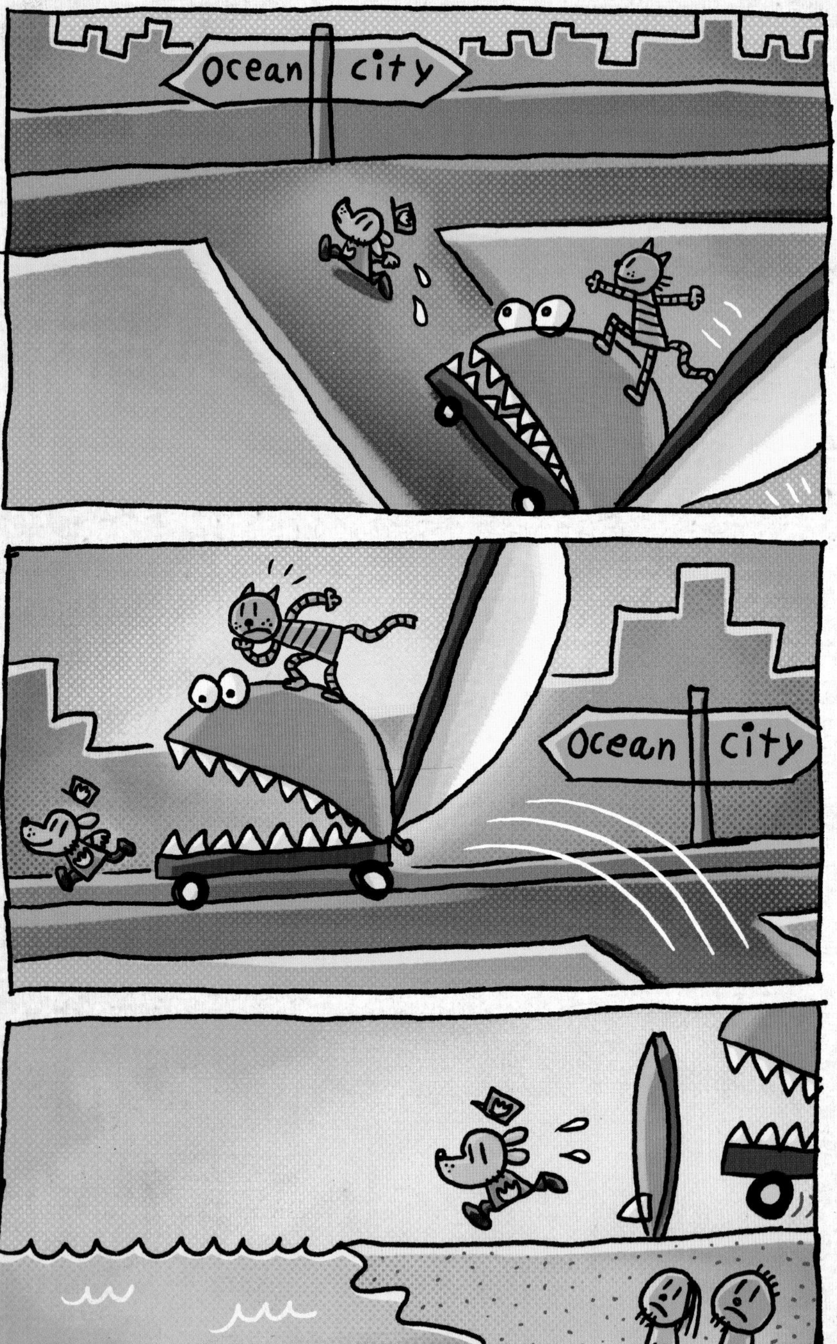
Ocean city
Ocean city

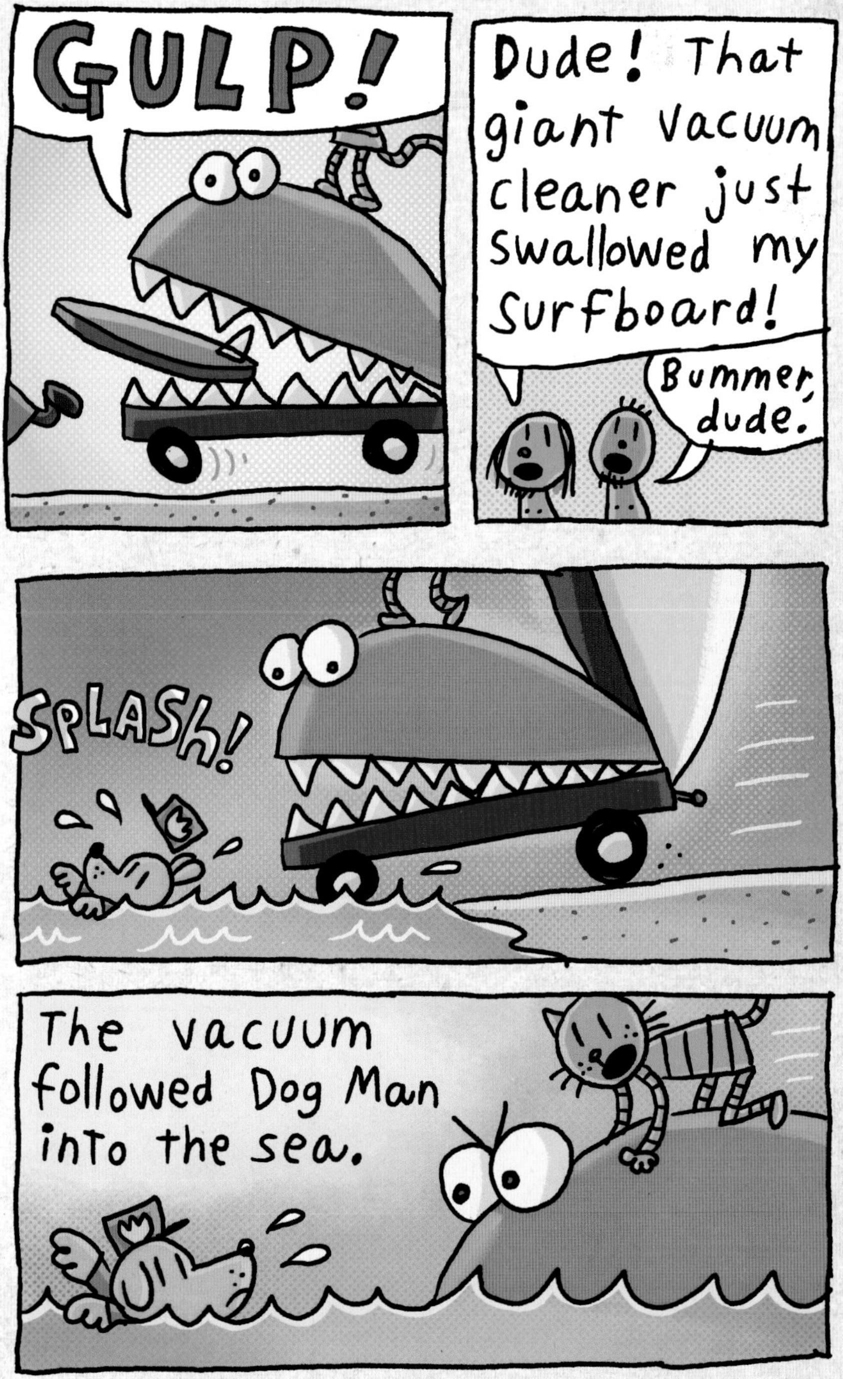
GULP!
Dude! That giant vacuum cleaner just swallowed my surfboard!
Bummer, dude.
SPLASH!
The vacuum followed Dog Man into the sea.

So the vacuum started sucking up the sea.

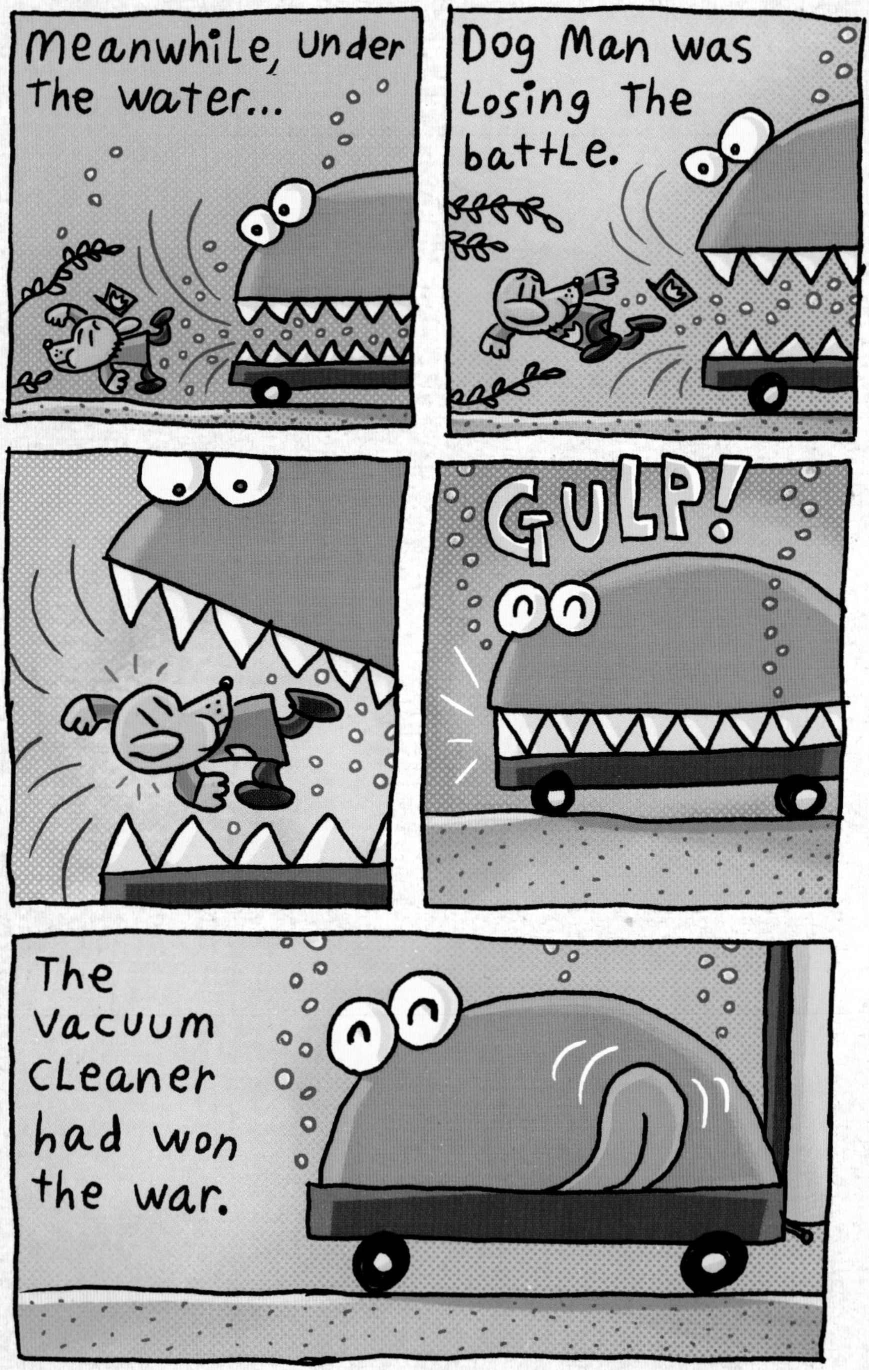
Meanwhile, under the water...
Dog Man was losing the battle.
GULP!
The vacuum cleaner had won the war.

or had he?

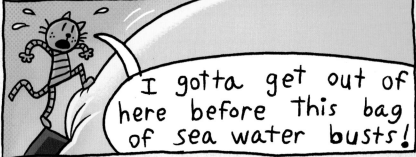

I gotta get out of here before this bag of sea water busts!

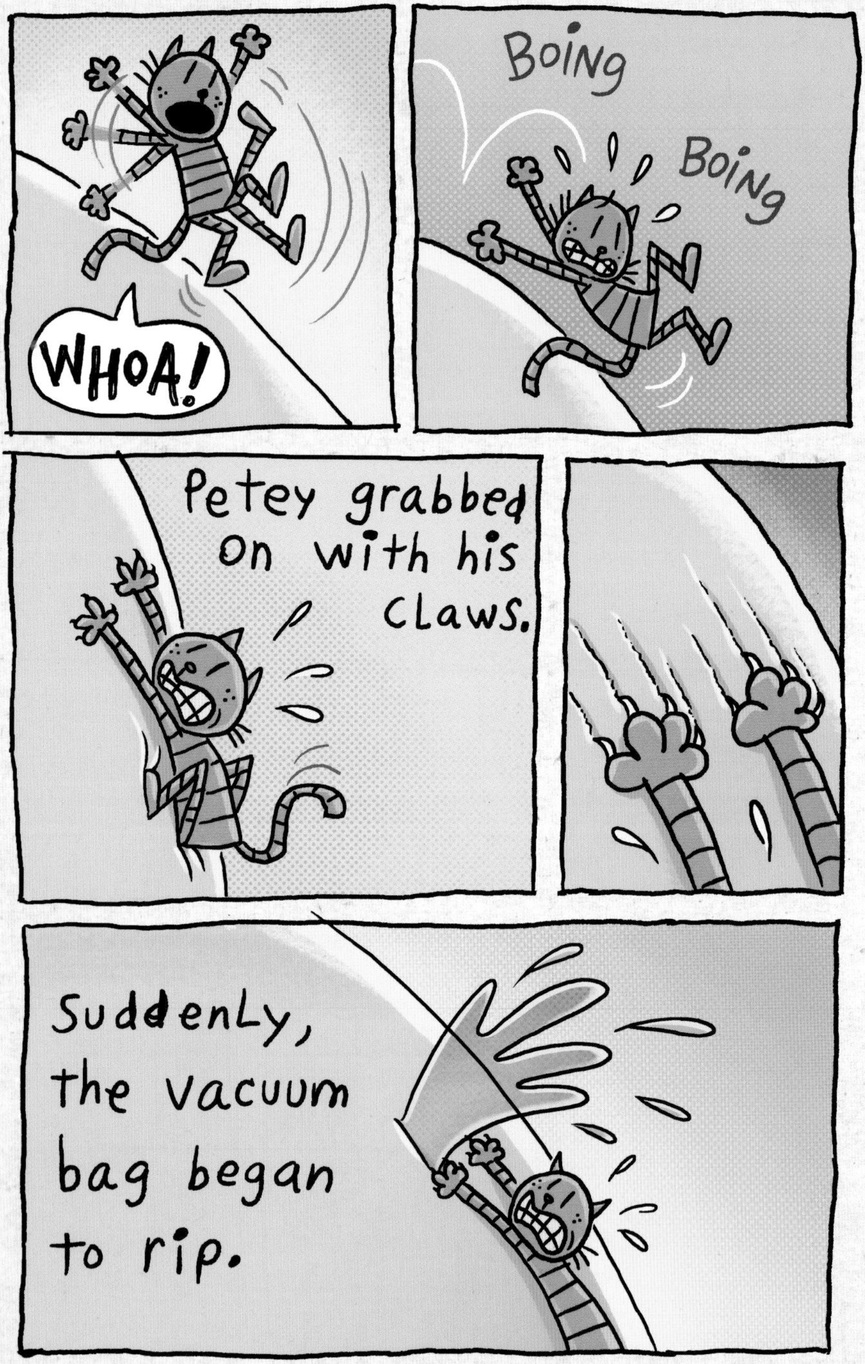
WHOA!
Boing
Boing
Petey grabbed on with his claws.
Suddenly, the vacuum bag began to rip.

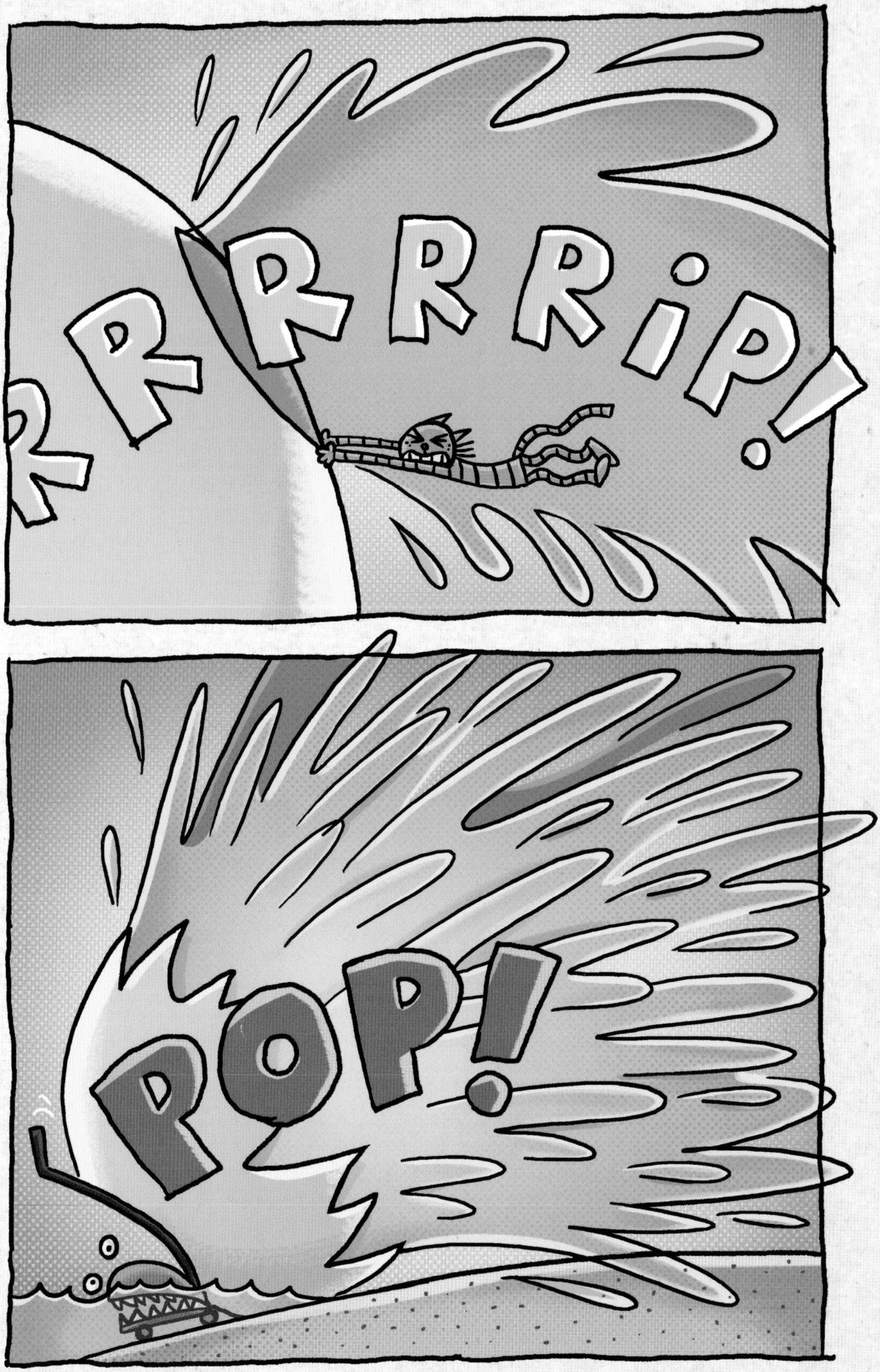
RRRRRRIP!
POP!

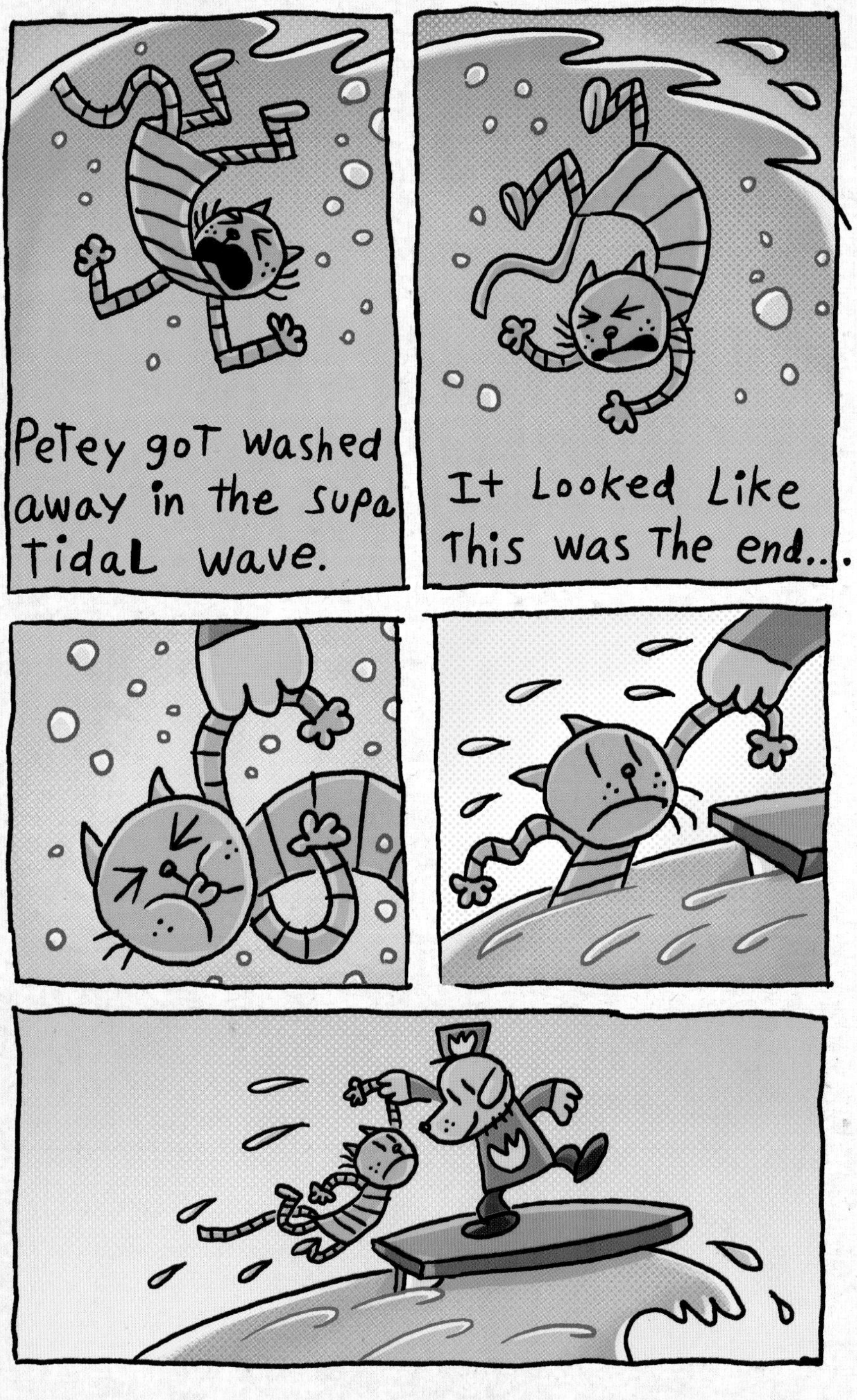

Petey got washed away in the supa Tidal wave.
It Looked Like This was The end...

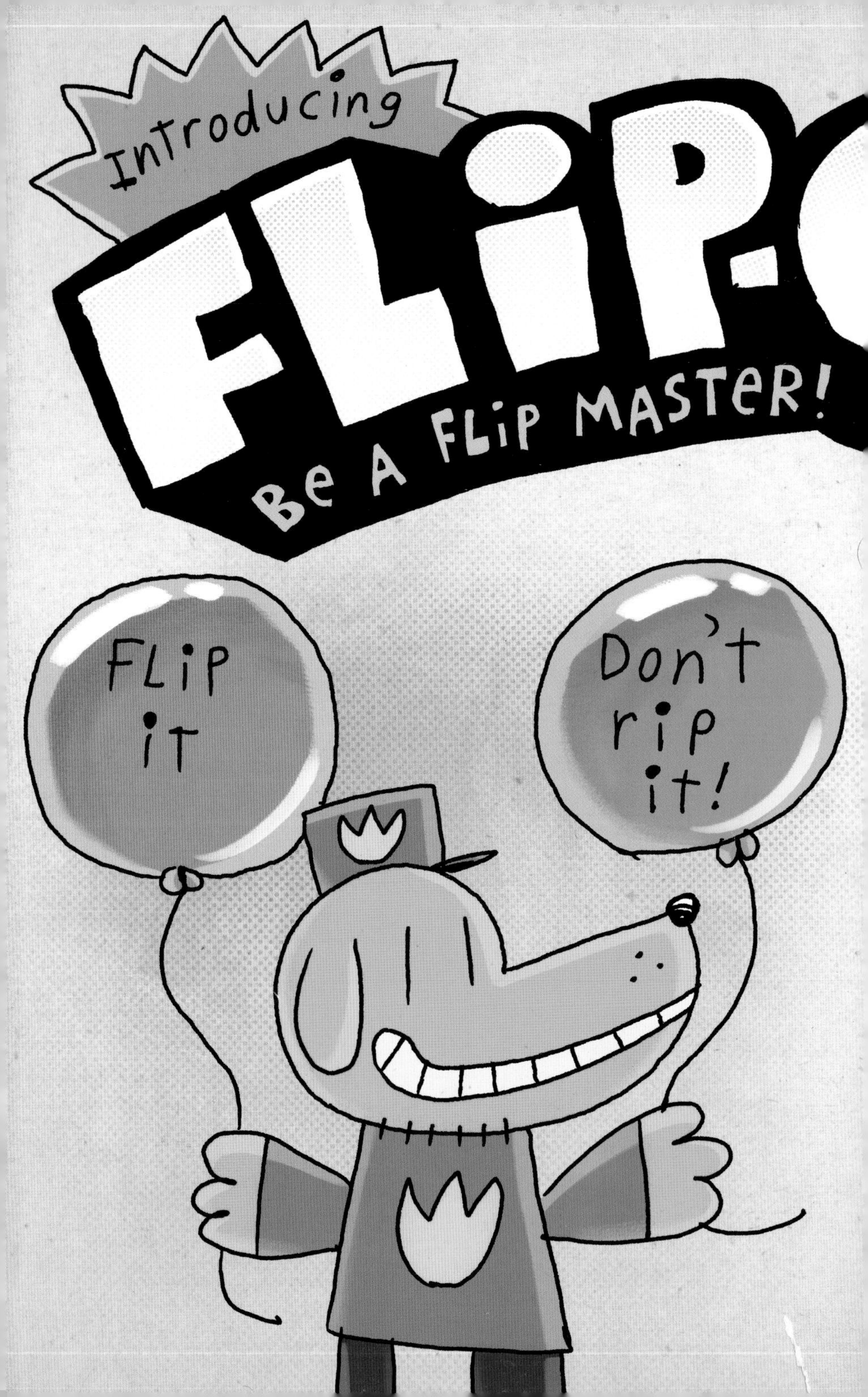

Introducing
FLIP-O
Be A FLIP MASTER!
FLIP it
Don't rip it!

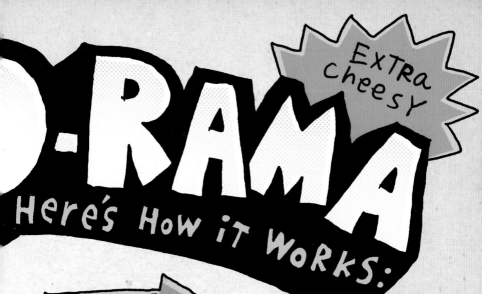

O-RAMA

EXTRA Cheesy

Here's How it WORKS:

STEP 1.
First, Place your Left hand inside the dotted Lines marked "Left hand here". Hold The book open FLAT!

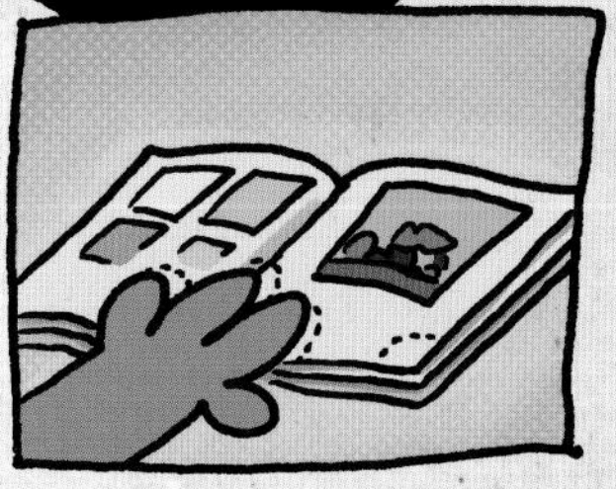

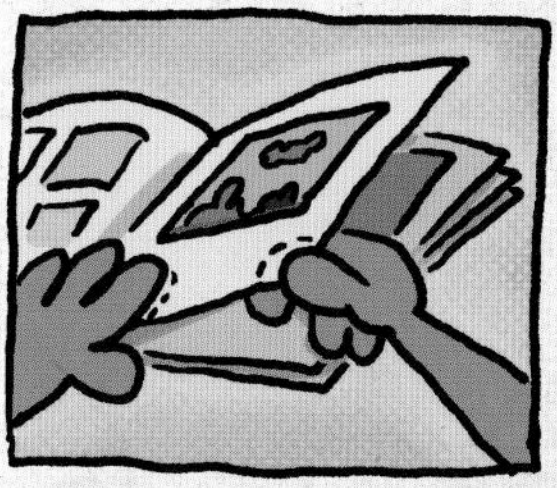

STEP 2:
Grasp the right-hand Page with your Thumb and index finger (inside the dotted Lines marked "Right Thumb Here").

STEP 3:
Now QUICKLY flip the right-hand page back and forth until the Picture appears to be Animated.

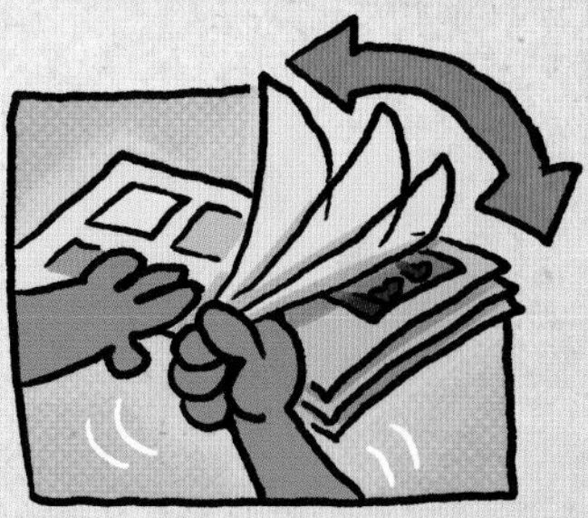

(for extra fun, try adding your own sound-effects!)

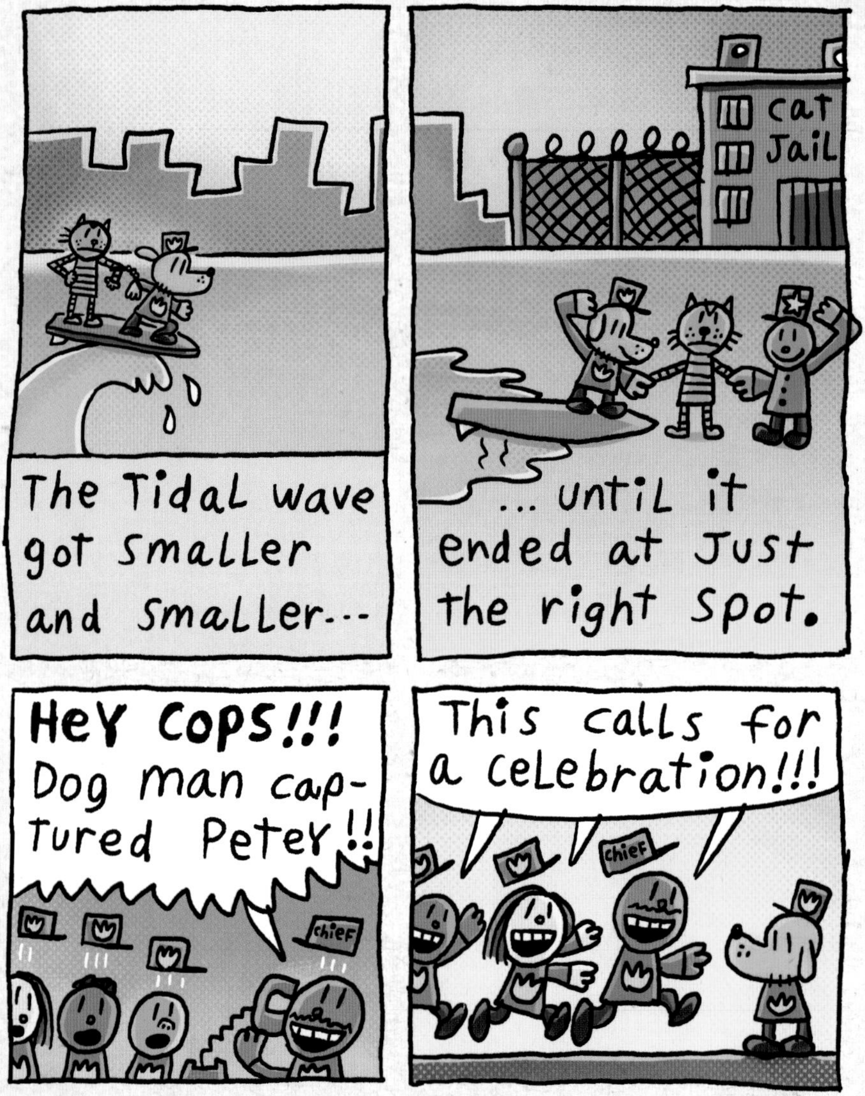
The Tidal wave got smaller and smaller...
CAT JAIL
...until it ended at just the right spot.
HEY COPS!!! Dog man captured Peter!!
chief
This calls for a celebration!!!
chief

Remember, flip only page 43.
Be sure you can see the picture on page 43 **AND** the one on page 45 while you flip.

Left hand here.

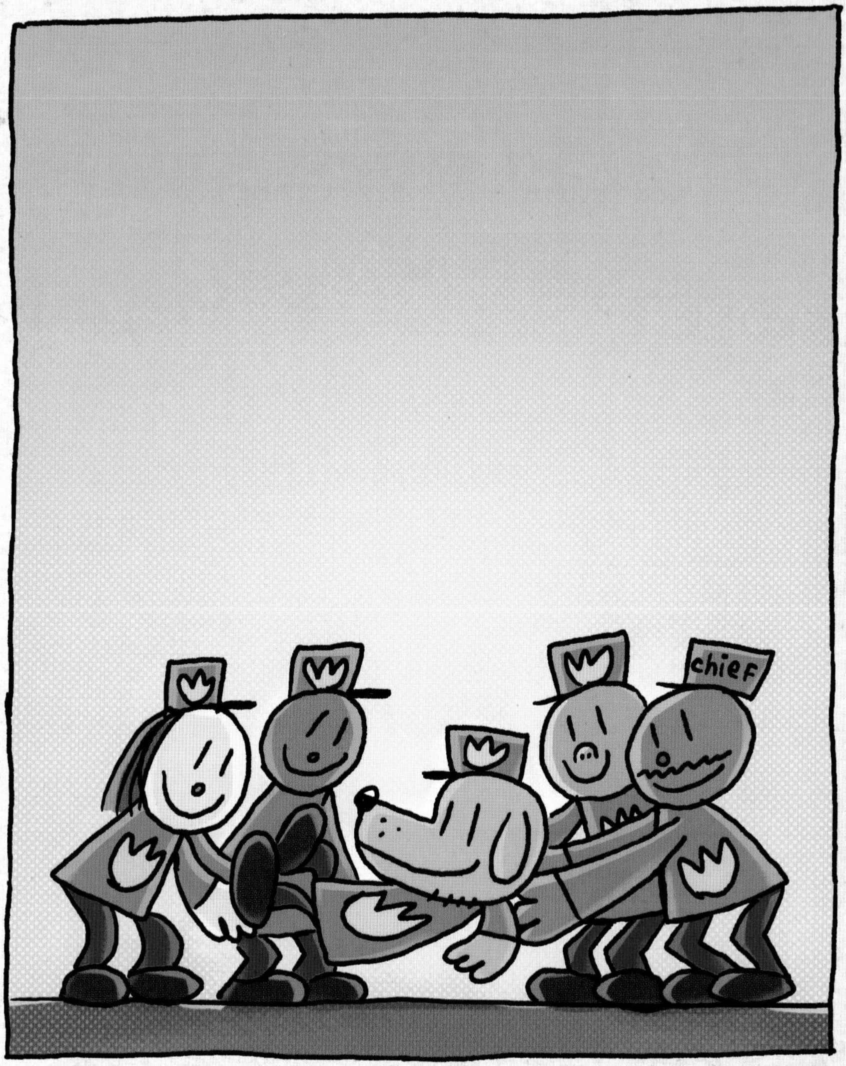
chief

For he's a
JoLLy good
doggy!

Right
Thumb
here.

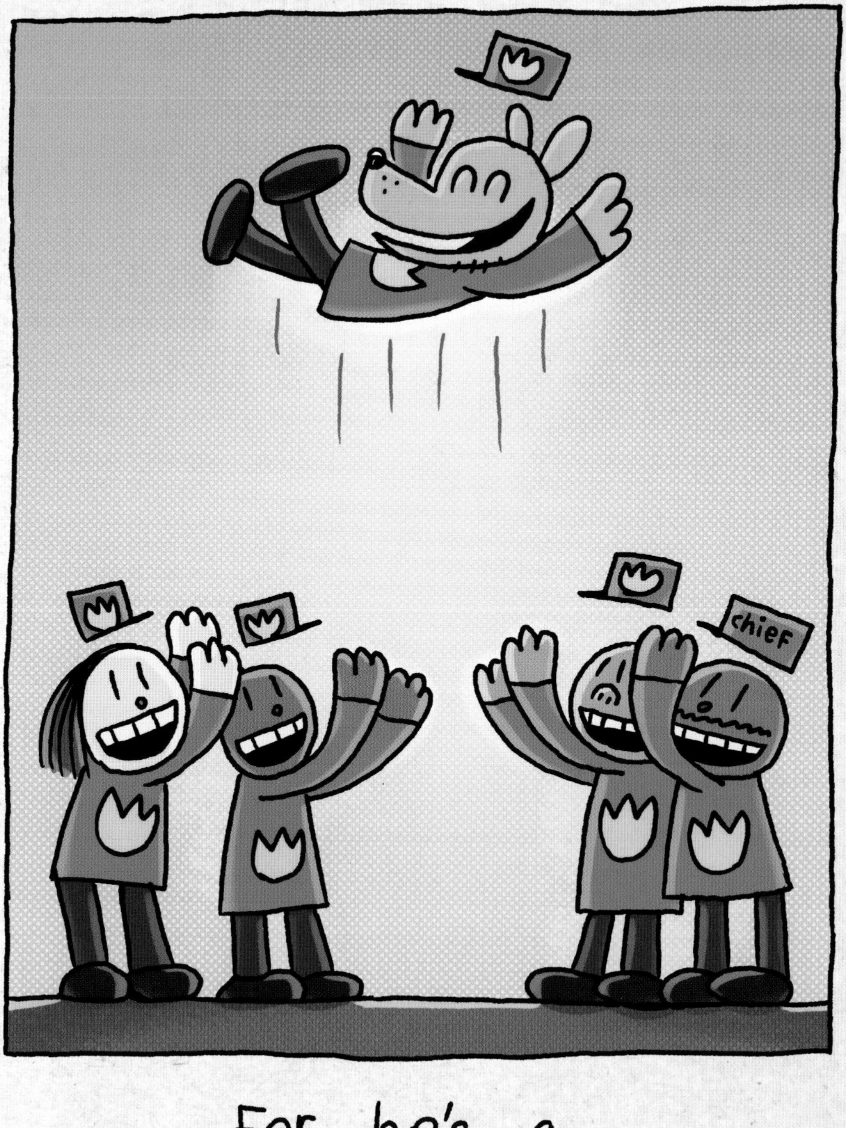
chief

For he's a JoLLy good doggy!

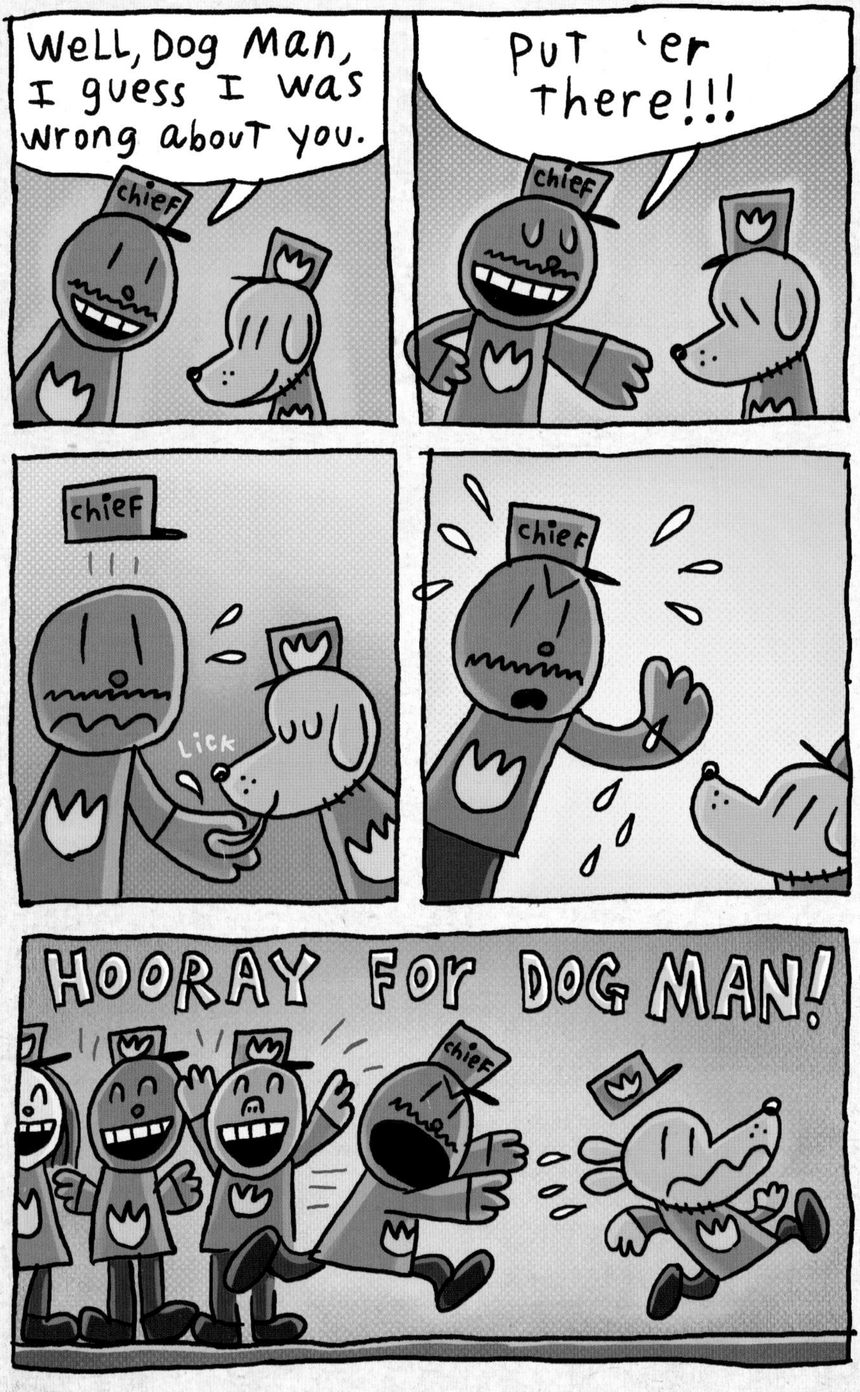
WeLL, Dog Man, I guess I was wrong about you.
chief
PuT 'er there!!!
chief
chief
chief
LICK
HOORAY For DOG MAN!
chief

CHAPTER 2
ROBO CHIEF

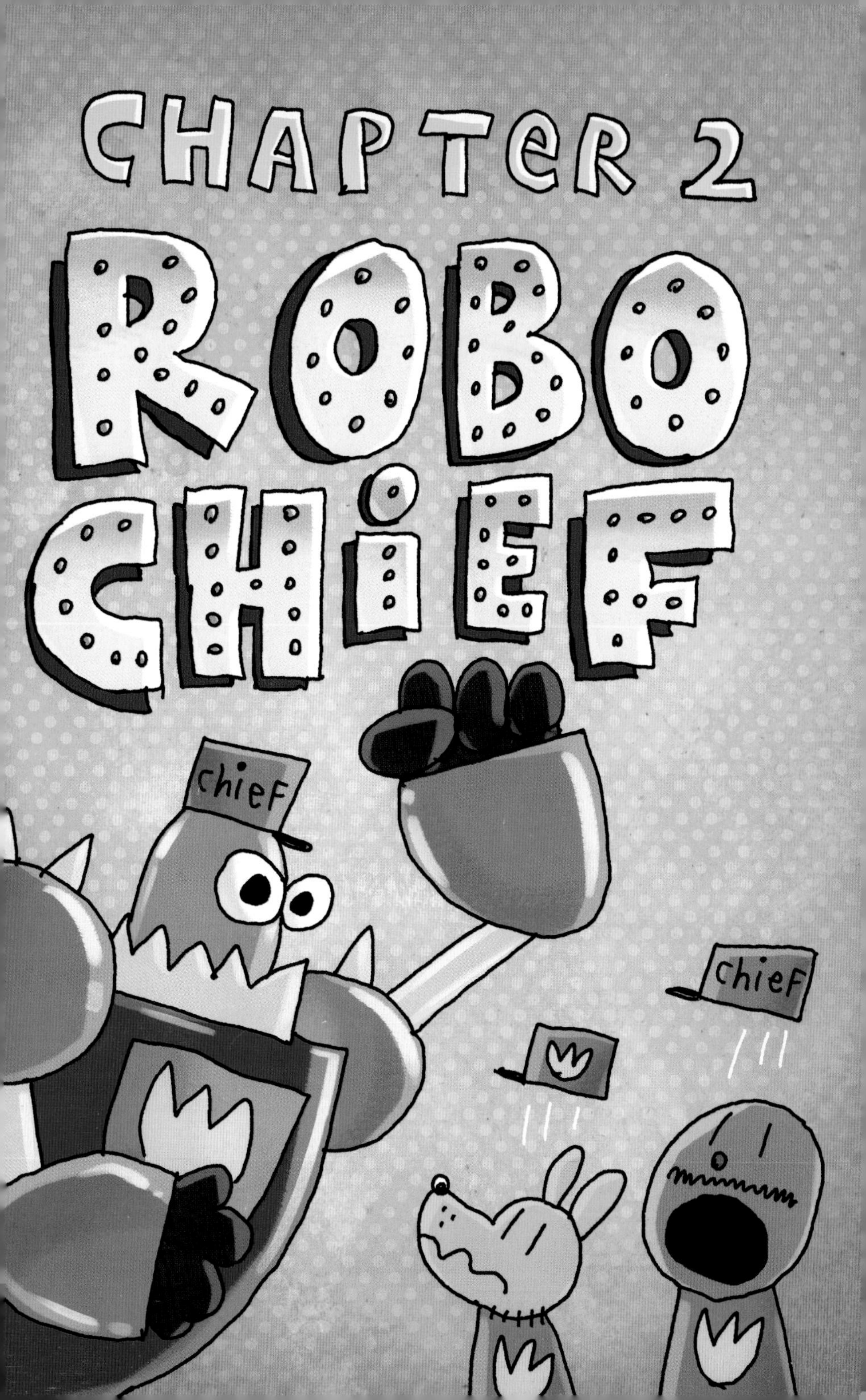
chief
chief

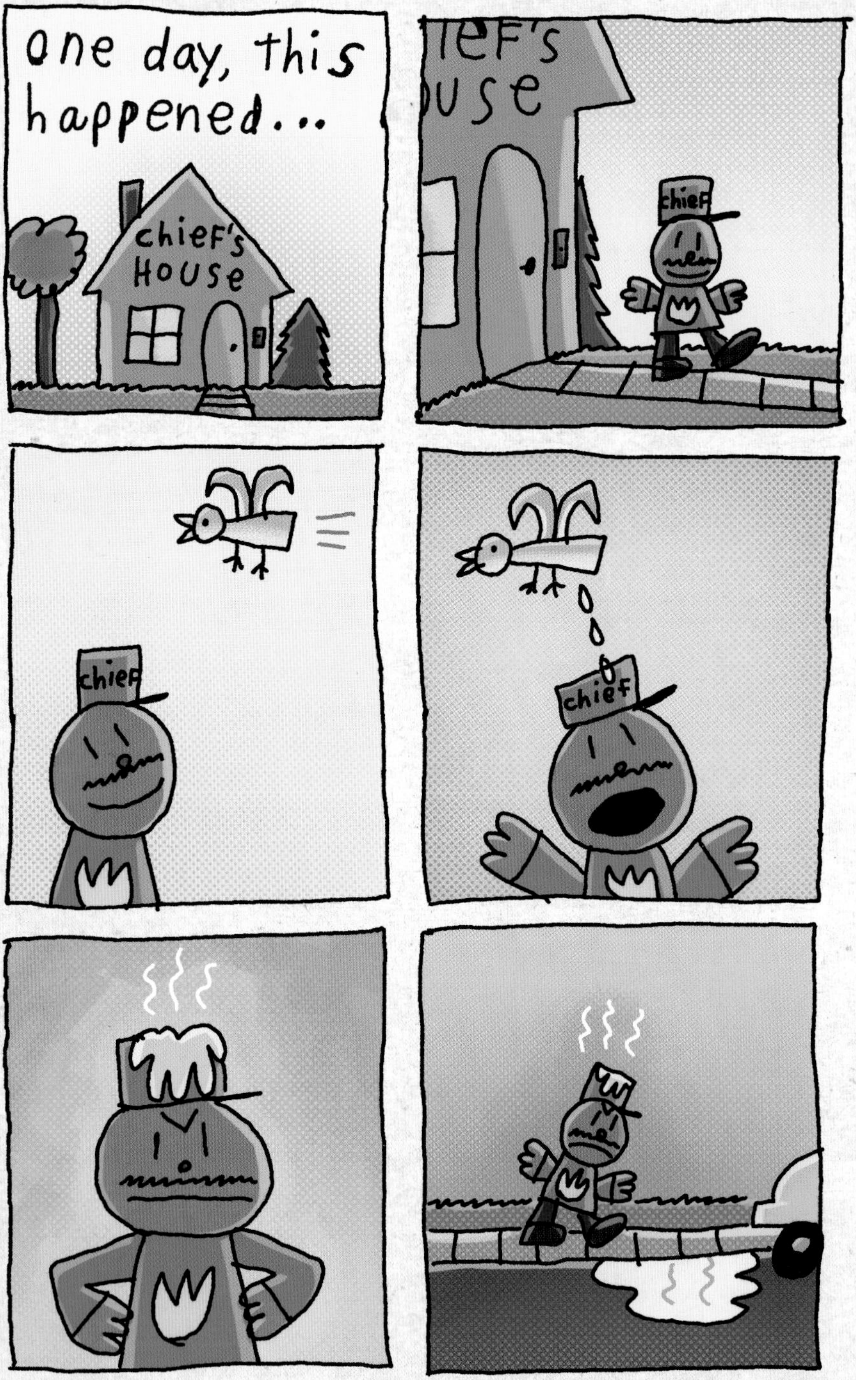
one day, this happened...
CHIEF'S HOUSE
IEF'S
USE
chief
chief
chief

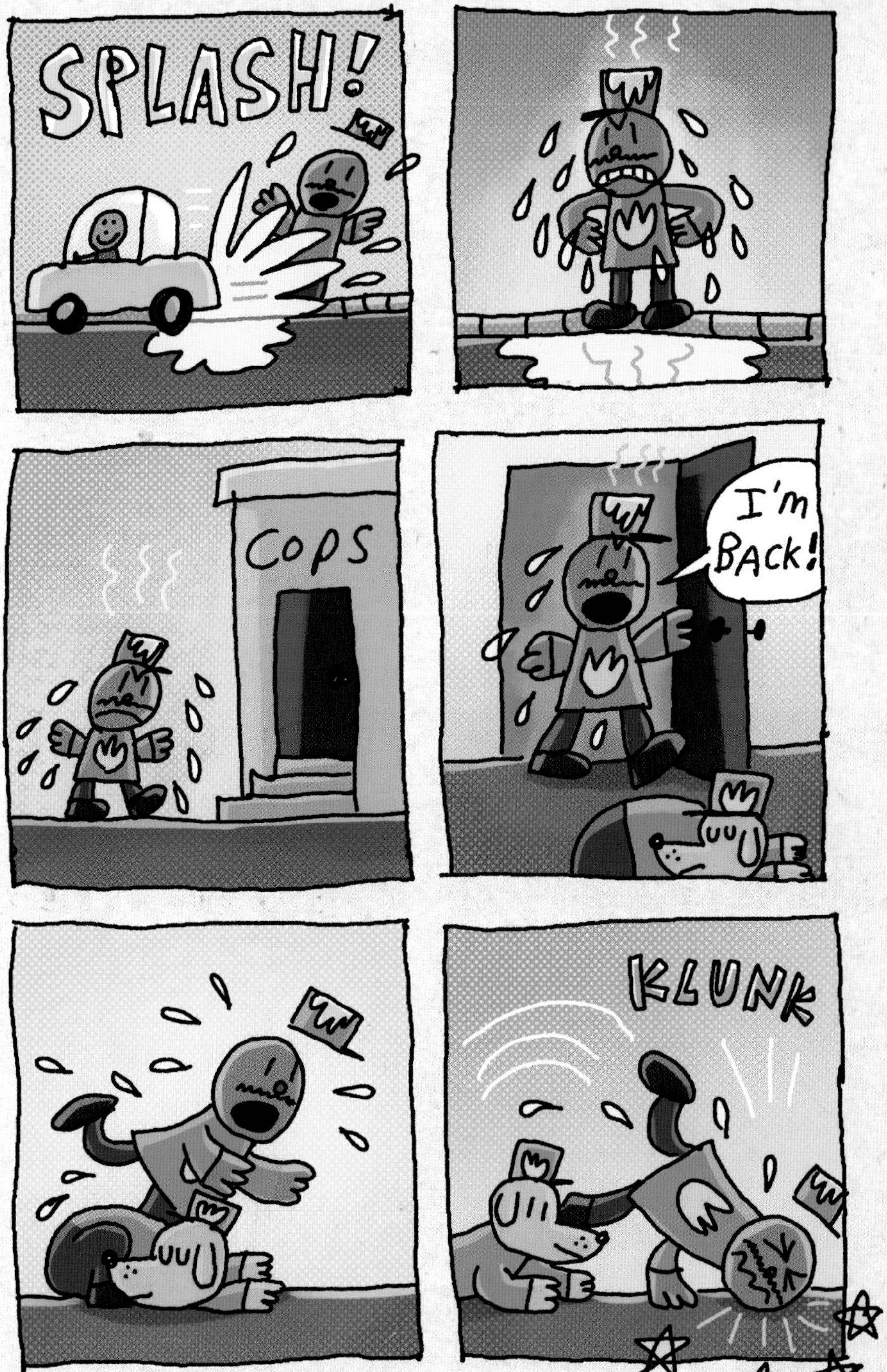
SPLASH!
COPS
I'm BACK!
KLUNK

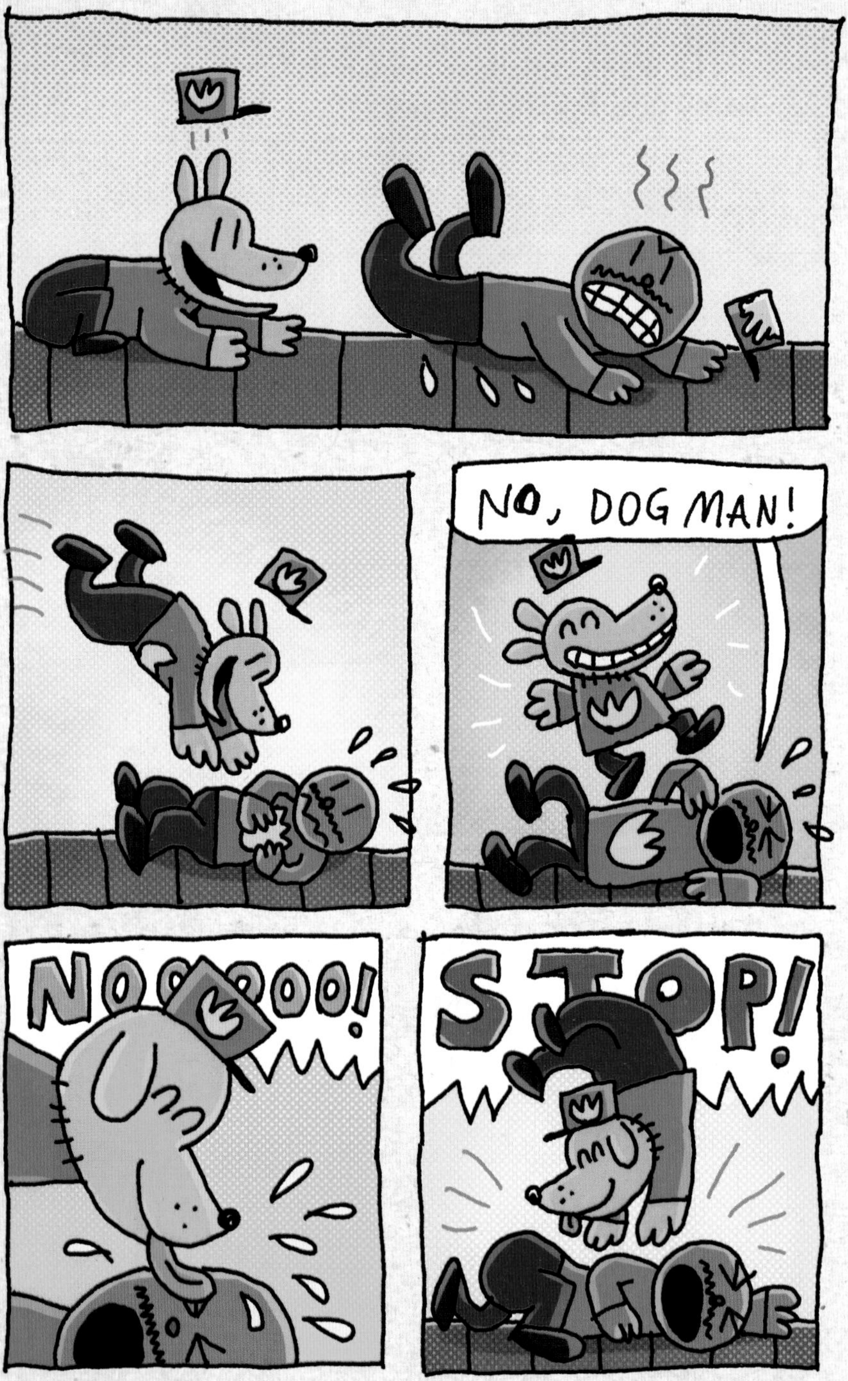
NO, DOG MAN!
NOOOOOO!
STOP!

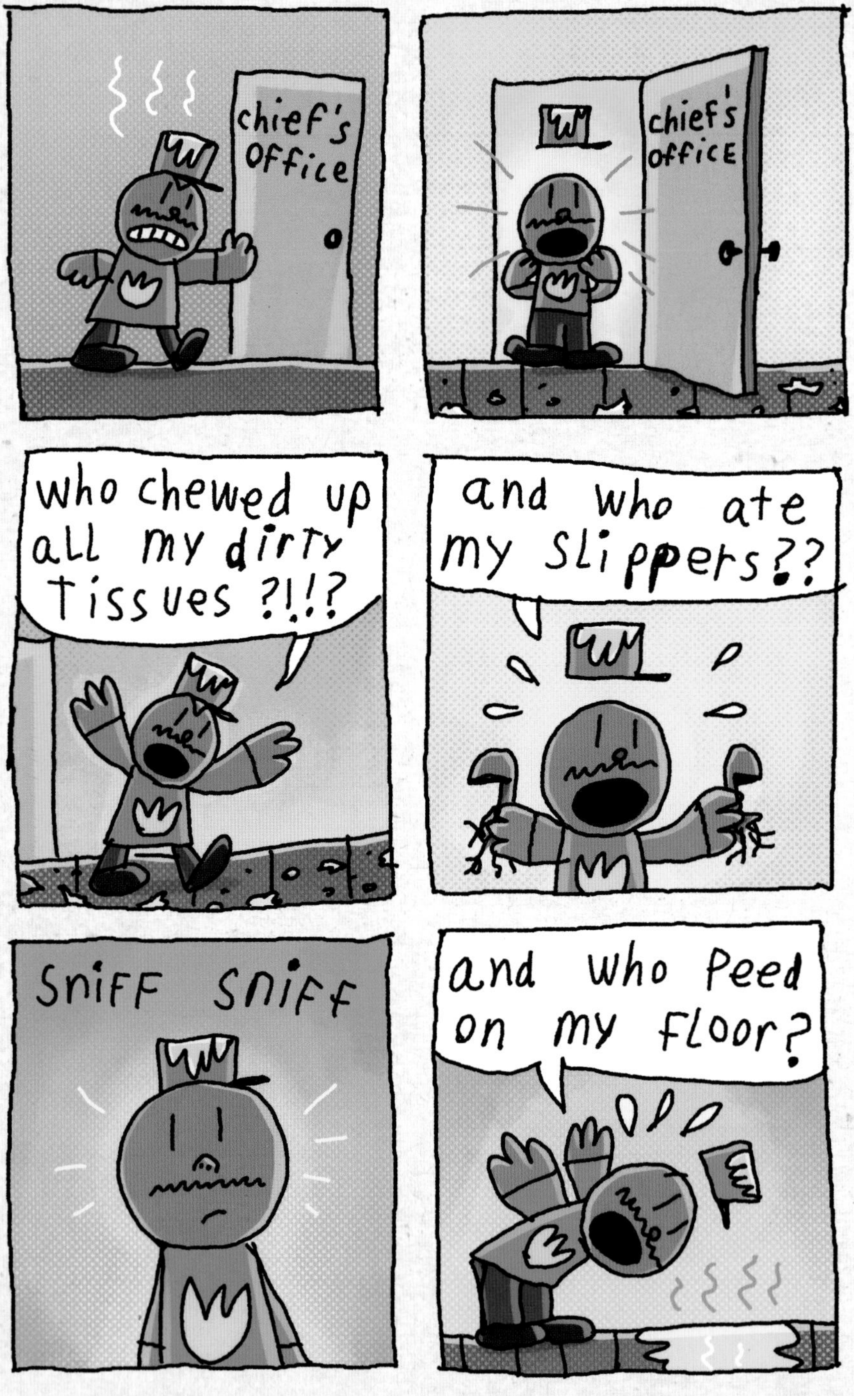
chief's office
chief's office
who chewed up all my dirty tissues ?!!?
and who ate my slippers??
sniff sniff
and who peed on my floor?

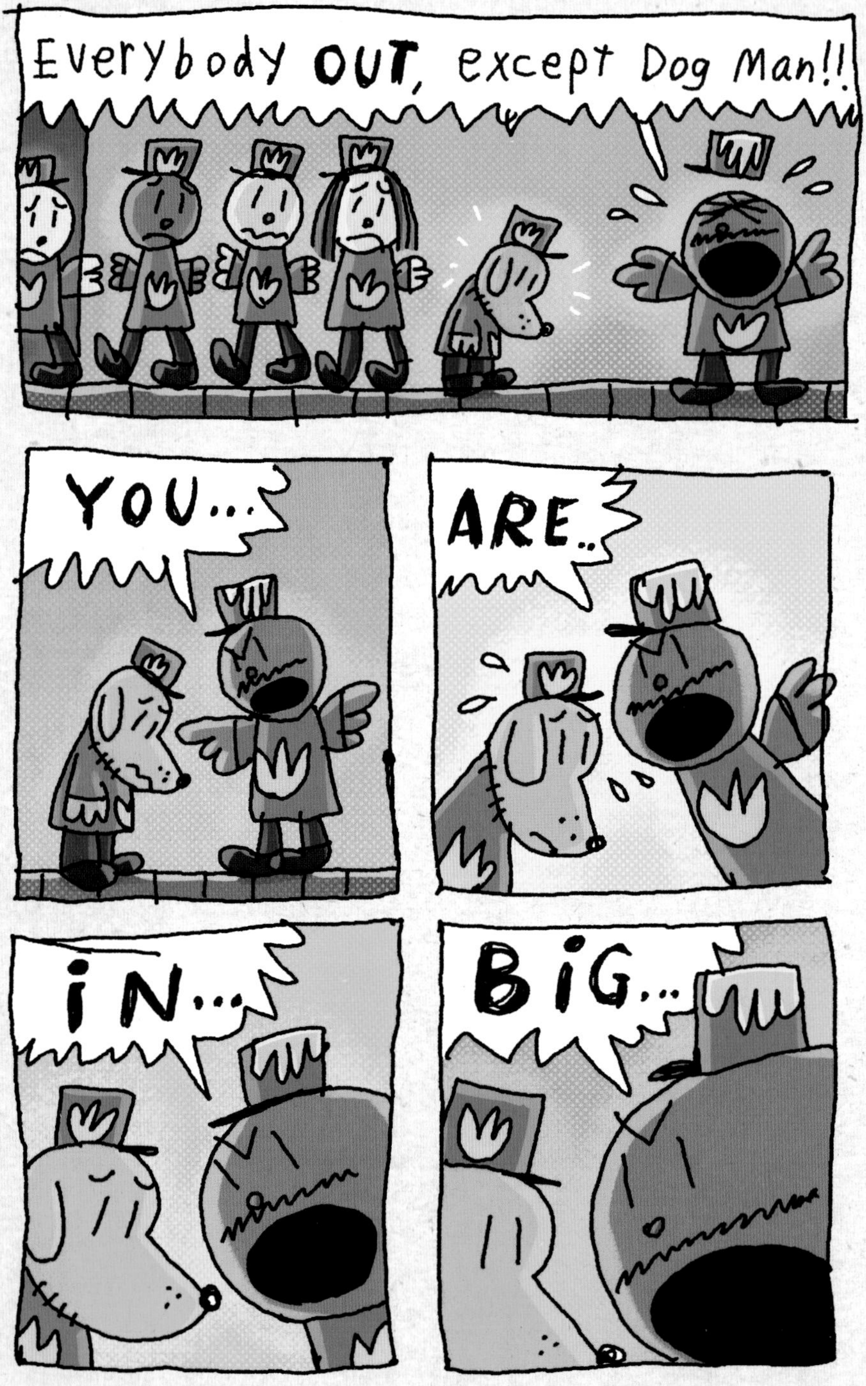
Everybody OUT, except Dog Man!!
YOU...
ARE...
iN...
BiG...

TROUBLE!!!
PSST! Hey Chief! The Mayor's here!
Uh-oh.
Heh heh... UH, Send her right in!!!
WHAM!
M

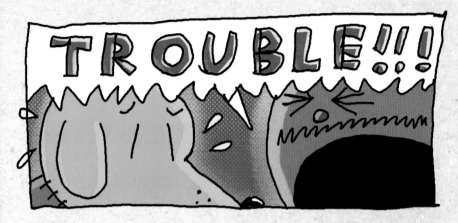

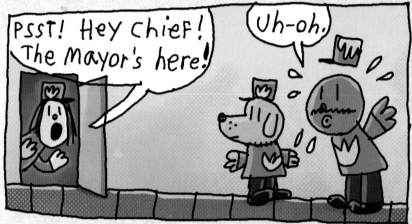

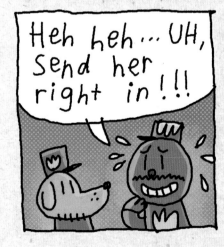

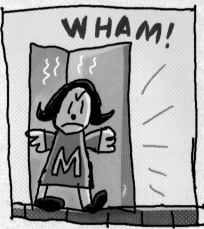

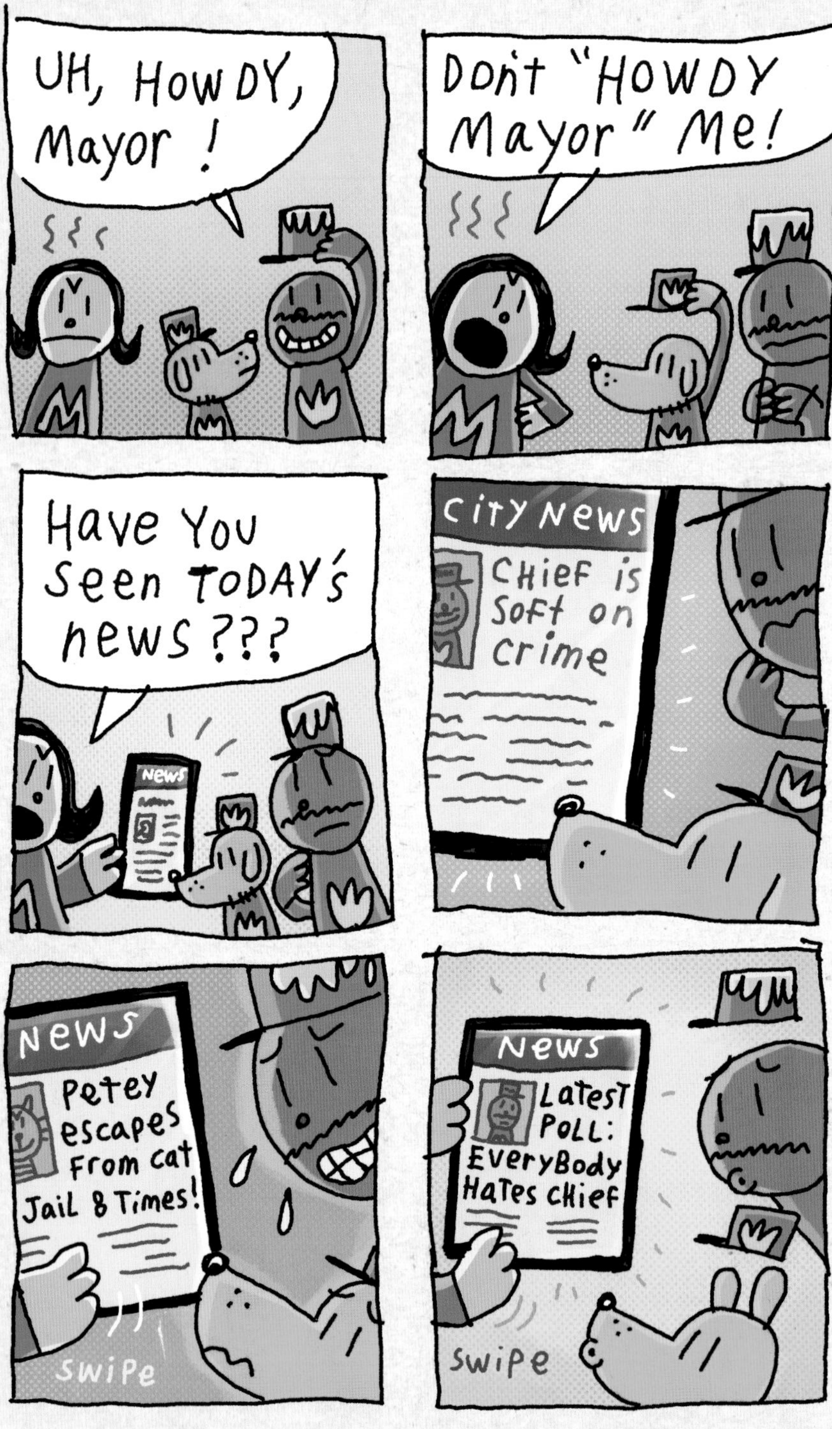
UH, HOWDY, Mayor!
Don't "HOWDY Mayor" Me!
Have You Seen TODAY's news???
News
City News
Chief is Soft on crime
News
Petey escapes From cat Jail 8 Times!
swipe
News
Latest Poll: EveryBody Hates Chief
swipe

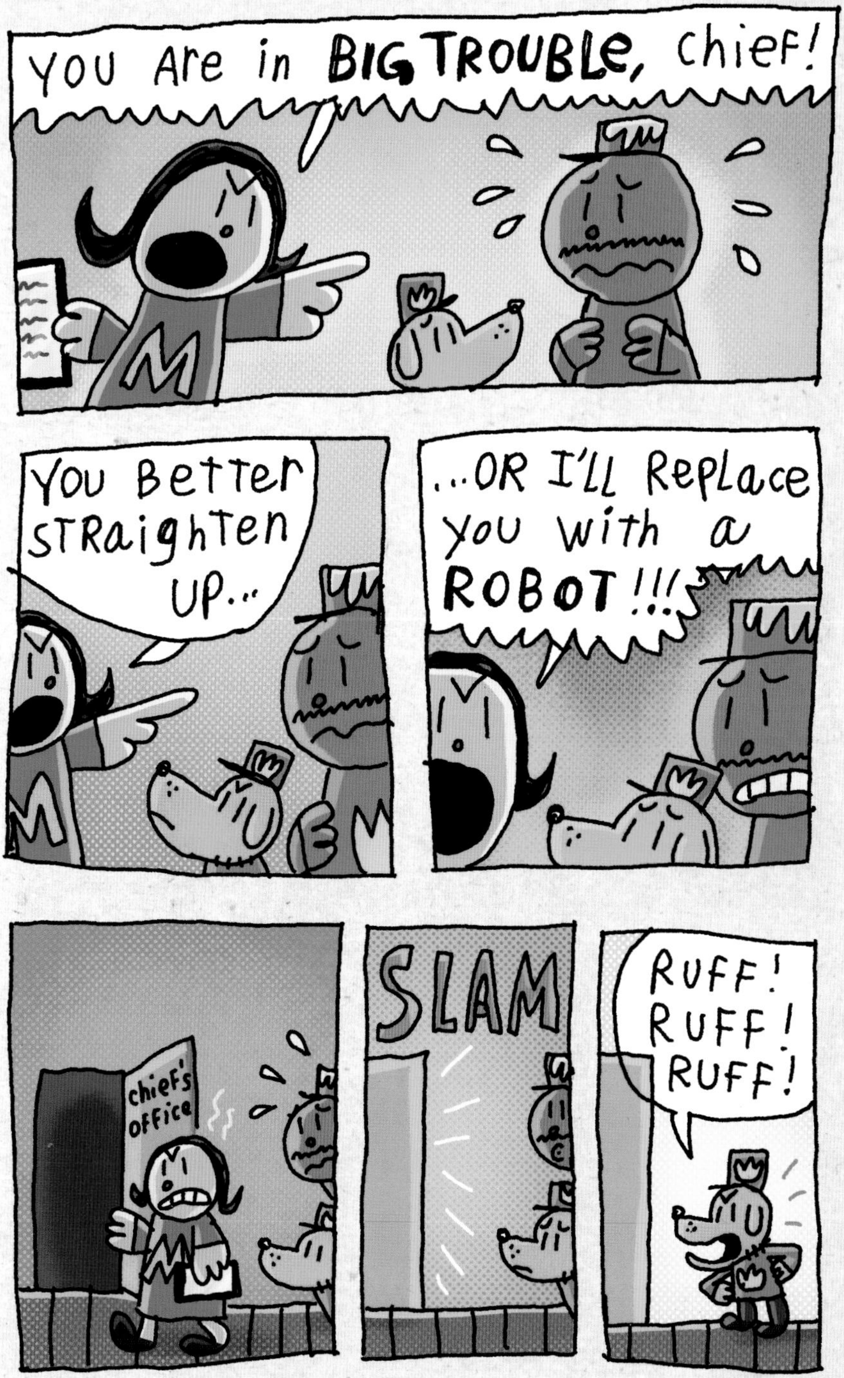
YOU ARE in BIG TROUBLE, chief!
You Better STRAIGHTEN UP...
...OR I'LL Replace you with a ROBOT!!!
chief's office
SLAM
RUFF! RUFF! RUFF!

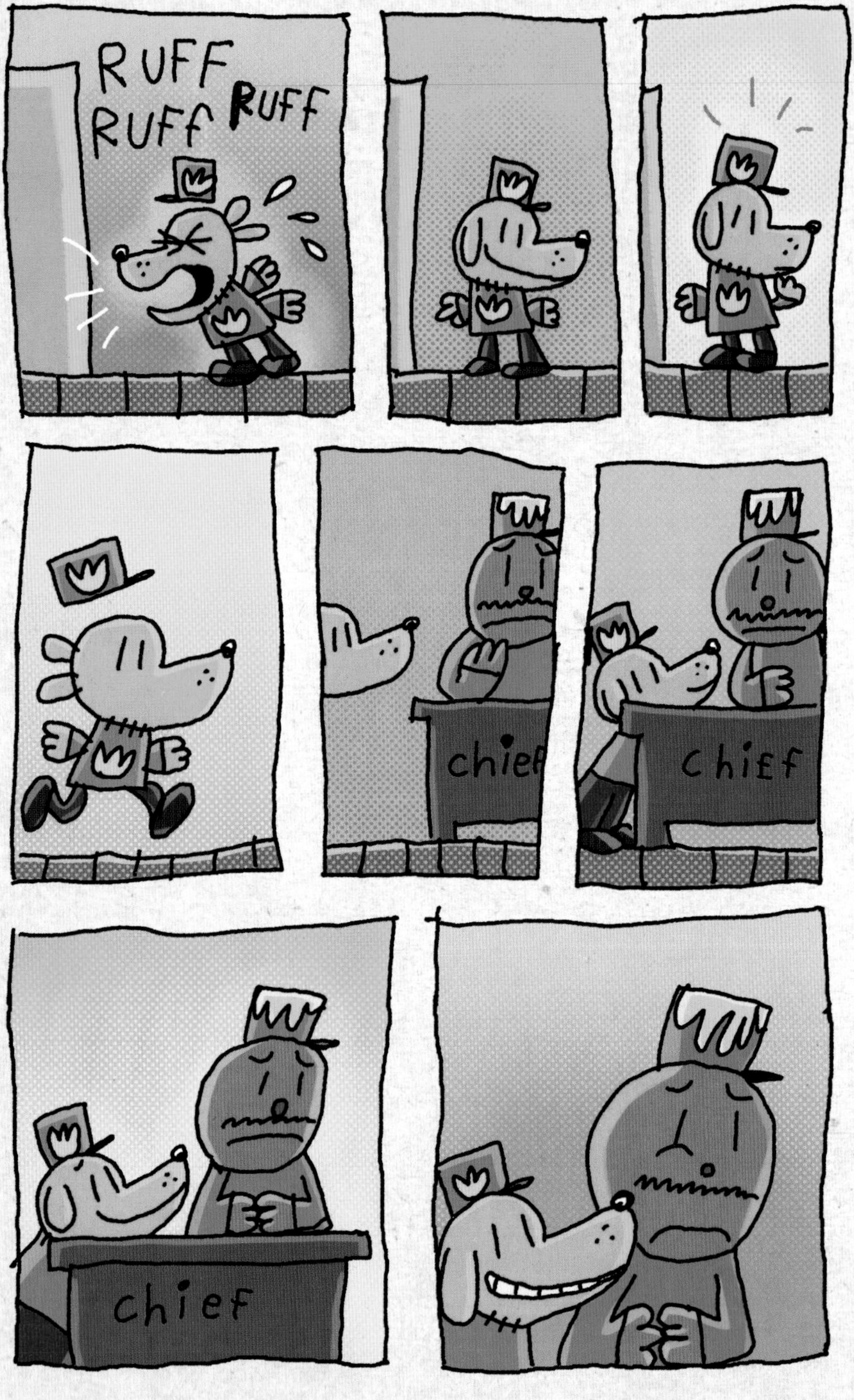
RUFF
RUFF RUFF
chief
Chief
chief

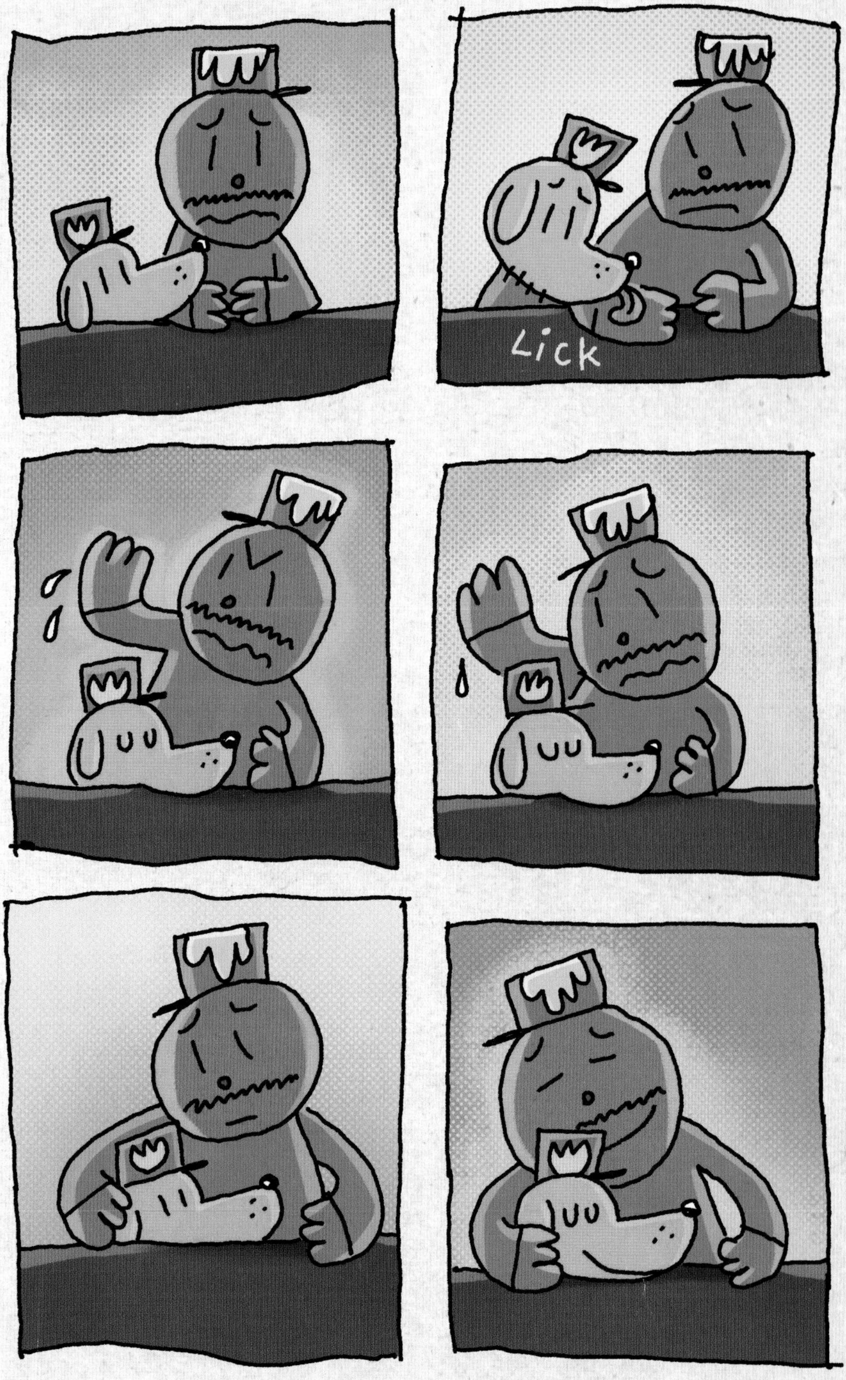
LICK

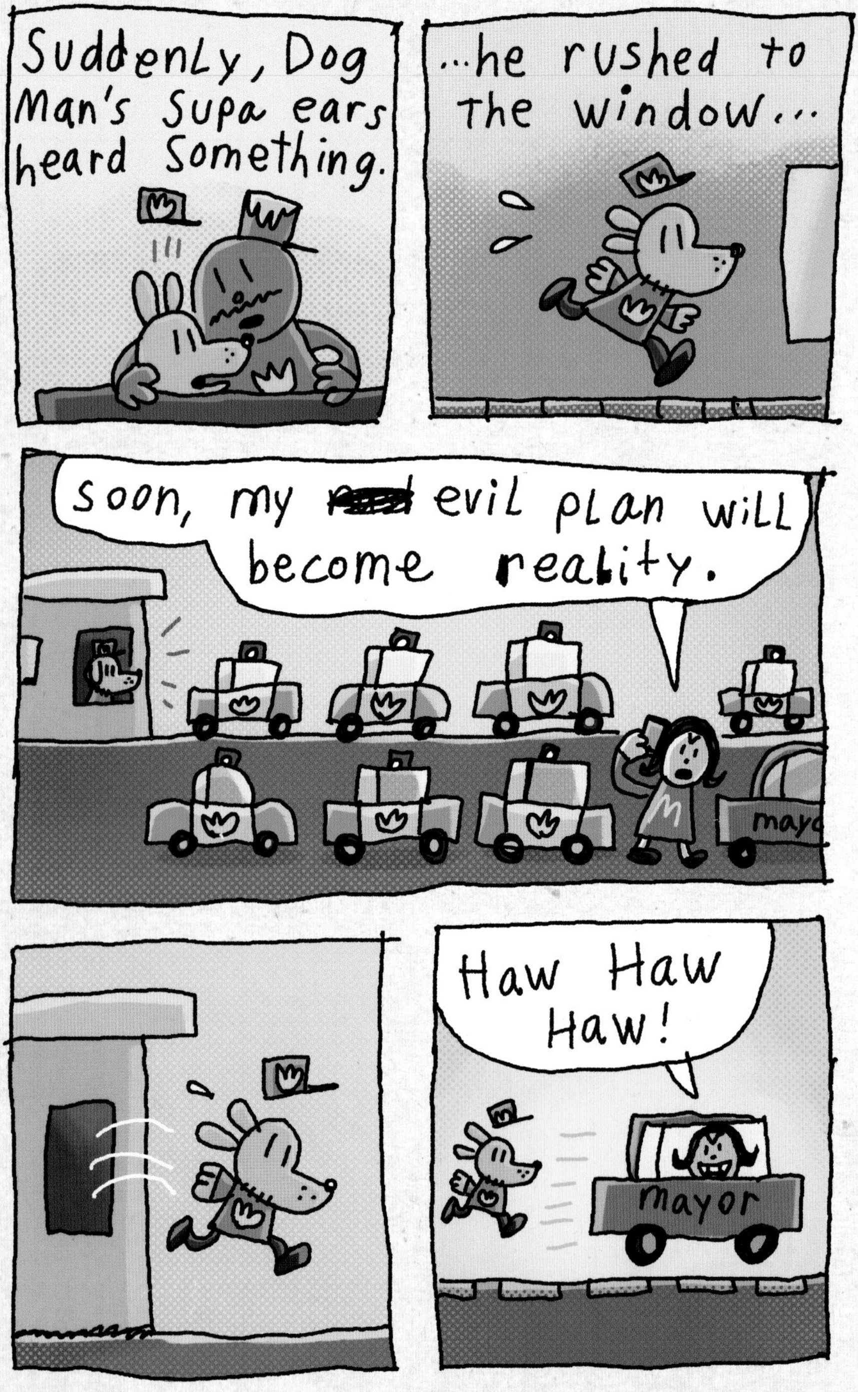
Suddenly, Dog Man's Supa ears heard Something.
...he rushed to The window...
soon, my [redacted] evil plan will become reality.
Haw Haw Haw!
mayor

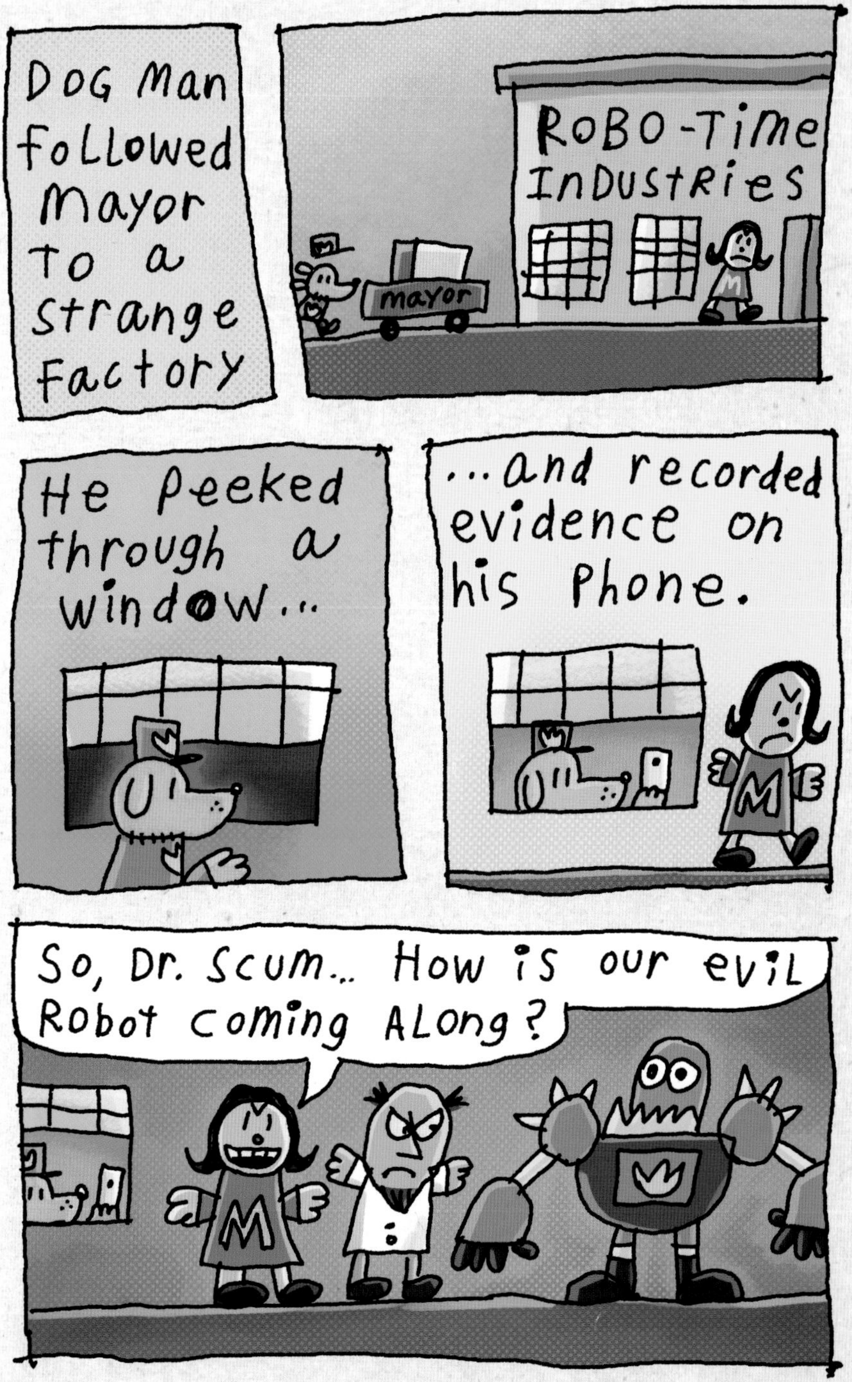
Dog Man followed Mayor to a strange Factory
ROBO-Time Industries
Mayor
He peeked through a window...
...and recorded evidence on his Phone.
So, Dr. Scum... How is our evil Robot coming Along?

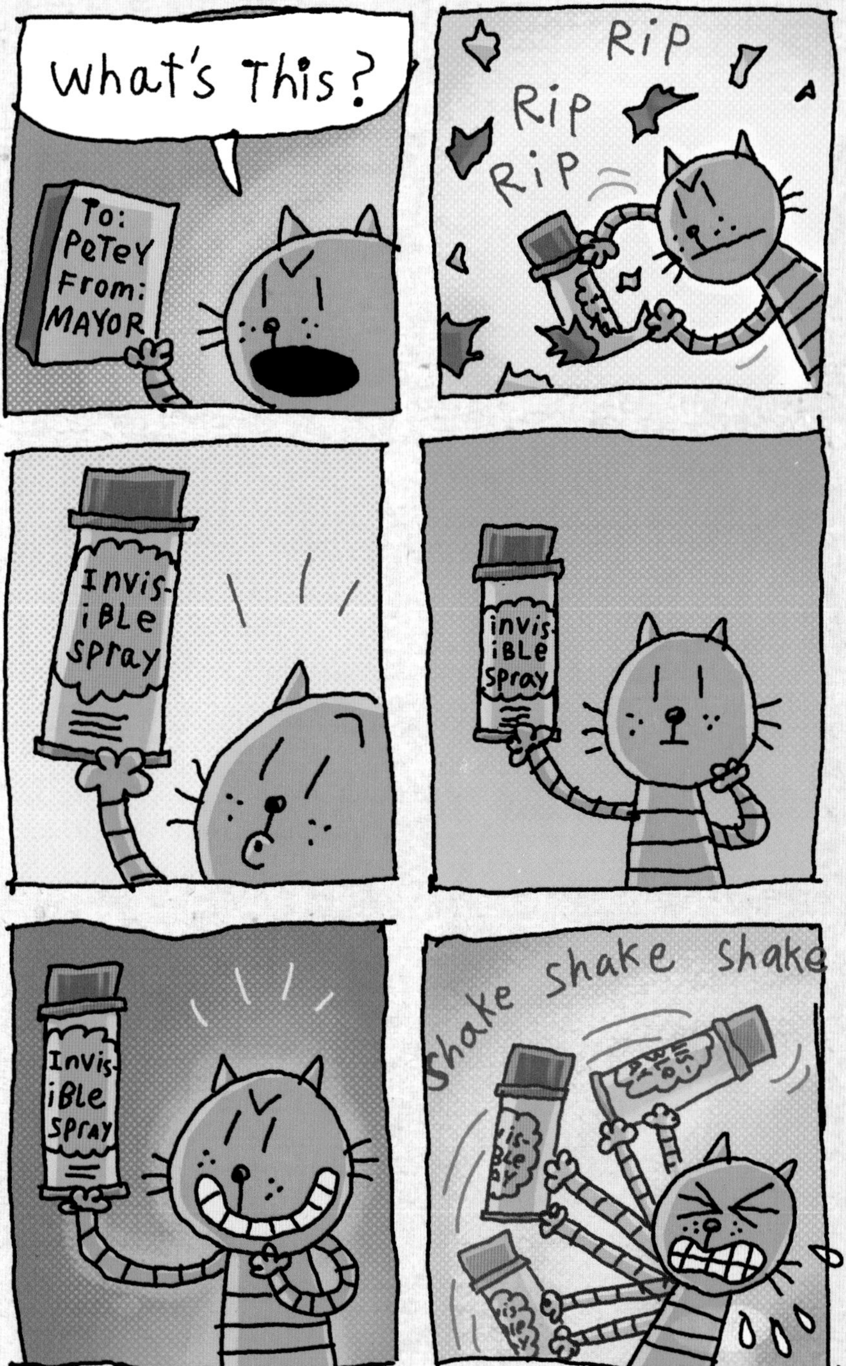
What's This?
To: Petey From: MAYOR
Rip
Rip
Rip
Invis-ible spray
invis-ible spray
Invis-ible spray
Shake shake shake

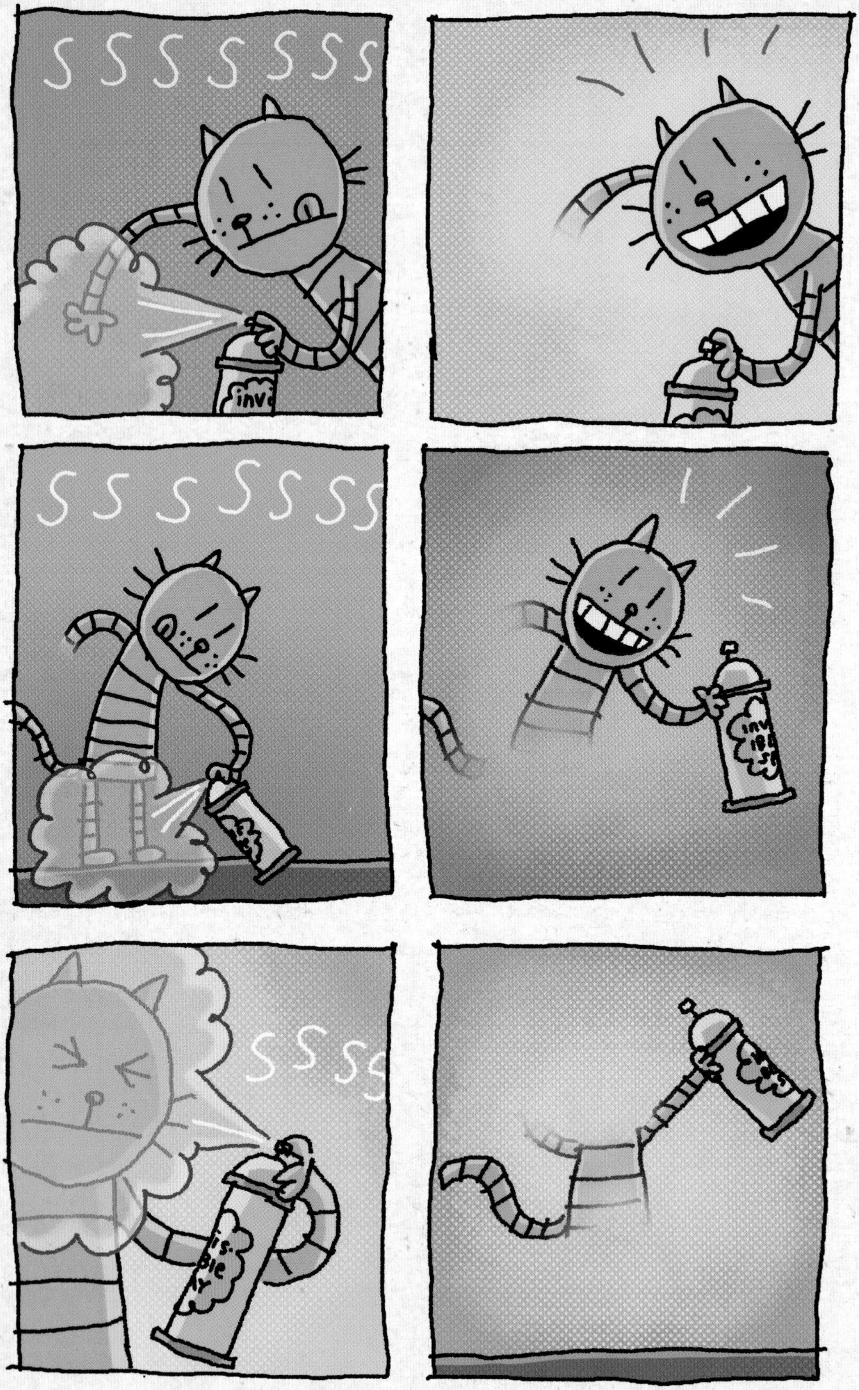
SSSSSSS
SSSSSSS
SSSS

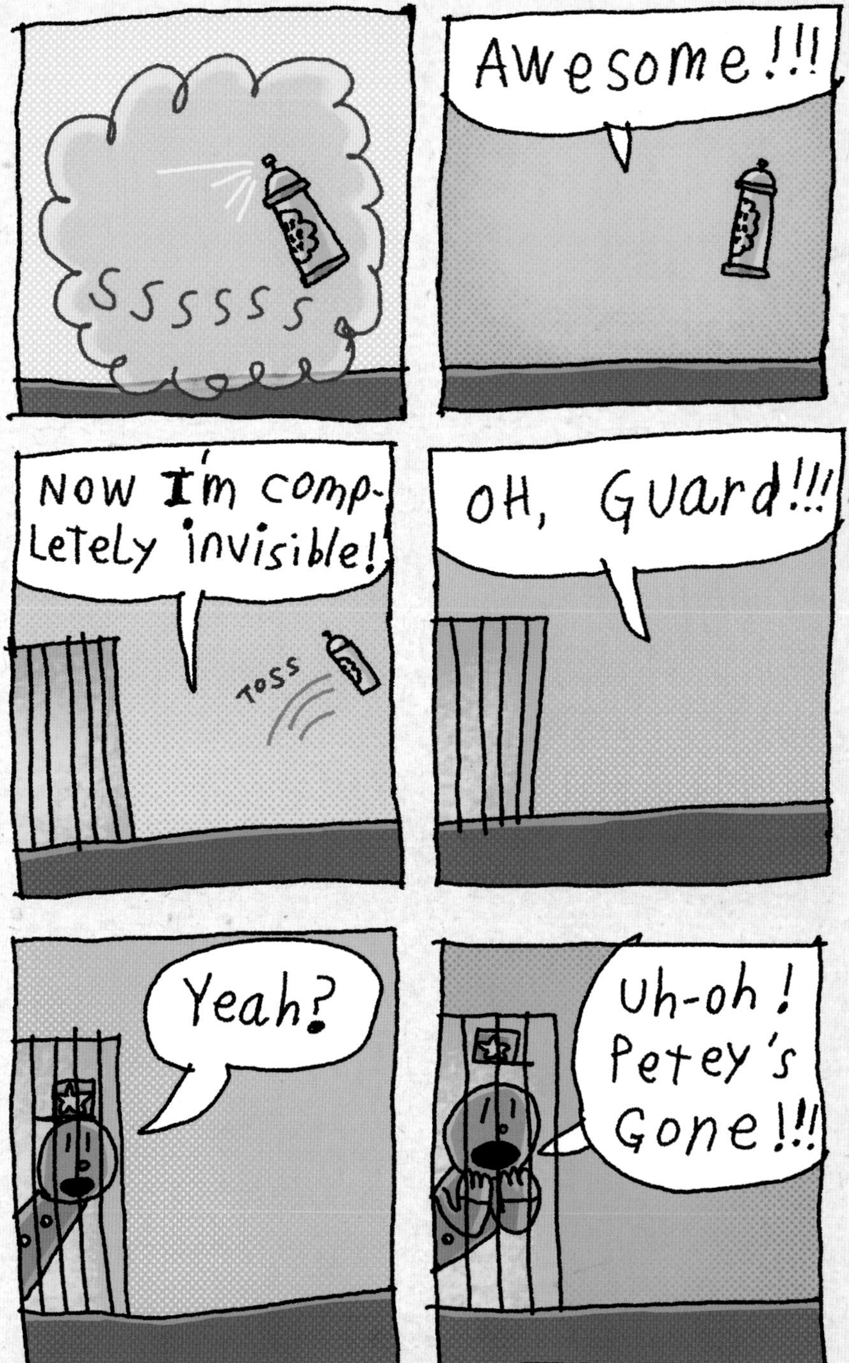
SSSSSS
Awesome!!!
Now I'm completely invisible!
TOSS
OH, Guard!!!
Yeah?
Uh-oh! Petey's Gone!!!

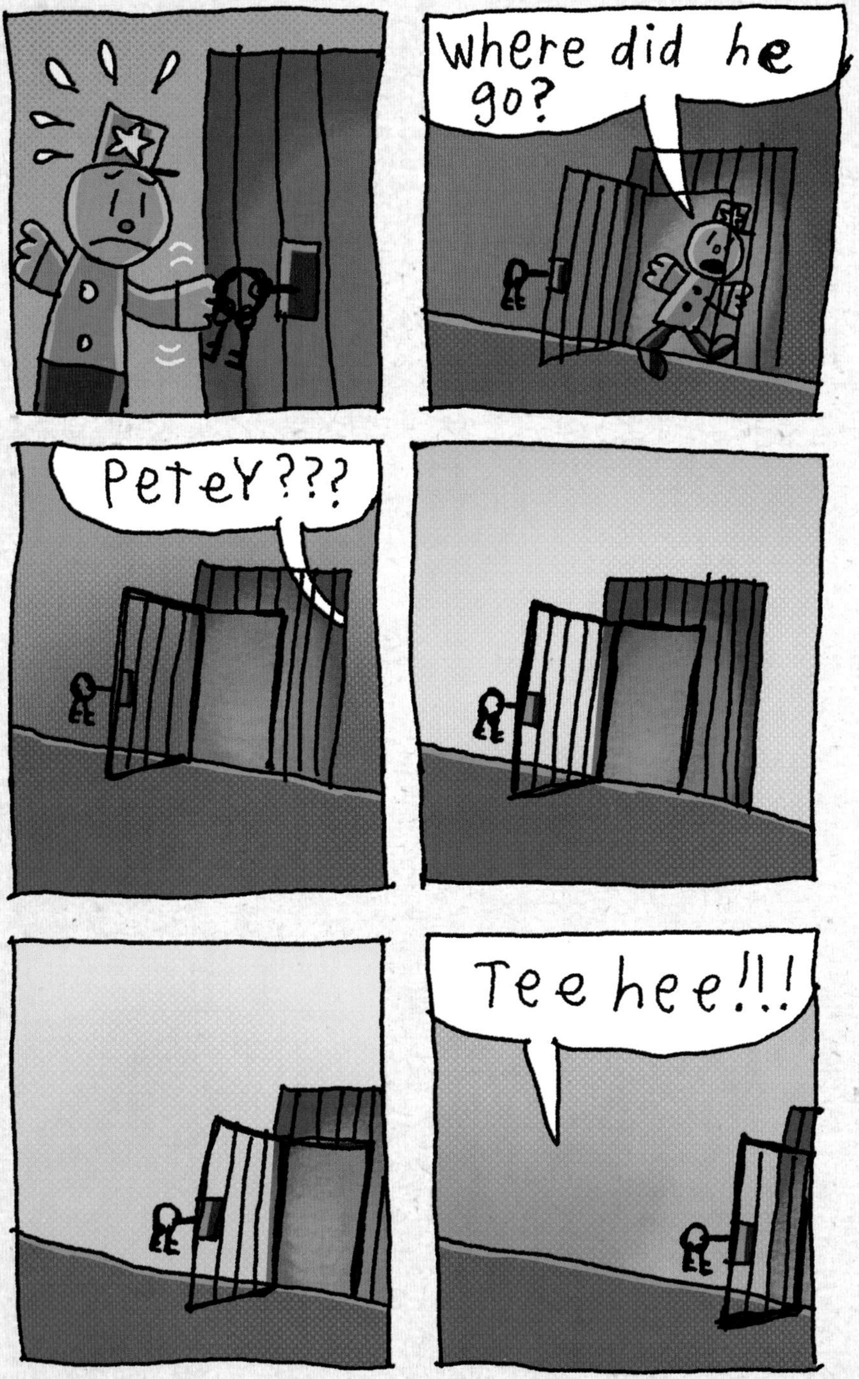
Where did he go?
PeteY???
Teehee!!!

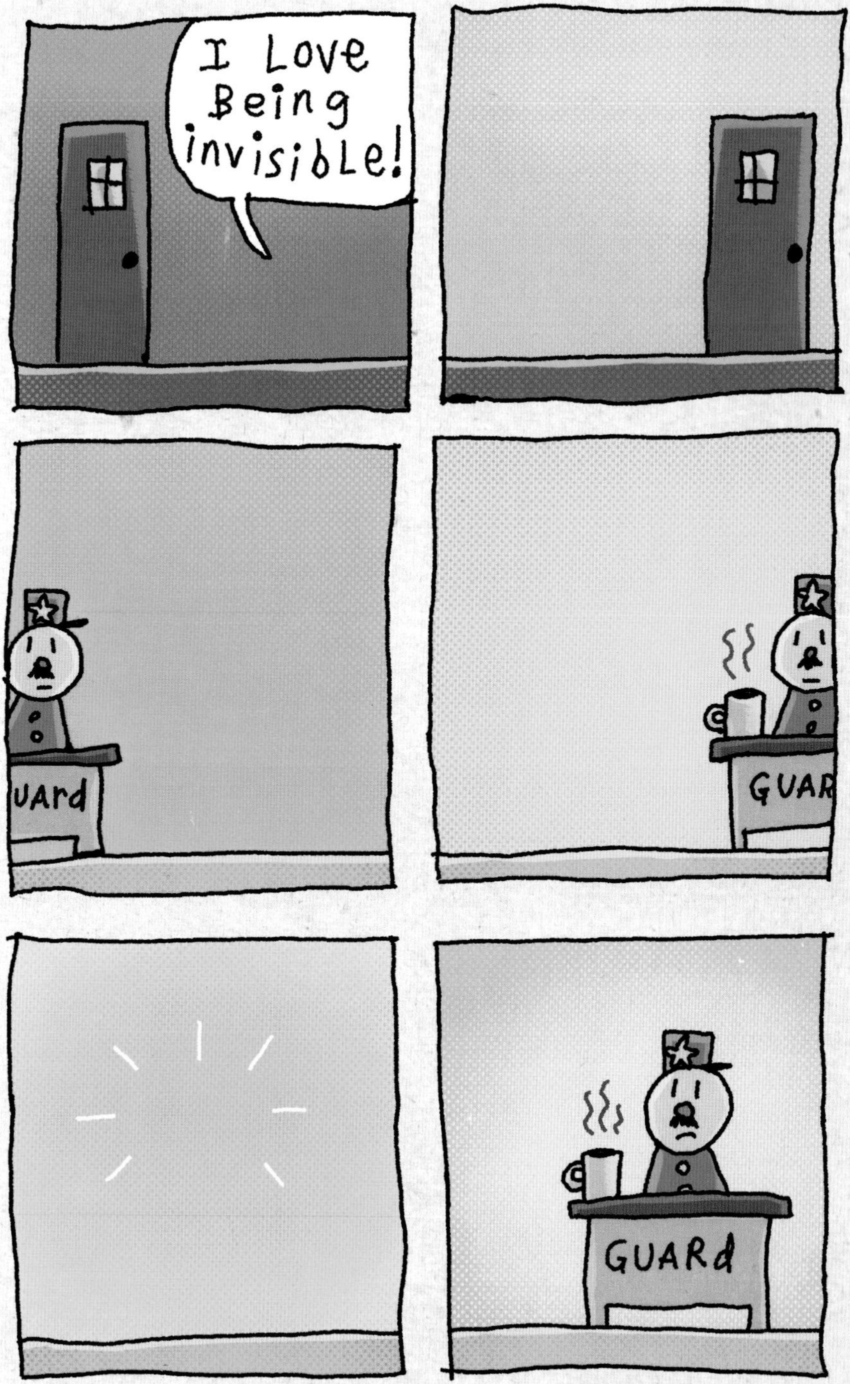
I Love Being invisible!
uArd
GUAR
GUARd

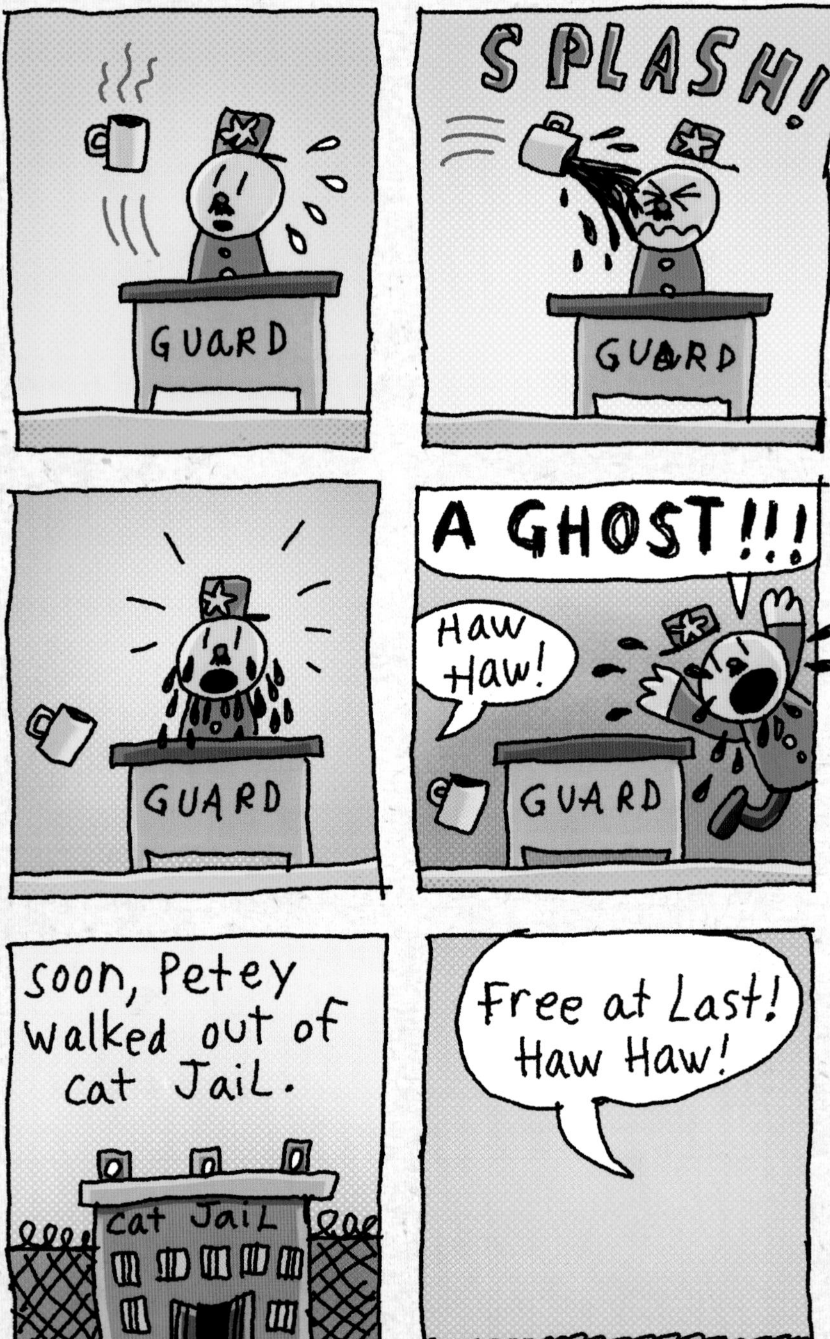
GUARD
SPLASH!
GUARD
GUARD
A GHOST!!!
Haw Haw!
GUARD
soon, Petey walked out of cat JaiL.
cat JaiL
Free at Last! Haw Haw!

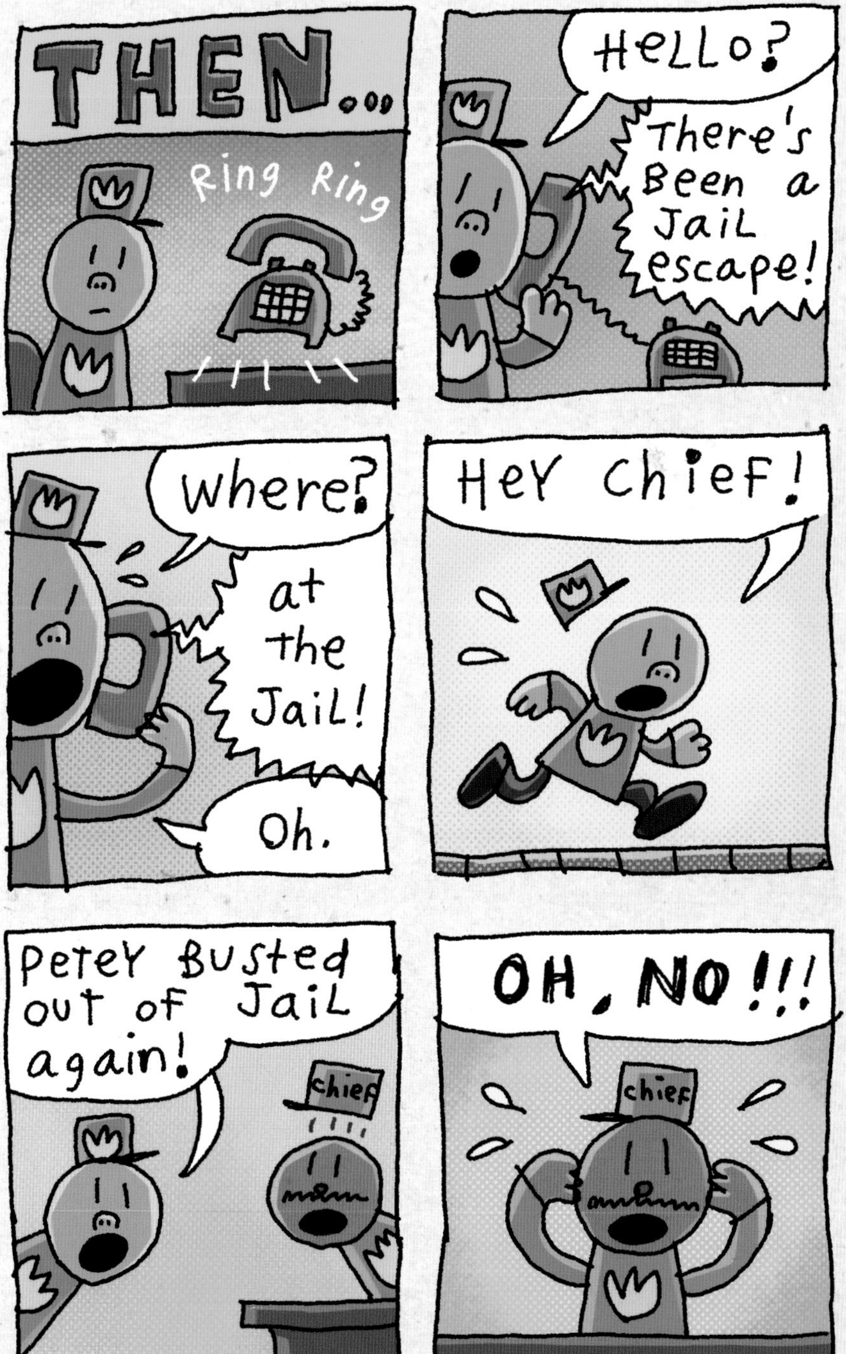
THEN...
Ring Ring
HELLO?
There's Been a JaiL escape!
Where?
at the JaiL!
Oh.
HEY ChieF!
PeteY BUSted out of JaiL again!
chief
chief
OH, NO!!!

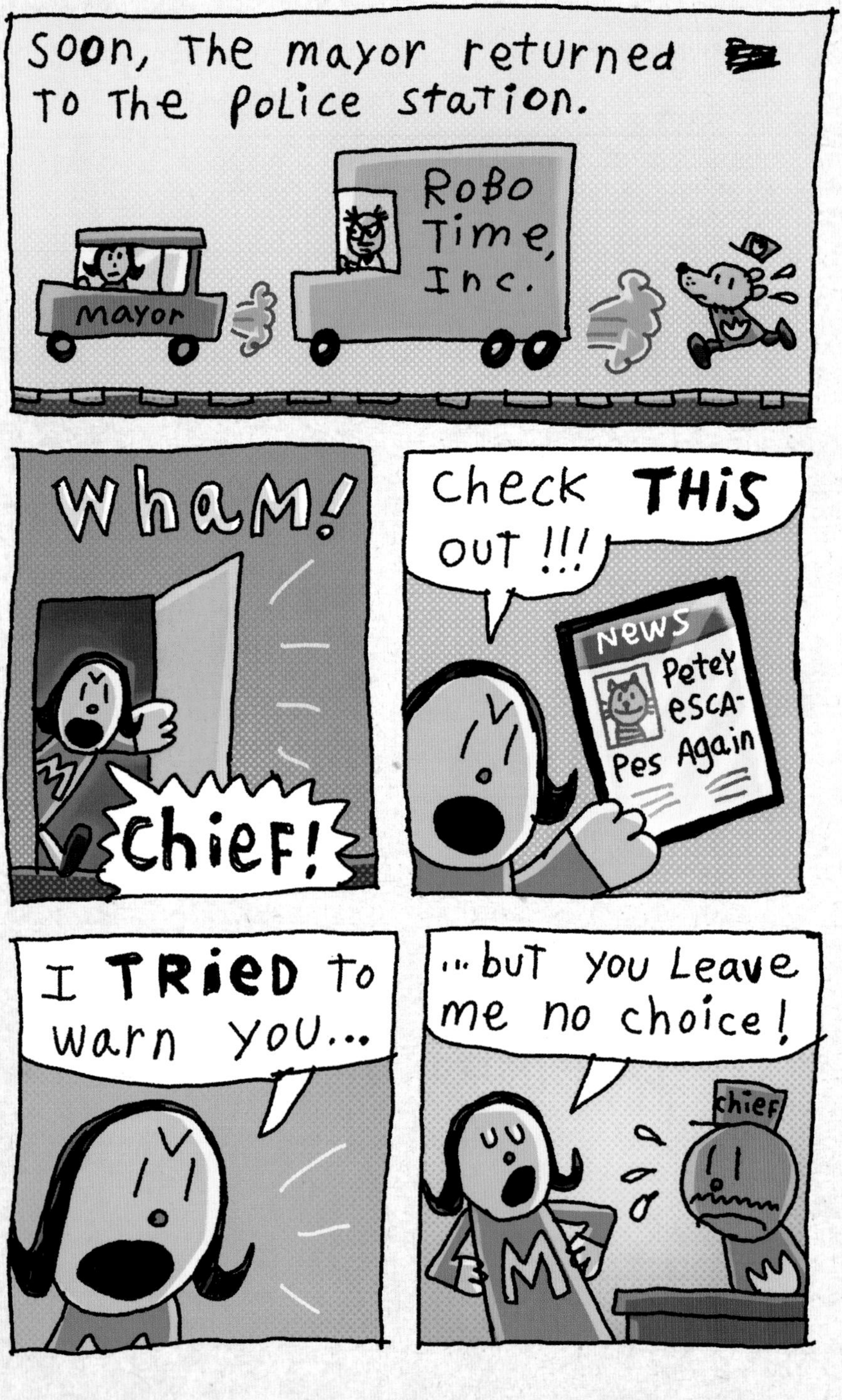

Soon, the mayor returned to the police station.
ROBO Time, Inc.
mayor
WHAM!
CHIEF!
Check THIS out!!!
NEWS
Petey ESCA-
PES Again
I TRIED to warn you...
...but you leave me no choice!
chief

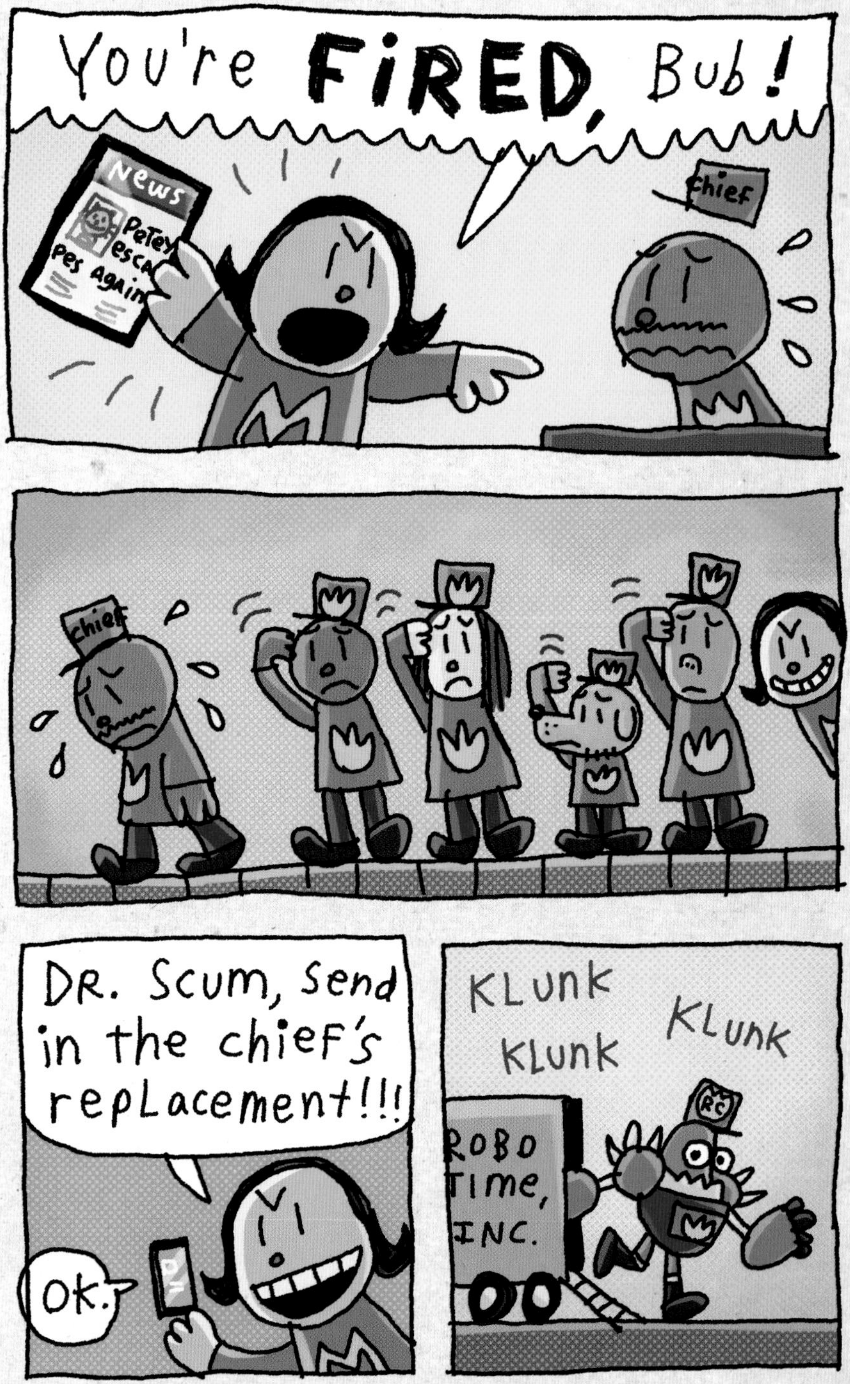
You're FIRED, Bub!
News
Petey escapes again
chief
chief
DR. Scum, send in the chief's replacement!!!
OK.
KLUNK
KLUNK
KLUNK
ROBO TIME, INC.
RC

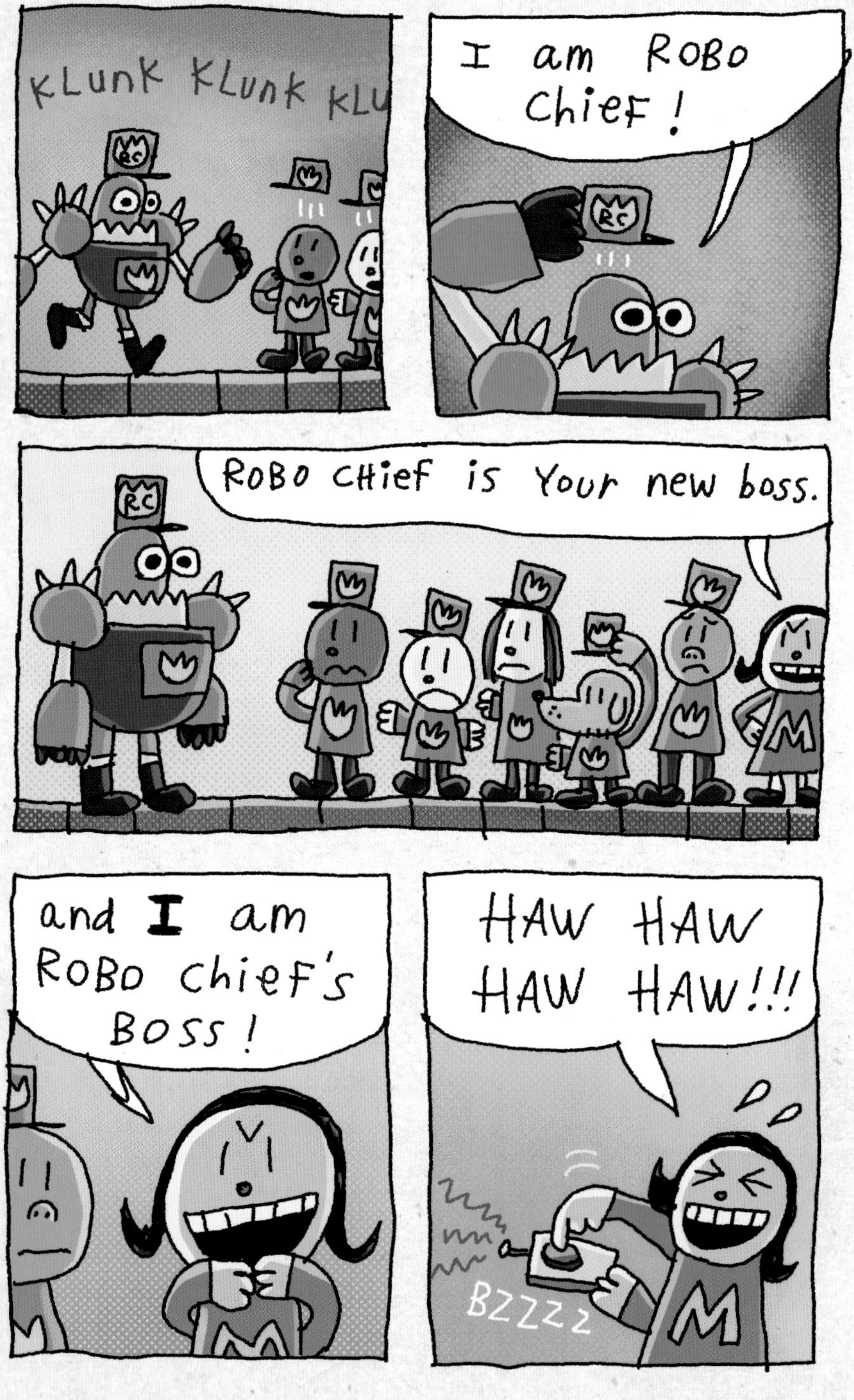
KLUNK KLUNK KLU
I am ROBO CHIEF!
ROBO CHIEF is Your new boss.
and I am ROBO chief's BOSS!
HAW HAW HAW HAW!!!
BZZZZ

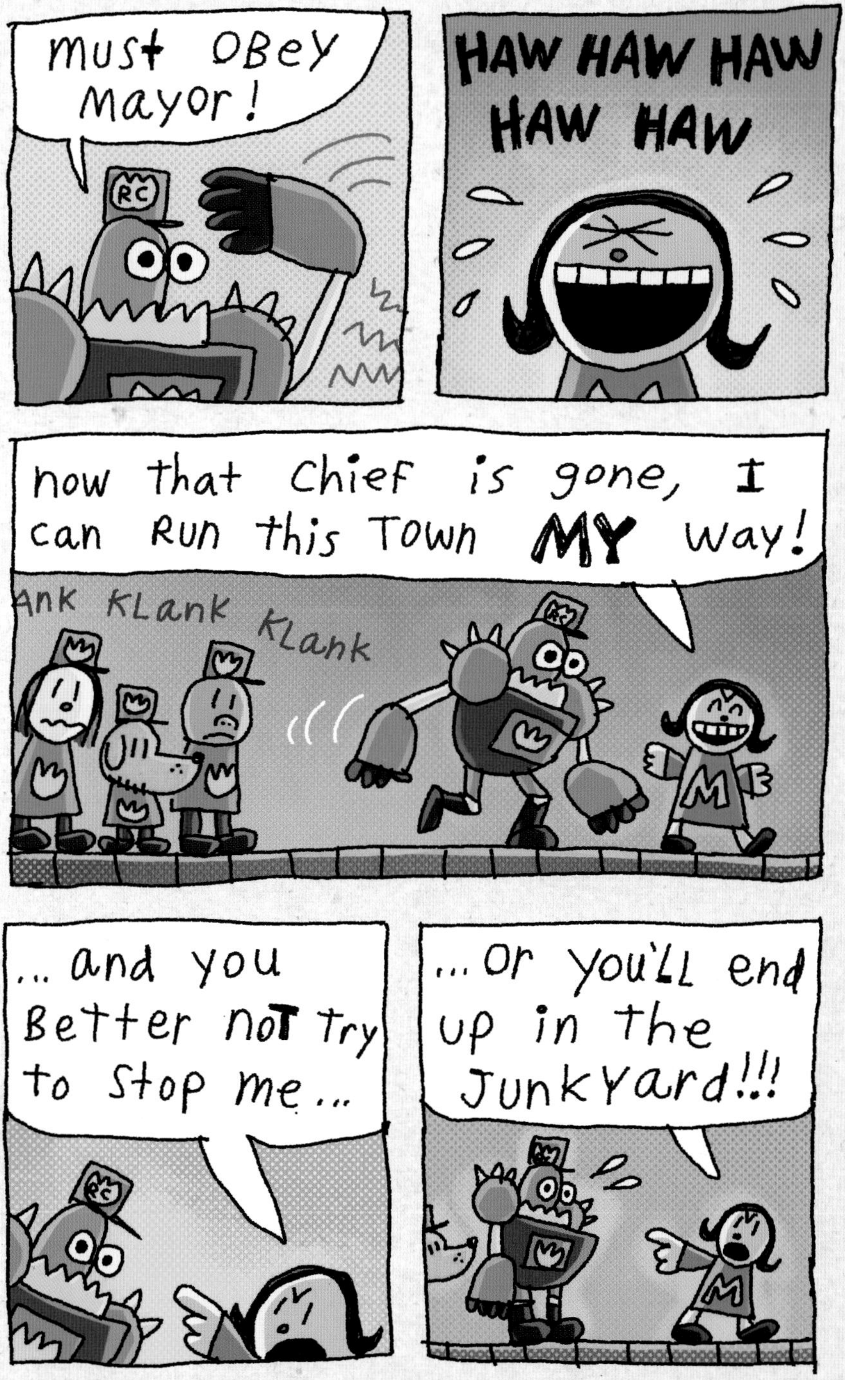
must OBey Mayor!
HAW HAW HAW HAW HAW HAW
now that Chief is gone, I can RUN this Town MY way!
Ank KLank KLank
... and you Better noT Try to Stop me...
... Or you'LL end up in the JunkYard!!!

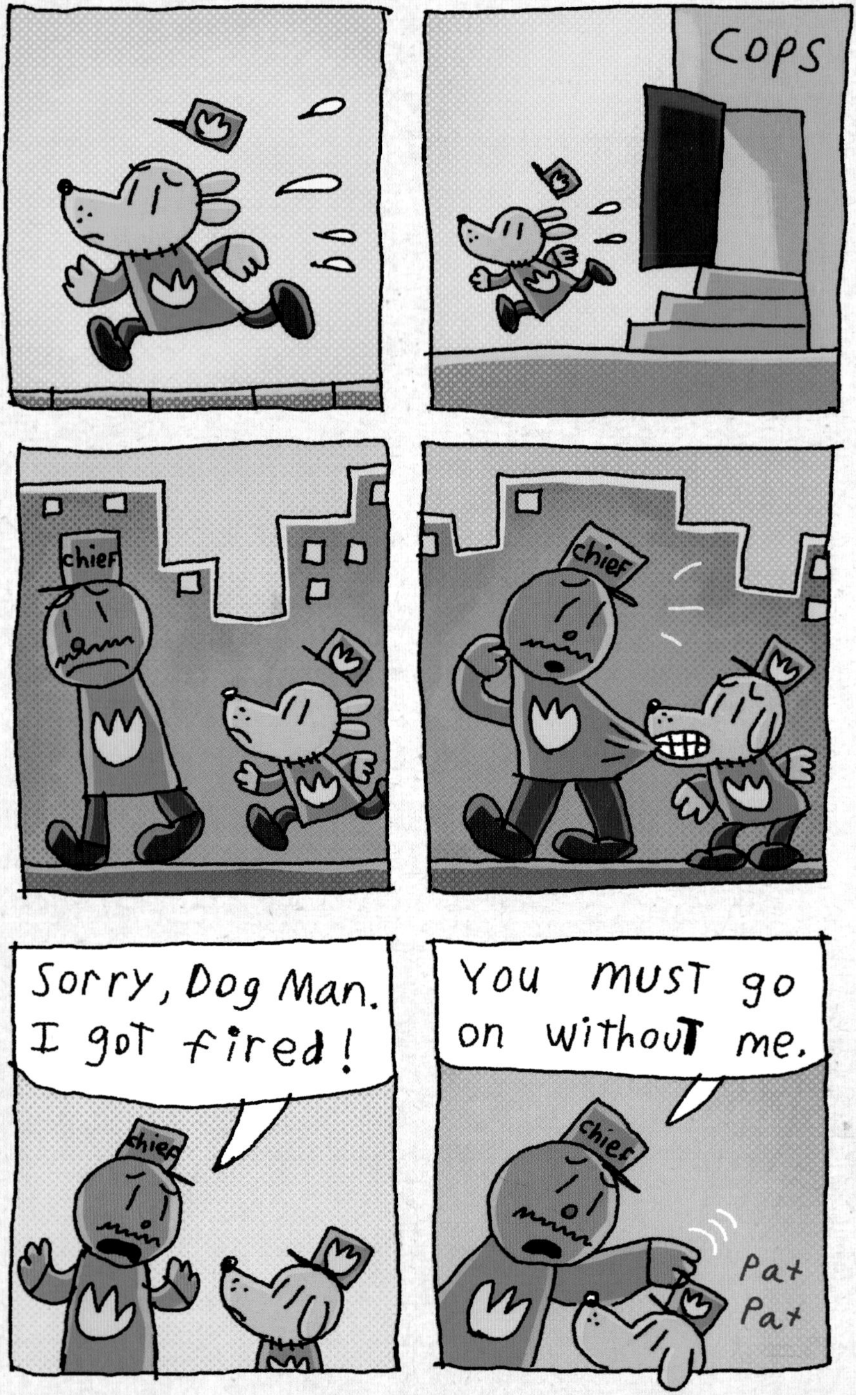
COPS
chief
chief
Sorry, Dog Man. I got fired!
chief
You MUST go on without me.
chief
Pat Pat

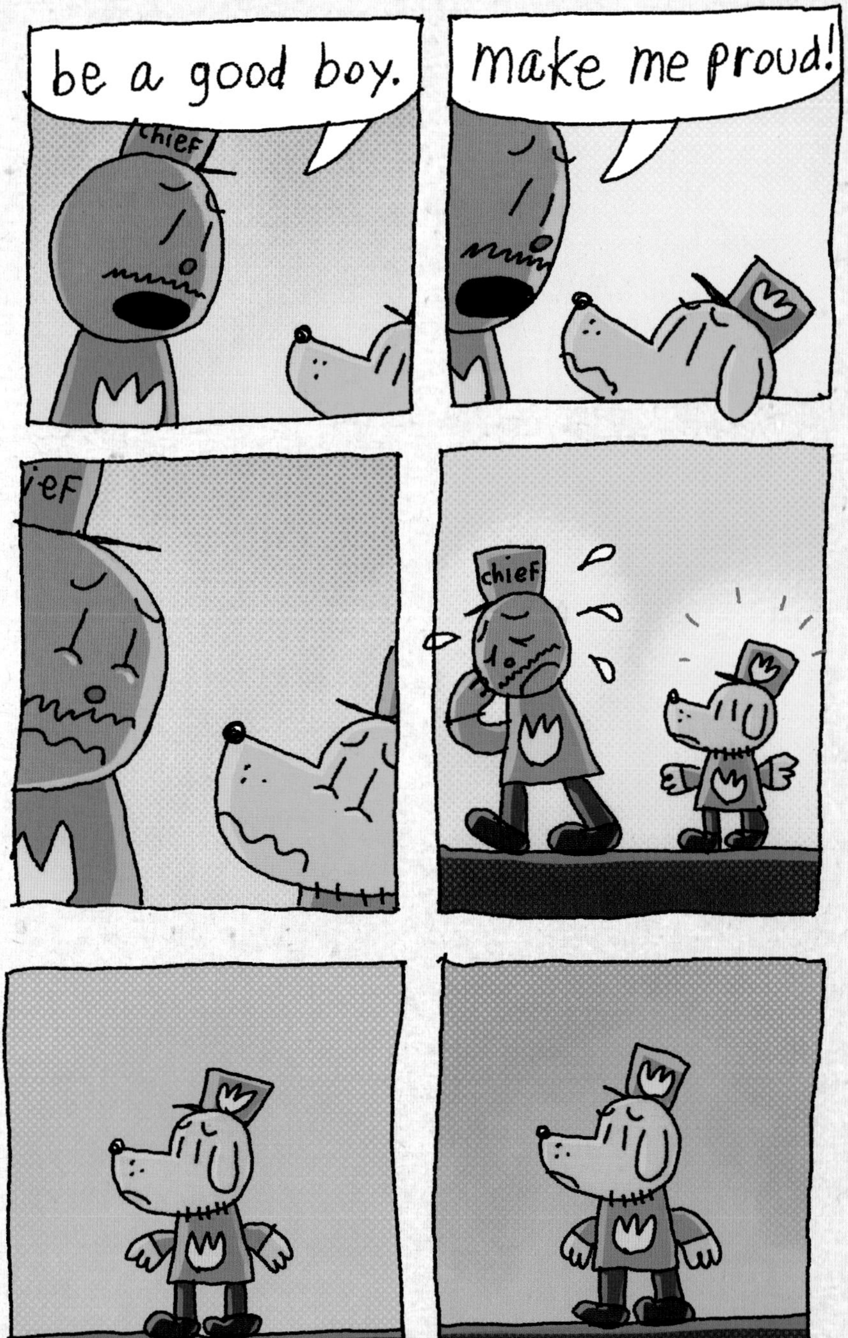
be a good boy.
make me proud!
chief
chief
chief

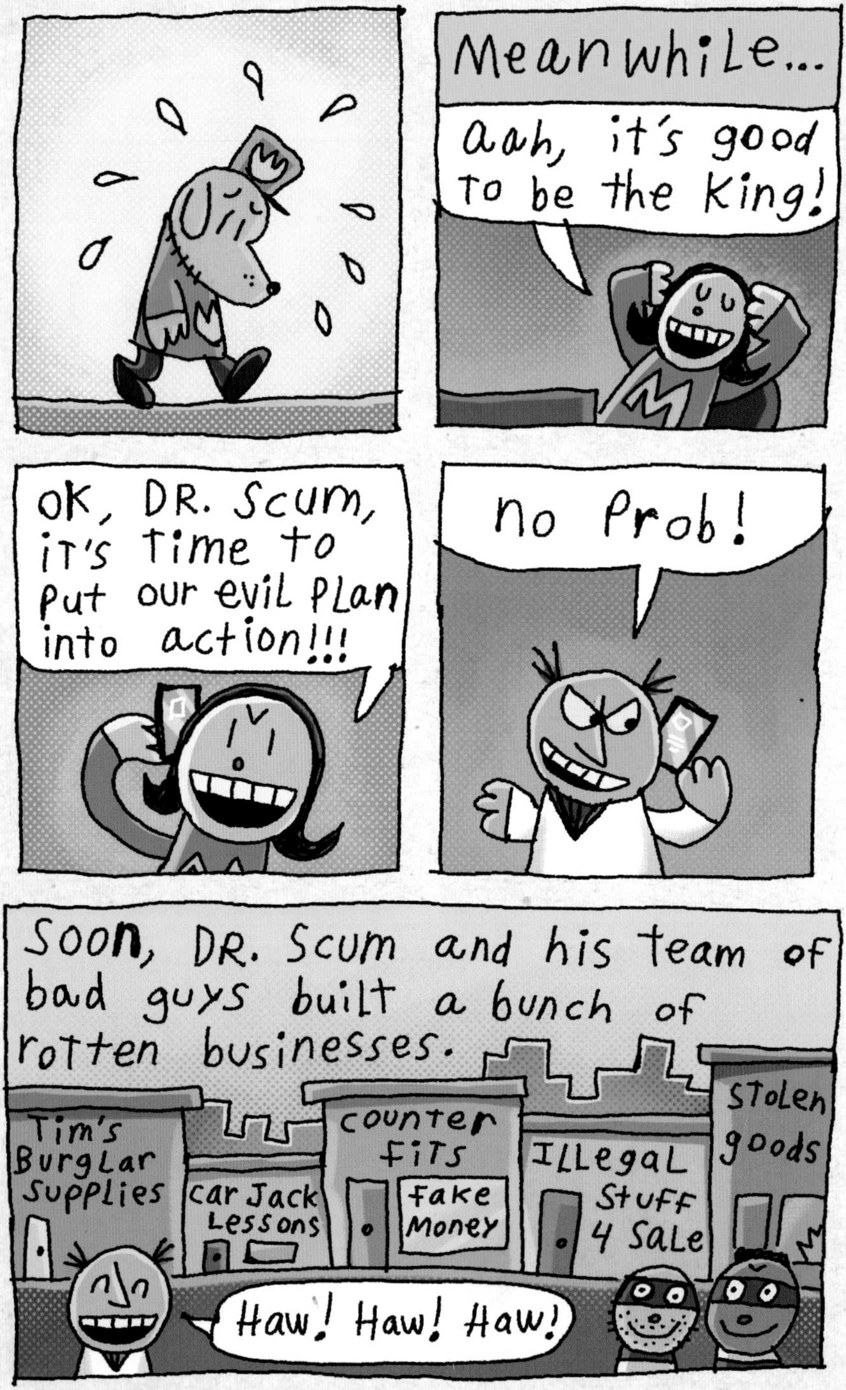
Meanwhile...
aah, it's good to be the King!
OK, DR. Scum, it's time to put our evil PLan into action!!!
no Prob!
Soon, DR. Scum and his team of bad guys built a bunch of rotten businesses.
Tim's Burglar Supplies
car Jack Lessons
counter fits
Fake Money
ILLegal Stuff 4 SaLe
StoLen goods
Haw! Haw! Haw!

and all cops were ordered to stay away.

it was the perfect crime...

...except for one thing!

Invisible Petey was not Happy!

Grrr!

Somebody is ~~trying~~ trying to muscle in on **MY** Territory!

I have to Stop those evil Jerks!

There can only be **ONE** villain in This town!!!

Invisible Petey got right to Work.

He Followed each customer into The rotten Stores...

BILL'S BomBs

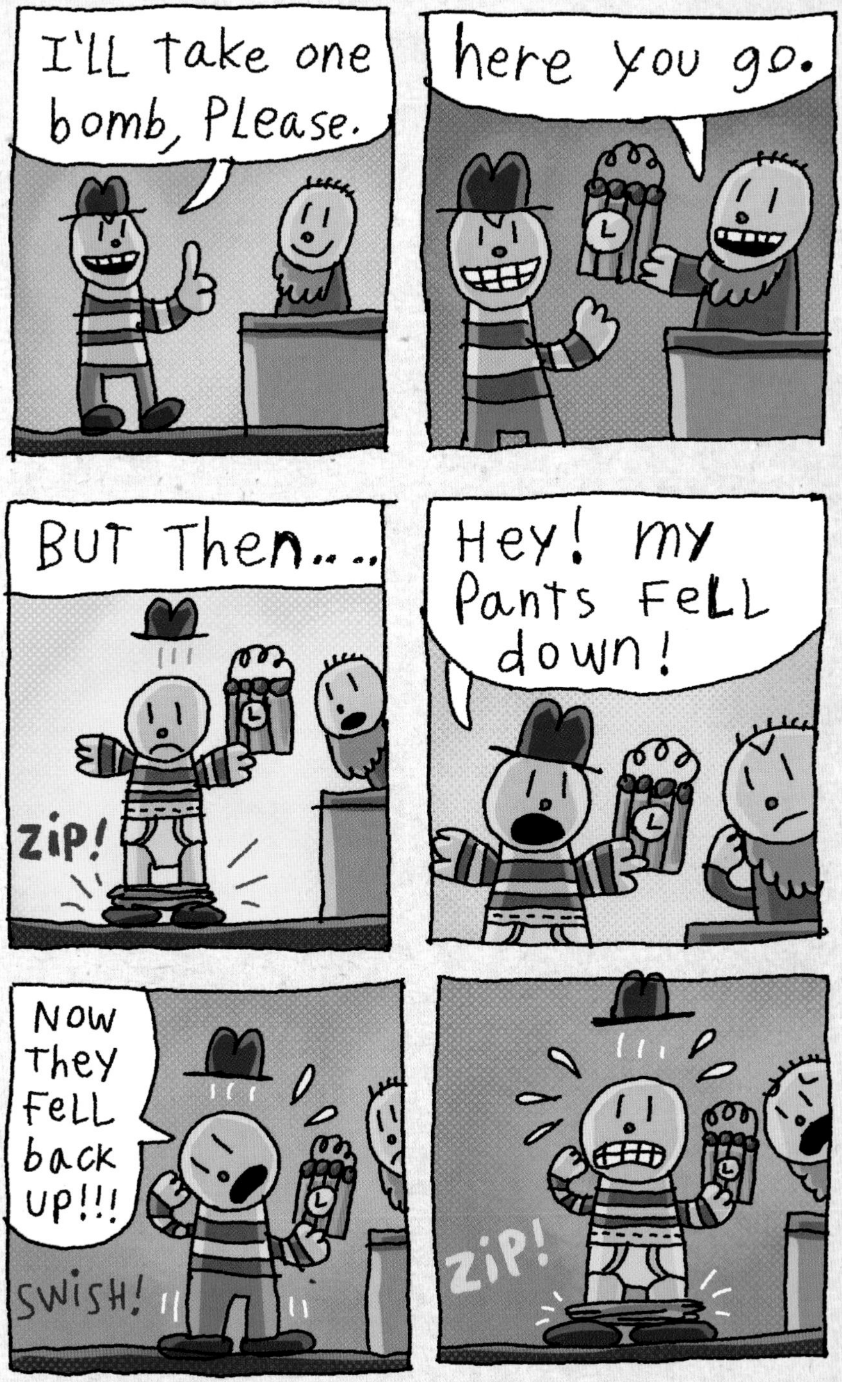
I'LL take one bomb, PLease.
here you go.
BUT Then....
ZIP!
Hey! my Pants FeLL down!
Now they FeLL back up!!!
SWISH!
ZIP!

TRIPLE FLIP-O-RAMAS

animate the action cheesily. Here's How:

Hold Book open Like this...

Flip Page Back and Forth.

add your own sound effects!

Left hand here.

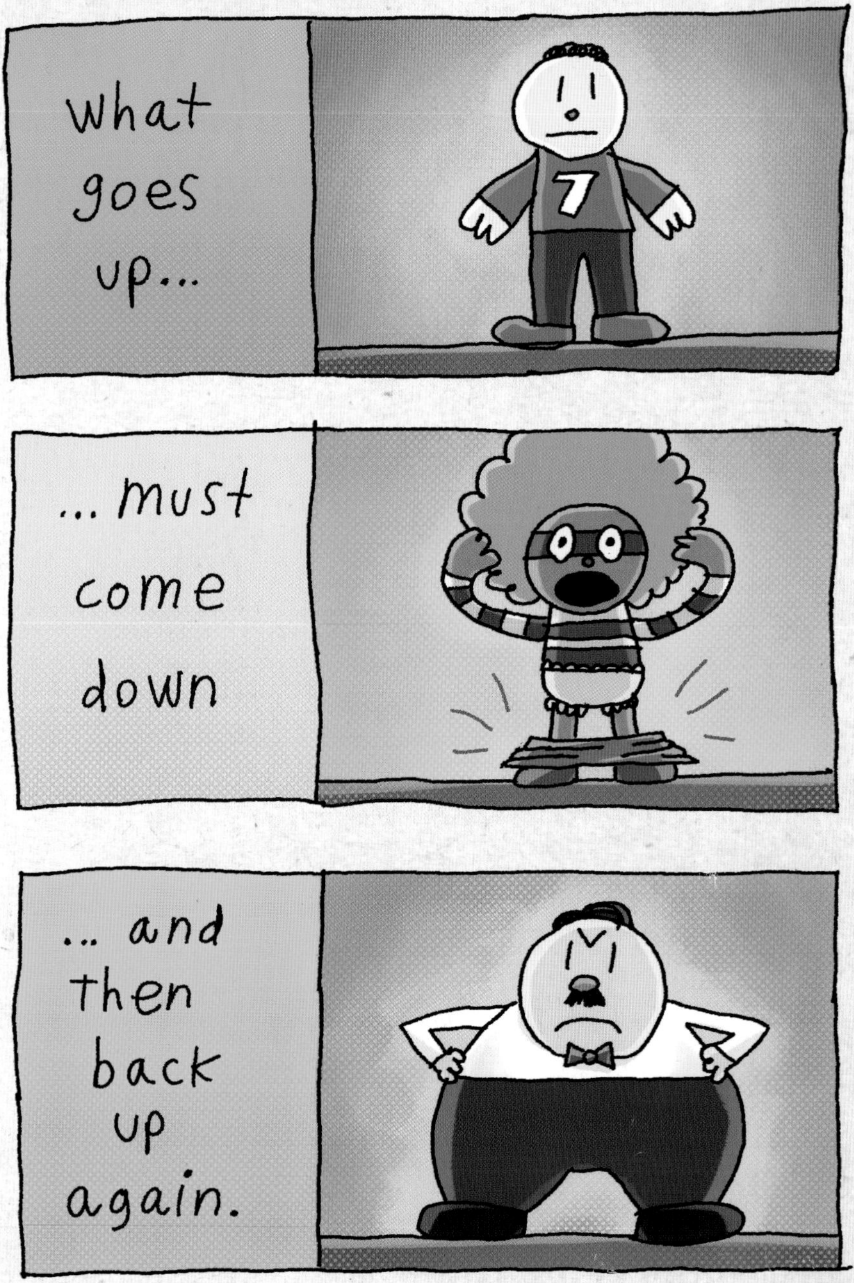
what goes up...
7
...must come down
... and then back up again.

Right Thumb here.

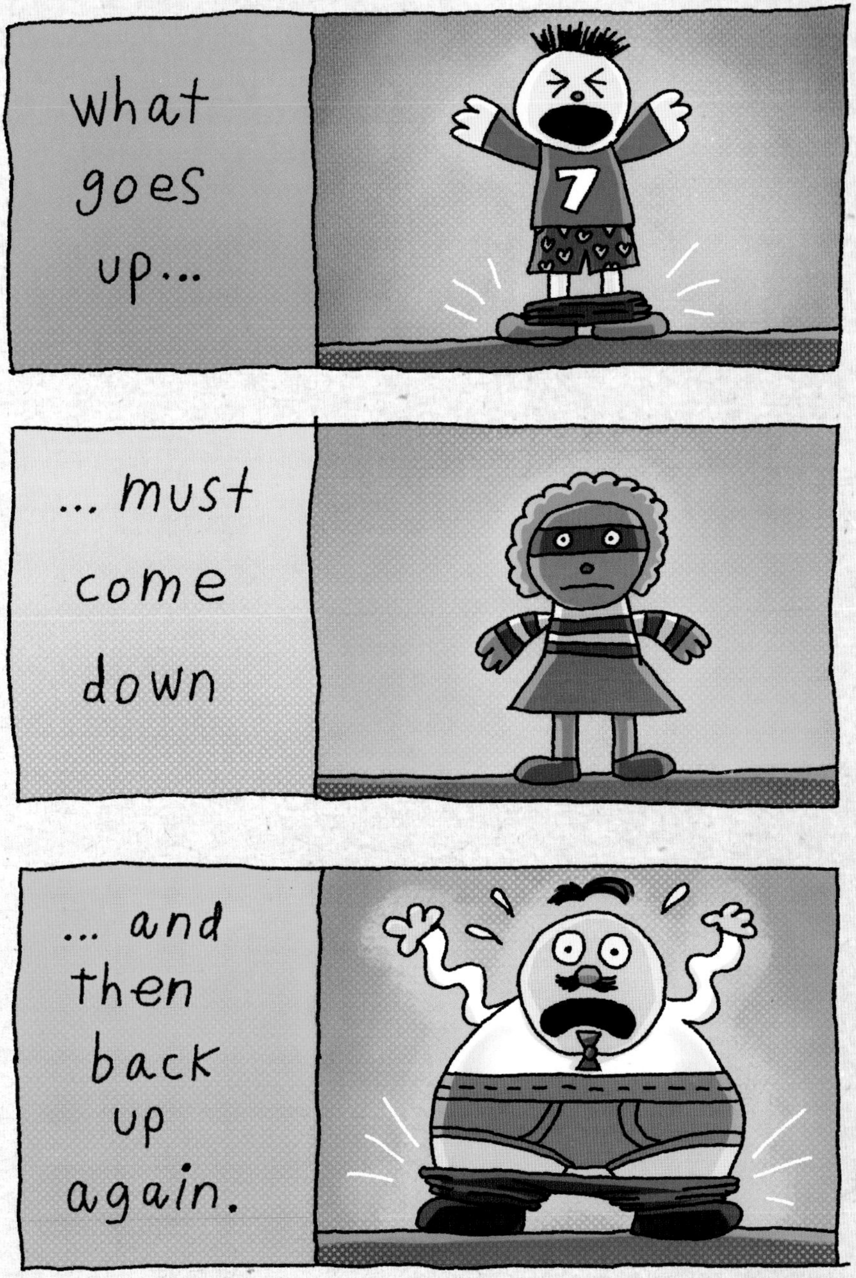
what goes up...
... must come down
... and then back up again.

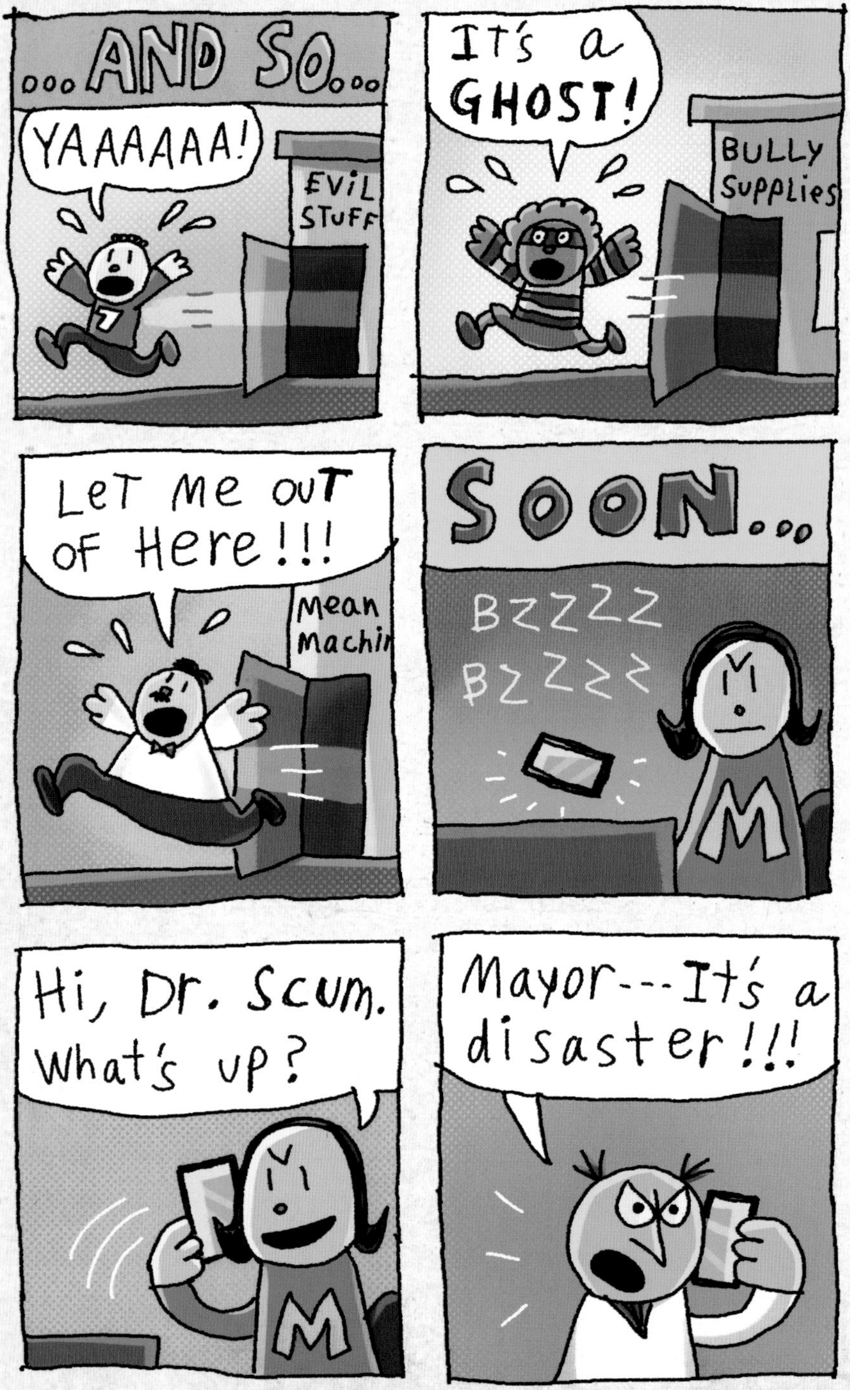
...AND SO...
YAAAAAA!
EVIL STUFF
It's a GHOST!
BULLY Supplies
Let me out of here!!!
Mean Machi
SOON...
BZZZZ
BZZZZ
Hi, Dr. Scum. What's up?
Mayor---It's a disaster!!!

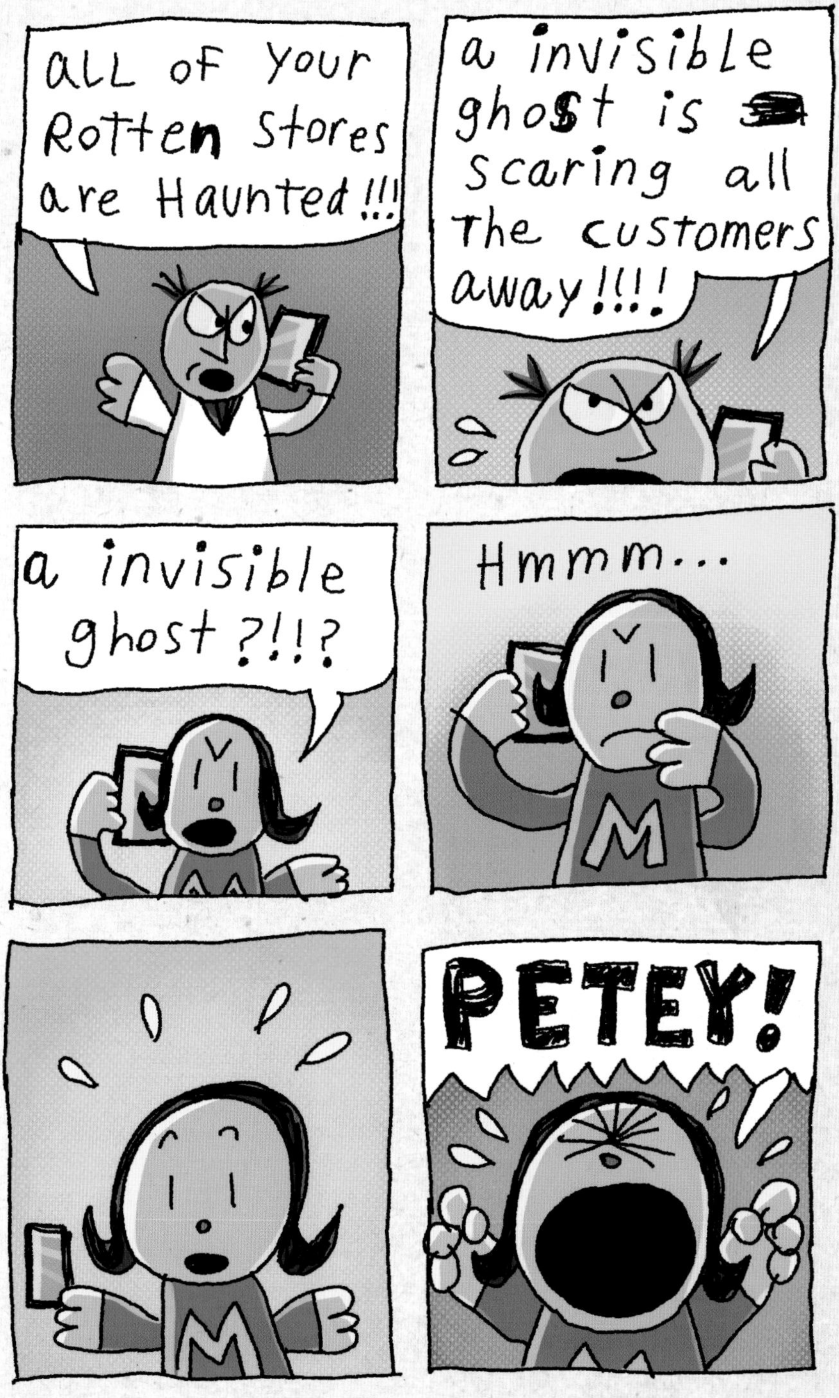
ALL OF YOUR ROTTEN STORES ARE HAUNTED!!!
A INVISIBLE GHOST IS SCARING ALL THE CUSTOMERS AWAY!!!!
A INVISIBLE GHOST?!!?
HMMM...
PETEY!

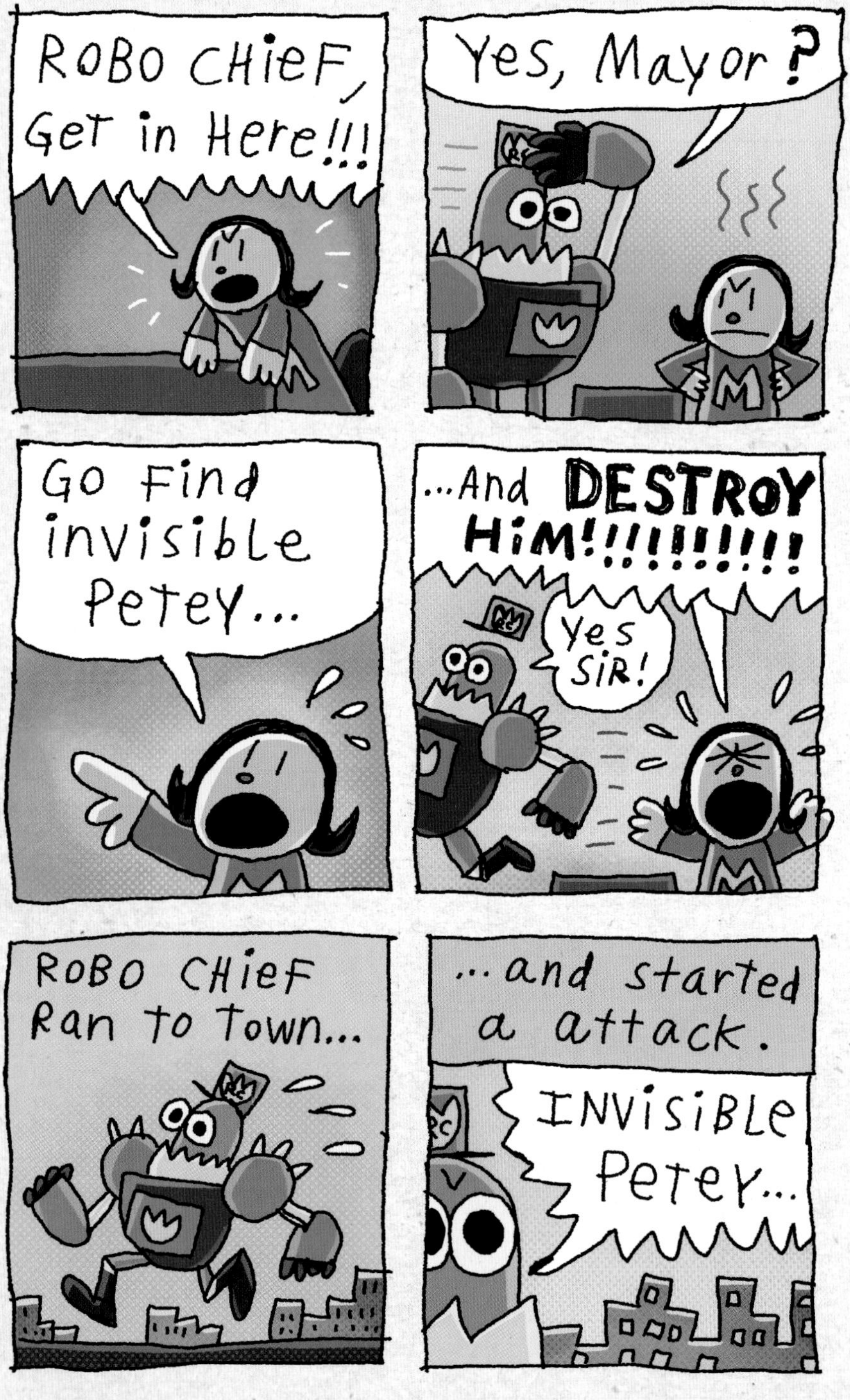
ROBO CHIEF, Get in Here!!!
Yes, Mayor?
Go Find invisible Petey...
...And DESTROY HIM!!!!!!!!!!!
Yes SIR!
ROBO CHIEF Ran to Town...
...and started a attack.
INVISIBLE Petey...

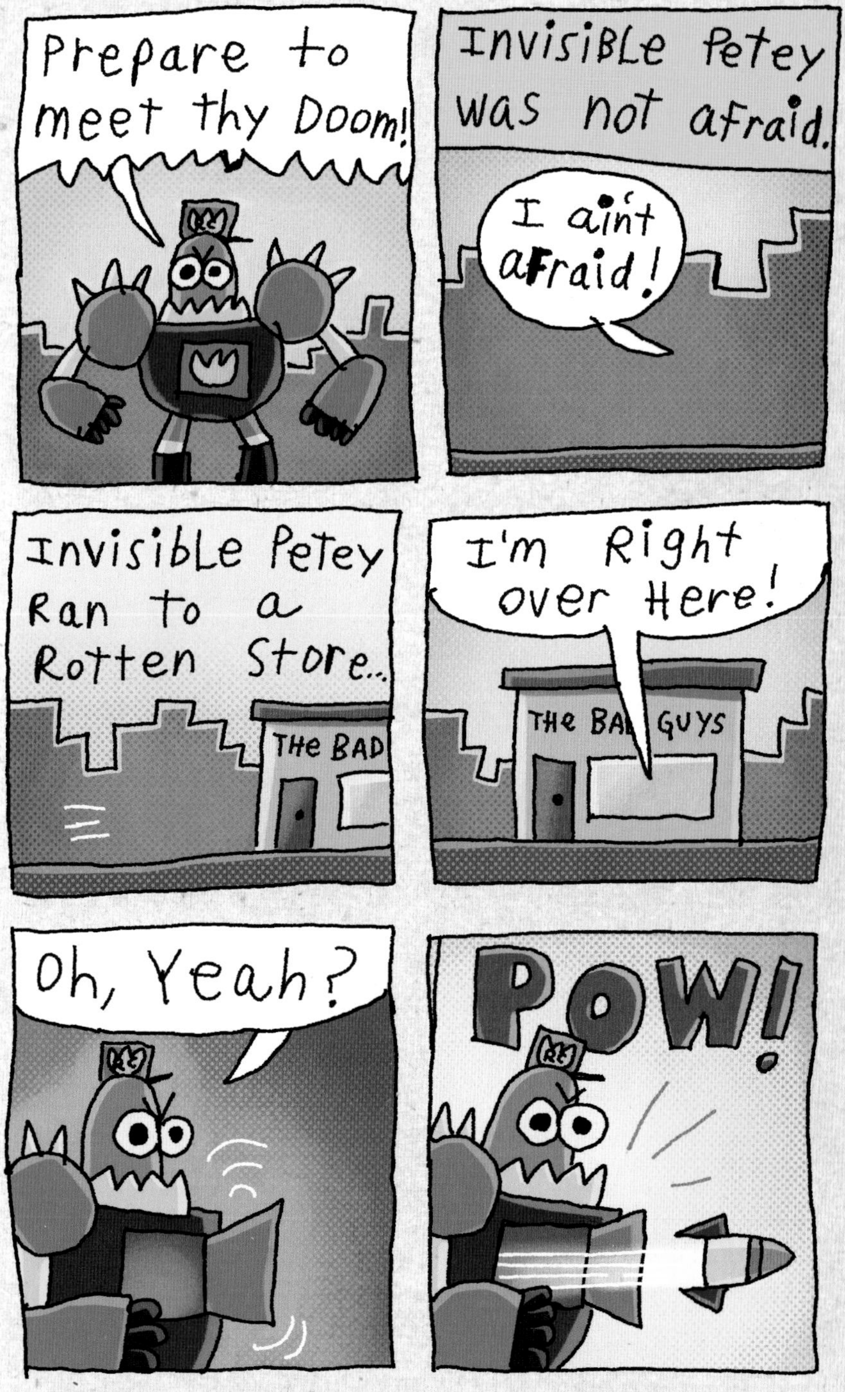
Prepare to meet thy Doom!
Invisible Petey was not afraid.
I ain't afraid!
Invisible Petey Ran to a Rotten Store...
THE BAD
I'm Right over Here!
THE BAD GUYS
Oh, Yeah?
POW!

Invisible Petey ~~had~~ had zipped away just in time.

Tee hee!

He ran to a-nother rotten store...

Haw! Haw!

EViL BiKES

HEY, RoBo DUDE! I'm over HERE now!!!

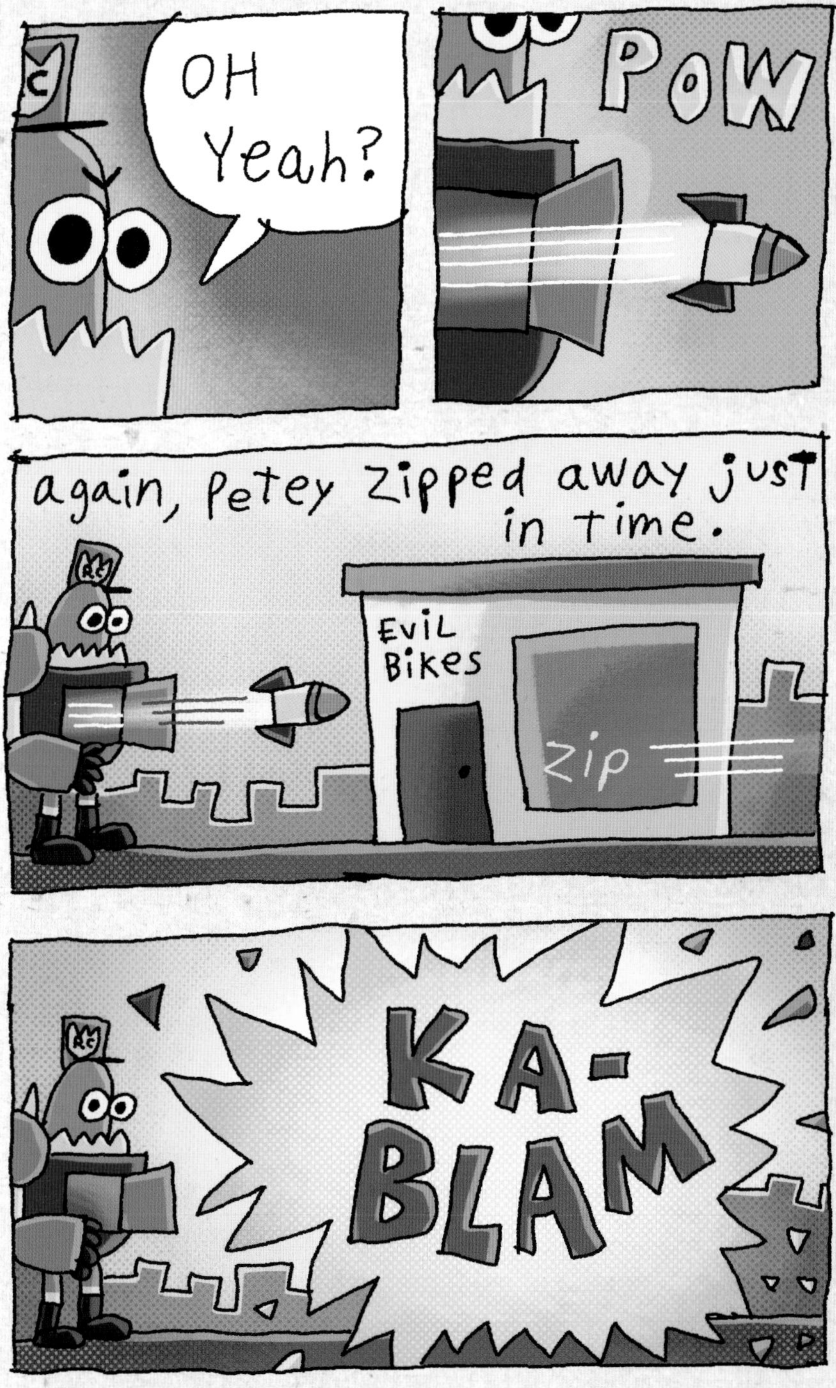
OH Yeah?
POW
again, Petey Zipped away just in time.
EVIL Bikes
Zip
KA-BLAM

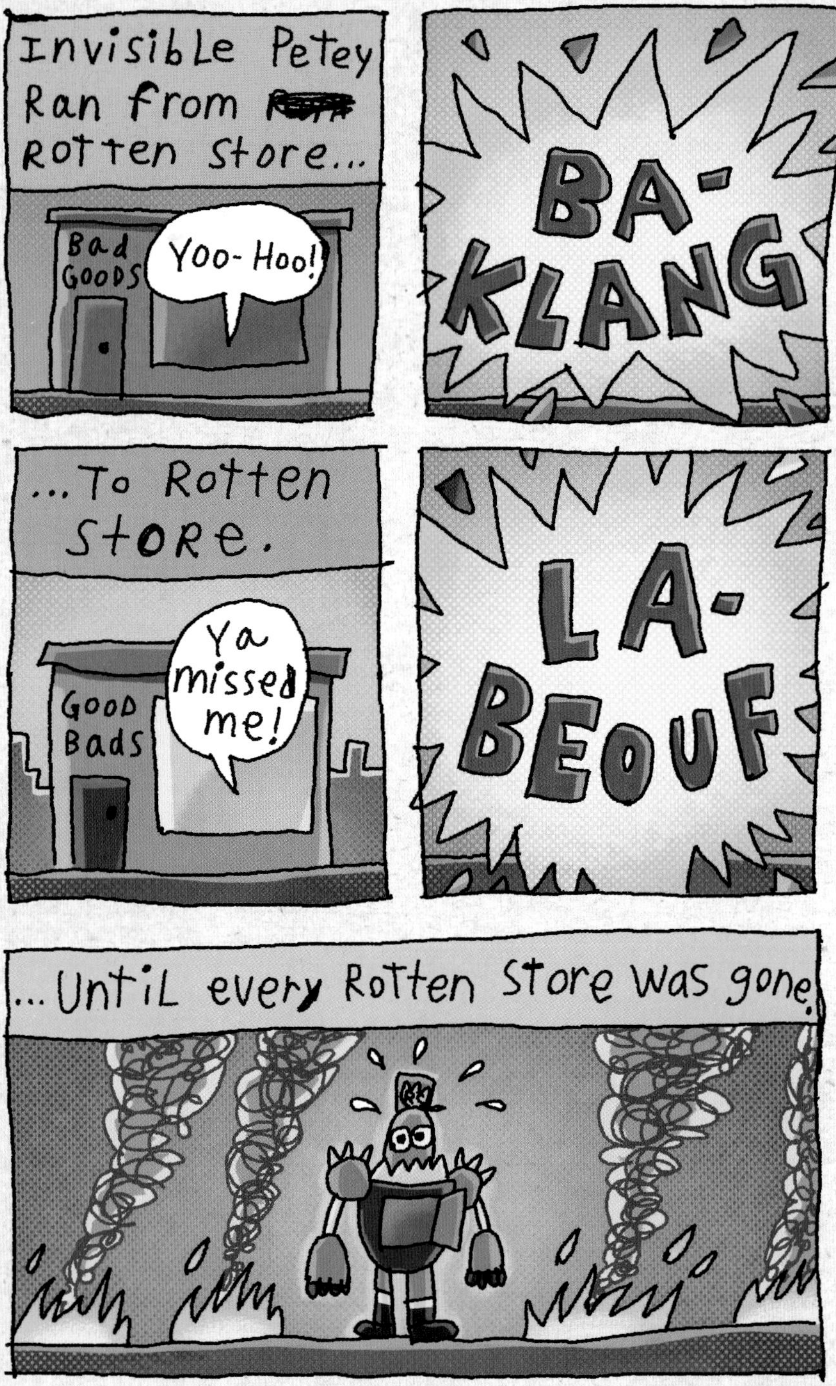
Invisible Petey Ran from Rotten Store...
Bad GOODS
Yoo-Hoo!
BA-KLANG
...To Rotten Store.
GOOD Bads
Ya missed me!
LA-BEOUF
...Until every Rotten Store was gone.

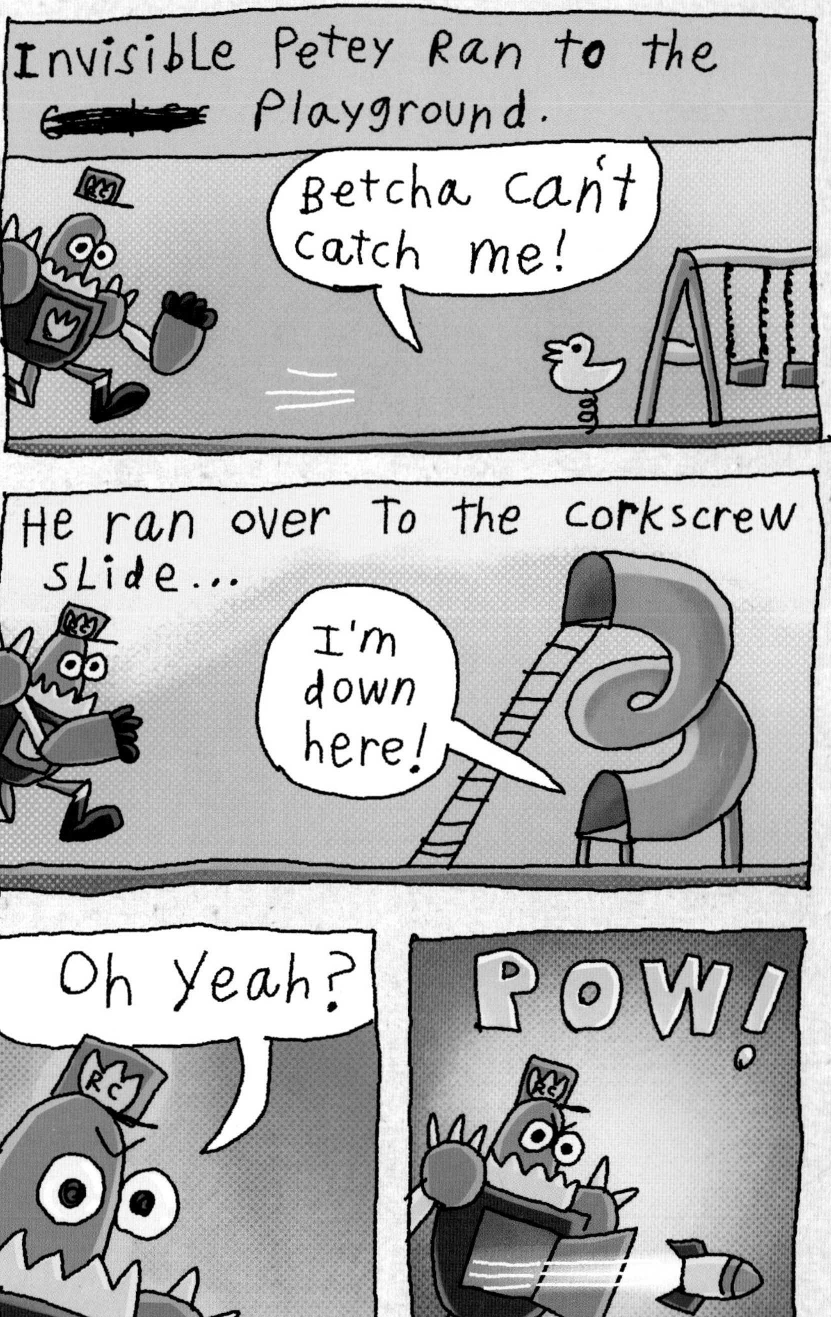

Invisible Petey Ran to the [redacted] Playground.
Betcha can't catch me!
He ran over To the corkscrew SLide...
I'm down here!
Oh Yeah?
POW!

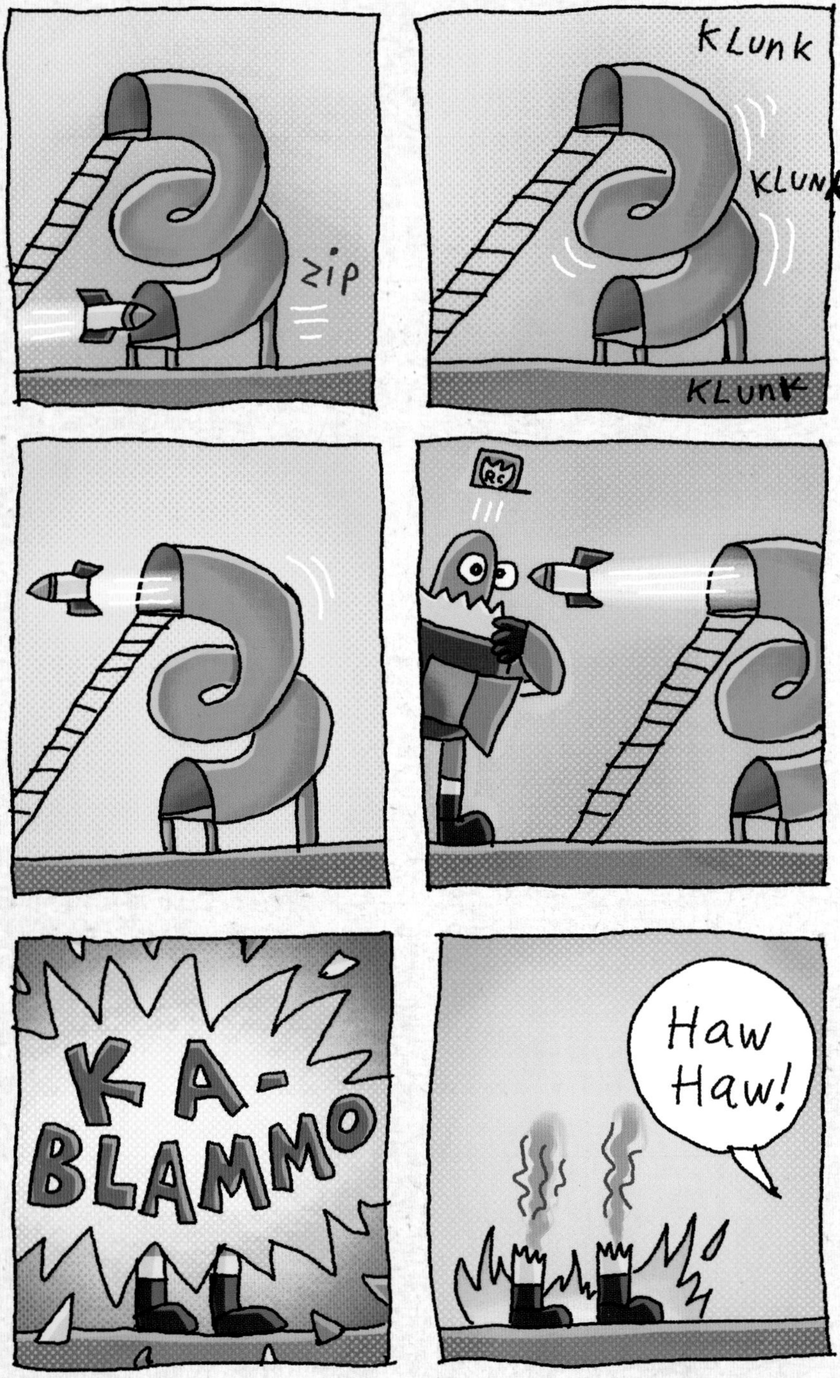
zip
KLunk
KLUNK
KLUNK
KA-BLAMMO
Haw Haw!

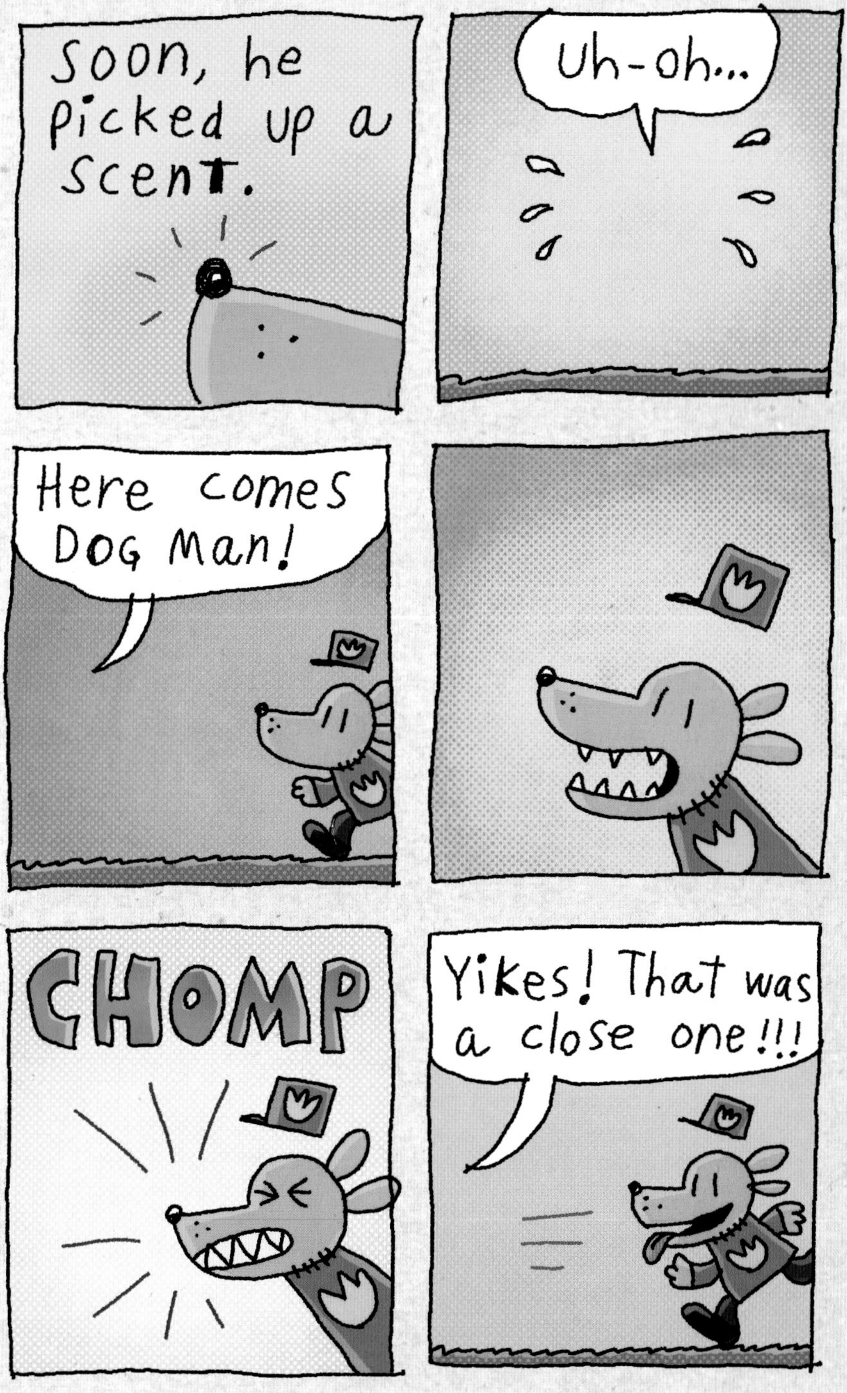
Soon, he picked up a scent.
Uh-oh...
Here comes DOG Man!
CHOMP
Yikes! That was a close one!!!

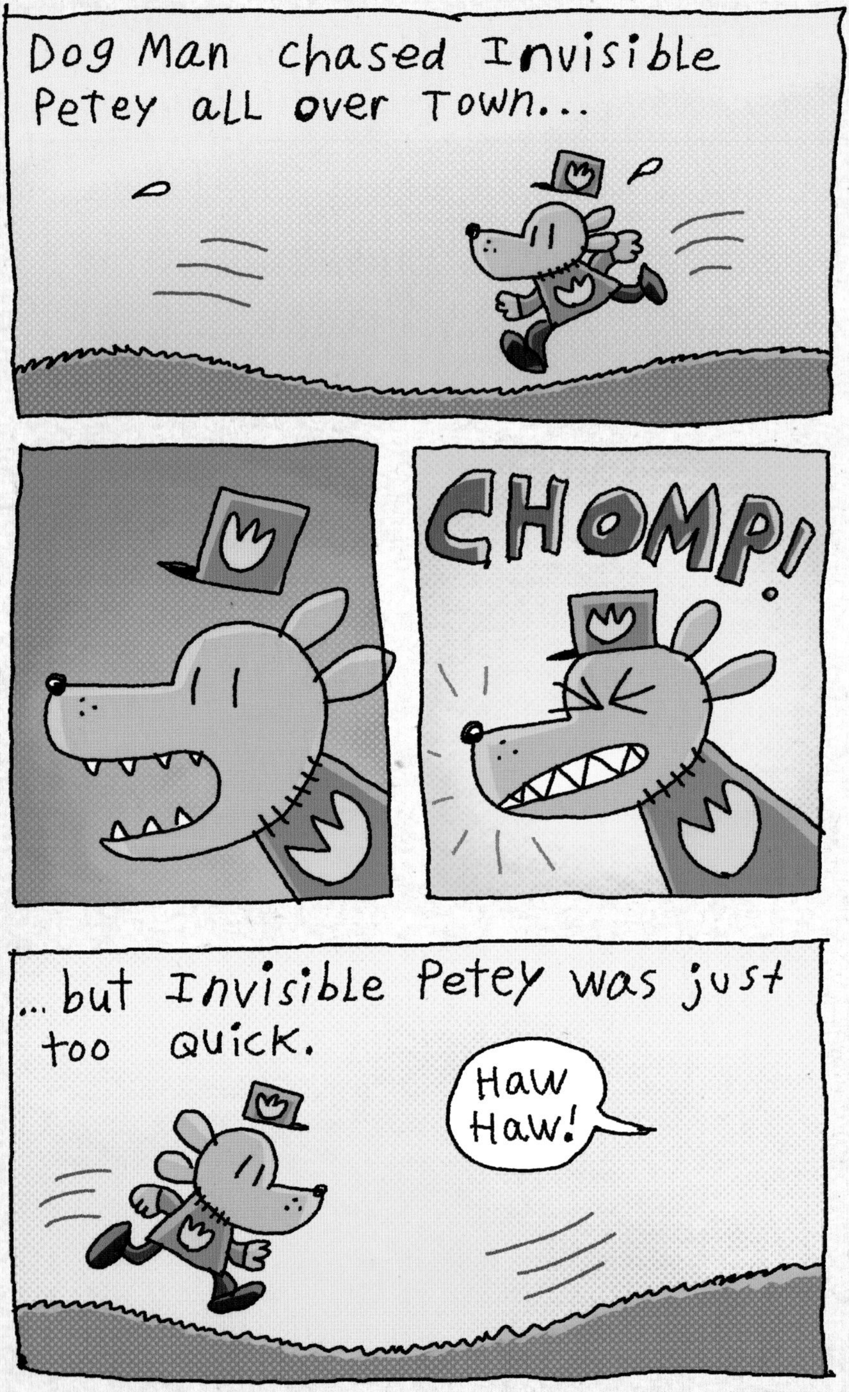
Dog Man chased Invisible Petey all over Town...
CHOMP!
...but Invisible Petey was just too quick.
Haw Haw!

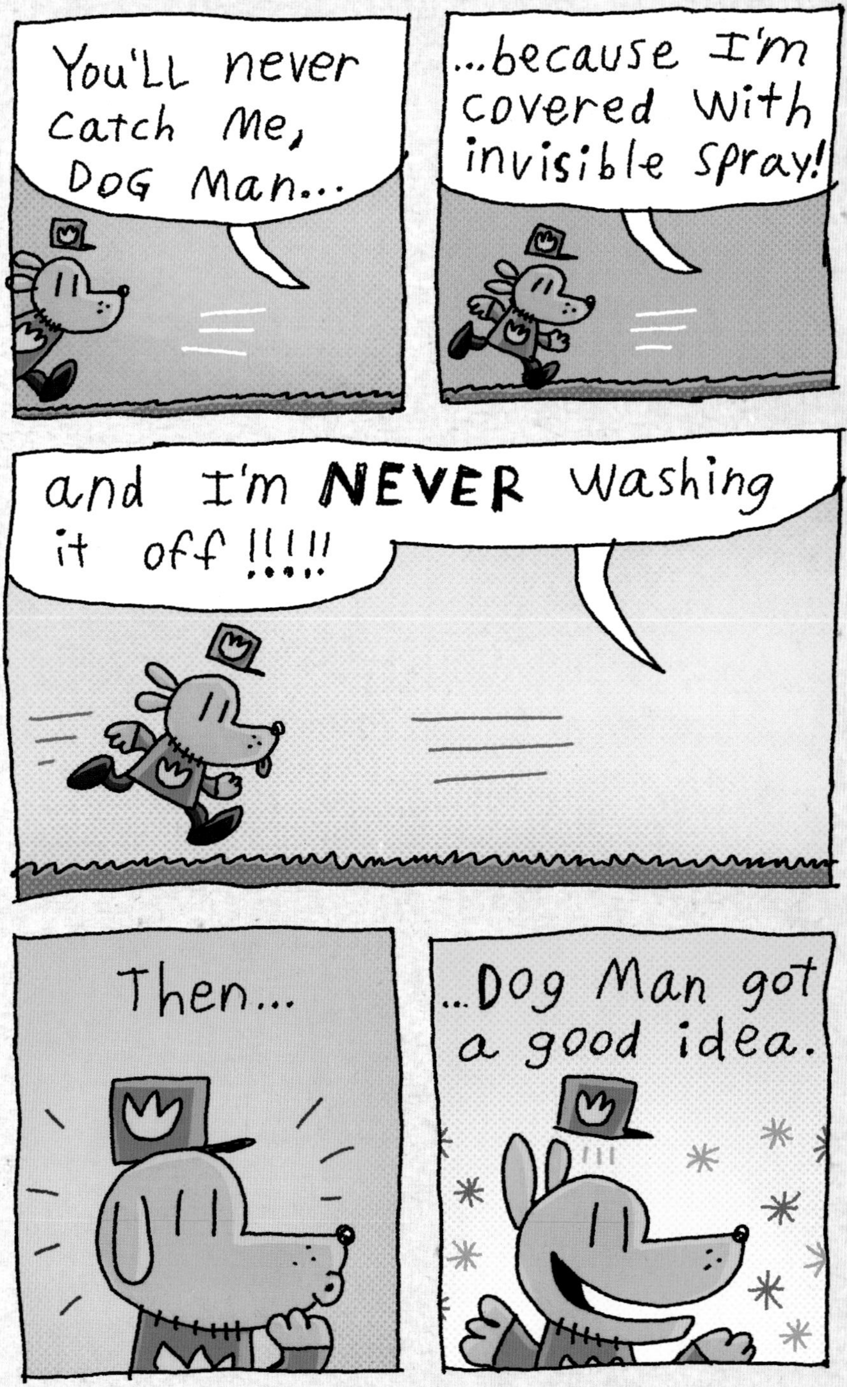
You'LL never catch me, DOG Man...
...because I'm covered with invisible spray!
and I'm NEVER washing it off!!!!!
Then...
...Dog Man got a good idea.

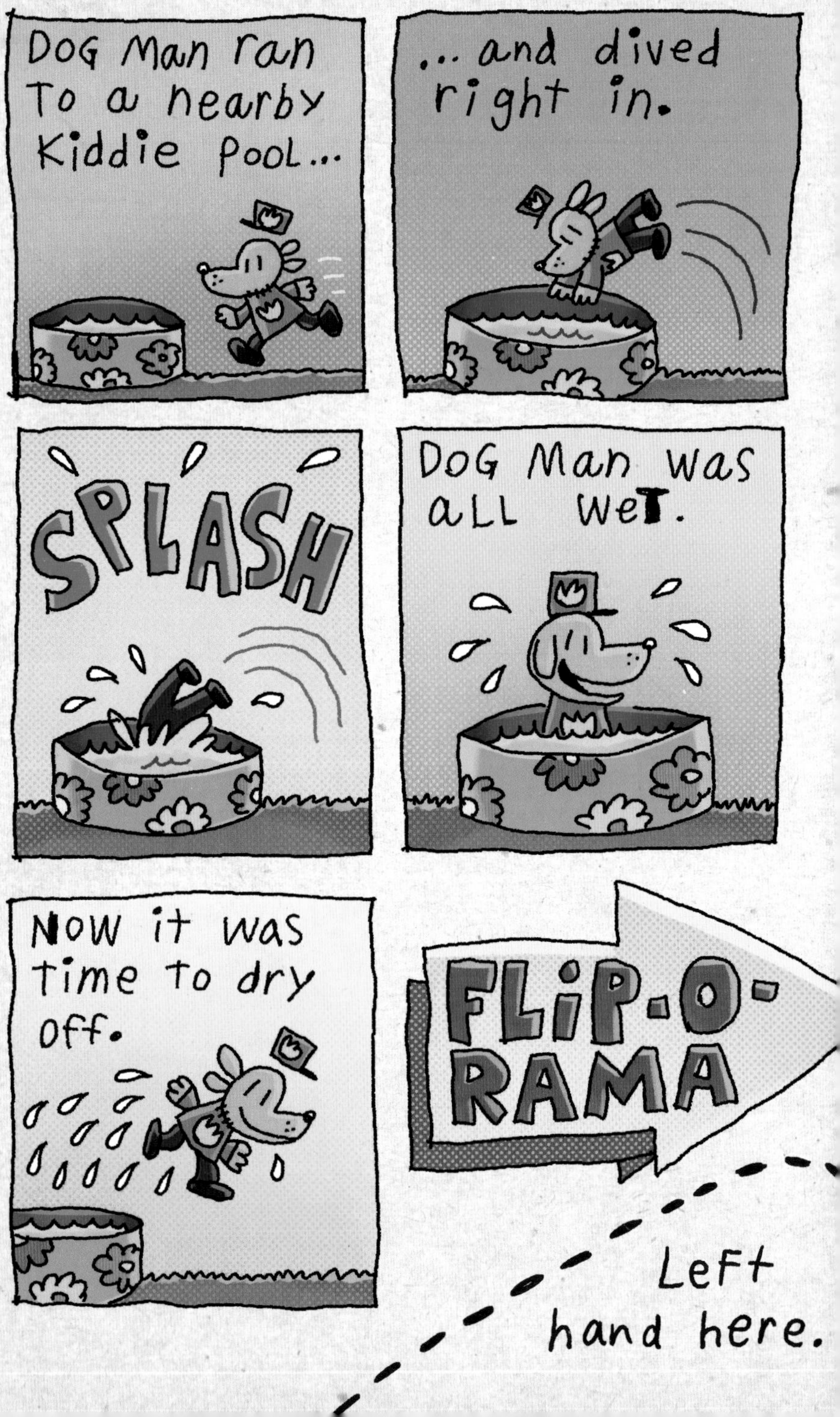
DOG Man ran To a nearby Kiddie PooL...
... and dived right in.
SPLASH
DOG Man was aLL weT.
NOW it was time to dry off.
FLiP-O-RAMA
Left hand here.

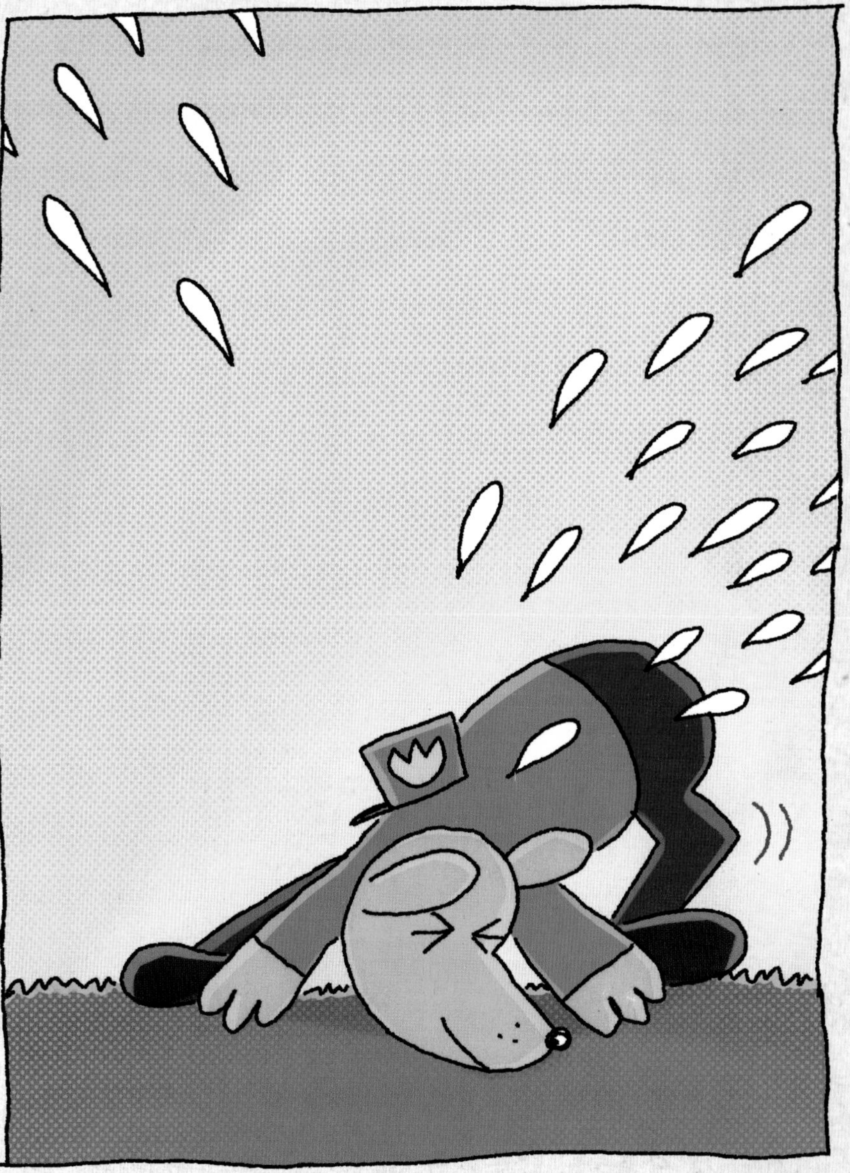

Supa
Soaker

Right
Thumb
here.

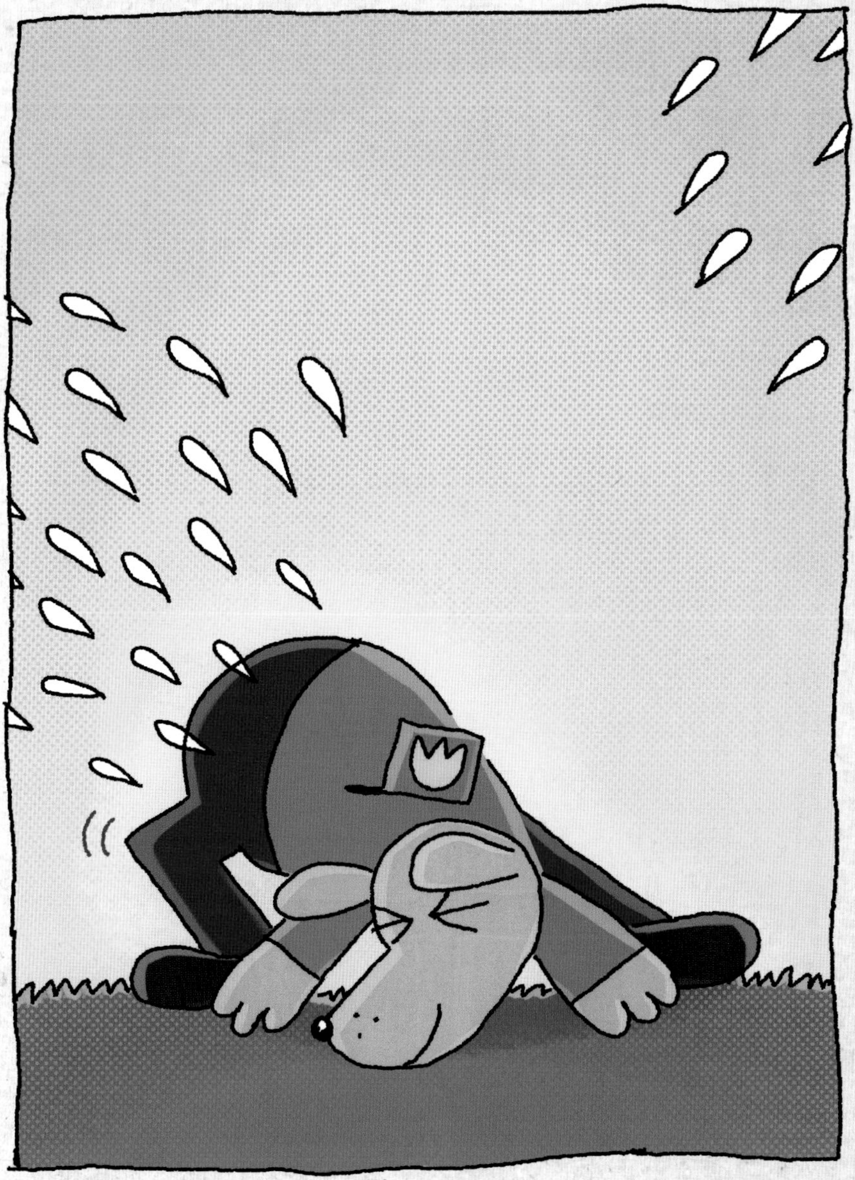

Supa soaker

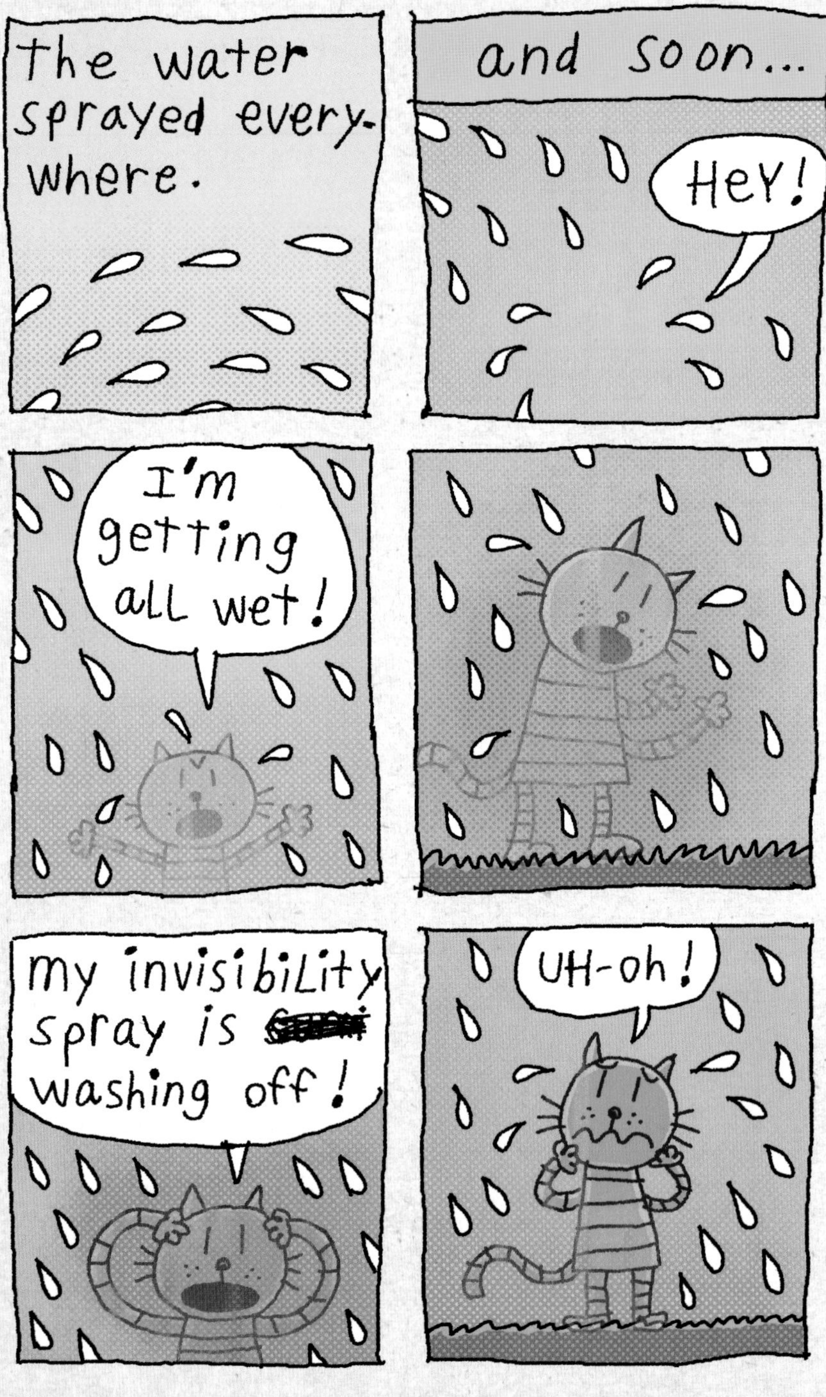
The water sprayed every-where.
and soon...
HEY!
I'm getting all wet!
my invisibility spray is [redacted] washing off!
UH-oh!

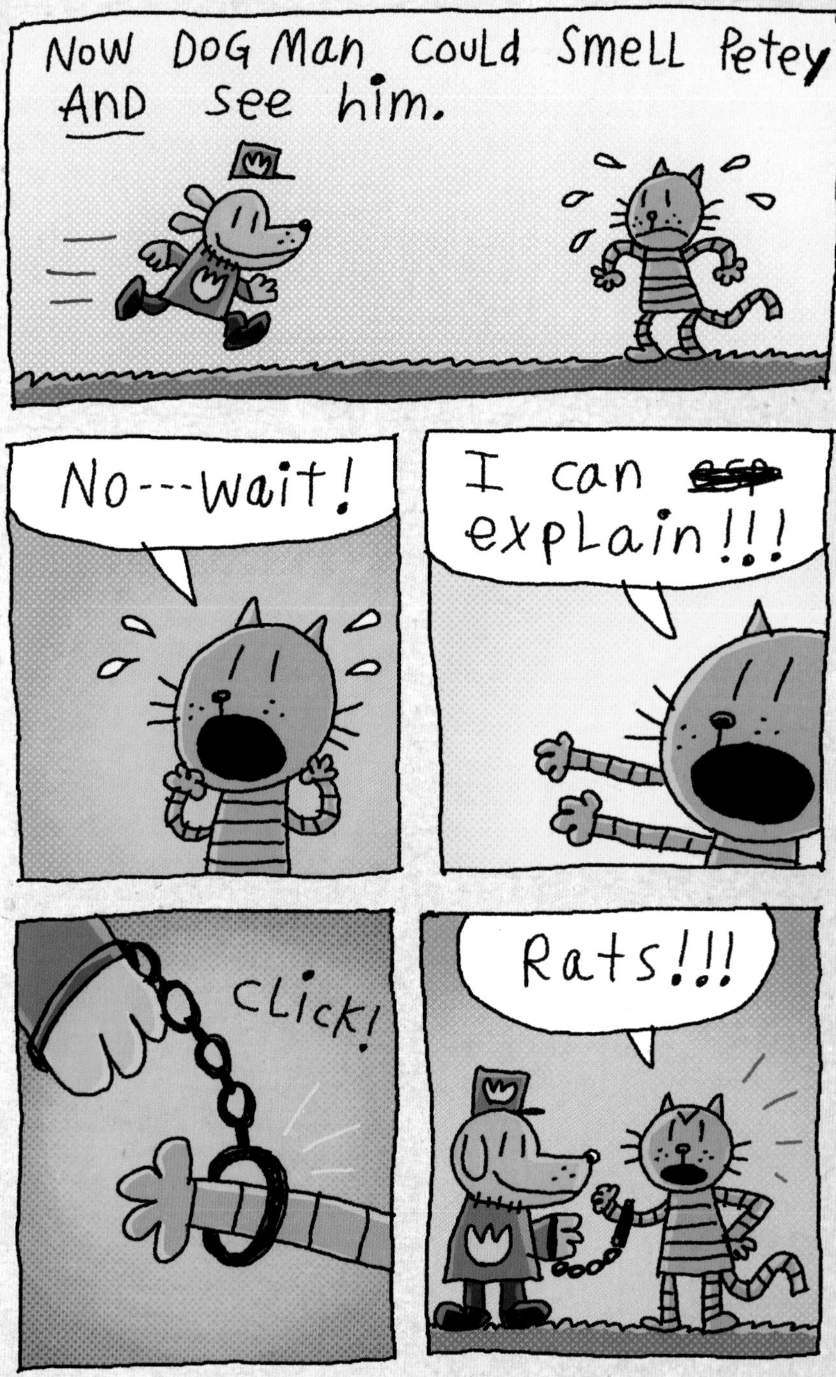
NOW DOG MAN COULD SMELL PETEY AND SEE HIM.
No---wait!
I can explain!!!
CLICK!
Rats!!!

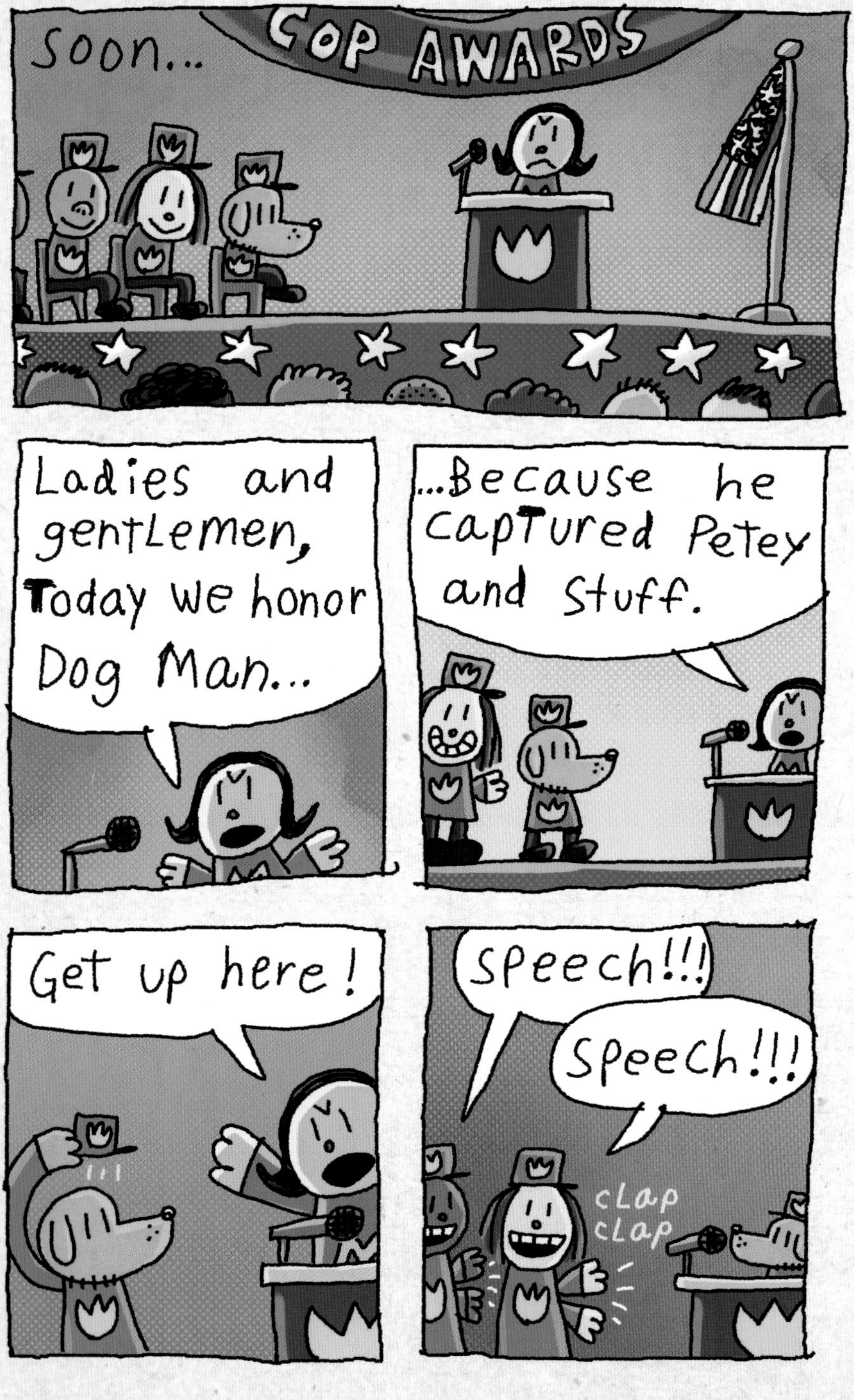
Soon...
COP AWARDS
Ladies and gentlemen, Today we honor Dog Man...
...Because he captured Petey and stuff.
Get up here!
Speech!!!
Speech!!!
clap clap

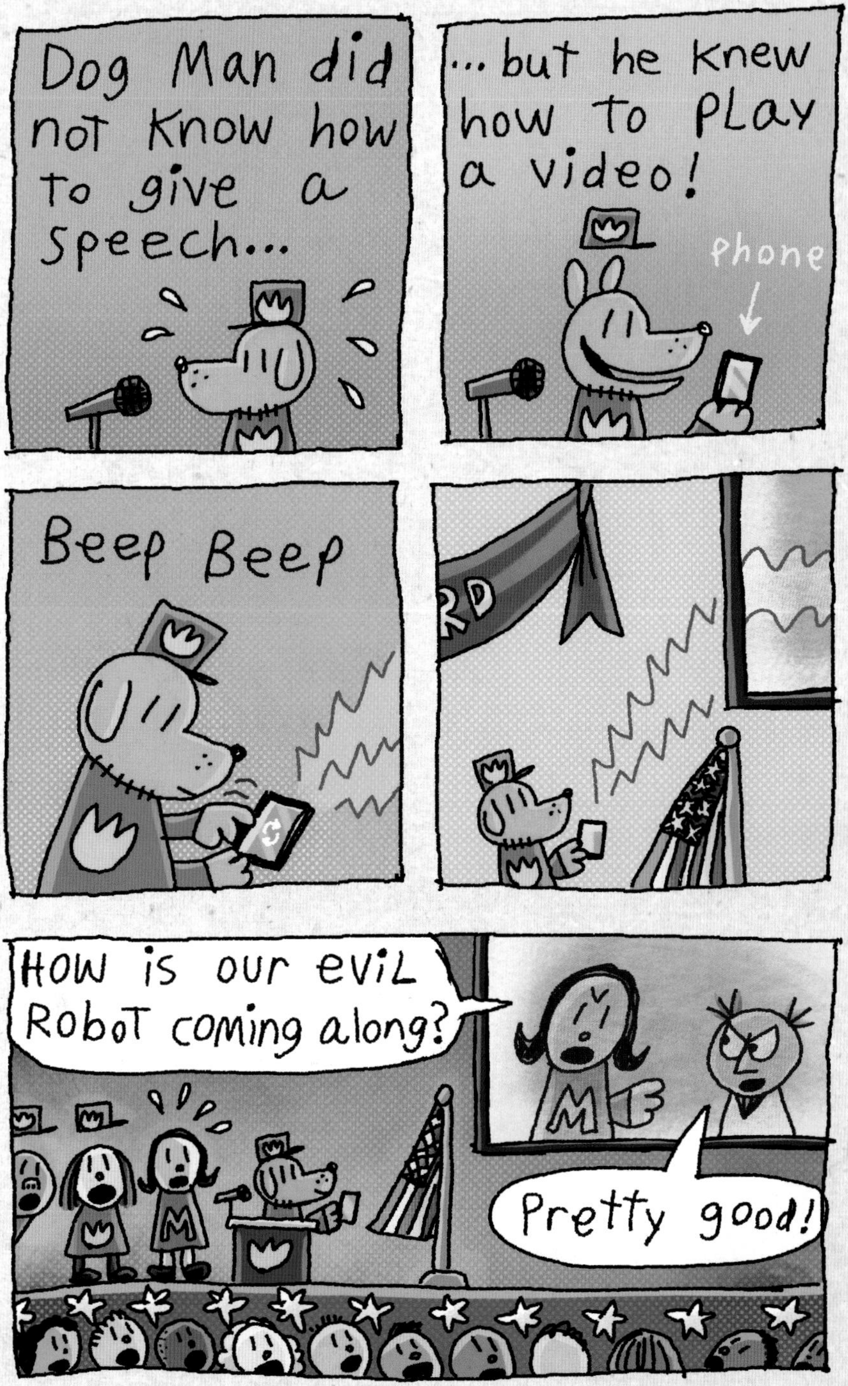
Dog Man did not know how to give a speech...
...but he knew how to play a video!
Phone
Beep Beep
RD
HOW is our evil Robot coming along?
Pretty good!

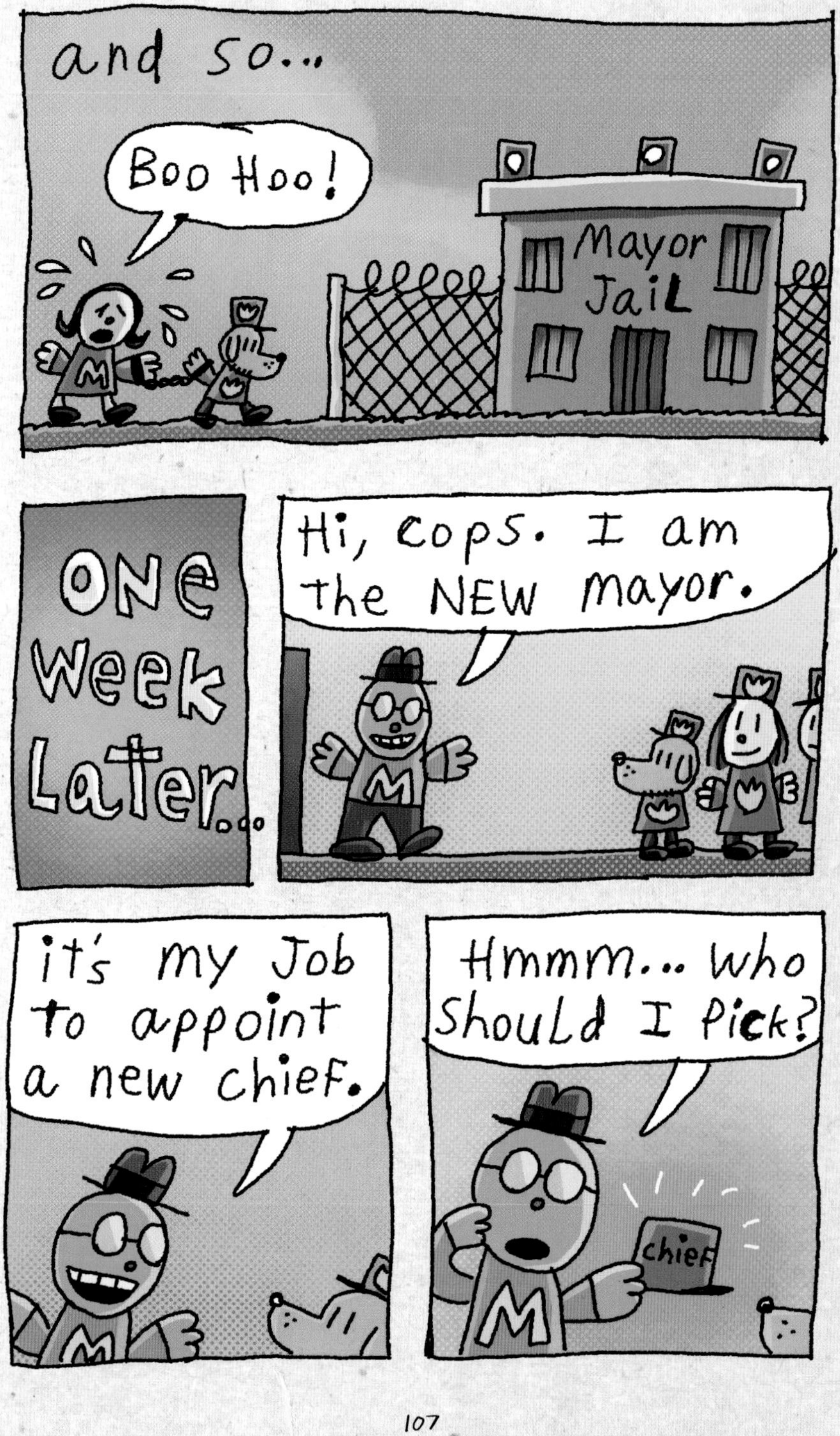
and so...
Boo Hoo!
Mayor Jail
One Week Later...
Hi, cops. I am the NEW mayor.
it's my Job to appoint a new chief.
Hmmm... who Should I Pick?
chief

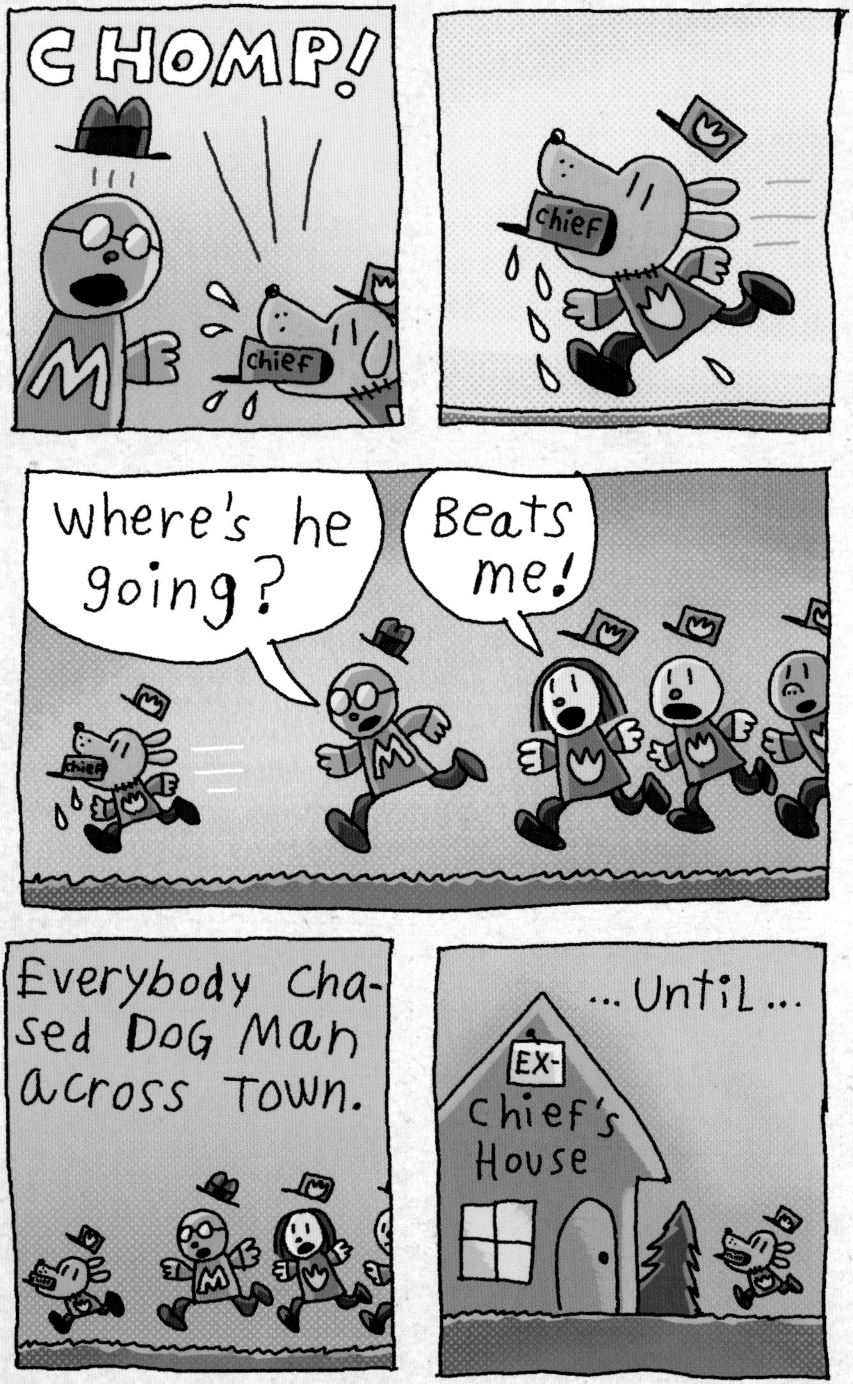
CHOMP!
chief
chief
Where's he going?
Beats me!
chief
Everybody Chased DOG Man across Town.
...Until...
EX-
Chief's House

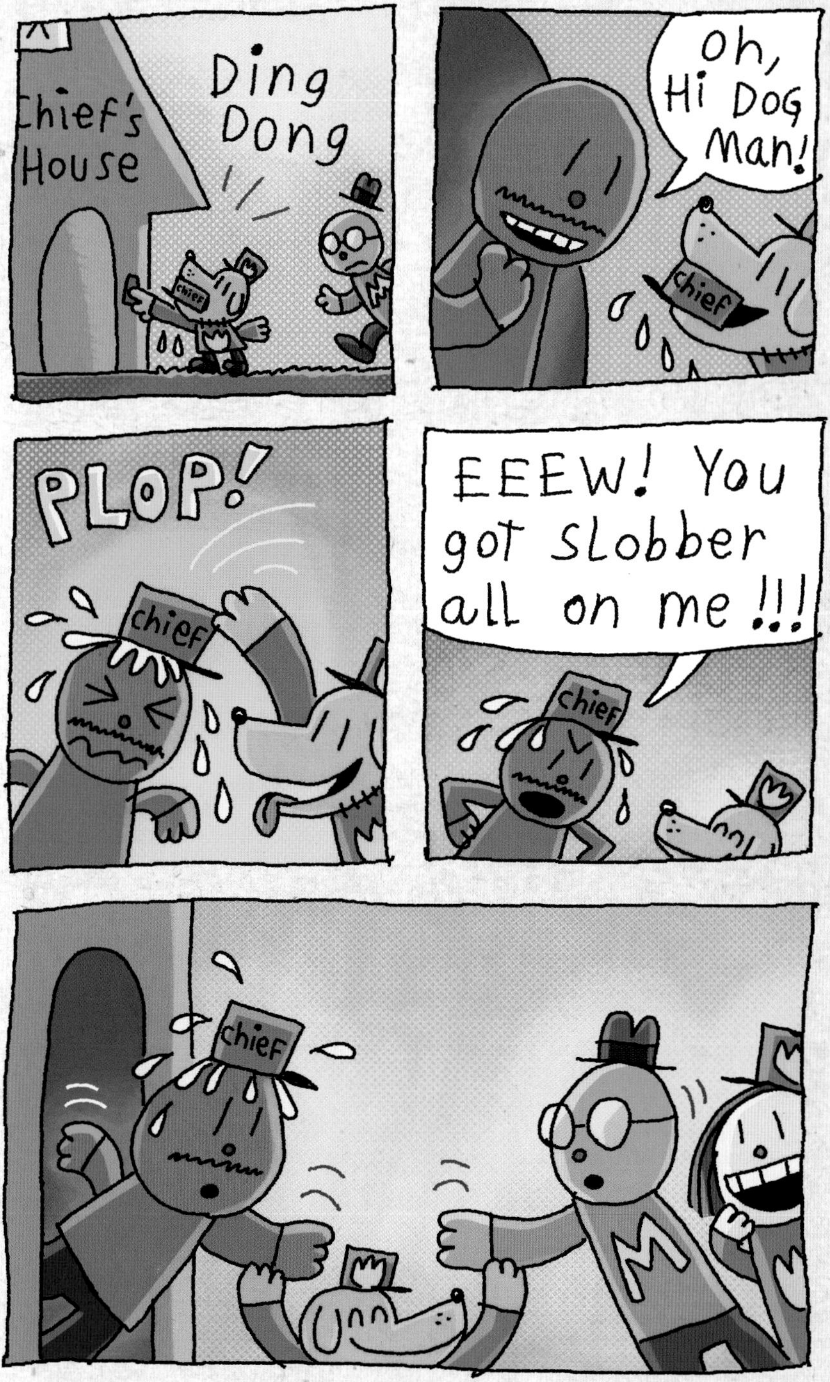
Chief's House
Ding Dong
Oh, Hi Dog Man!
PLOP!
EEEW! You got slobber all on me!!!

So Chief got his old job back...

and soon, everything was back to normal.

Hey!!!

CHAPTER 3

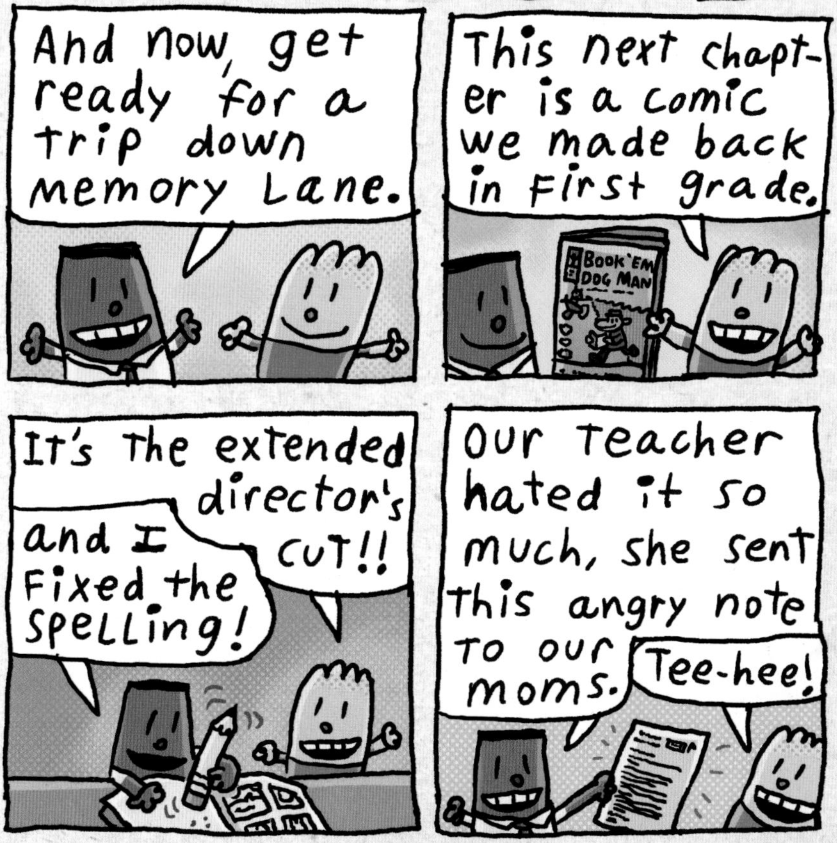

And now, get ready for a trip down memory Lane.
This next chapter is a comic we made back in First grade.
BOOK 'EM DOG MAN
It's the extended director's cut!!
and I Fixed the spelling!
Our Teacher hated it so much, she sent this angry note to our moms.
Tee-hee!
We hope you Like it...
...better than she did!
Tree House comix Presents
BOOK 'EM, DOG MAN!
a graphic novella
ACTION
LAFFS

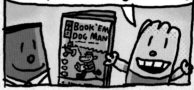

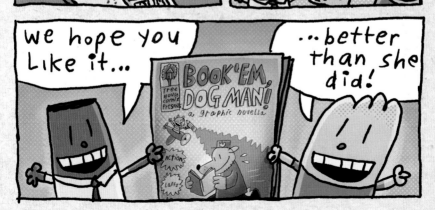

Jerome Horwitz Elementary School

We put the "ow" in Knowledge

Dear Mr. and Mrs. Beard,

Once again I am writing to inform you of your son's disruptive activity in my classroom.

The assignment was to create a WRITTEN public service message to promote reading. Your son and his friend, Harold Hutchins (I am sending a nearly identical letter to Harold's mother), were specifically told NOT to make a comic book for this assignment.

As usual, they did exactly what they were told not to do (see attached comic book). When I confronted George about his disobedience, he claimed that this was not a comic book, but a "graphic novella." I am getting fed up with George's impudence.

I have told both boys on numerous occasions that the classroom is no place for creativity, yet they continue to make these obnoxious and offensive "comix." As you will see, this comic book contains multiple references to human and/or animal feces. It also features a very questionable scene of disregard for homeless/hungry individuals. There are scenes of smoking, violence, nudity, and don't get me started on the spelling and grammar. Frankly, I found the little trash bag "baby" at the end to be very disturbing. I mean, how is that even possible?!!?

George's silly, disruptive behavior, as well as these increasingly disgusting and scatological comic books, are turning my classroom into a zoo. I have spoken to Principal Krupp about Dog Man on numerous occasions. We both believe that you should consider psychological counseling for your son, or at the very least some kind of behavior modification drug to cure his "creative streak."

Regretfully,

Ms. Construde

Ms. Construde
Grade 1 Teacher

BOOK 'EM, DOG MAN

Tree House Comix

BY George B. and Harold H.

One day Petey sat in his jail cell feeling sad.

News
DOG man wins again

Rats! Every time I have a evil plan, DOG man always **OUT-**smarts me!

How come He's so Darn smart ???

So Petey De-cided to find out!

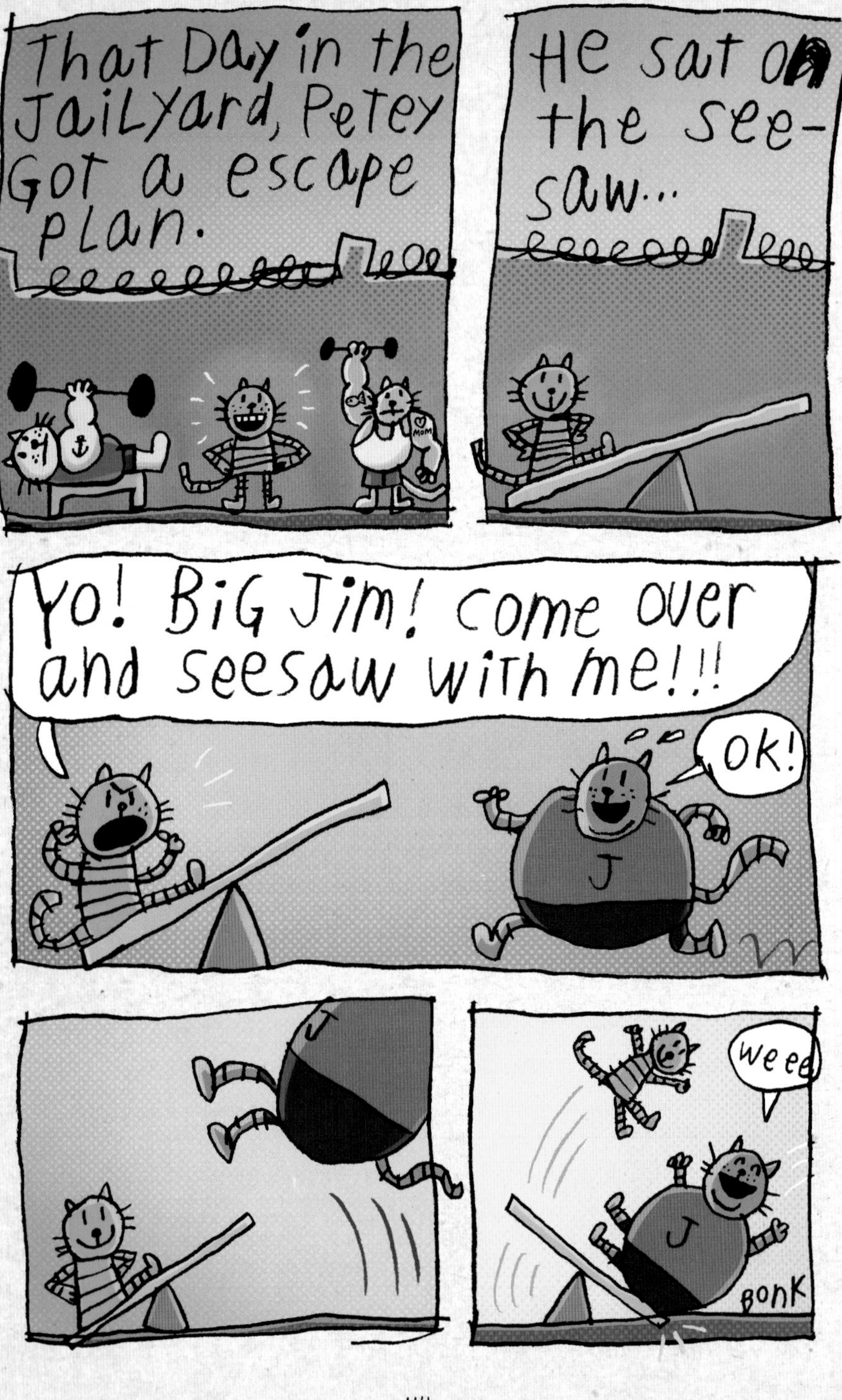
That Day in the JaiLyard, Petey Got a escape plan.
MOM
He sat on the See-saw...
Yo! BiG Jim! come over and seesaw with me!!!
OK!
J
J
weee
J
BONK

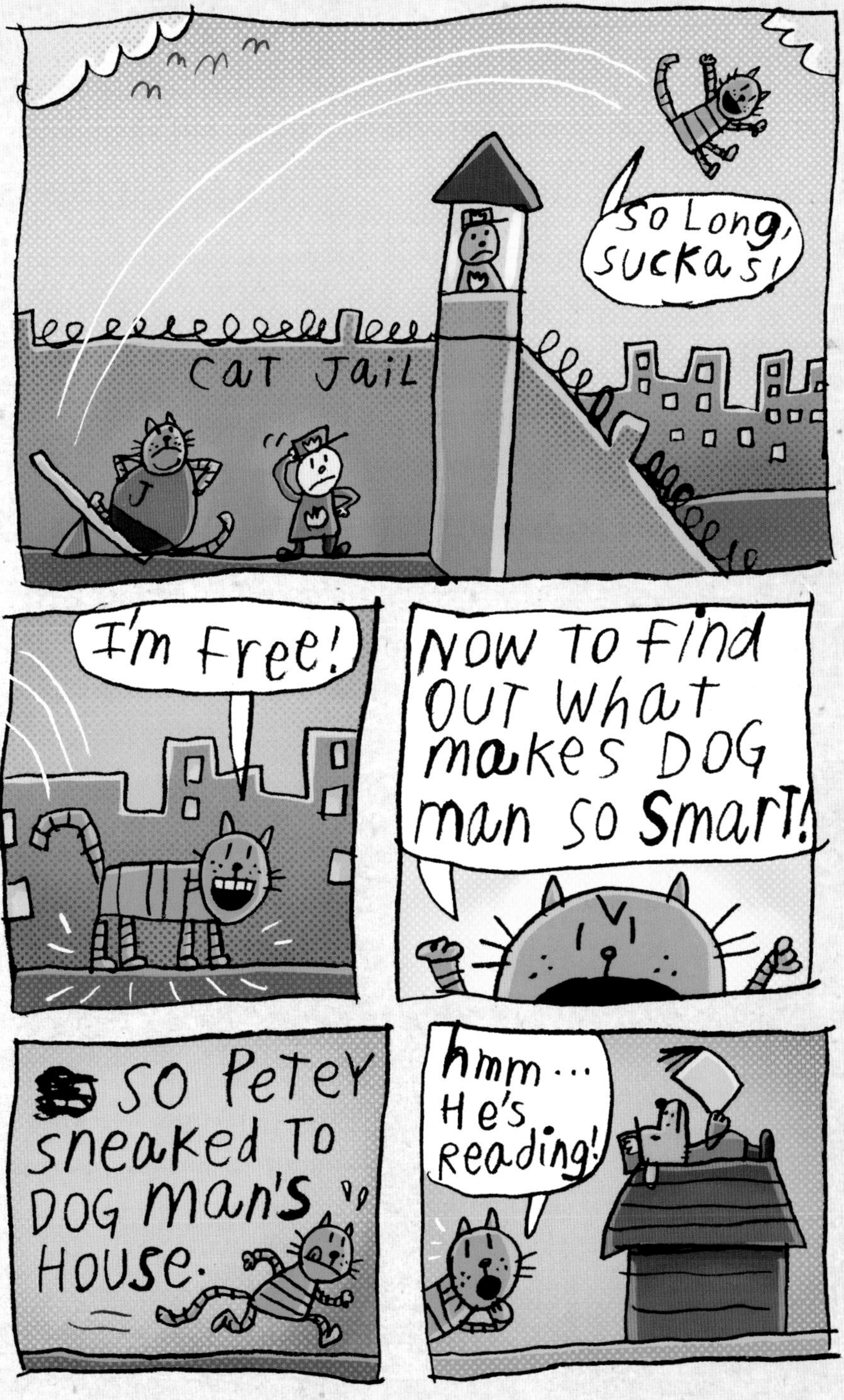
CAT JAIL
So Long, SUCKas!
I'm Free!
NOW TO Find OUT What makes DOG man SO SmarT!
SO Petey sneaked To DOG man'S HOUSe.
hmm... He's Reading!

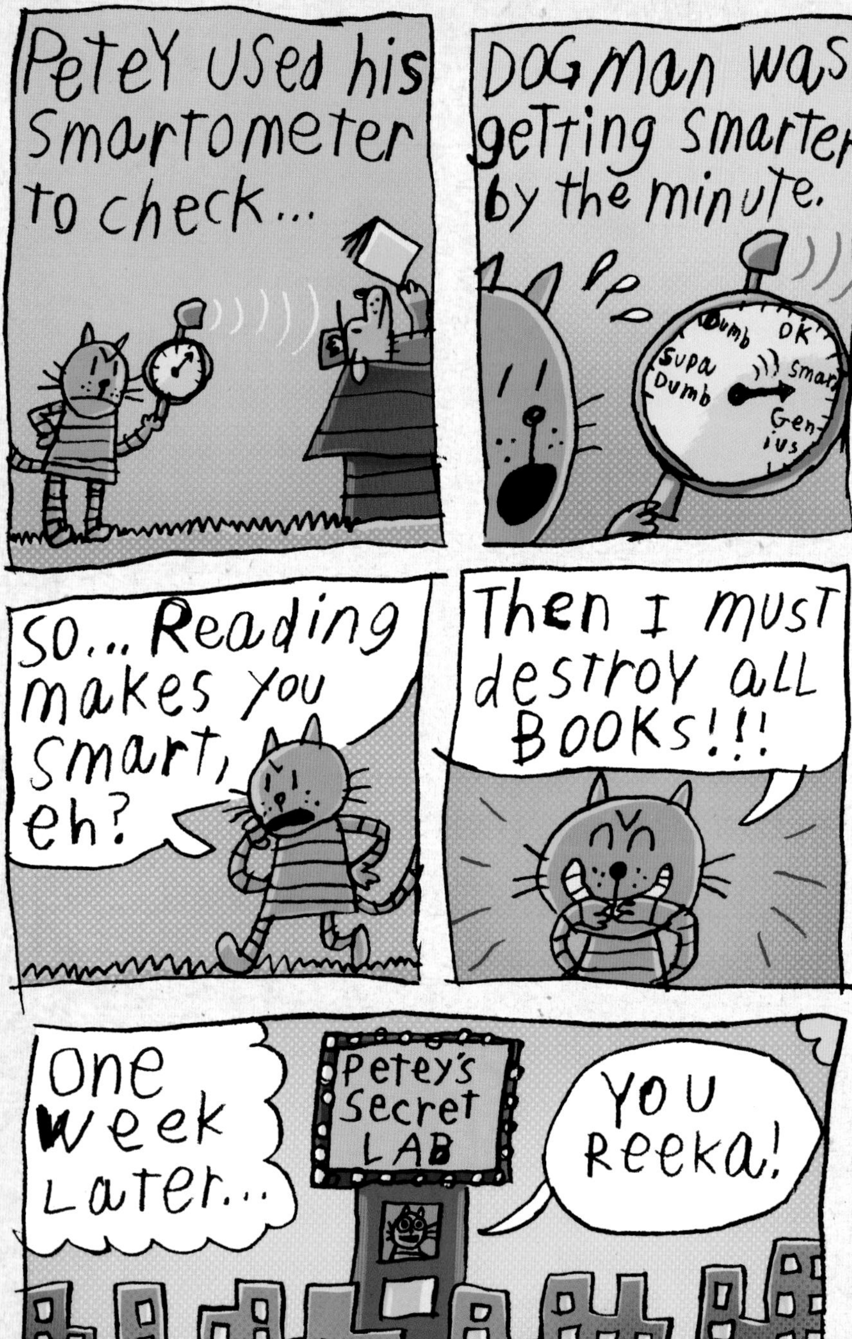
Petey used his Smartometer to check...
Dog Man was getting smarter by the minute.
Dumb
OK
Supa Dumb
Smar
Gen ius
So... Reading makes you smart, eh?
Then I must destroy all Books!!!
One week later...
Petey's Secret LAB
You Reeka!

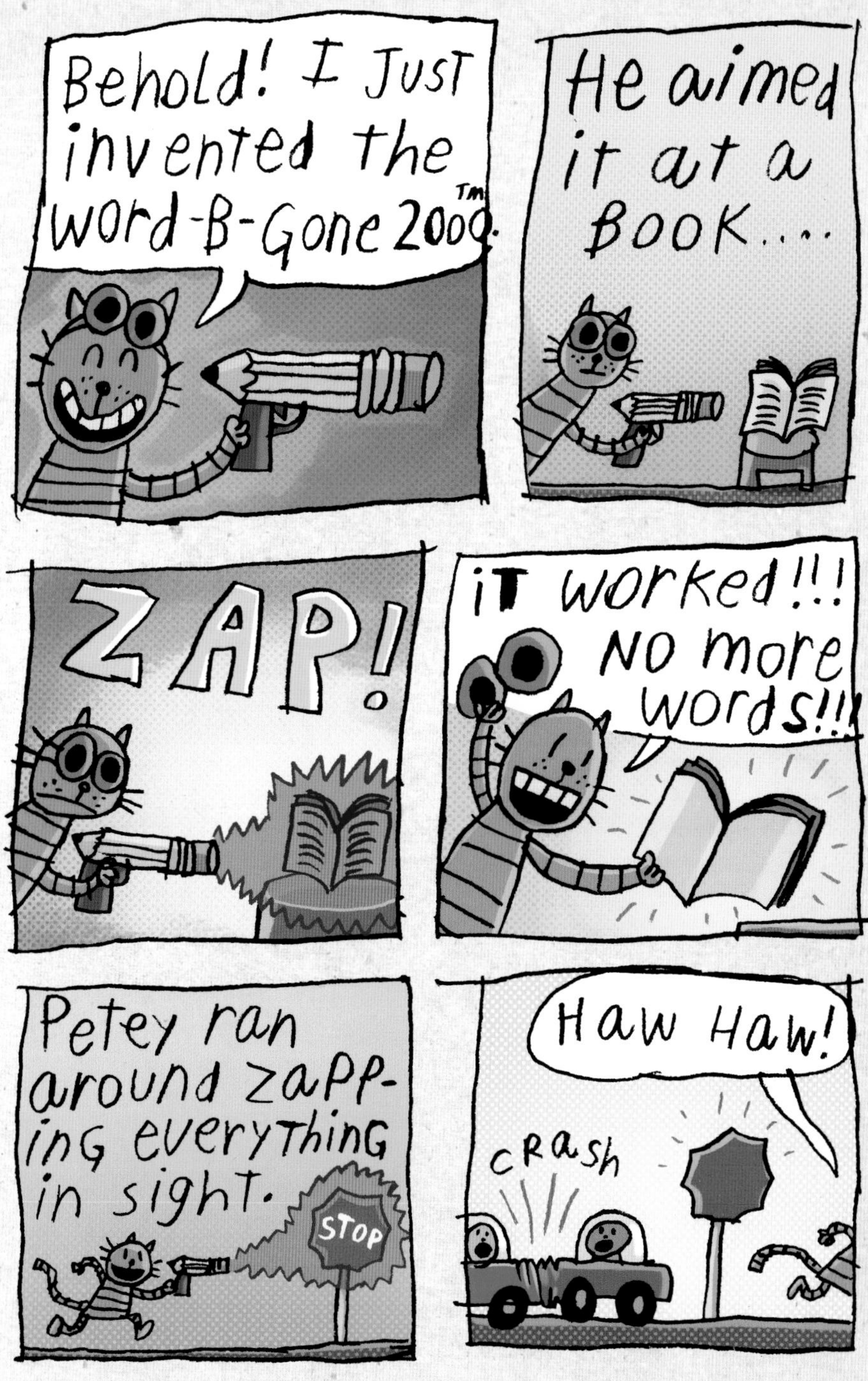
Behold! I JUST invented the word-B-Gone 2000™.
He aimed it at a BOOK....
ZAP!
iT worked!!! NO more words!!!
Petey ran around zapp-ing everyThinG in sight.
STOP
Haw Haw!
cRash

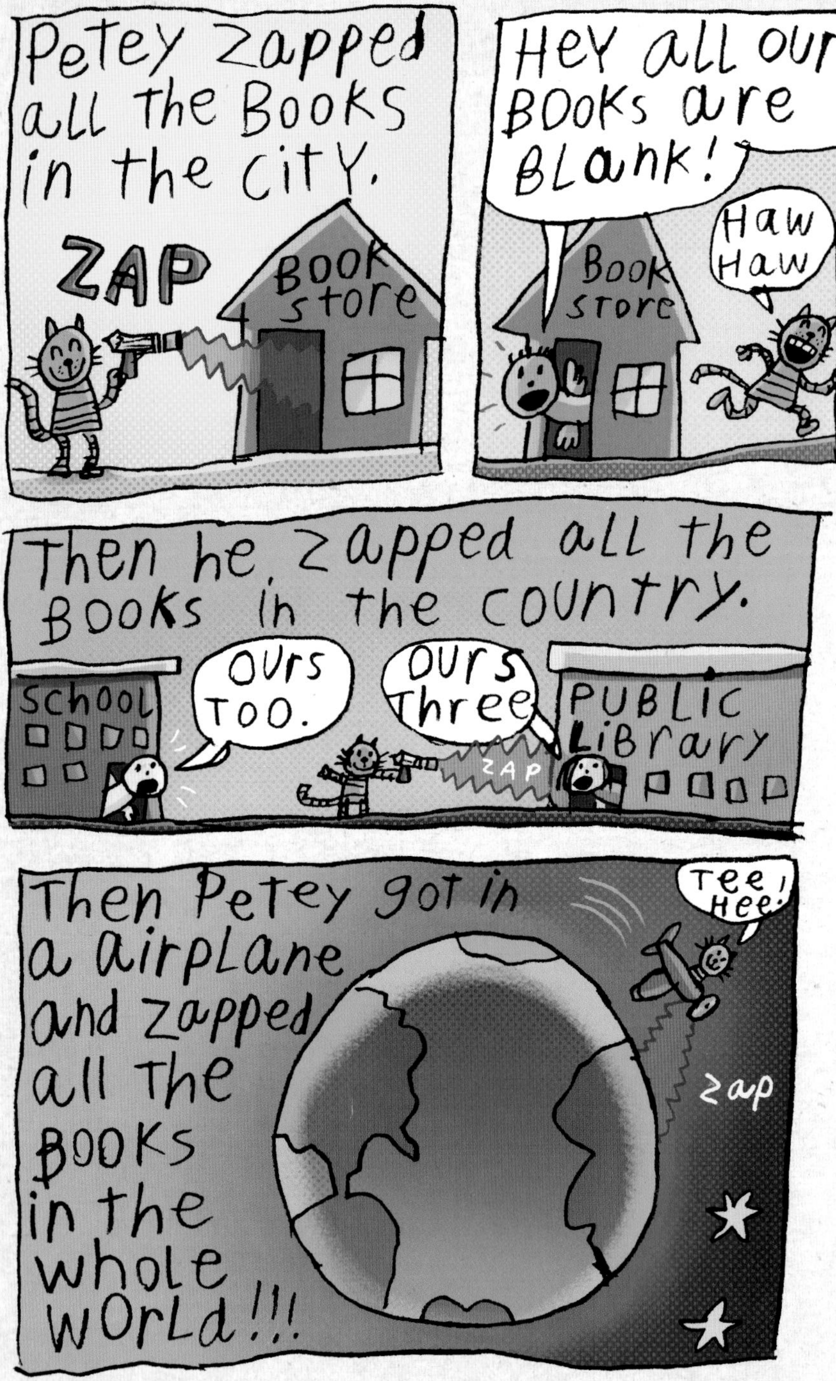
Petey Zapped all the Books in the City.
ZAP
BOOK Store
HEY all our BOOKs are BLank!
Haw Haw
Book Store
Then he zapped all the BOOKs in the country.
SCHOOL
OUrs TOO.
OUrs Three
PUBLIC Library
ZAP
Then Petey got in a airplane and zapped all the BOOKS in the whole WOrLd!!!
Tee! Hee!
Zap

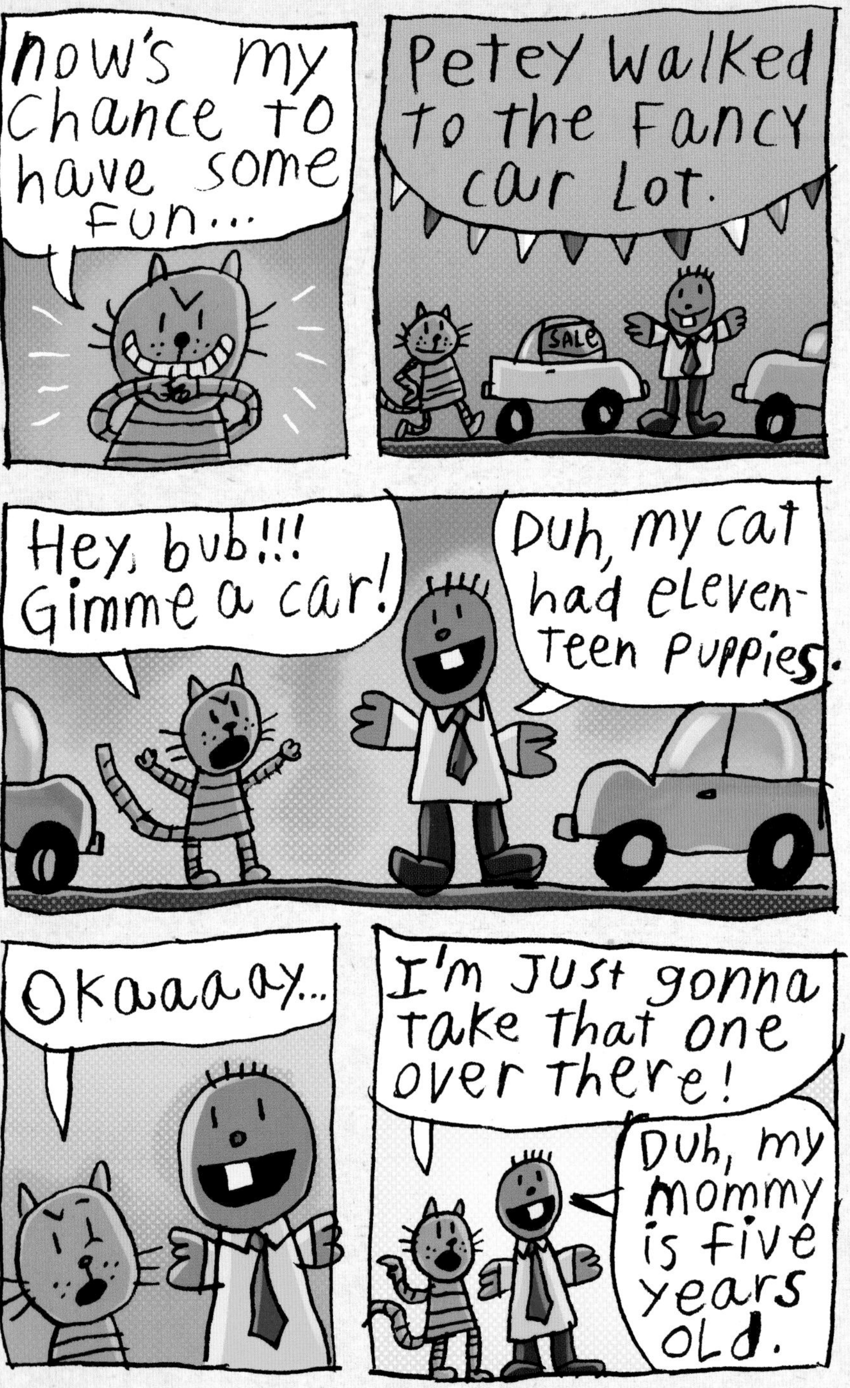
Now's my chance to have some fun...
Petey walked to the fancy car lot.
SALE
Hey, bub!!! Gimme a car!
Duh, my cat had eleven-teen puppies.
Okaaaay...
I'm just gonna take that one over there!
Duh, my mommy is five years old.

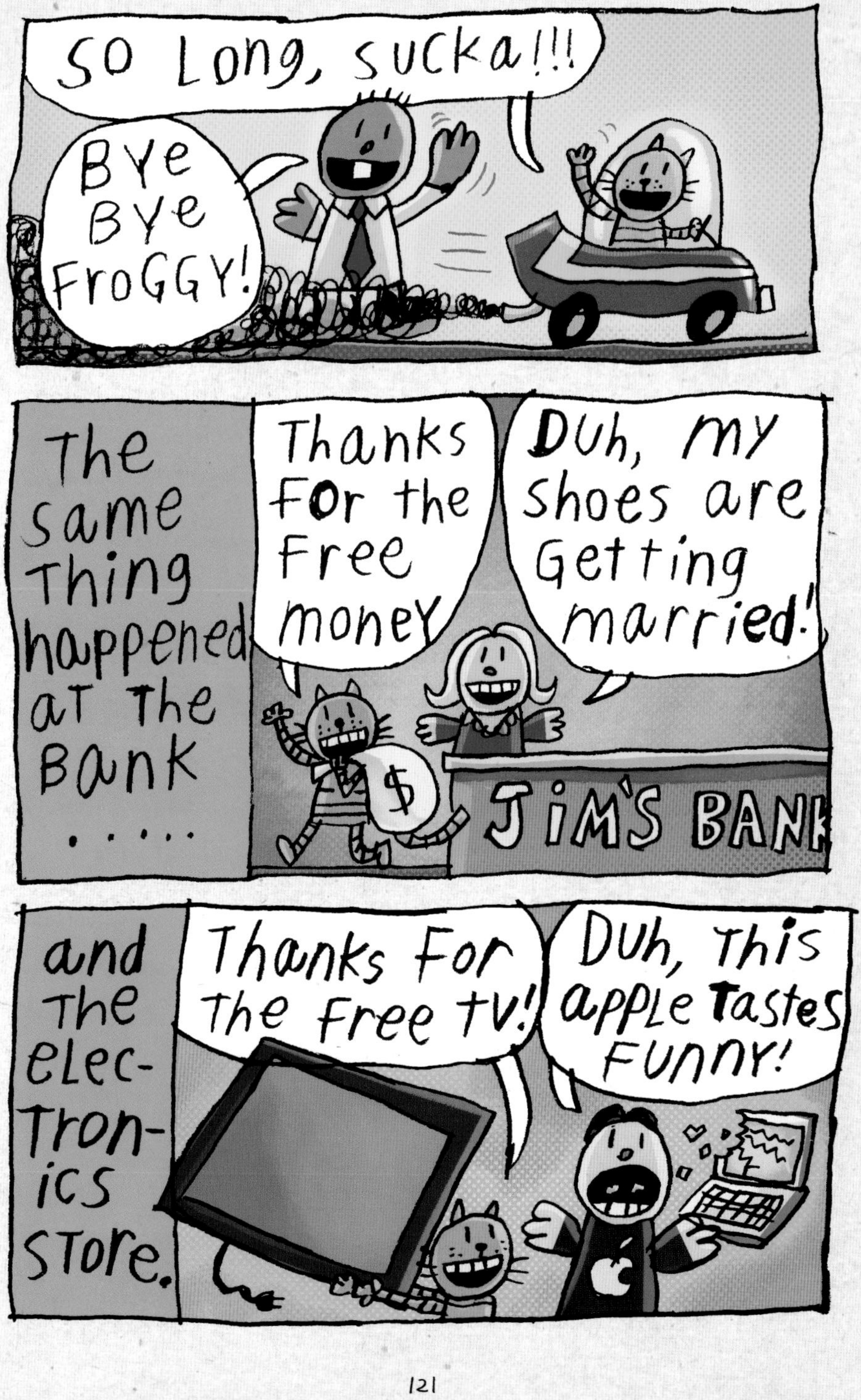
SO LONG, SUCKA!!!
BYE BYE FROGGY!
The same Thing happened at The Bank . . . . .
Thanks FOr the Free money
DUh, my shoes are Getting married!
JIM'S BANK
and The elec-Tron-ics STore.
Thanks For The Free TV!
DUh, This apple Tastes FUNNY!

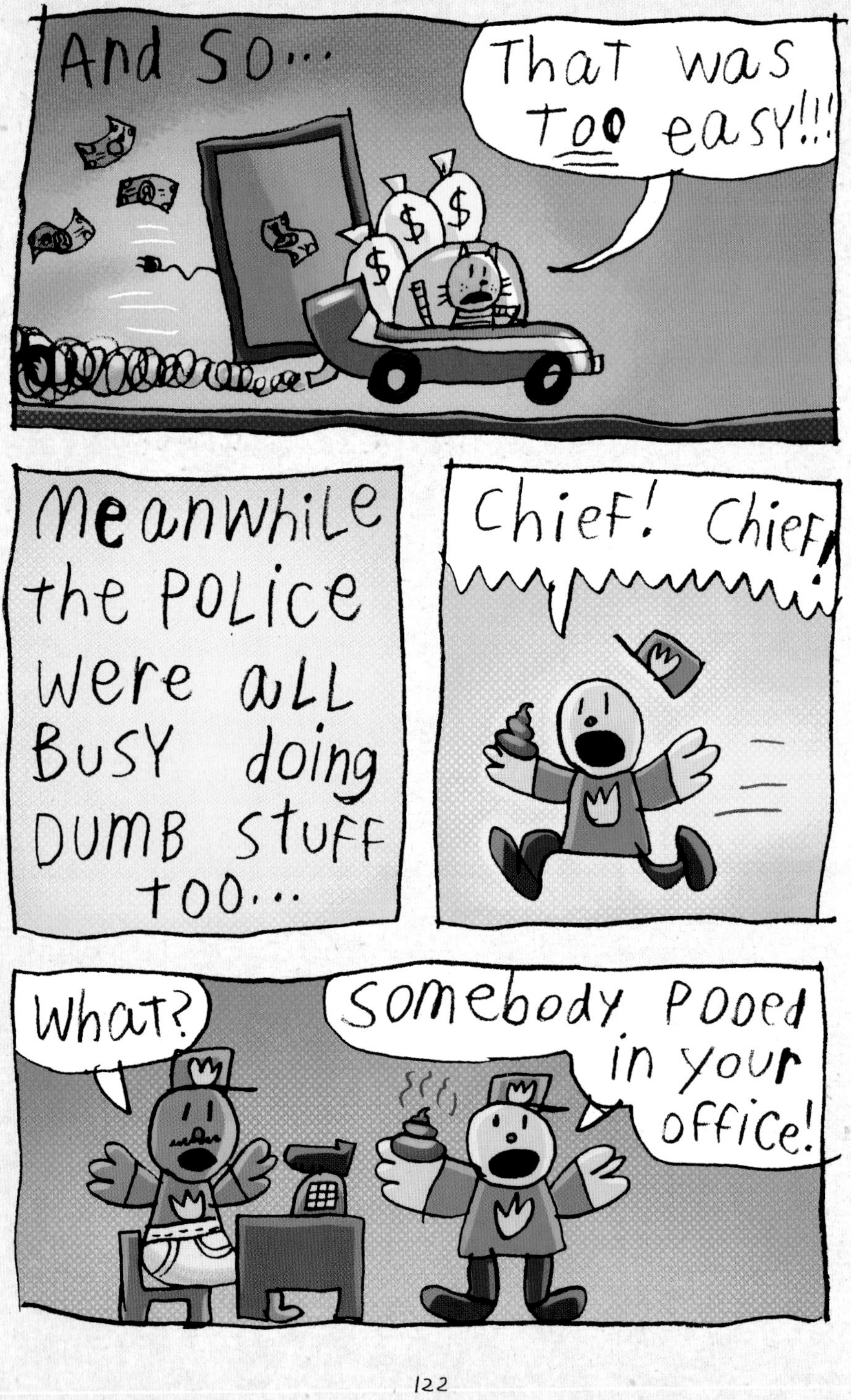
And so...
That was TOO easy!!!
Meanwhile the police were all busy doing dumb stuff too...
Chief! Chief!
What?
Somebody pooed in your office!

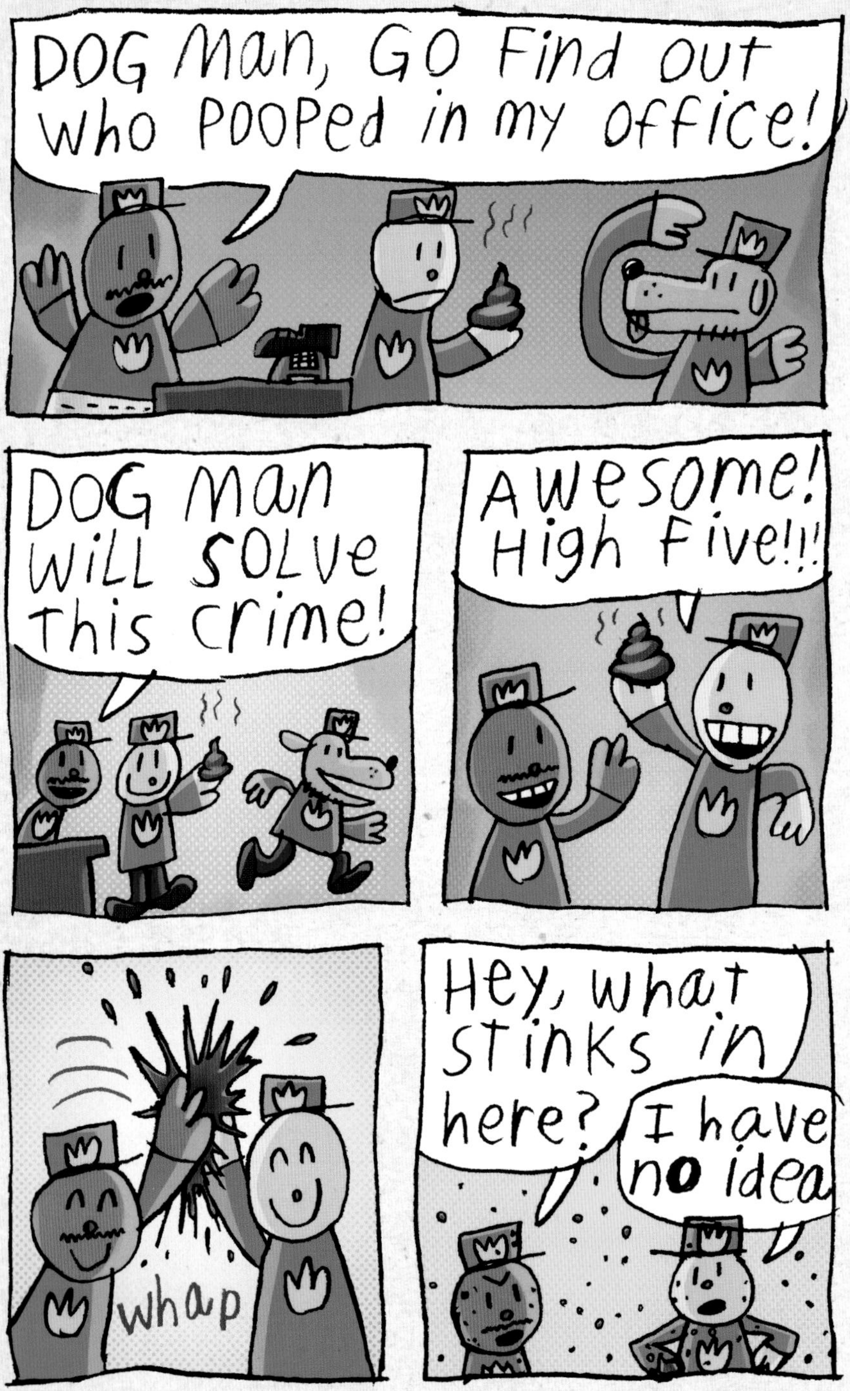
DOG Man, GO Find out who POOPed in my office!
DOG Man WiLL SOLVe This crime!
Awesome! High Five!!!
whap
Hey, what stinks in here?
I have no idea

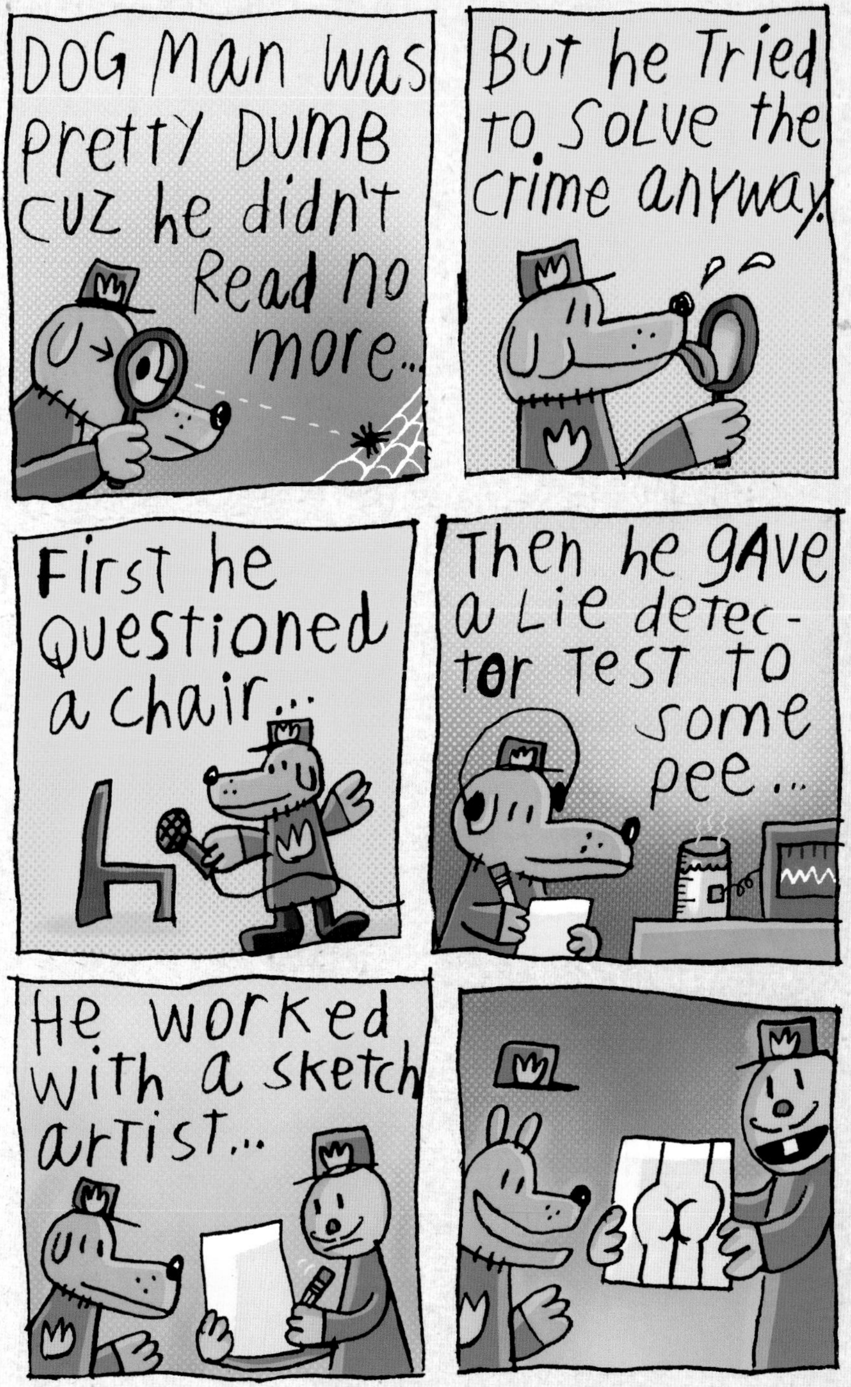
DOG Man was pretty DUMB cuz he didn't Read no more...
But he Tried to SOLVE the crime anyway.
First he Questioned a chair...
Then he gAve a Lie detector TEST to some pee...
He worked with a sketch artist...

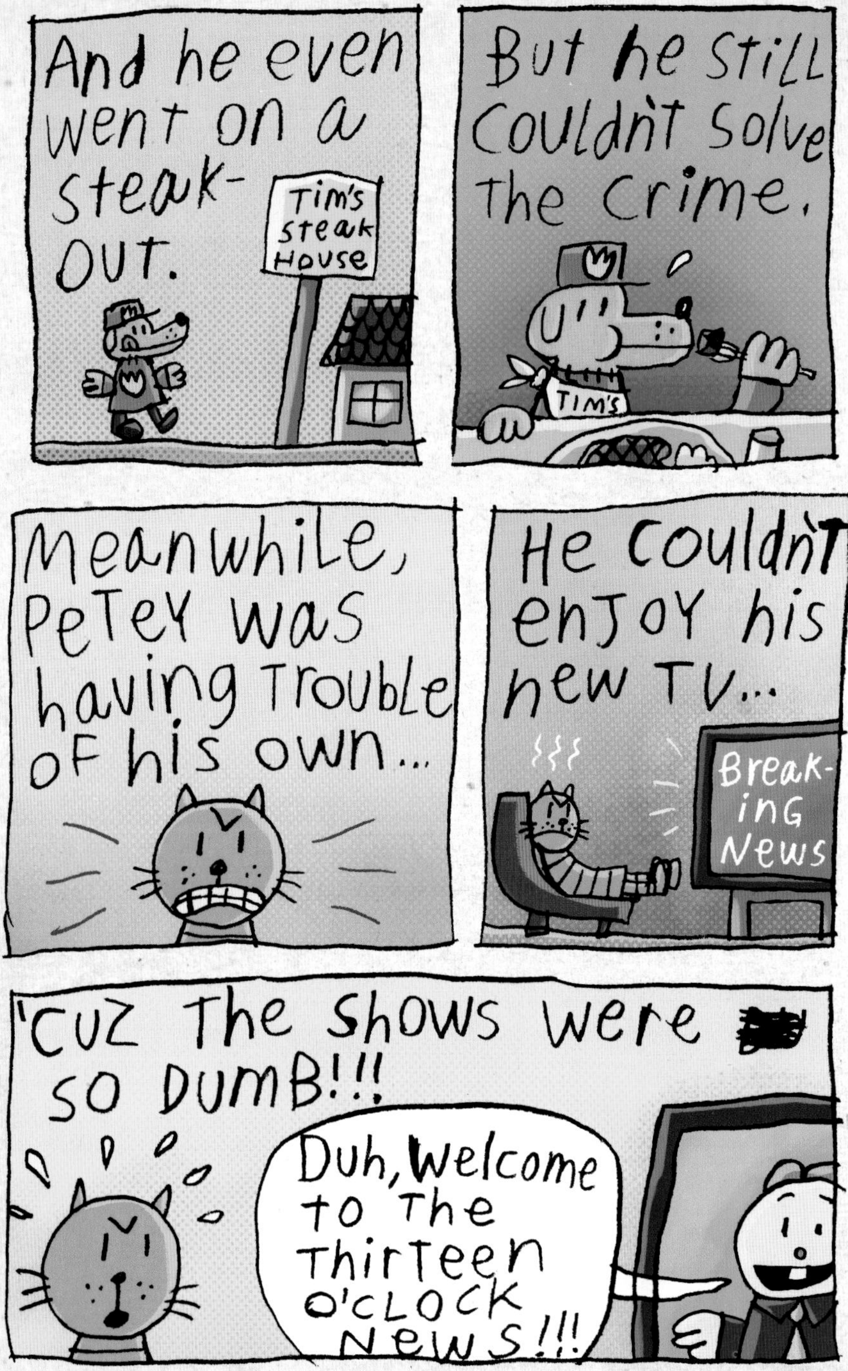
And he even went on a steak-out.
Tim's Steak House
But he still couldn't solve the crime.
Tim's
Meanwhile, Petey was having trouble of his own...
He couldn't enjoy his new TV...
Break-ing News
'Cuz the shows were so DUMB!!!
Duh, welcome to the thirteen o'clock News!!!

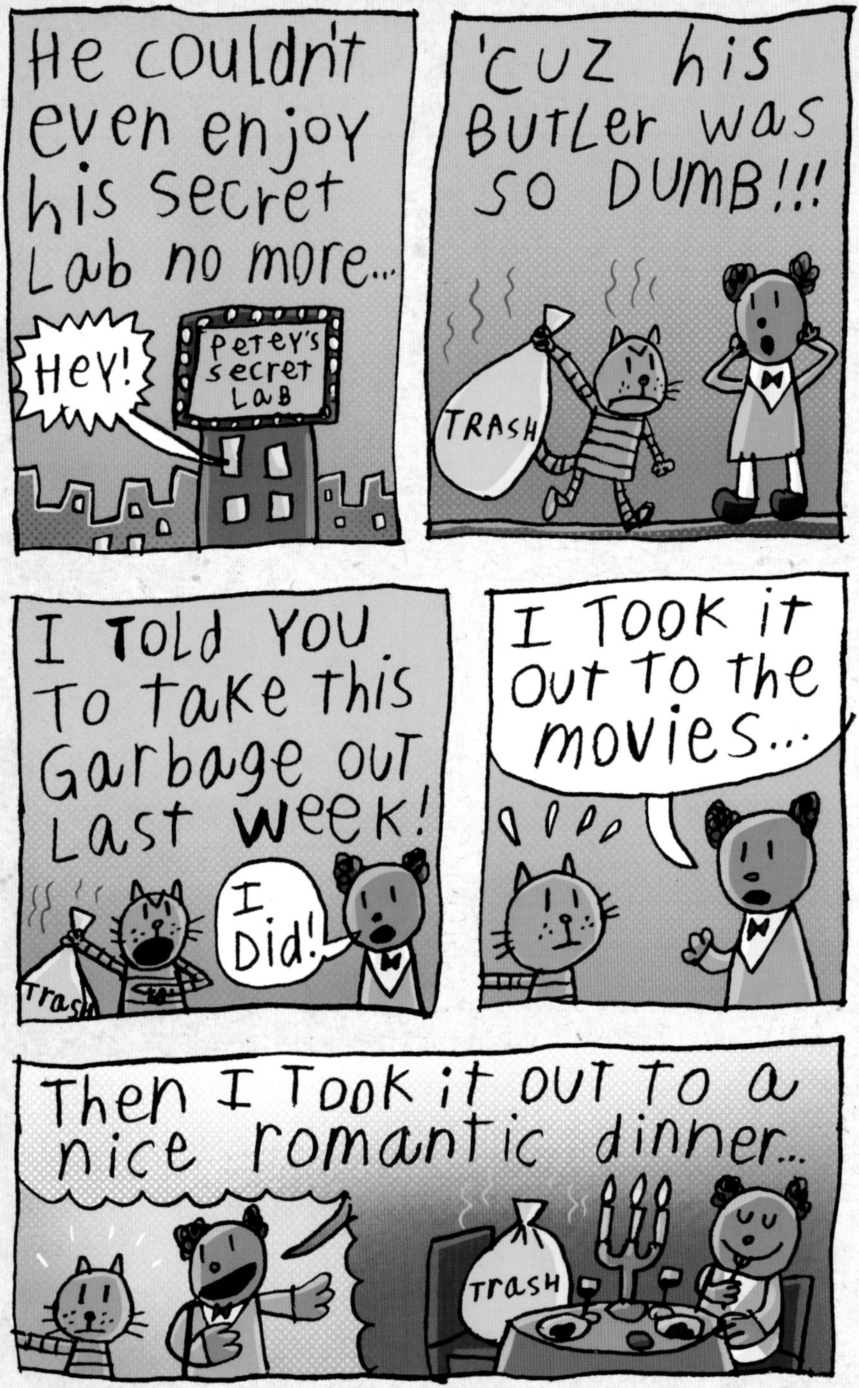
He couldn't even enjoy his secret Lab no more...
HEY!
PETEY'S SECRET LAB
'CUZ his BUTLER was SO DUMB!!!
TRASH
I TOLD YOU TO TAKE THIS GARBAGE OUT LAST WEEK!
I Did!
TRASH
I TOOK it OUT TO the movies...
Then I Took it OUT TO a nice romantic dinner...
TRASH

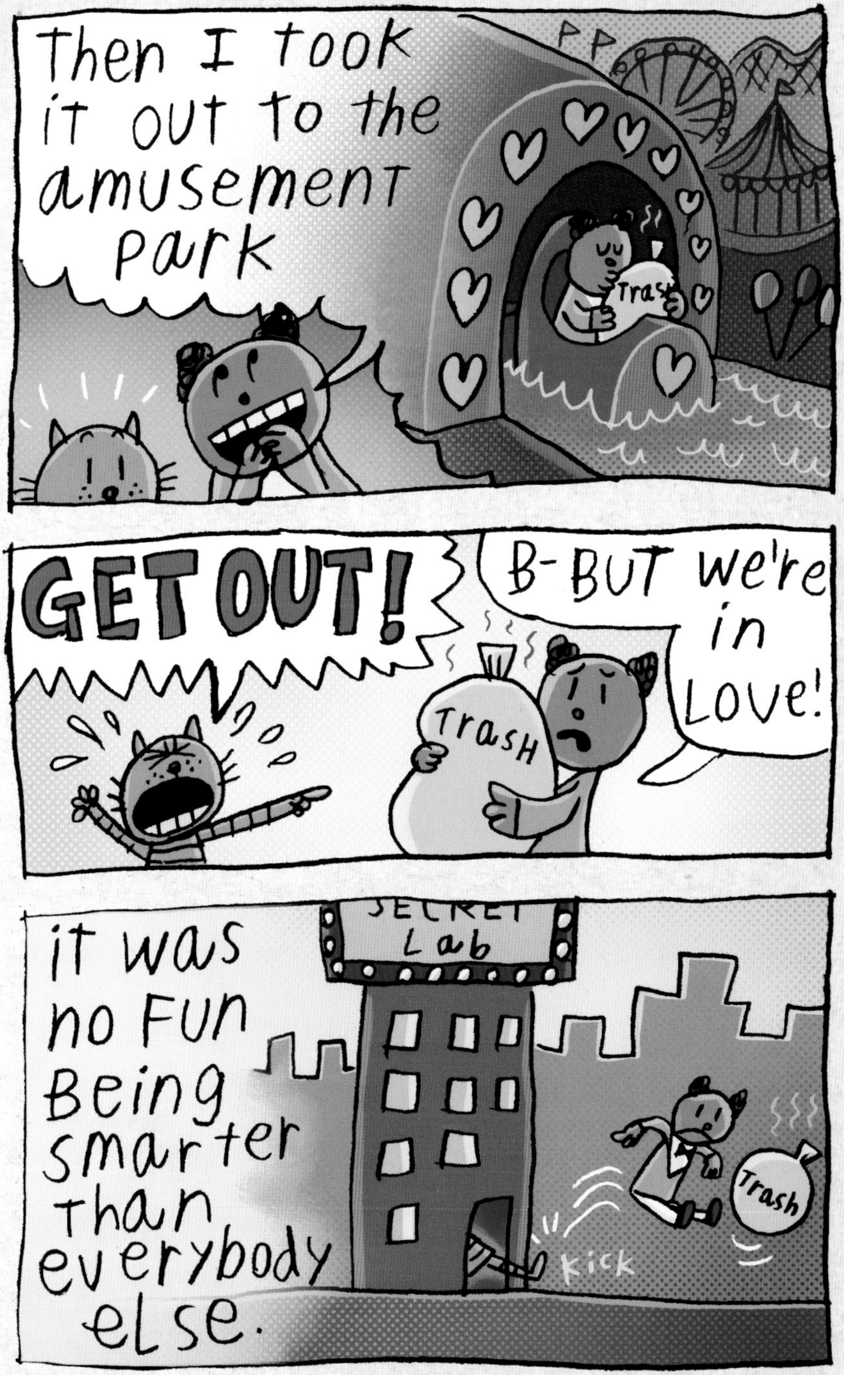
Then I took it out to the amusement park
Trash
GET OUT!
B-BUT we're in Love!
Trash
SECRET Lab
it was no Fun Being smarter than everybody else.
Kick
Trash

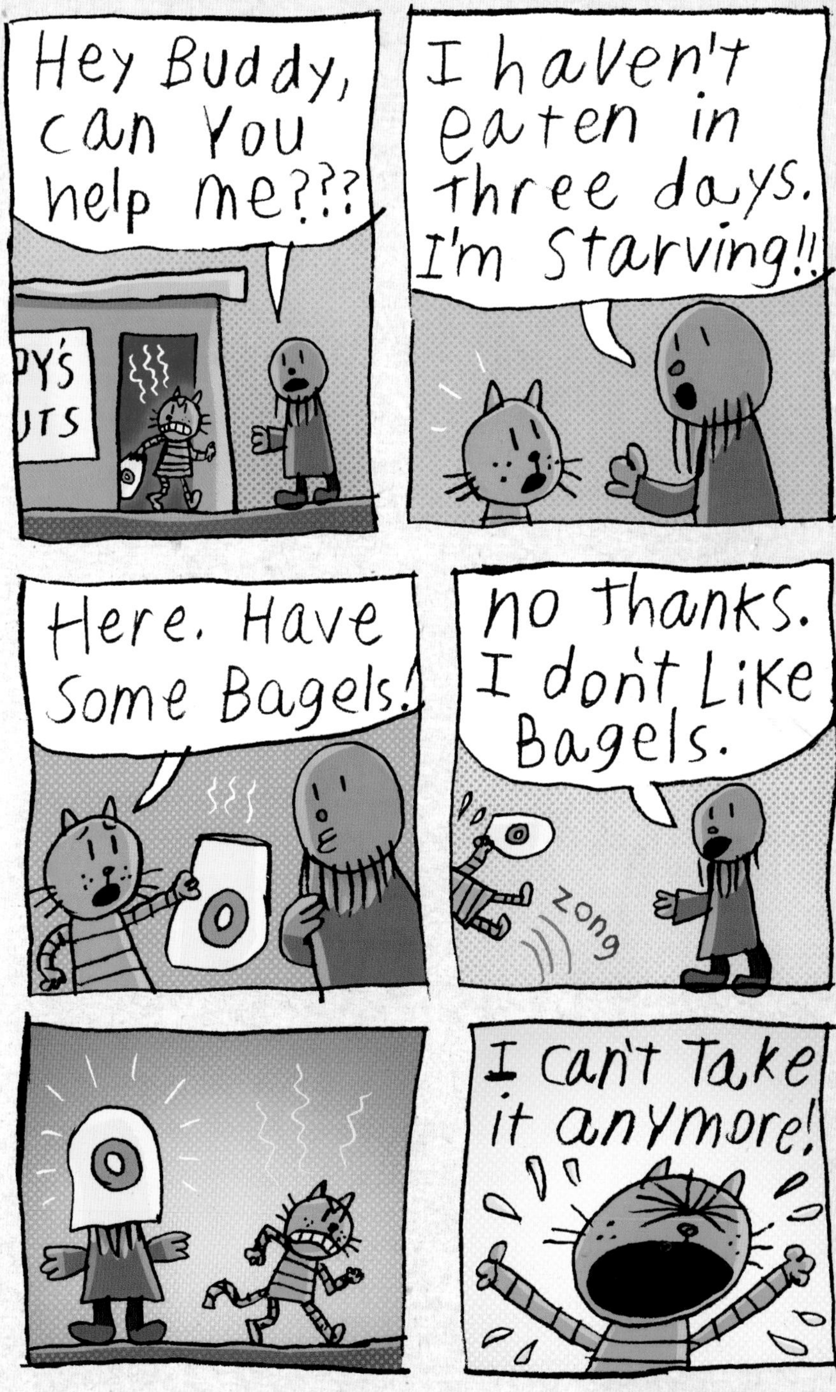
Hey Buddy, can You help me???
I haven't eaten in three days. I'm Starving!!
Here. Have Some Bagels!
no thanks. I don't Like Bagels.
zong
I can't Take it anymore!

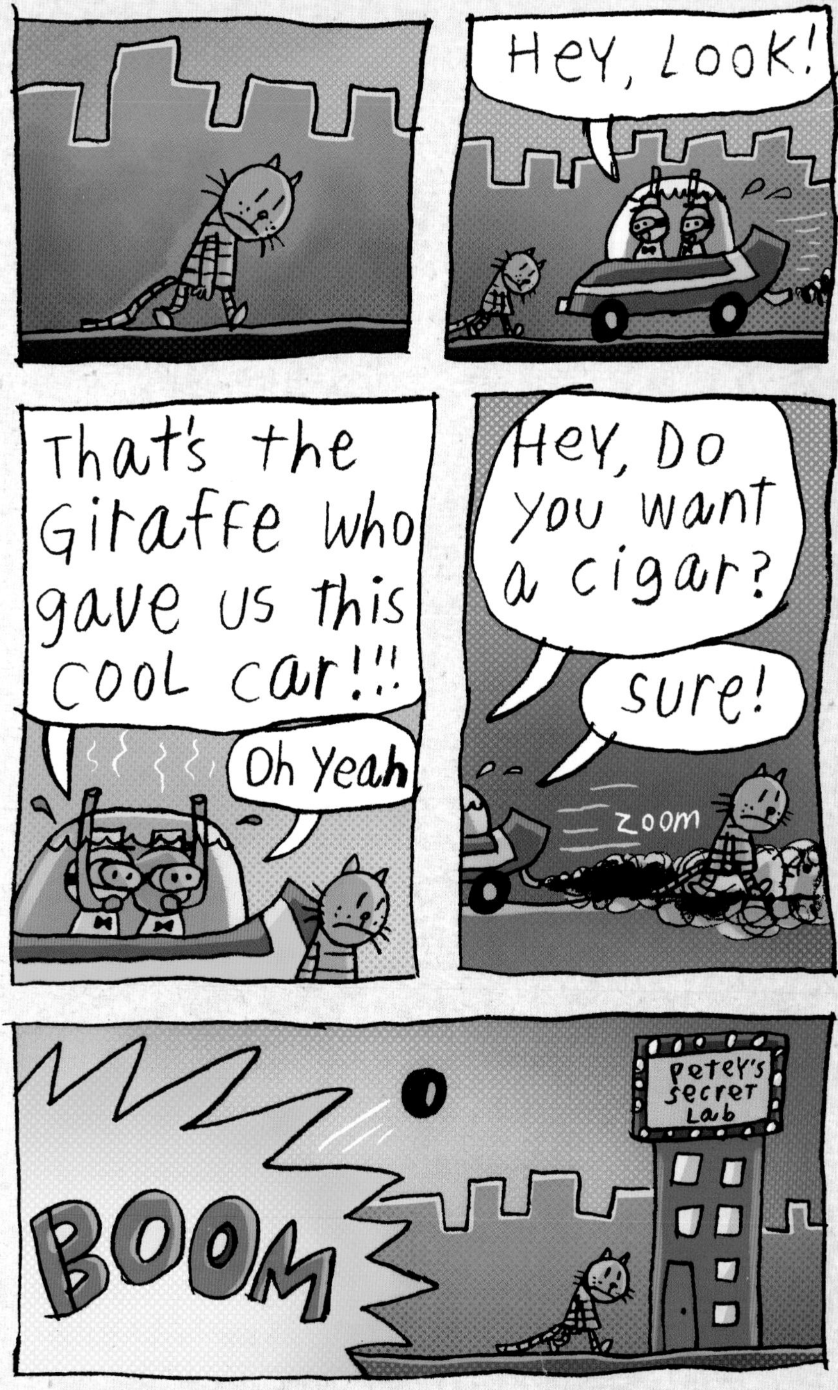
HEY, LOOK!
That's the Giraffe who gave us this cool car!!!
Oh Yeah
Hey, Do you want a cigar?
sure!
zoom
BOOM
petey's secret Lab

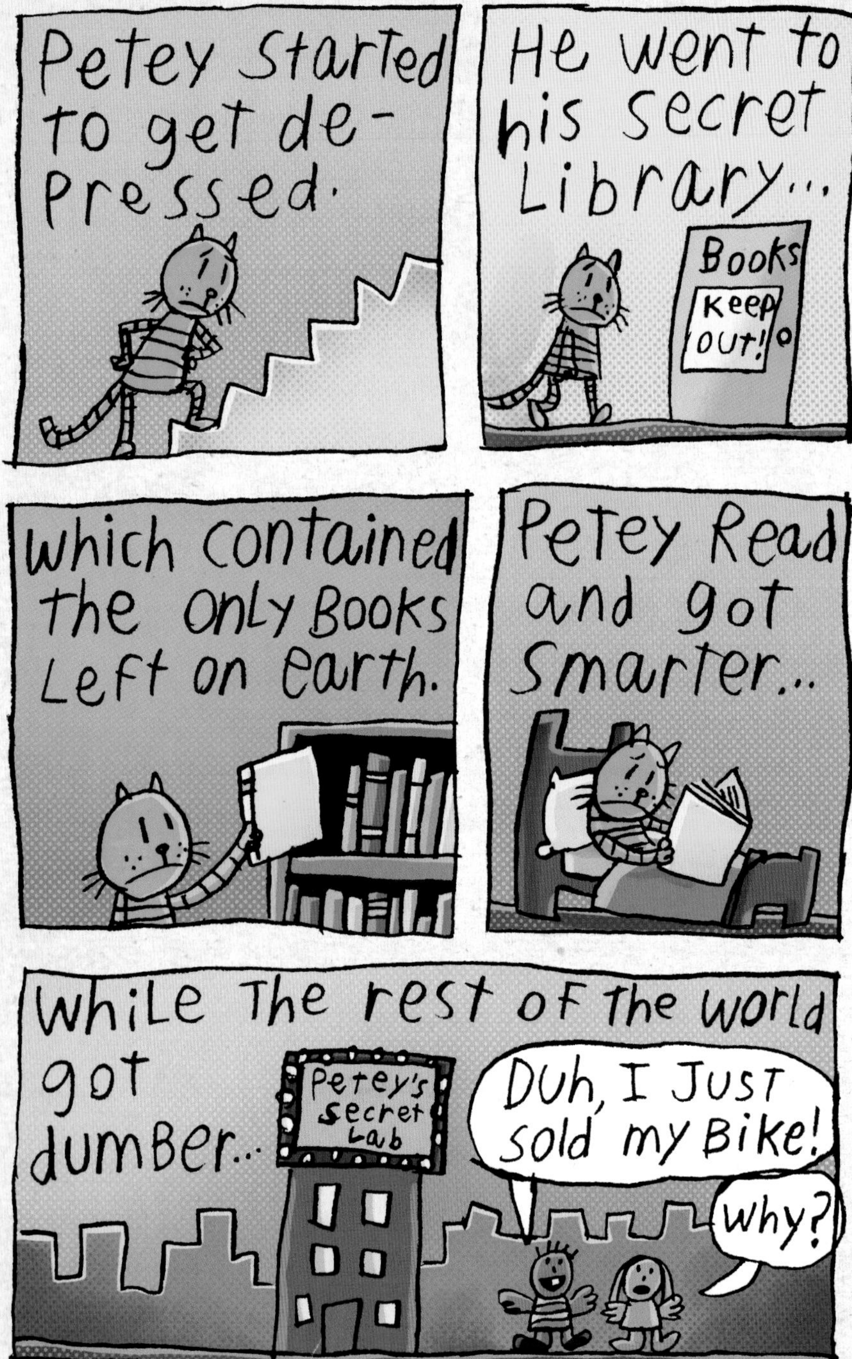
Petey Started to get de-pressed.
He went to his secret Library...
Books
Keep OUT!
which contained the only Books Left on earth.
Petey Read and got Smarter...
While The rest of The world got dumBer...
Petey's Secret Lab
DUh, I JUST sold my Bike!
why?

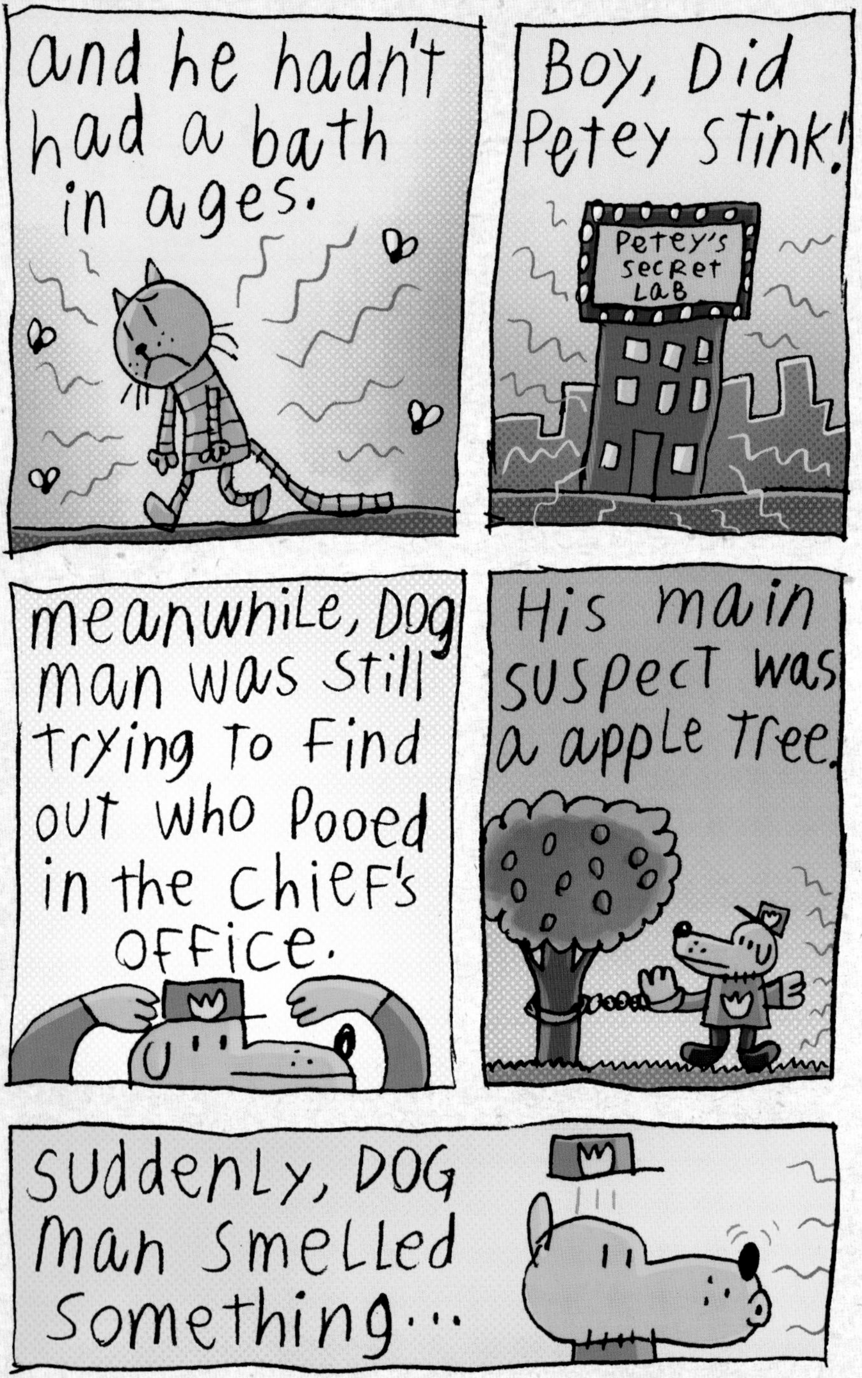
and he hadn't had a bath in ages.
Boy, Did Petey Stink!
Petey's secret Lab
meanwhile, Dog man was still trying to Find out who Pooed in the Chief's office.
His main suspect was a apple Tree.
suddenly, DOG man smelled something...

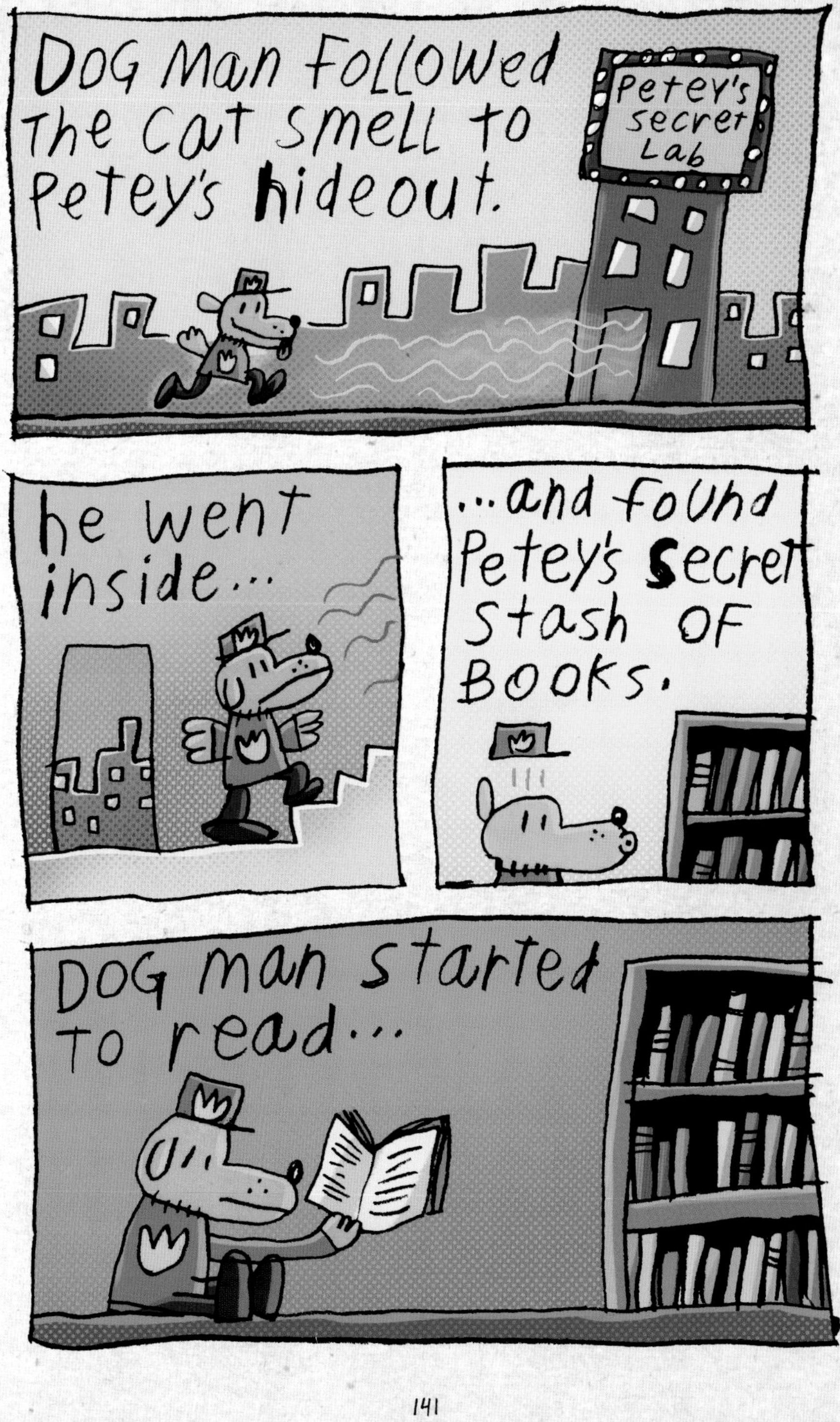
DOG Man FOLLOWed The Cat SmeLL to Petey's hideout.
Petey's Secret Lab
he went inside...
...and found Petey's Secret Stash OF BOOKS.
DOG man started To read...

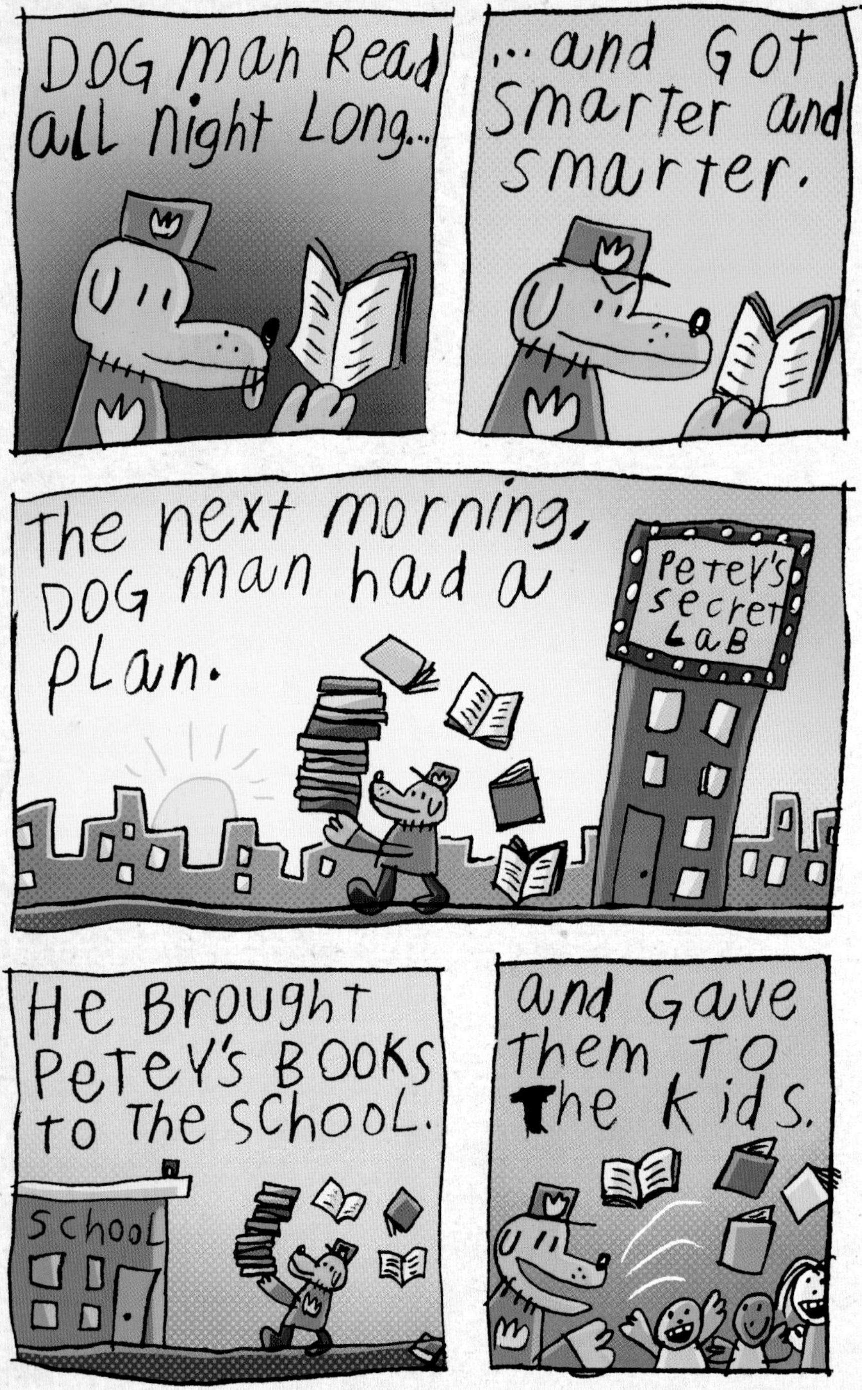
DOG man Read all night Long...
...and Got Smarter and smarter.
The next morning, DOG man had a plan.
Petey's secret LaB
He Brought Petey's BOOKS to The SchooL.
SchooL
and Gave them To The kids.

The kids read and Read.

and Then...

HOORAY!

We're smart again!

SOON, PETEY woke up...

...To a shock!

MY BOOKS!

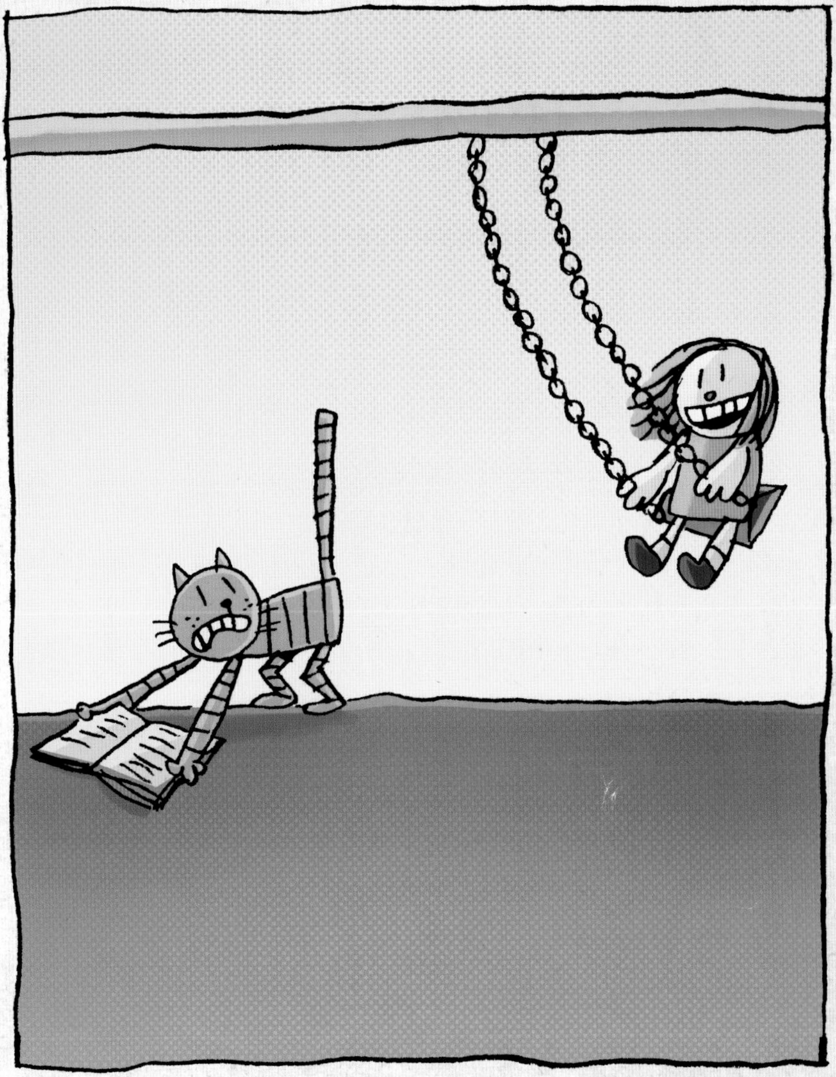

The swing set smacker

Right Thumb here.

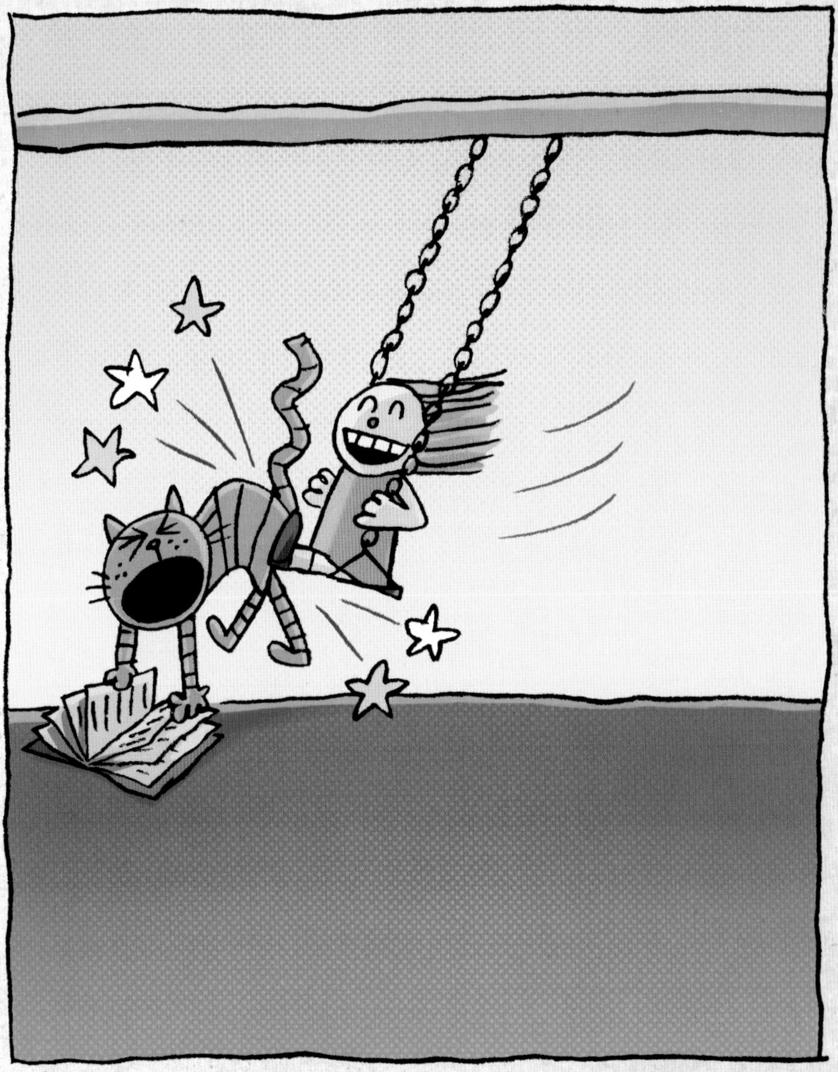

The Swing Set Smacker

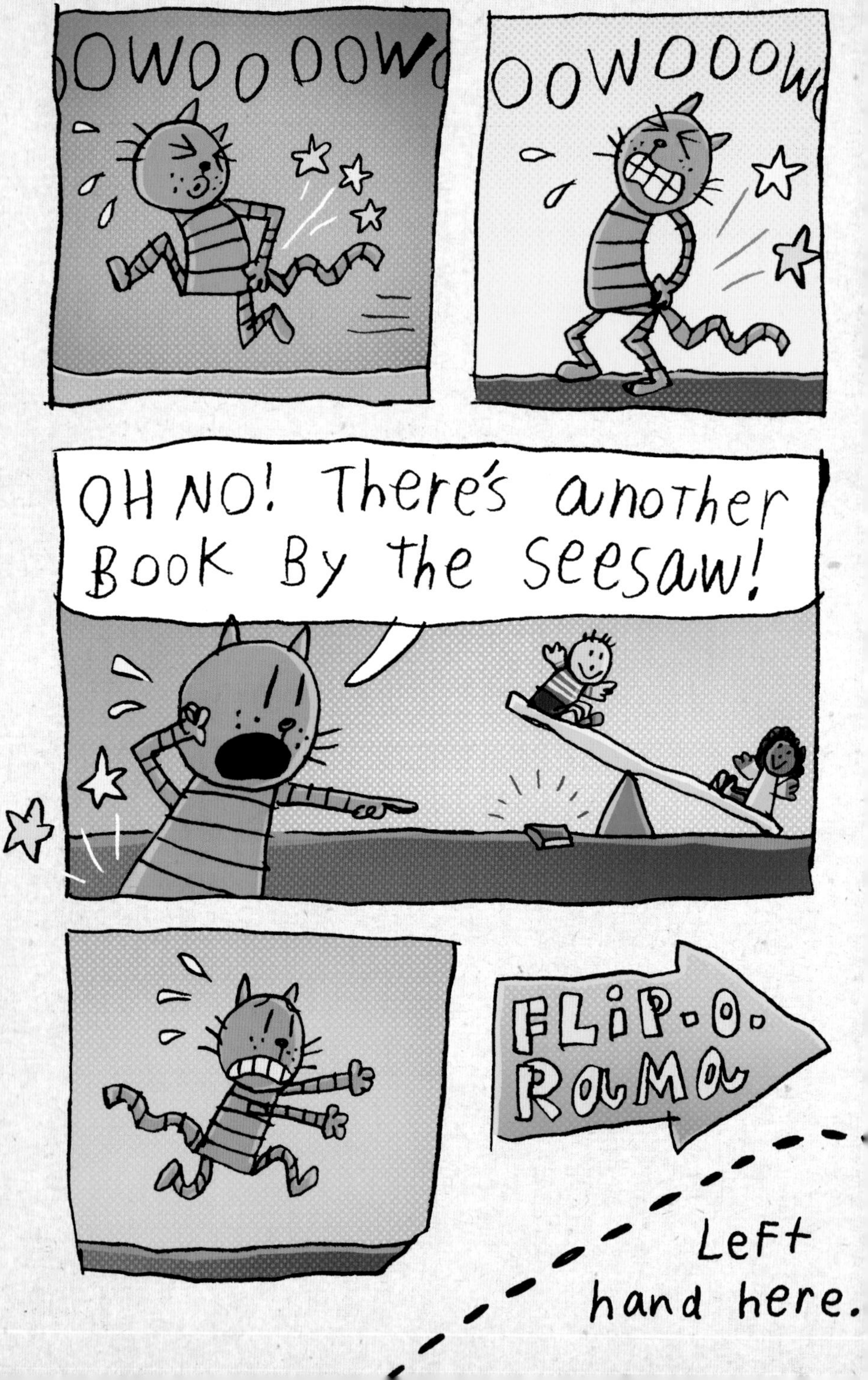
OOWOOOOOW
OOWOOOOW
OH NO! There's another Book By the seesaw!
FLIP-O-RAMA
Left hand here.

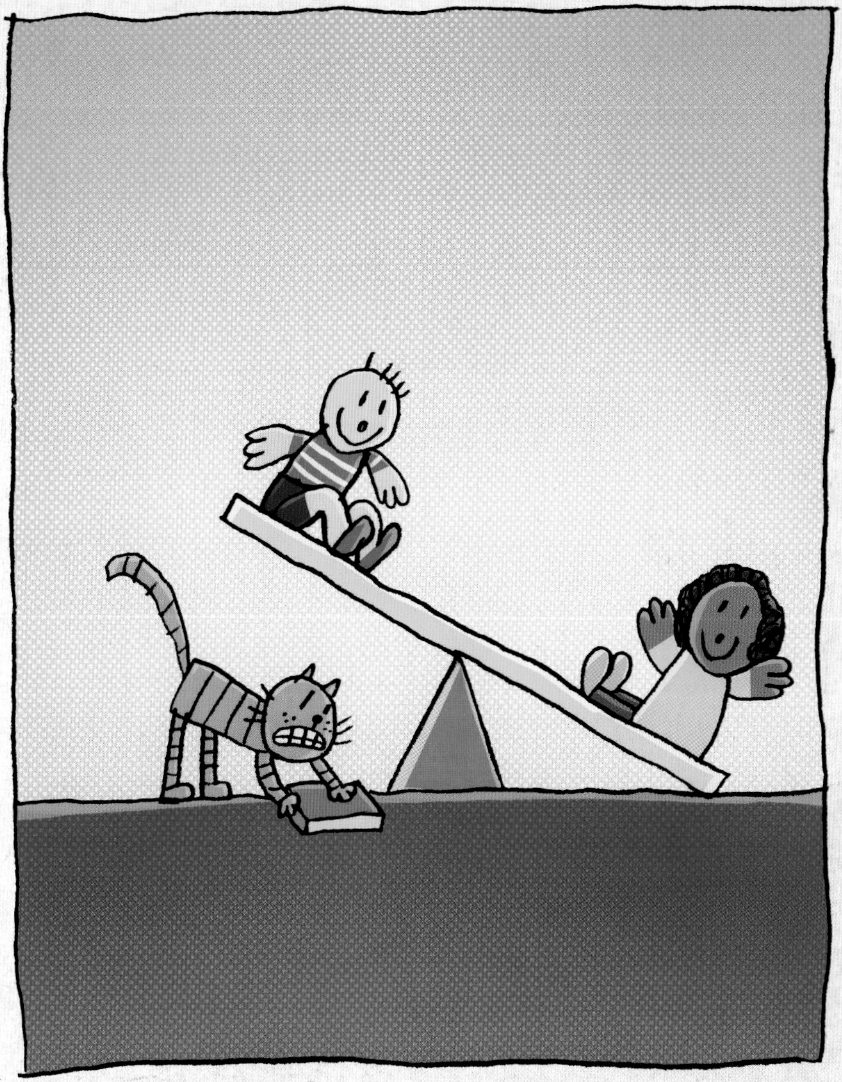

The Seesaw Smoosher

Right Thumb here.

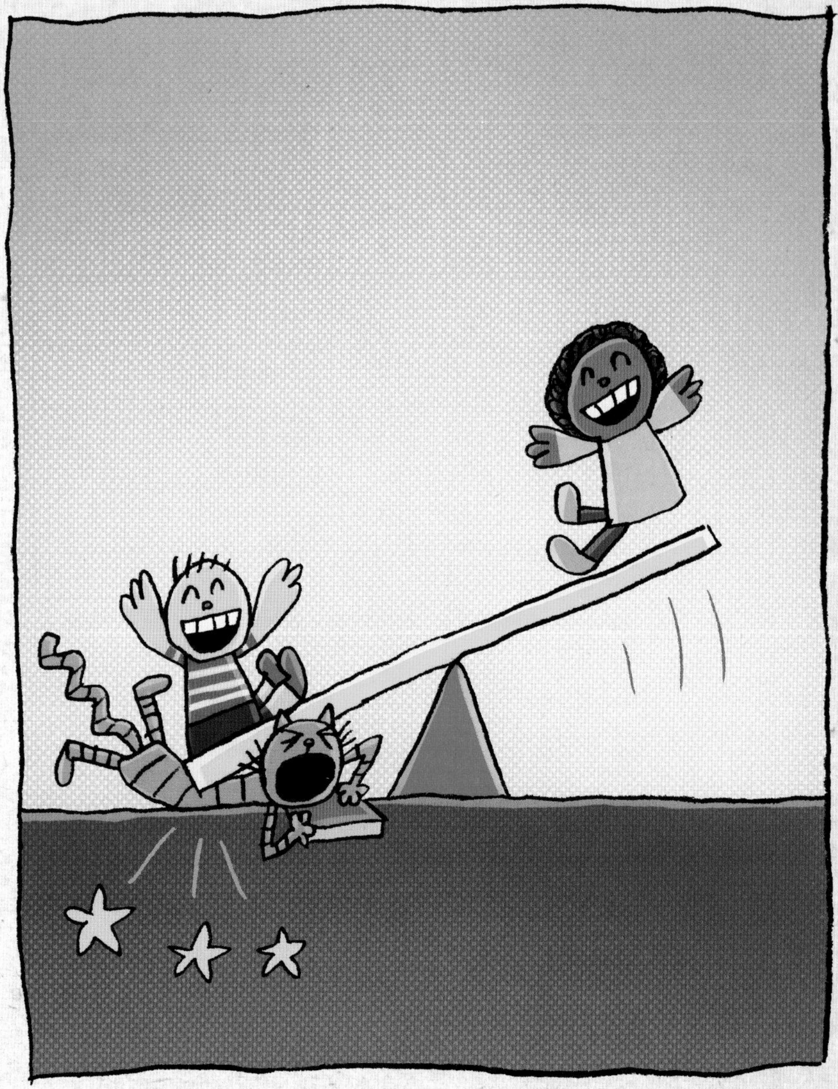

The Seesaw Smoosher

OH, NO!!! There's another Book By the spring riders!!!

Left hand here.

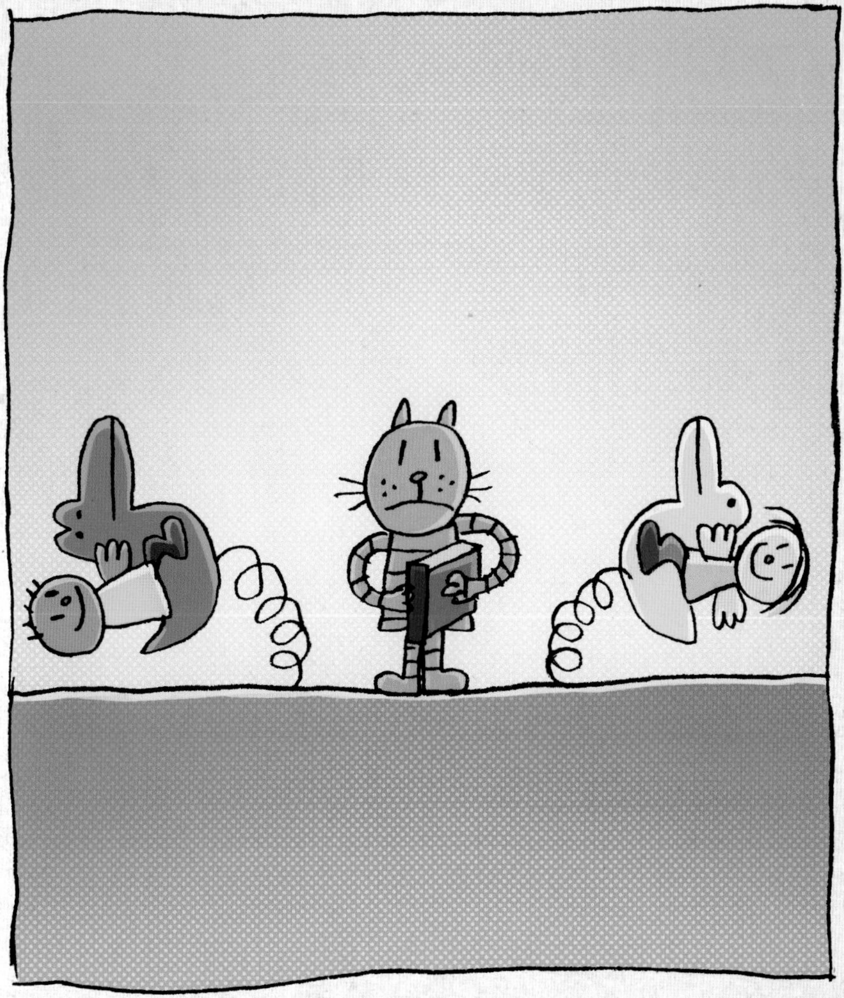

Spring Break

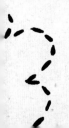

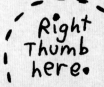

Right Thumb here.

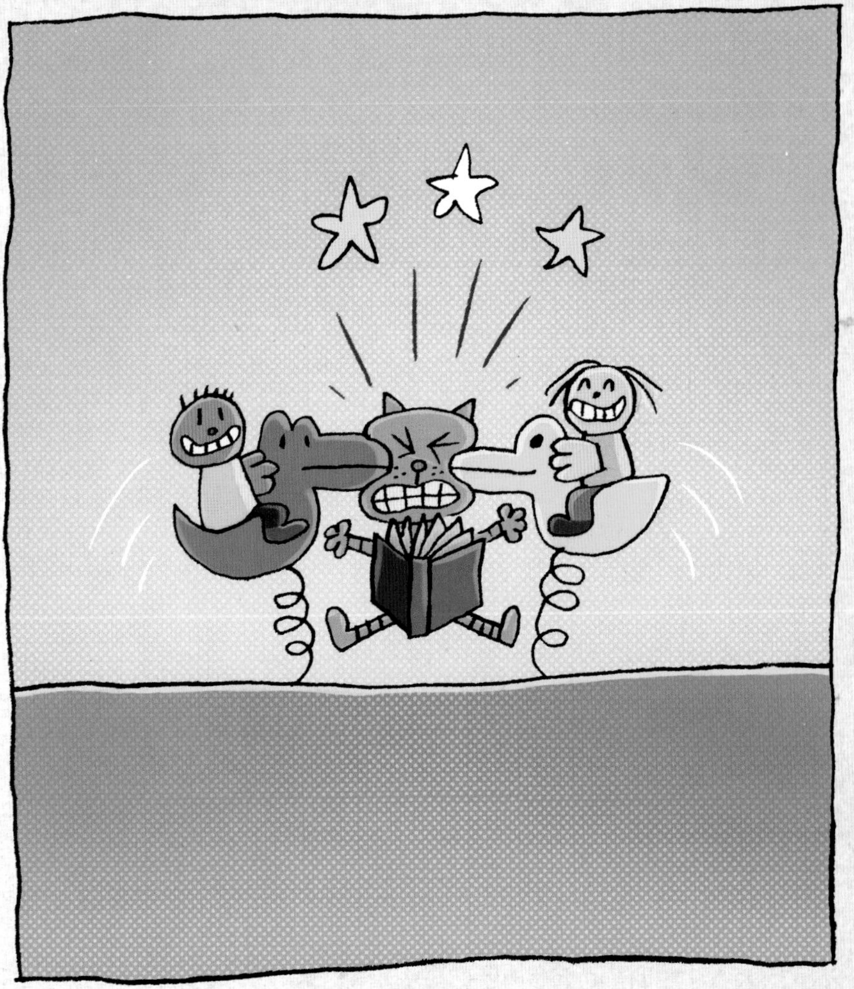

Spring Break

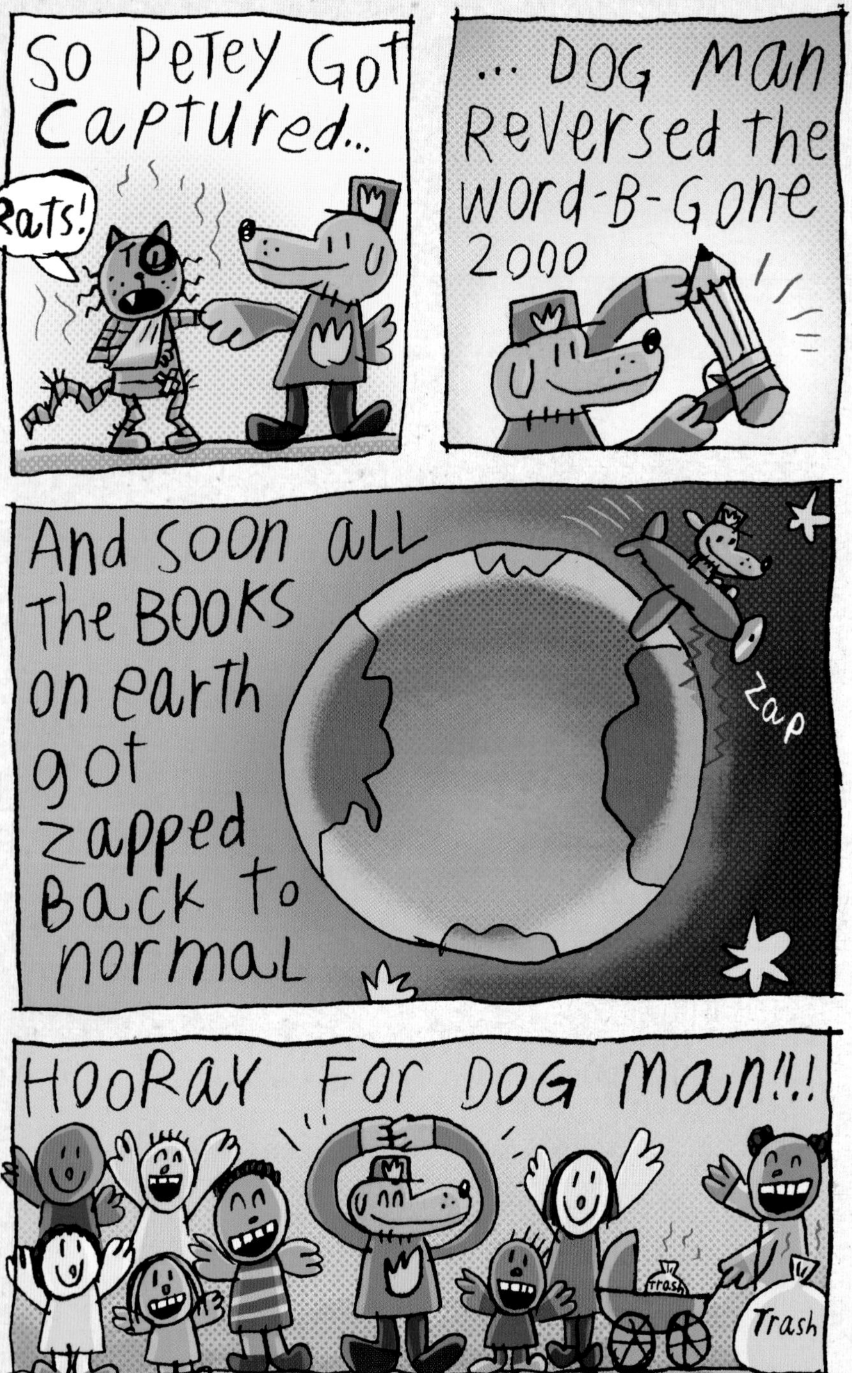
So Petey Got Captured...
Rats!
... DOG Man Reversed the Word-B-Gone 2000
And soon all The BOOKS on earth got zapped Back to normal
Zap
HOORAY FOR DOG Man!!!
Trash
Trash

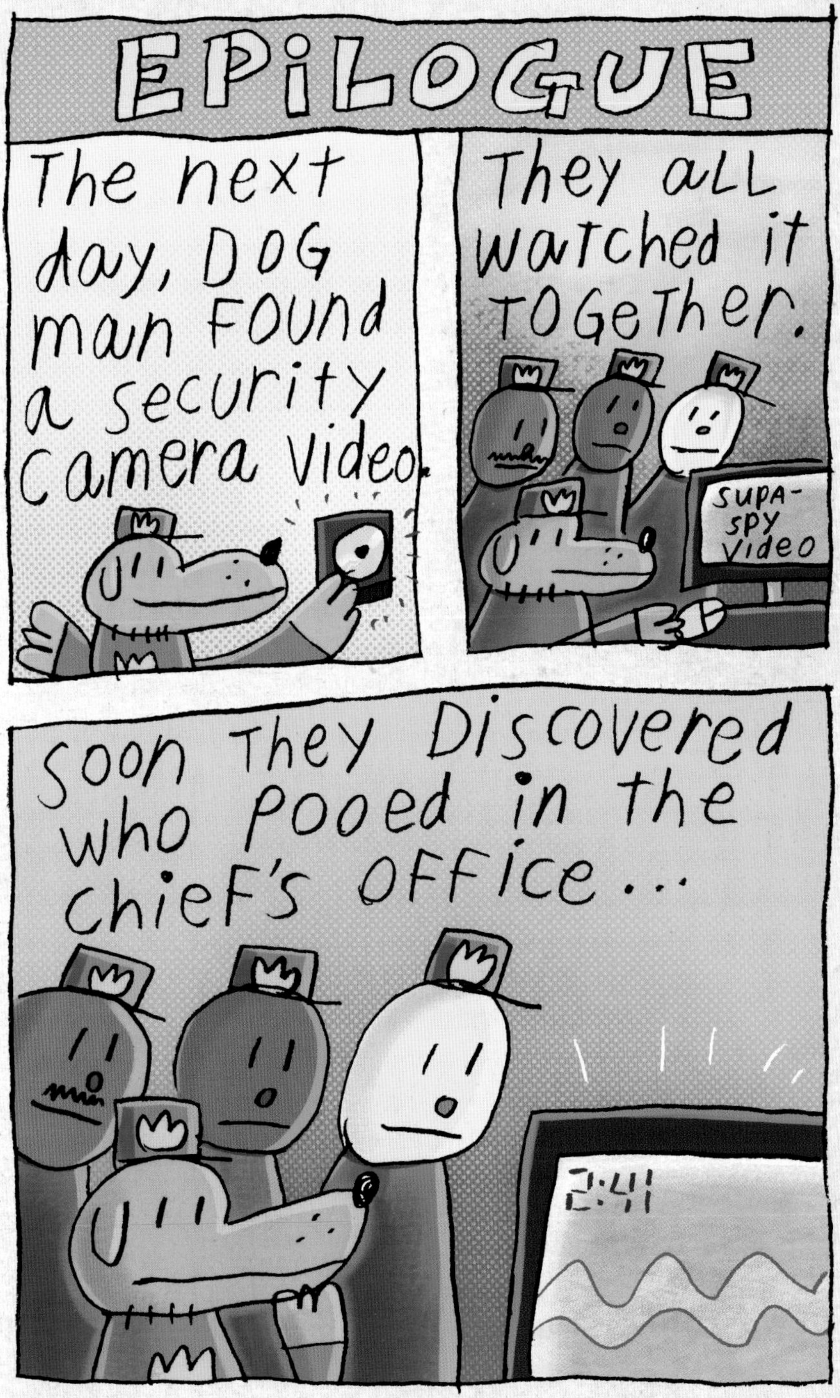
EPiLOGUE
The next day, DOG man FOUND a security camera video.
They aLL watched it TOGeTher.
SUPA-SPY Video
Soon They Discovered who Pooed in the chieF's OFFice...
2:41

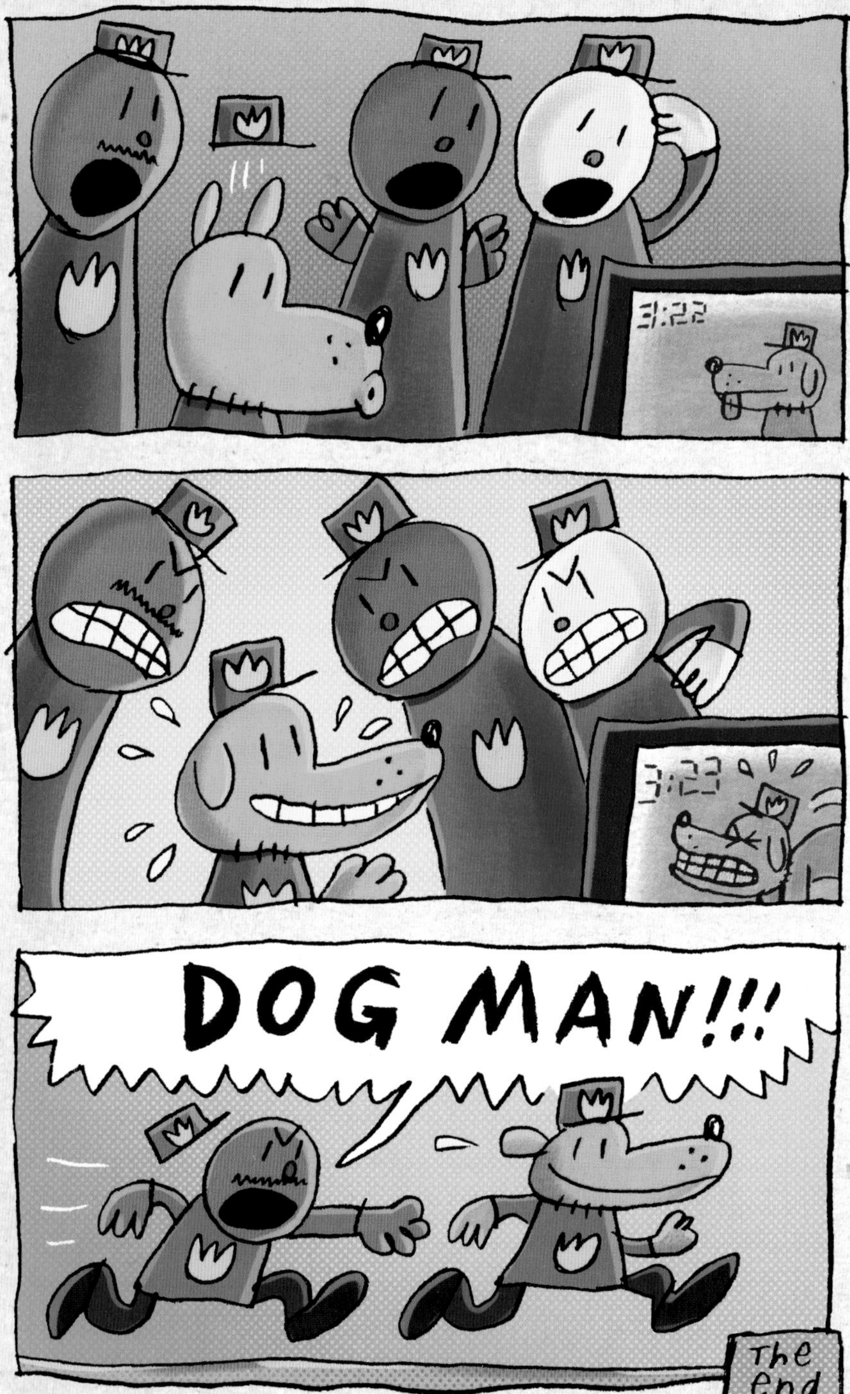
3:22
3:23
DOG MAN!!!
The end

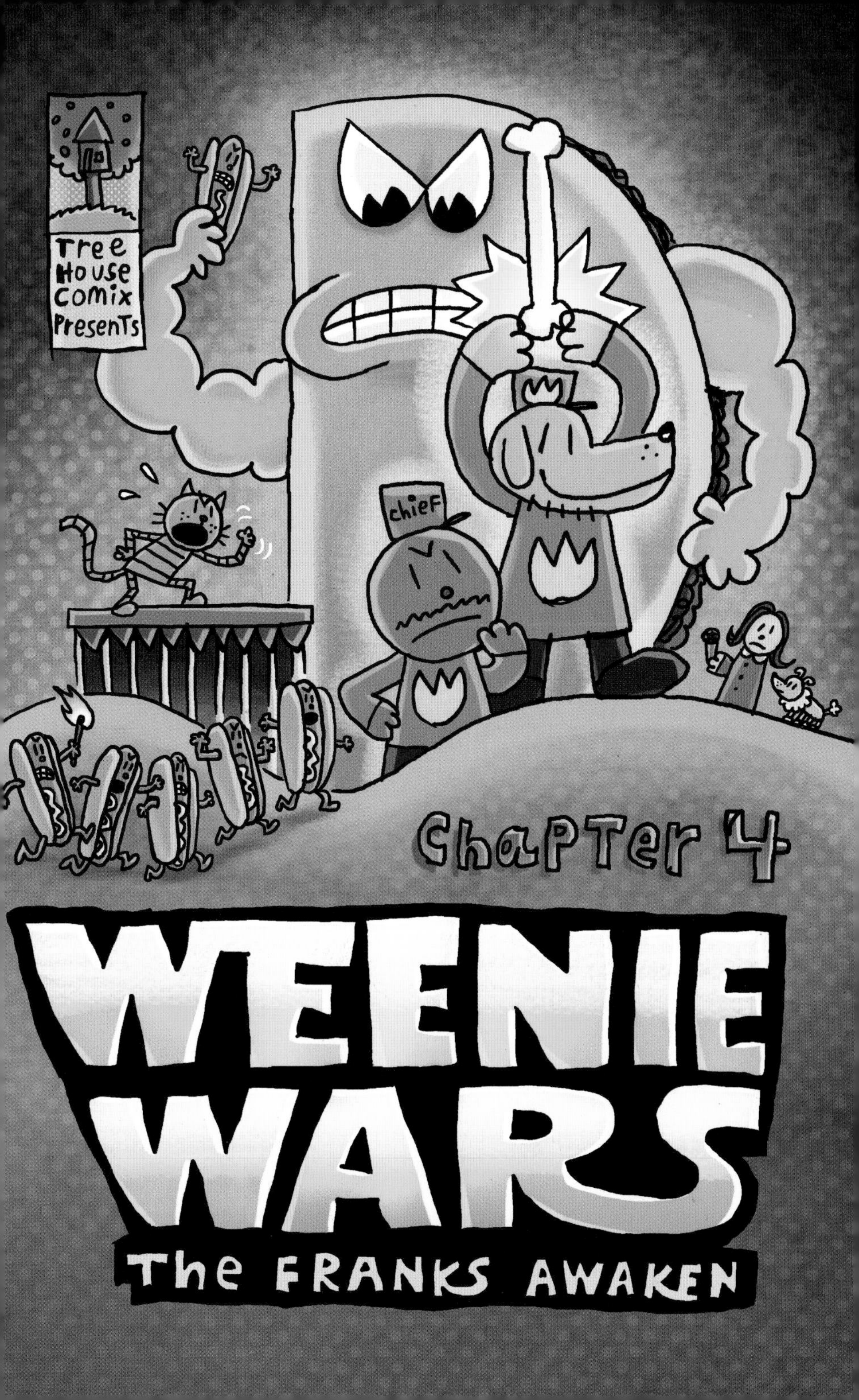
Tree House Comix Presents
chief
Chapter 4
WEENIE WARS
The FRANKS AWAKEN

DOG MAN in
WEENIE WARS:
THE FRANKS awaken

One Time at cat Jail ...

mail de-livery time!

Here, Fluffy, you got a Letter.

Thanks.

Here, Big Jim. You got candy.

Yay!

Gummy mice

Big Jim

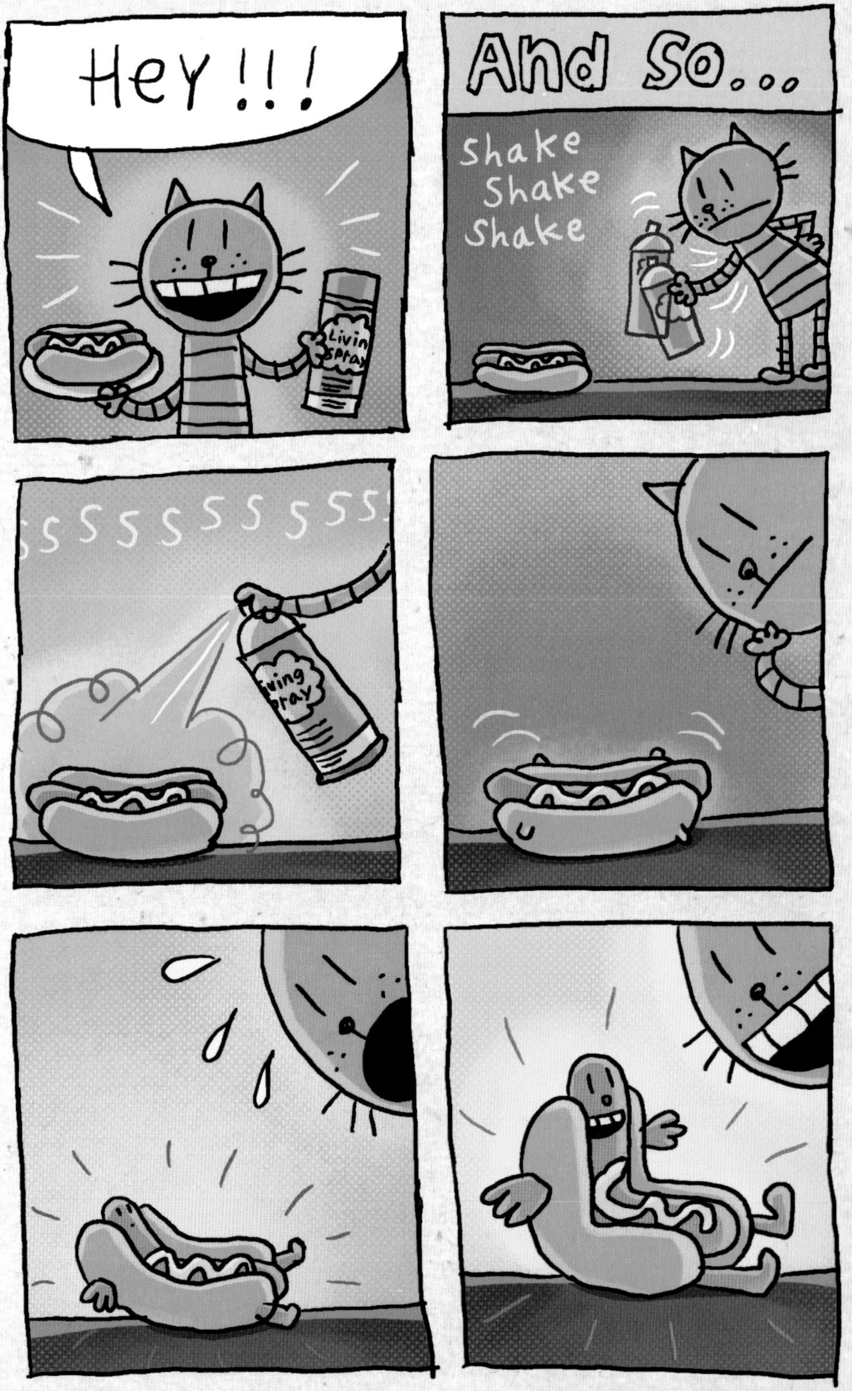
Hey!!!
And So...
Shake
Shake
Shake
SSSSSSSSSS

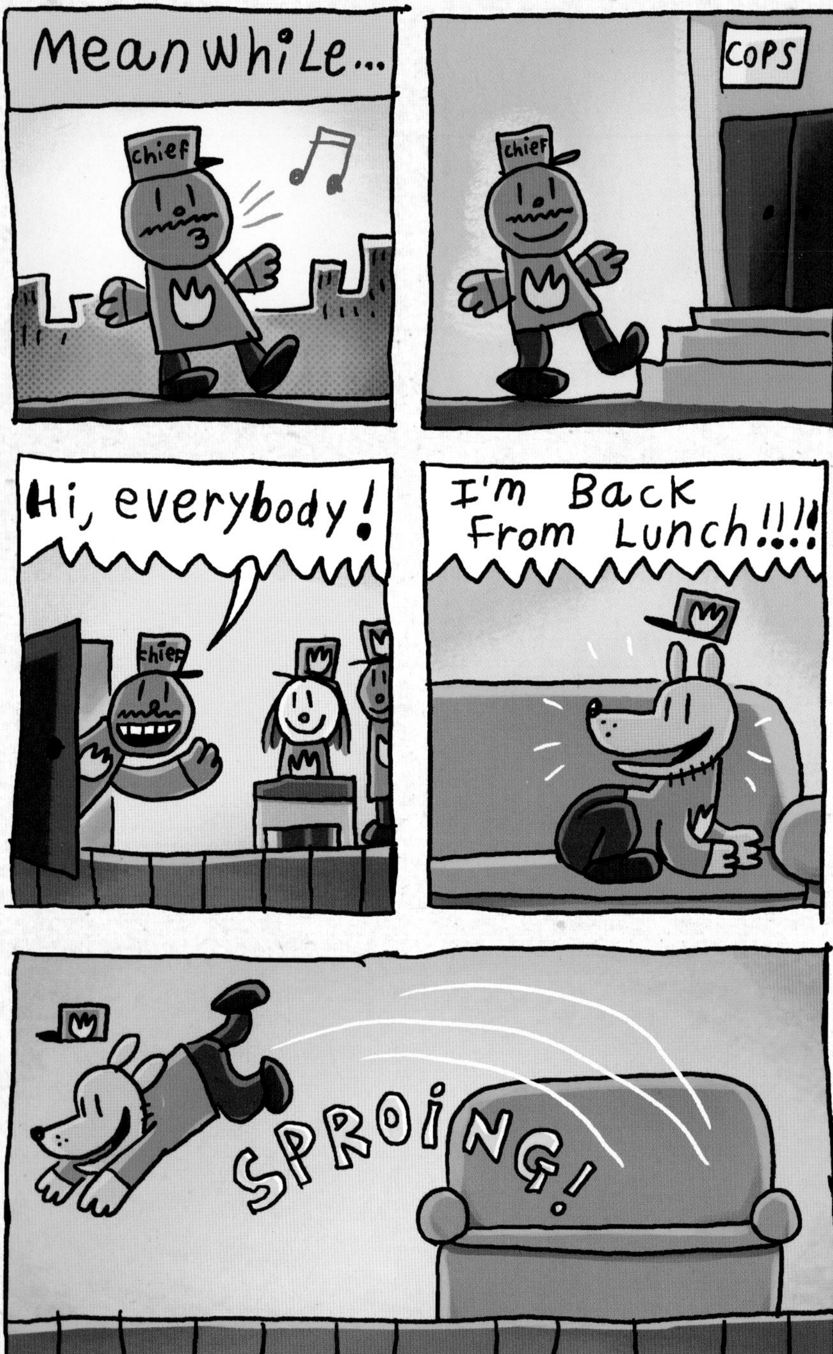
Meanwhile...
COPS
chief
Hi, everybody!
I'm Back From Lunch!!!!
SPROING!

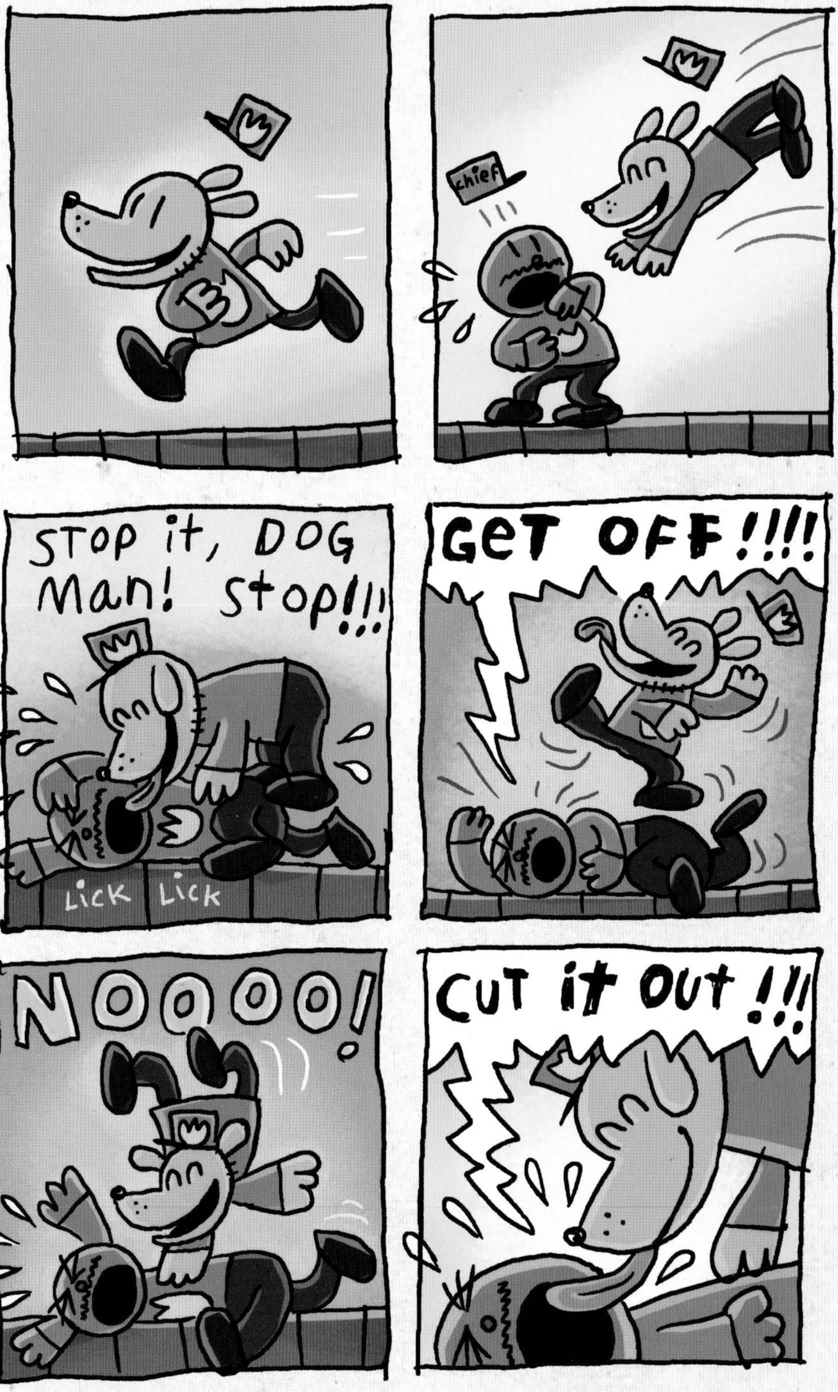
chief
STOP it, DOG Man! stop!!!
LiCK LiCK
GeT OFF!!!!
NOOOO!
CuT it OUT!!!

Remember--- Flip it,
Don't Rip it!!!!!!

Left
hand here.

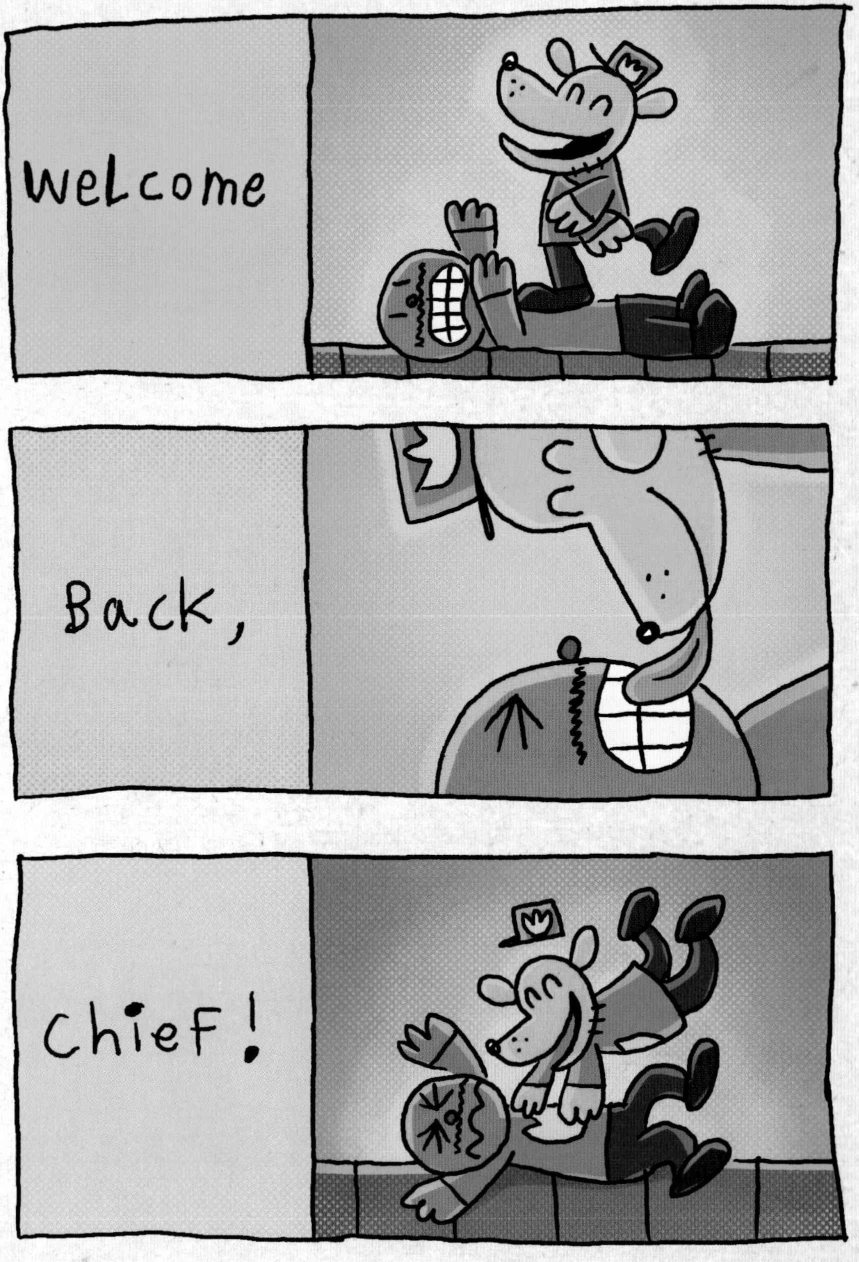
Welcome
Back,
Chief!

Right Thumb here.

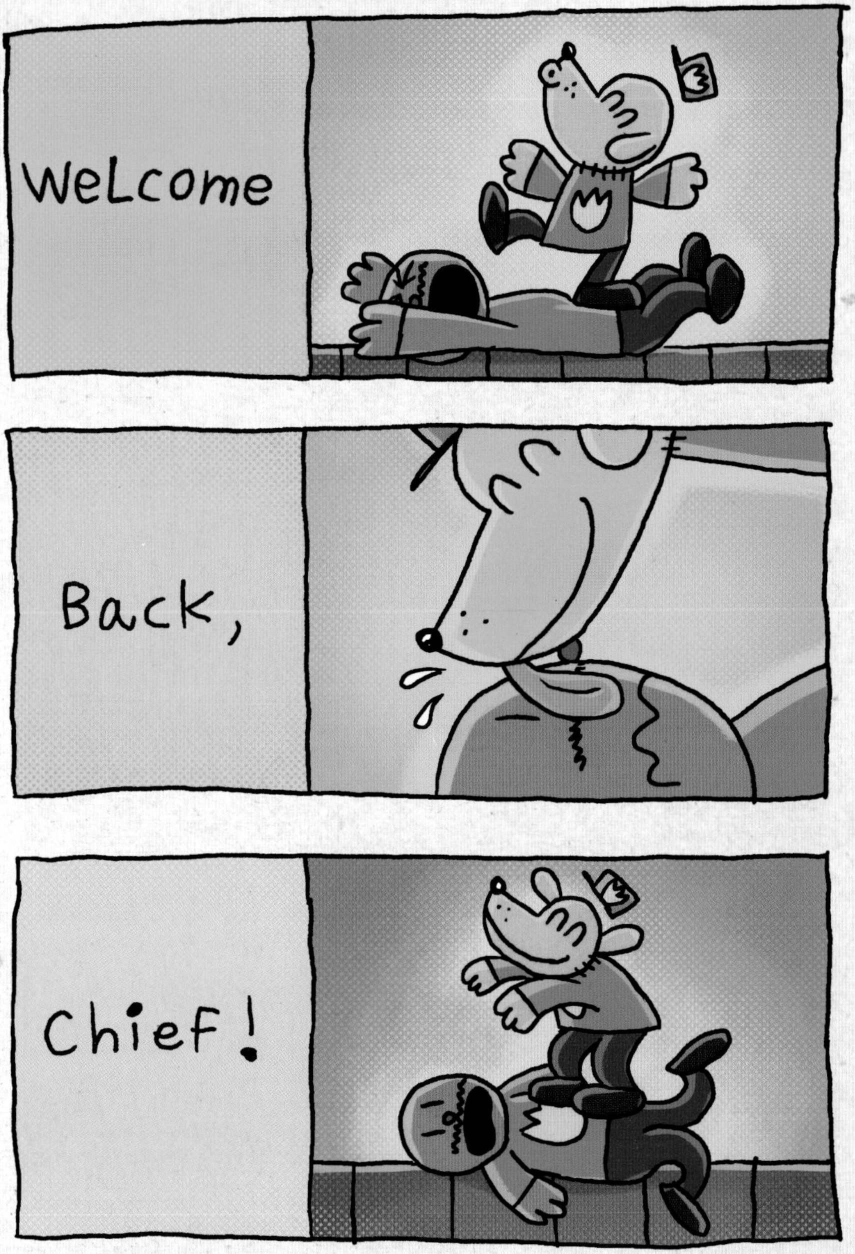
Welcome
Back,
Chief!

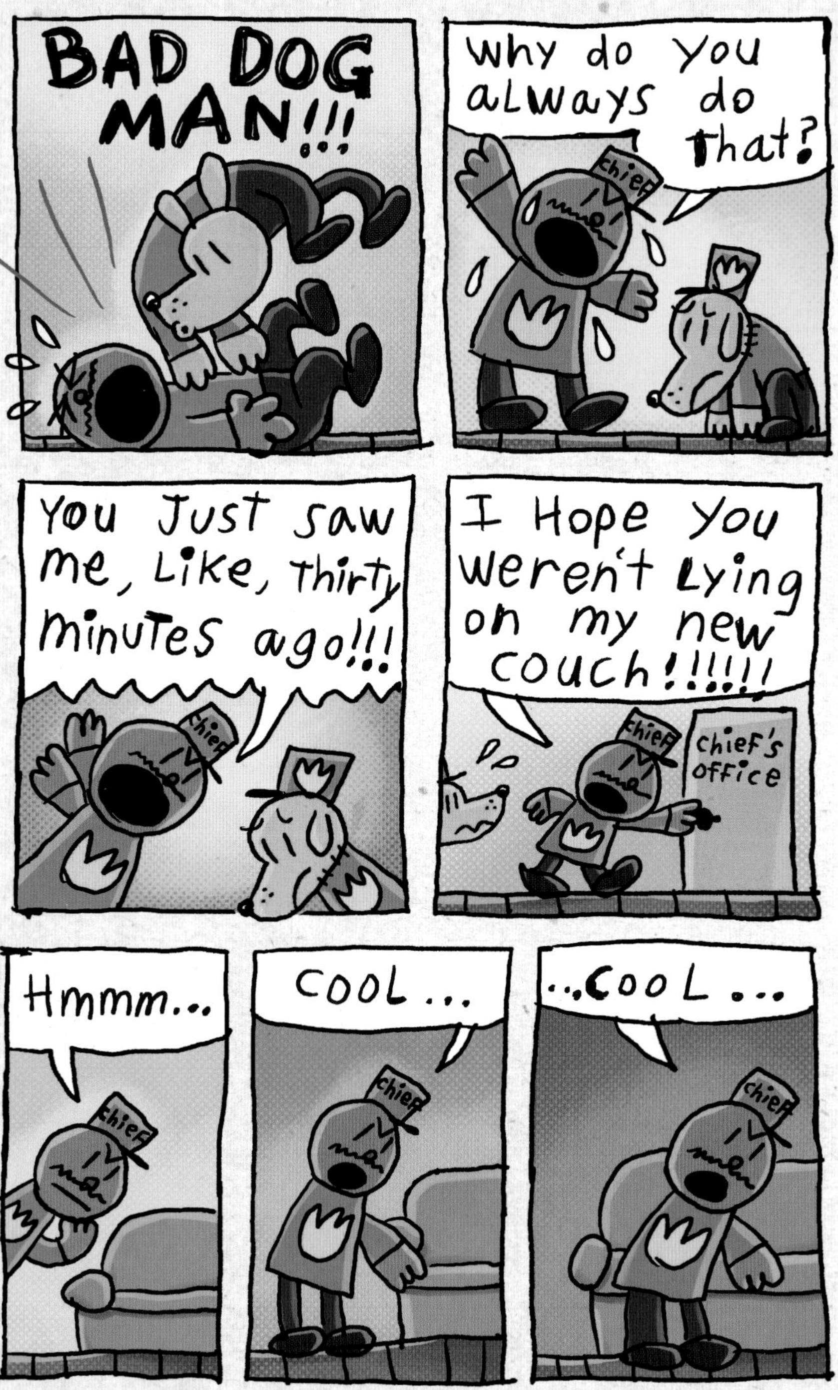
BAD DOG MAN!!!
Why do you always do that?
You just saw me, like, thirty minutes ago!!!
I hope you weren't lying on my new couch!!!!!!
chief's office
Hmmm...
cool...
...cool...

Get aLong, Little doggies!

That's right... in you go!!!!

Soon, every Dog will be in my Trap!

... Including DOG Man!!!

Meanwhile, back at Cat JaiL...

Stupid cat!!! I'LL Show him!!!

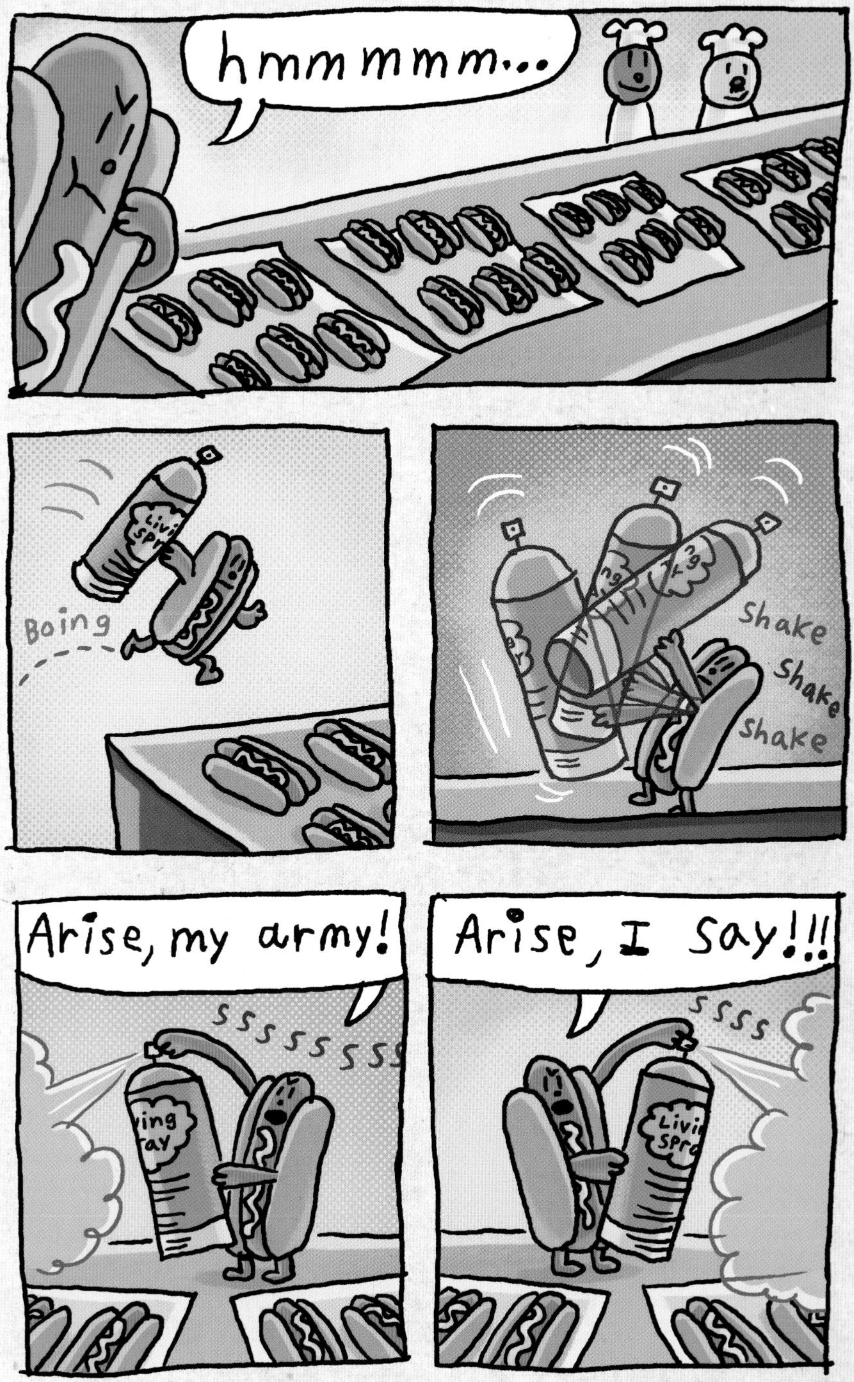
hmmmmmm...
Boing
Shake
Shake
Shake
Arise, my army!
SSSSSSSS
Arise, I say!!!
SSSS

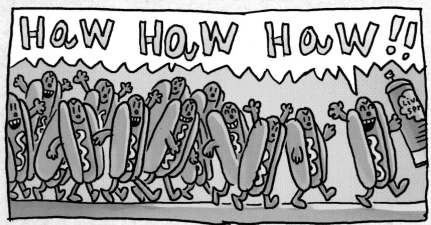

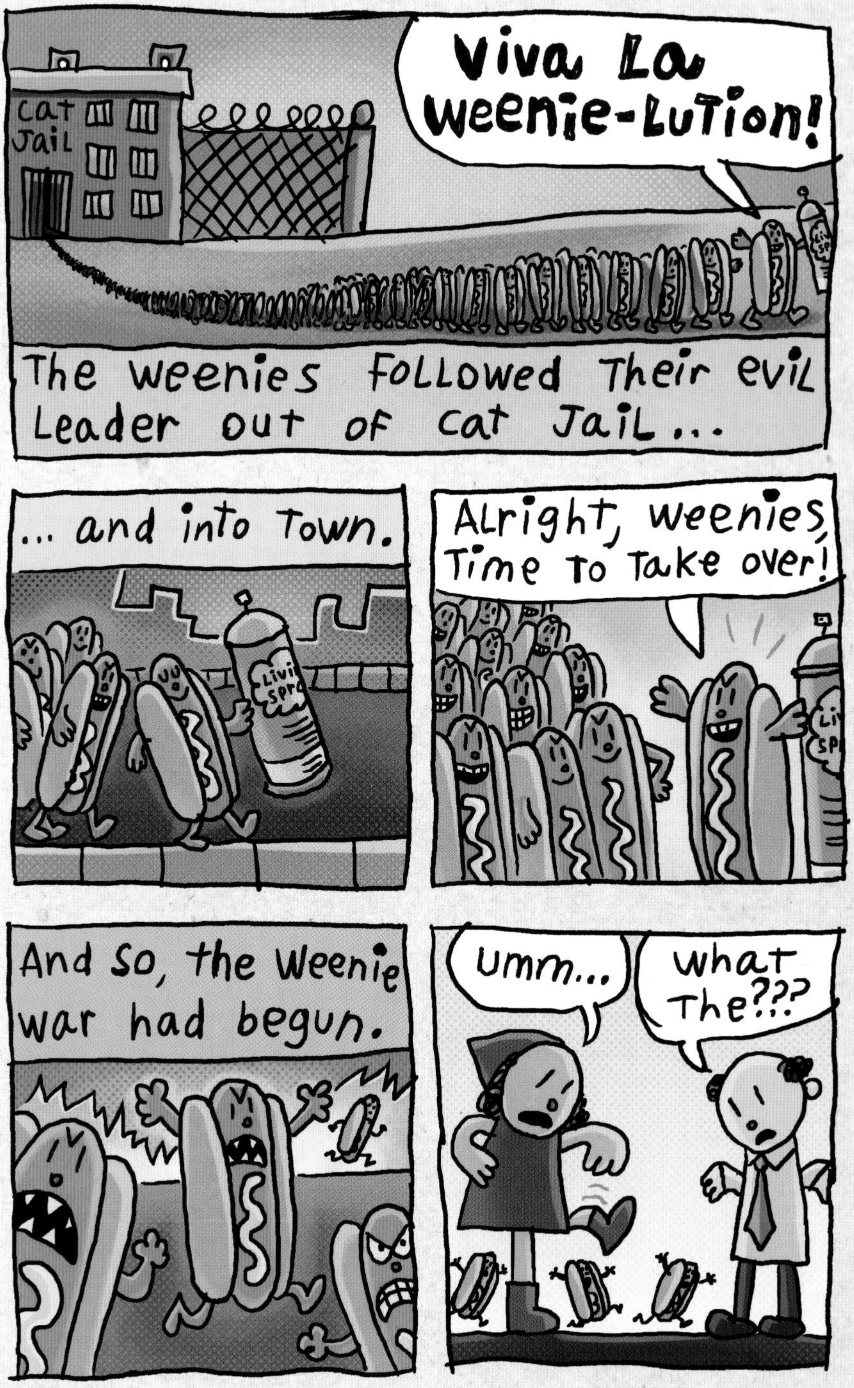
Viva La Weenie-Lution!
The weenies followed their evil leader out of Cat Jail...
CAT JAIL
... and into town.
Alright, weenies, time to take over!
And so, the weenie war had begun.
Umm...
What the???

It was True! DOG Man was Trapped...

...and all his human Strength didn't help.

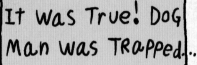

OH, NO!!! DOG Man is doomed!

why was I so mean to him???

There, there, chief.

DOG Man WILL Save the day! You'll see!

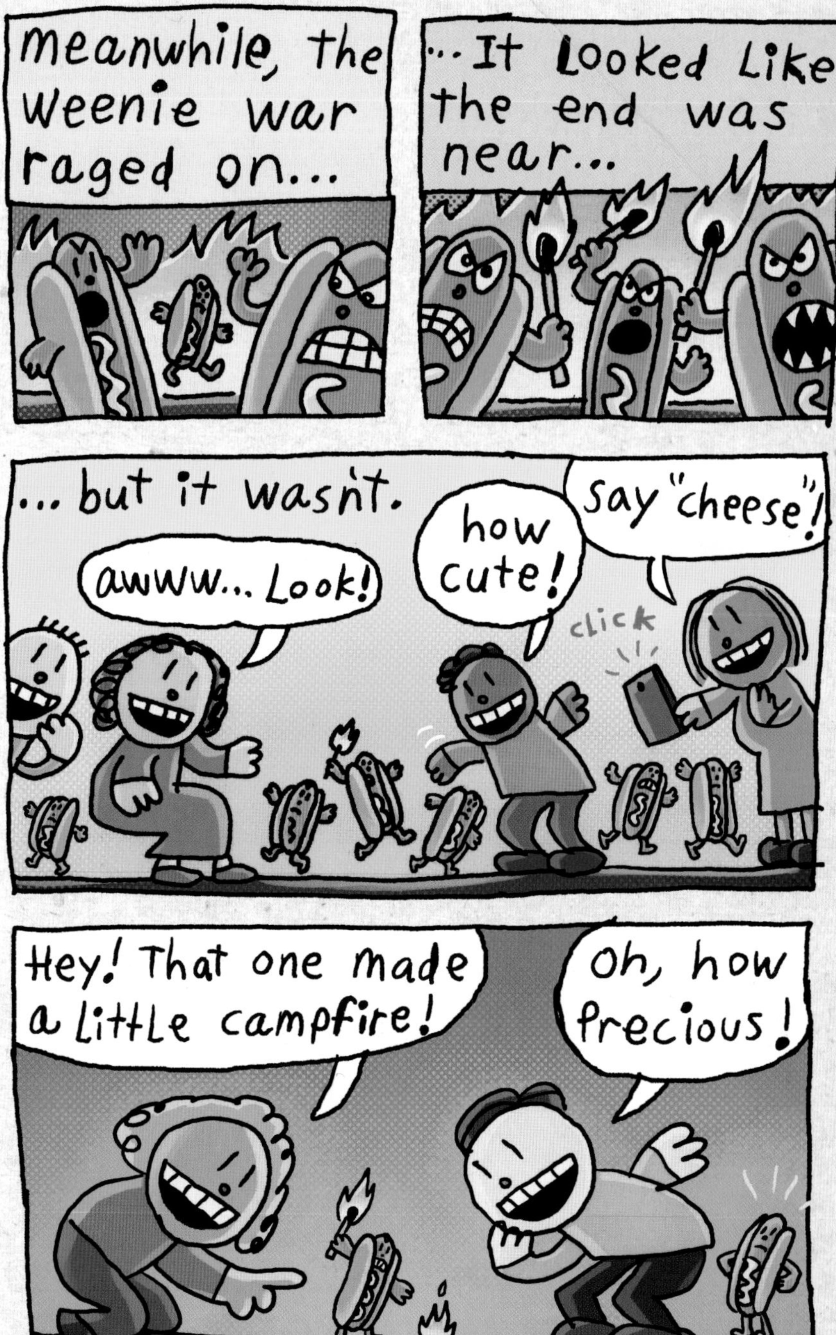
meanwhile, the weenie war raged on...
...It Looked Like the end was near...
...but it wasn't.
awww... Look!
how cute!
Say "cheese"!
click
Hey! That one made a Little campfire!
Oh, how Precious!

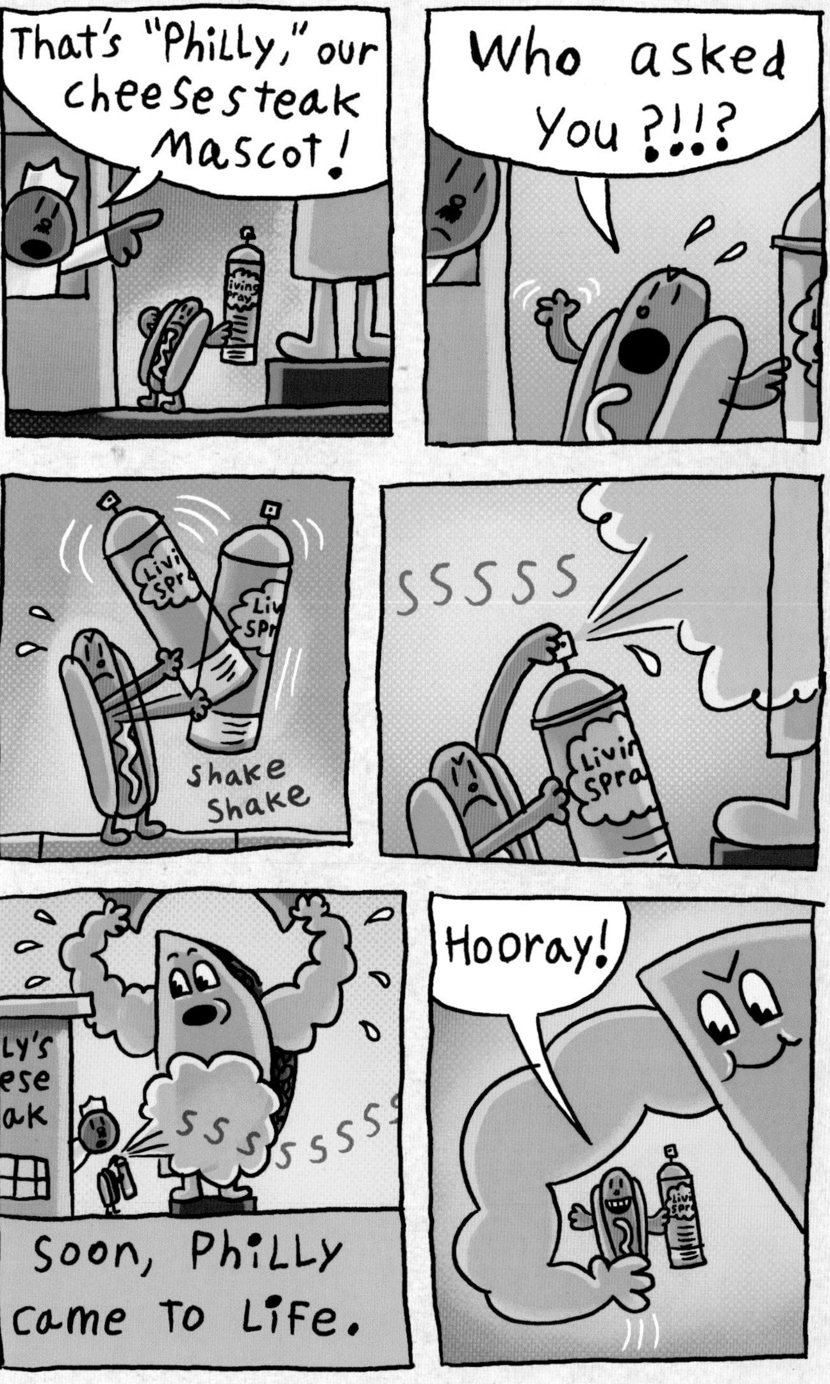
That's "Philly," our cheesesteak mascot!
Who asked you?!!?
shake shake
SSSSS
Soon, Philly came to life.
Hooray!

DOG MAN TRIED TO STOP THE CRUSHING POINTY THINGIES...

...but his human strength was giving out.

Oh, the caninity!!!!

HOW could things get any worse?

chief

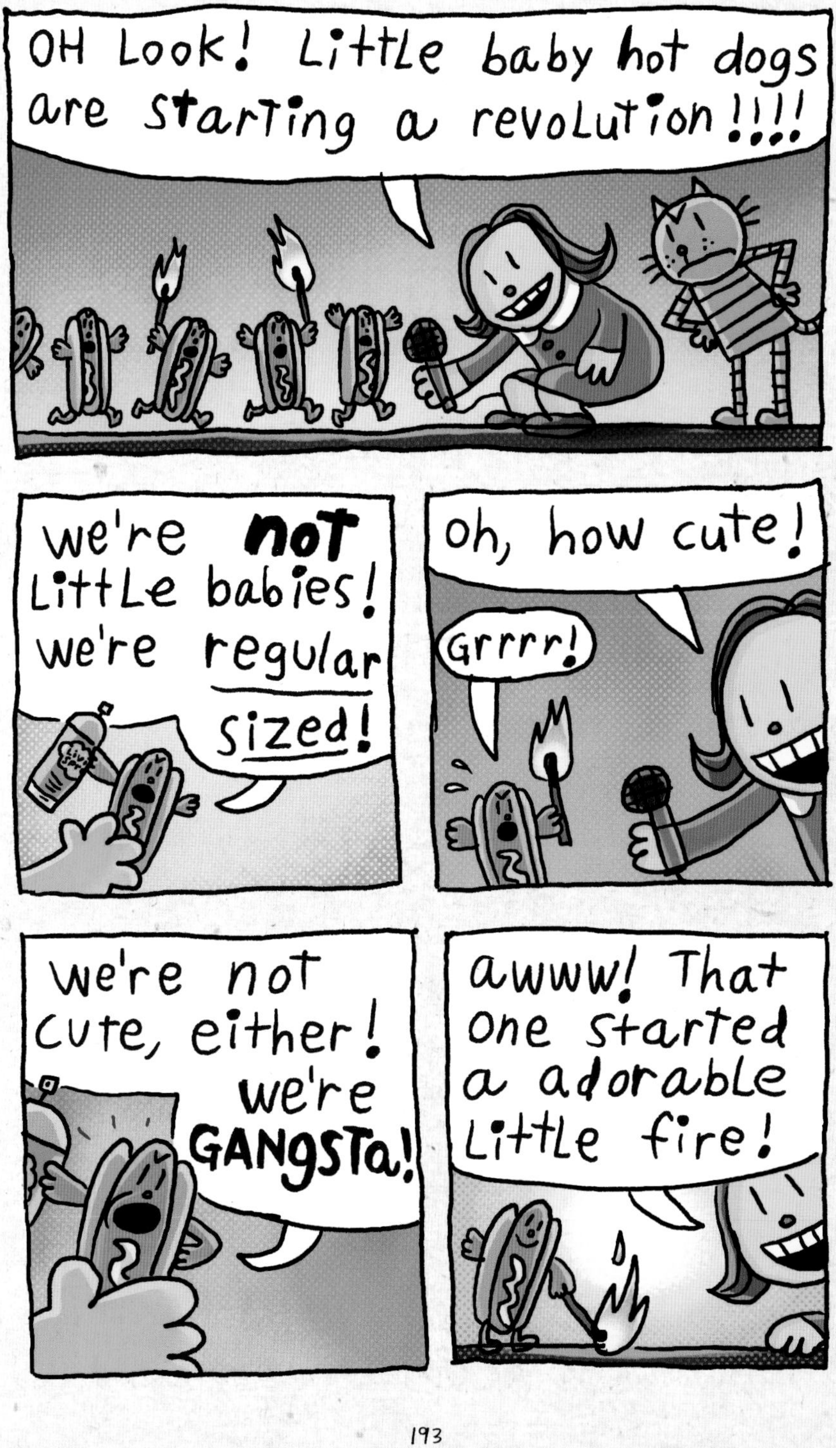
OH Look! Little baby hot dogs are starting a revolution!!!!
we're not little babies! we're regular sized!
oh, how cute!
Grrrr!
we're not cute, either! we're GANGSTA!
awww! That one started a adorable little fire!

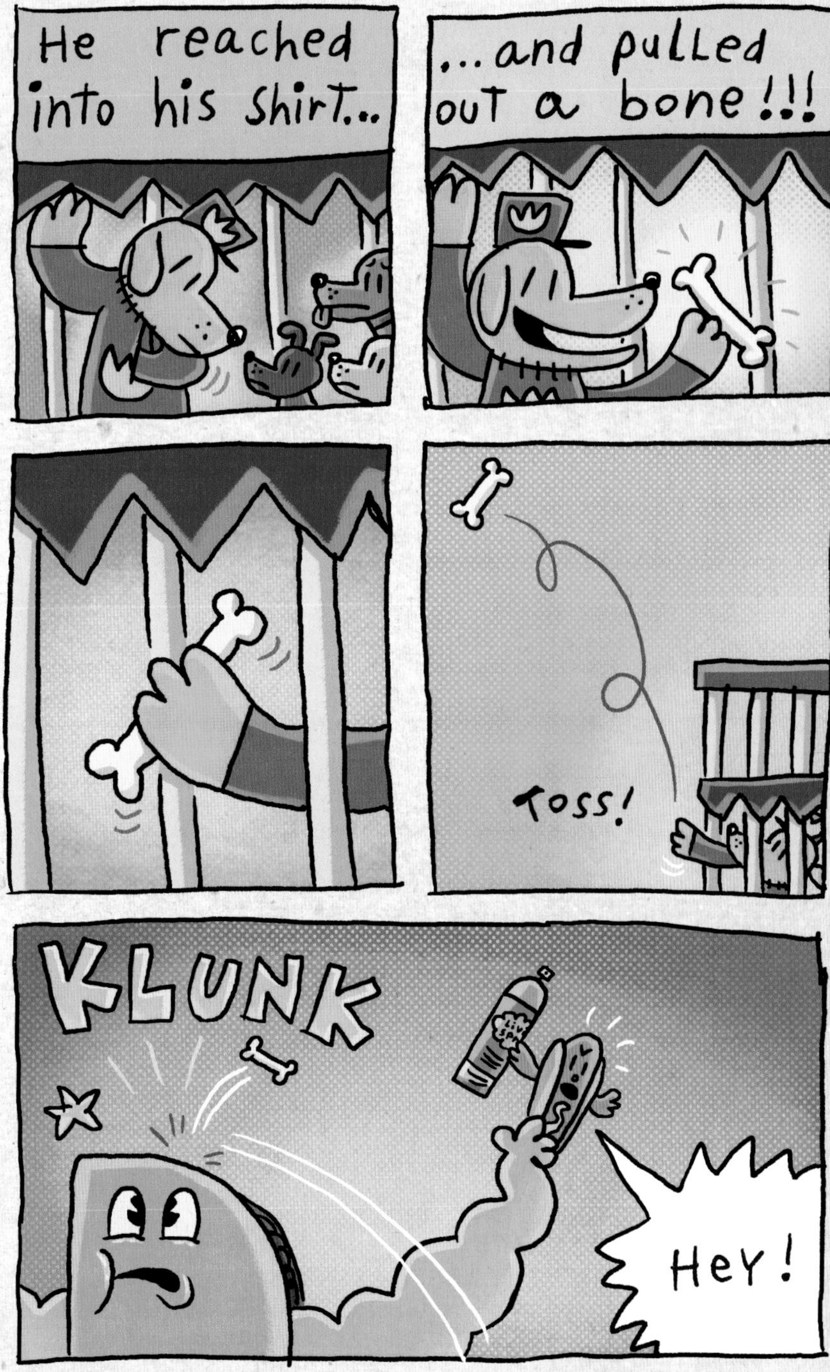
He reached into his shirt...
...and pulled out a bone!!!
TOSS!
KLUNK
HEY!

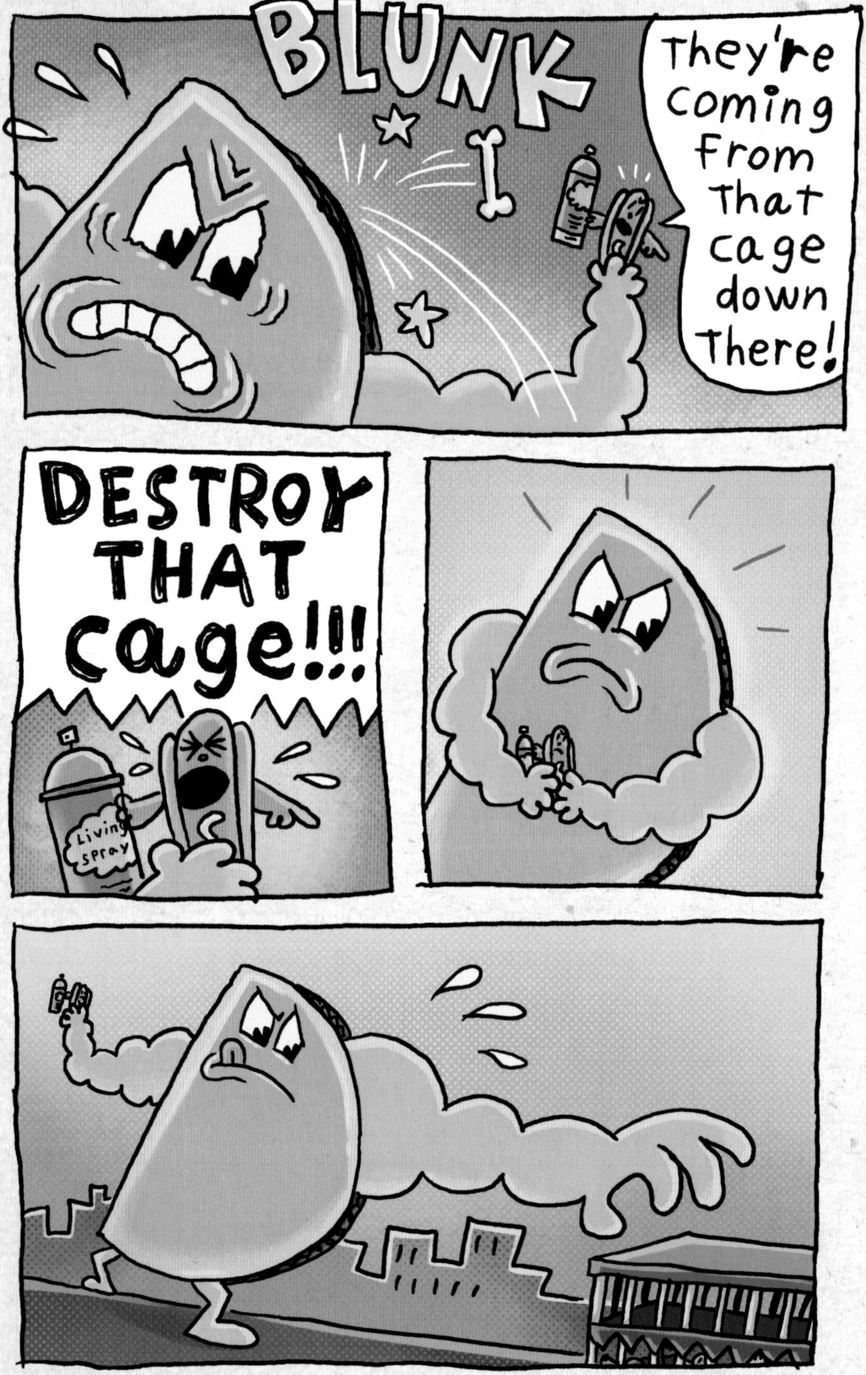
BLUNK
They're coming from That cage down There!
DESTROY THAT cage!!!
Living spray

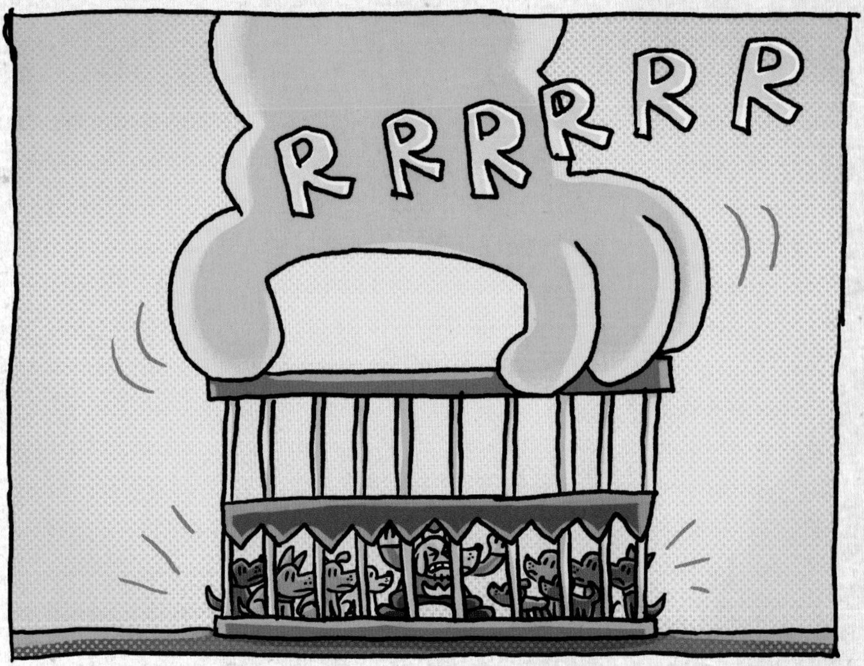
RRRRRRR

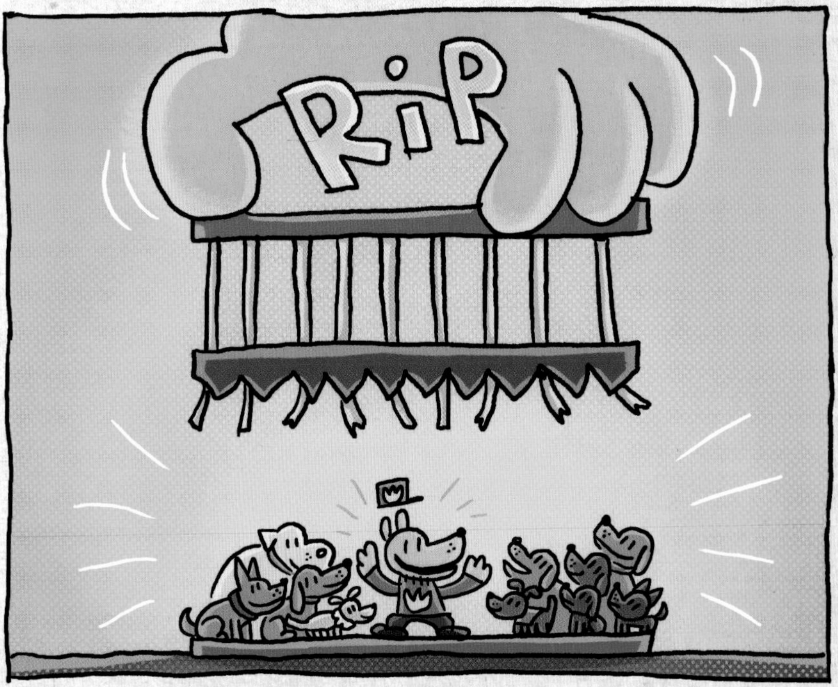
RIP

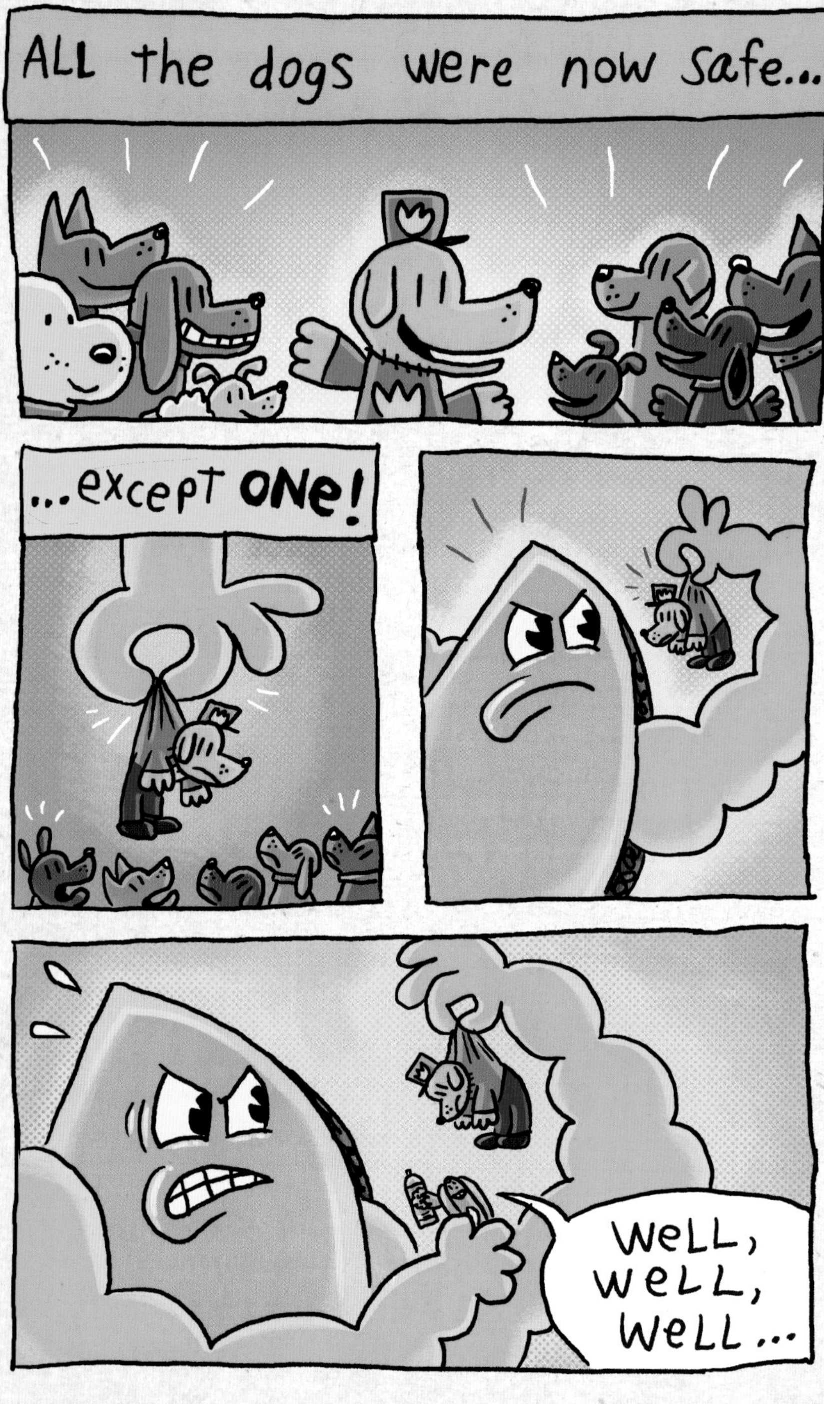
ALL the dogs were now safe...
...except ONE!
Well,
well,
well...

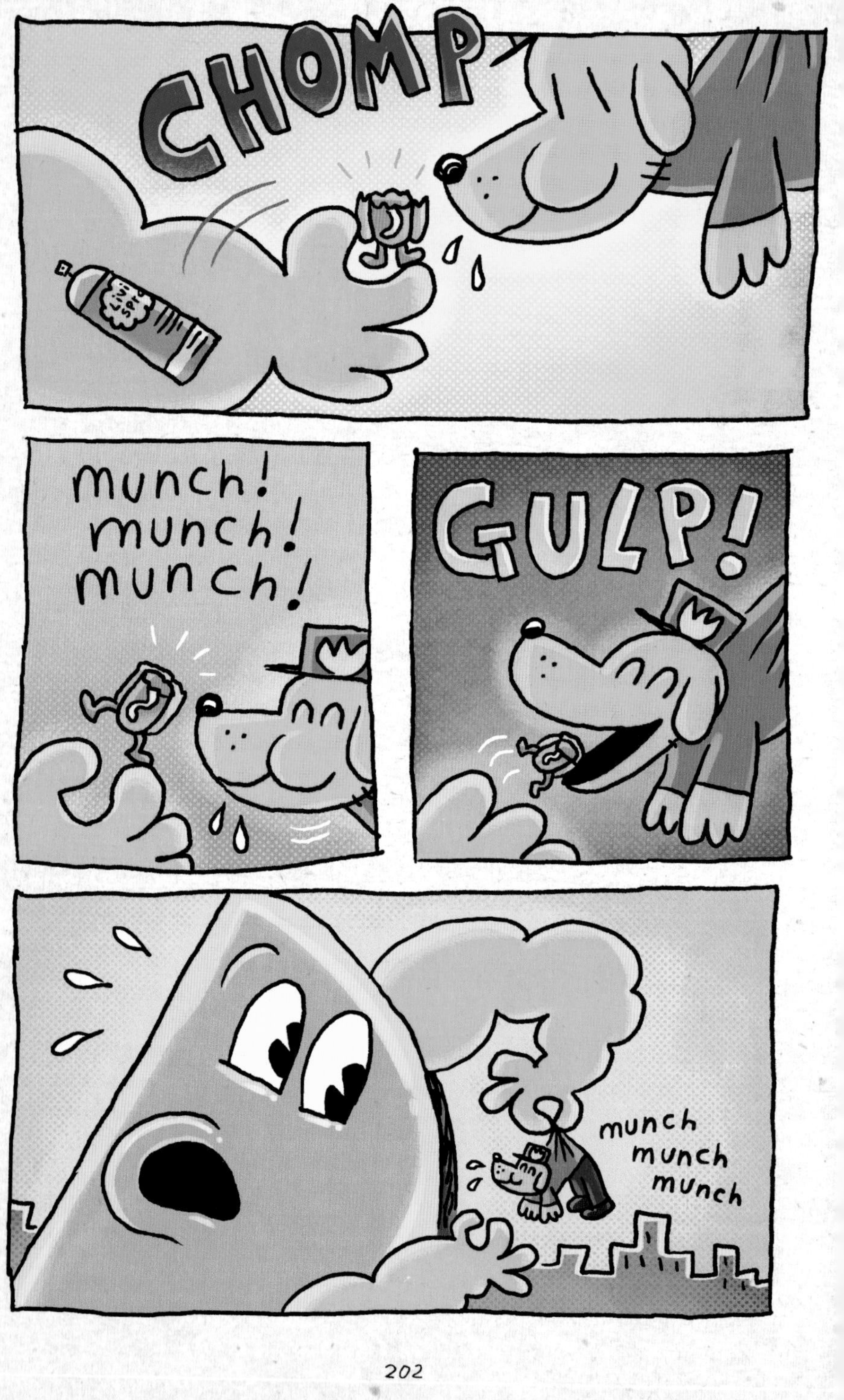
CHOMP
munch! munch! munch!
GULP!
munch munch munch

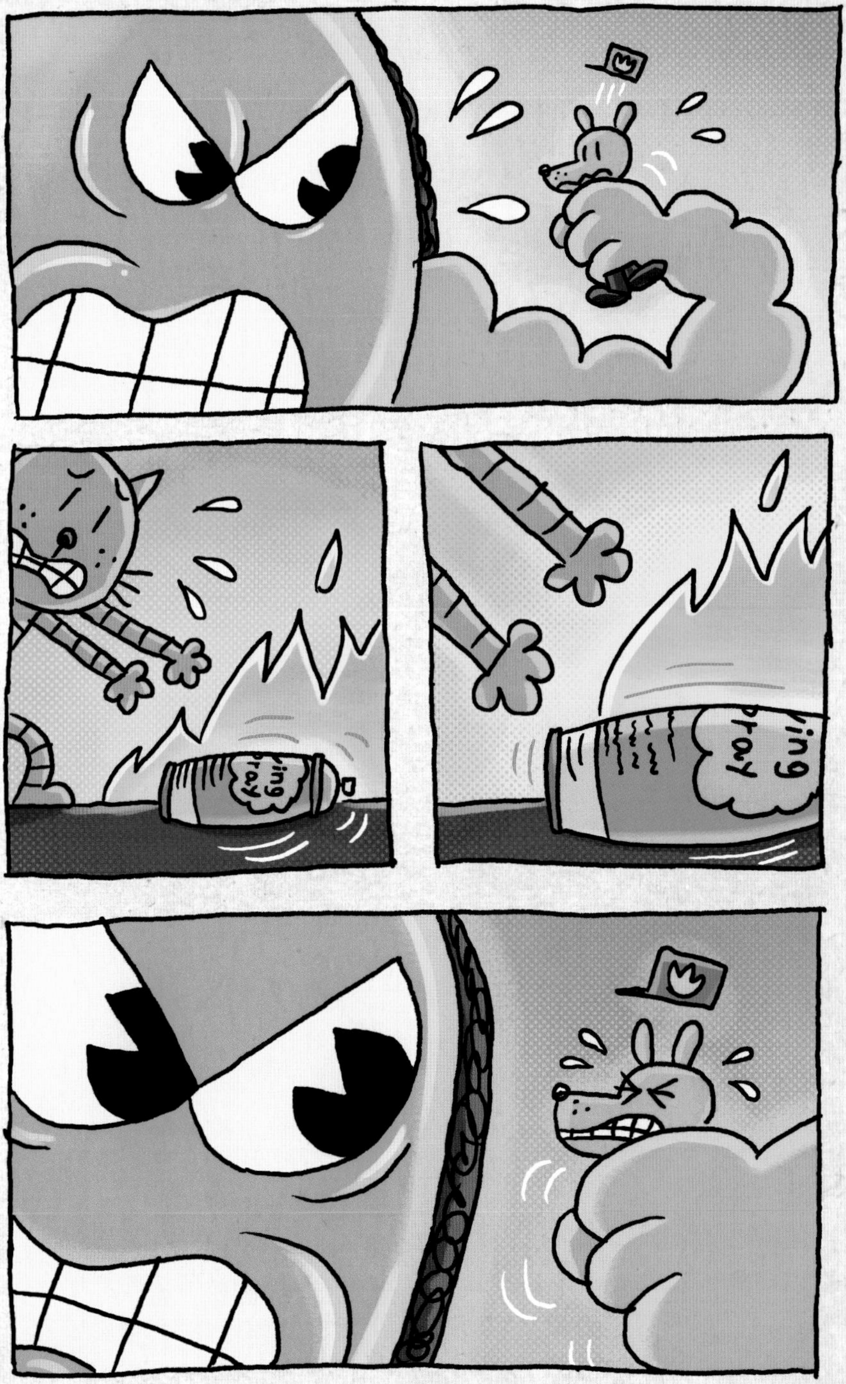

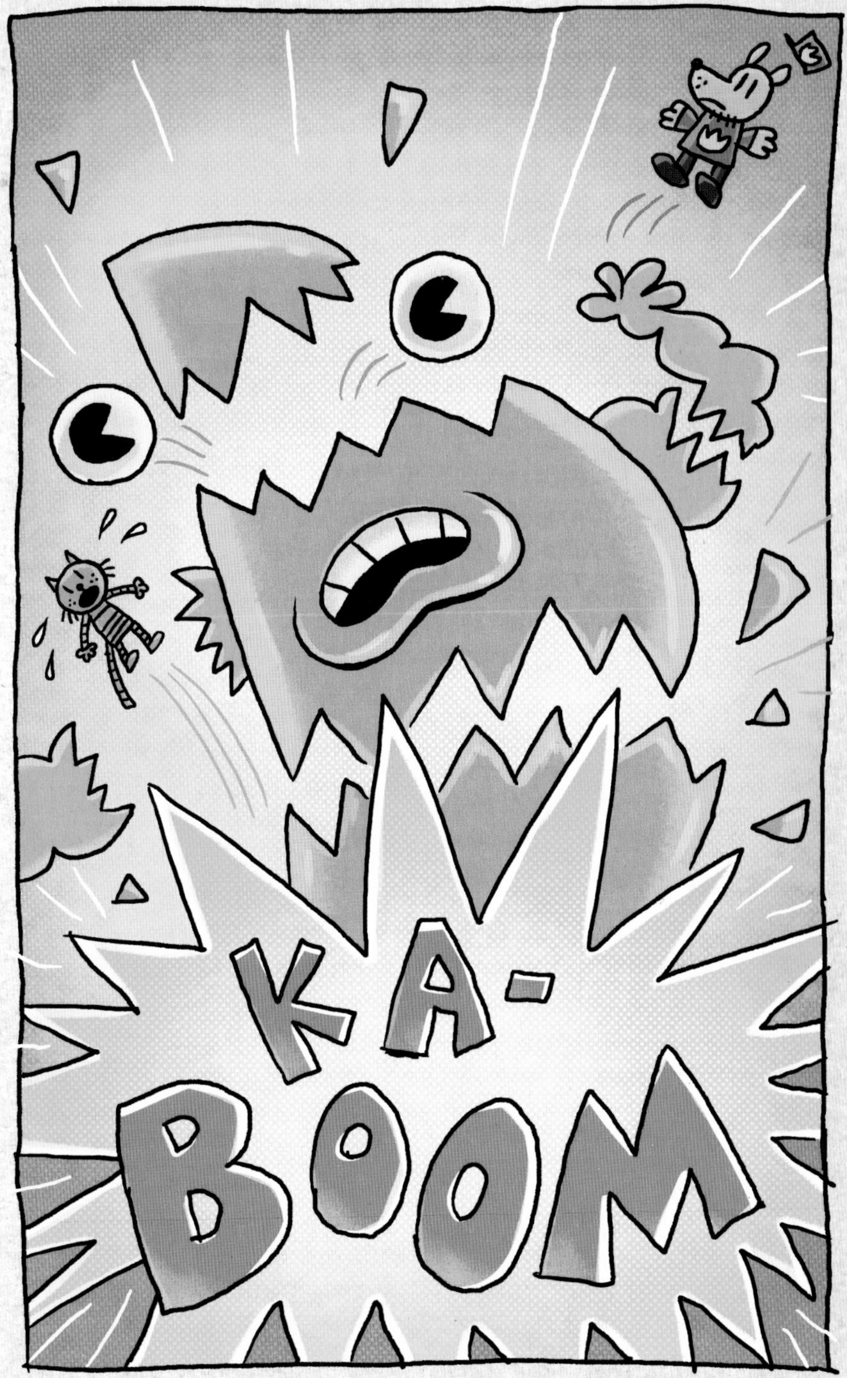
KA-BOOM

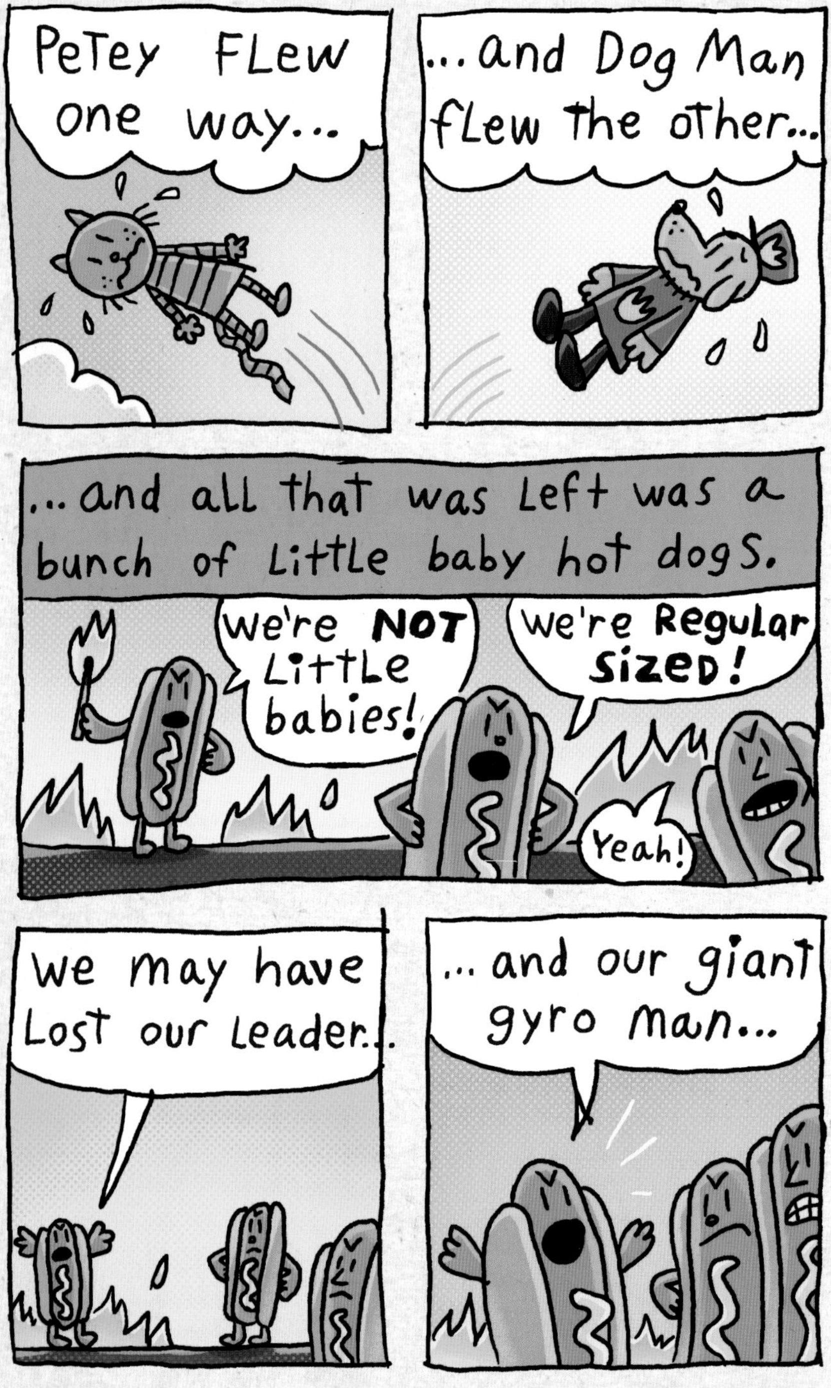
Petey flew one way...
...and Dog Man flew the other...
...and all that was left was a bunch of little baby hot dogs.
We're NOT little babies!
We're Regular SIZED!
Yeah!
We may have lost our leader...
...and our giant gyro man...

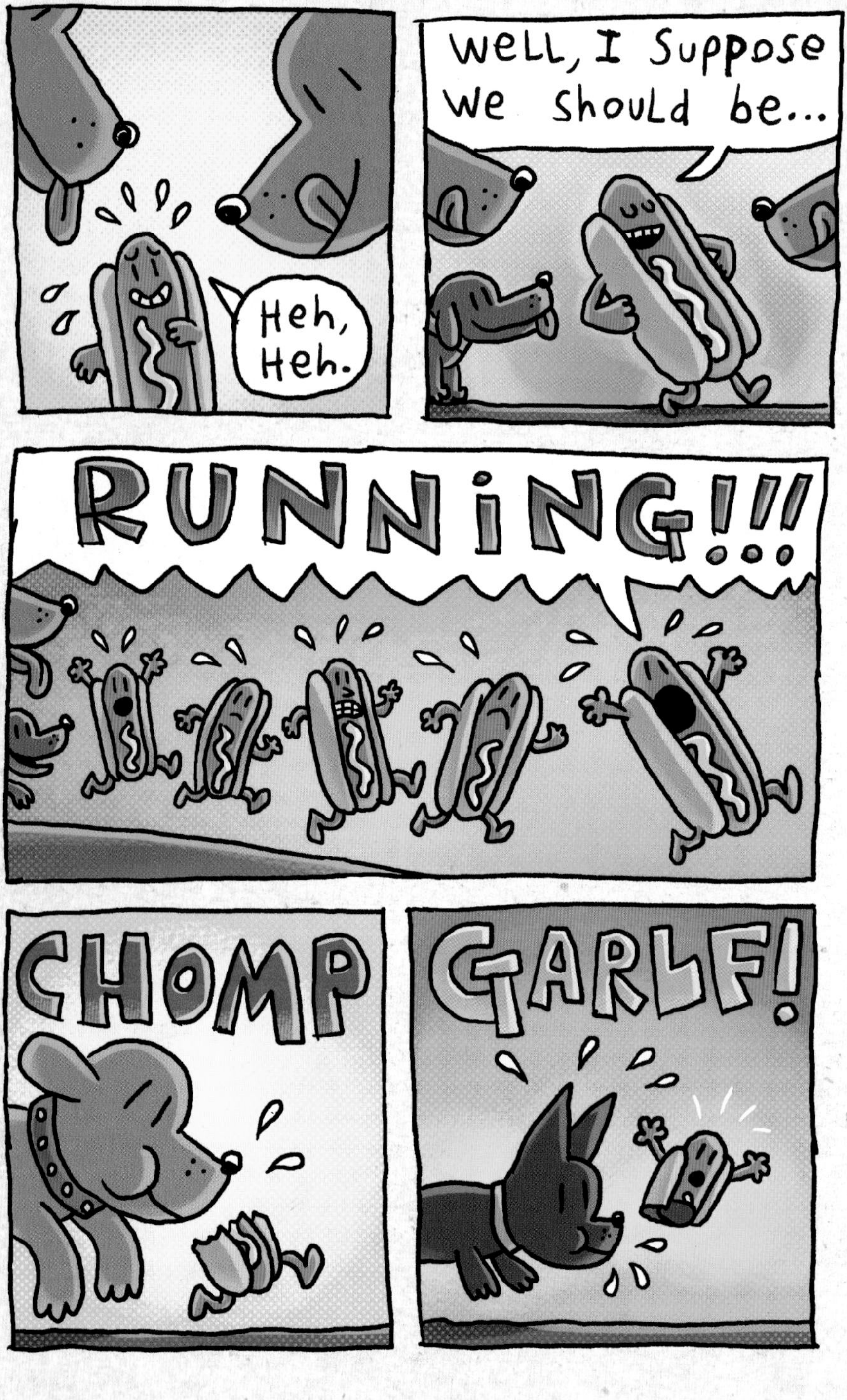
Heh, Heh.
WELL, I Suppose we should be...
RUNNING!!!
CHOMP
GARLF!

Looks like it's a DOG-EAT-HOT-DOG world after all!

BUT whatever happened to DOG Man and Petey?

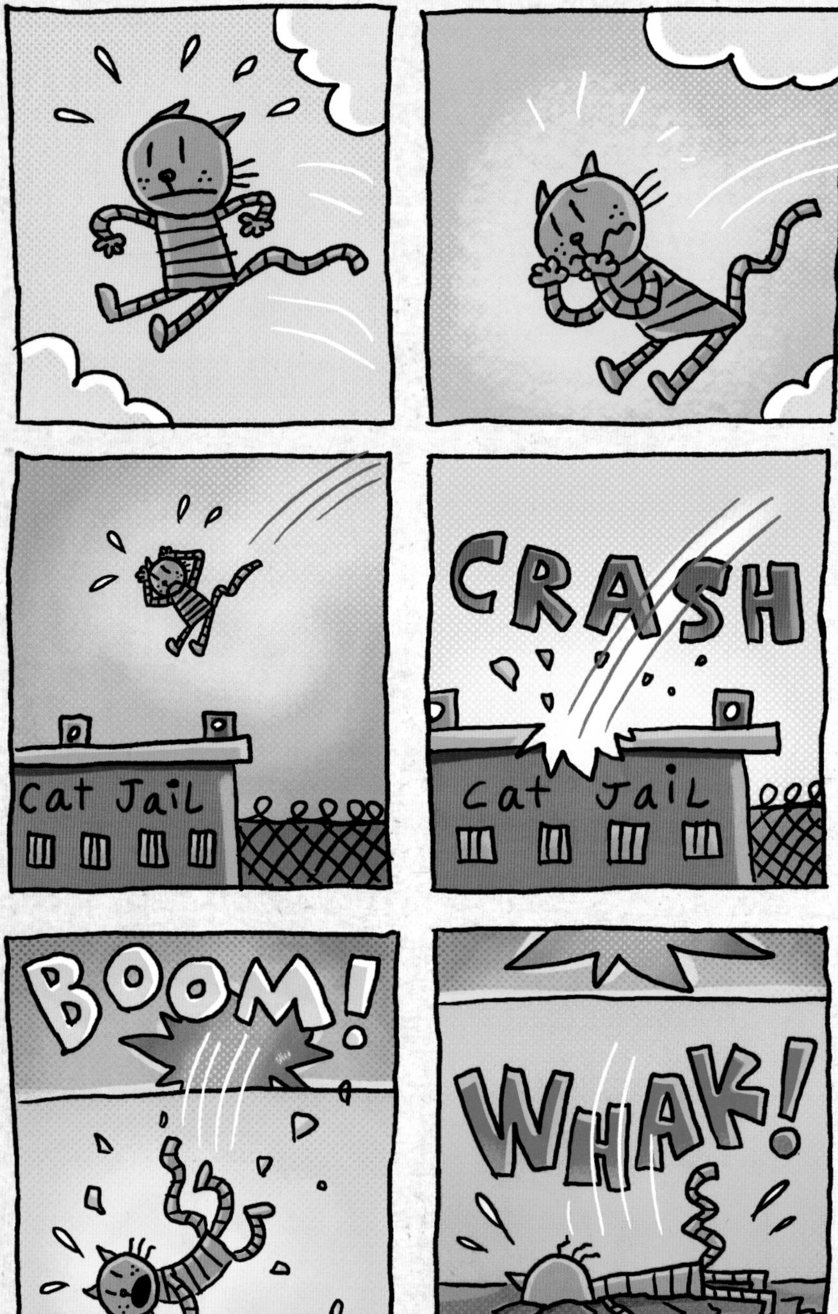
Cat Jail
CRASH
Cat Jail
BOOM!
WHAK!

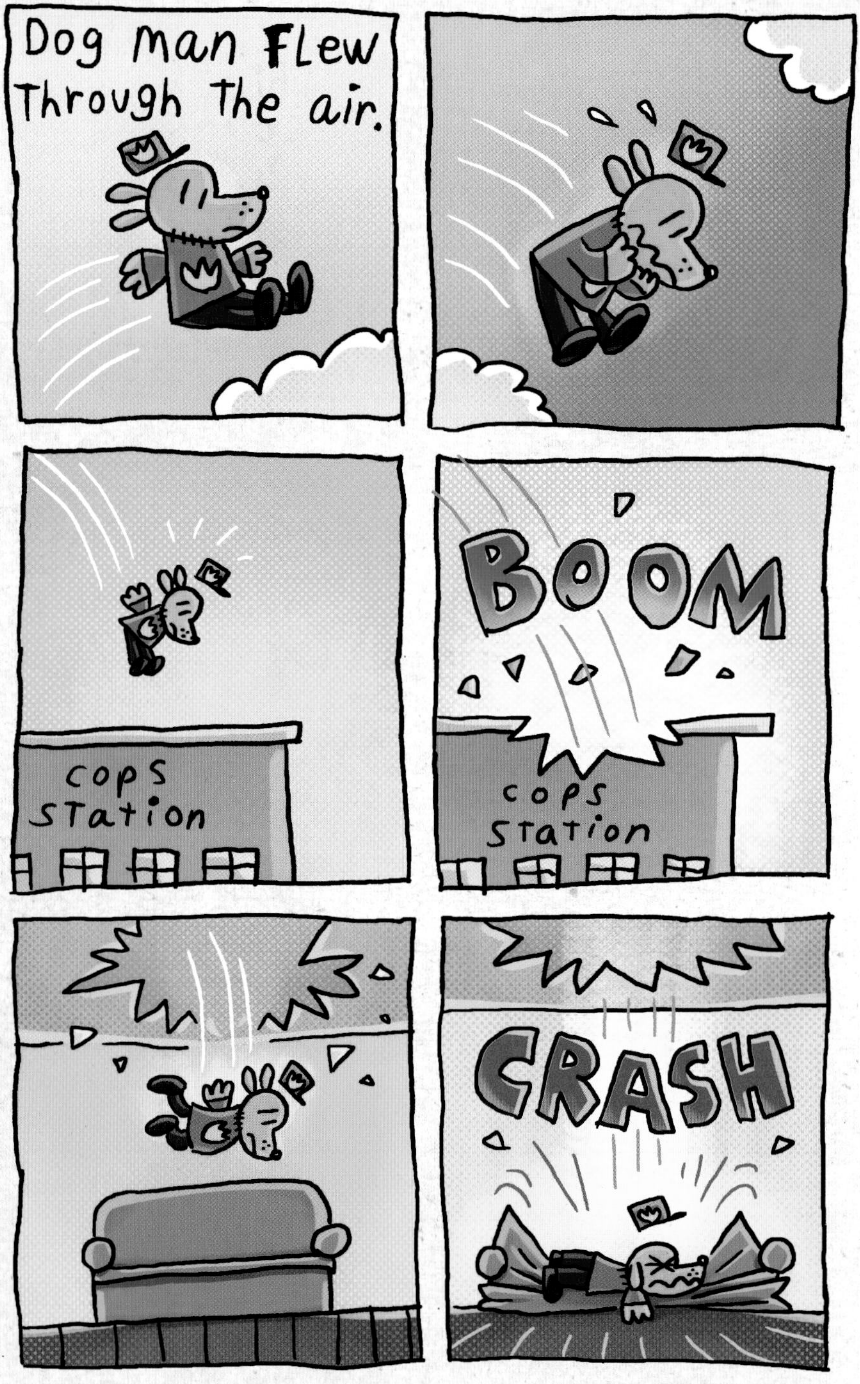
Dog Man Flew Through the air.
cops station
BOOM
cops station
CRASH

Hip!

Hip!

Hooray!!!

Right
Thumb
here.

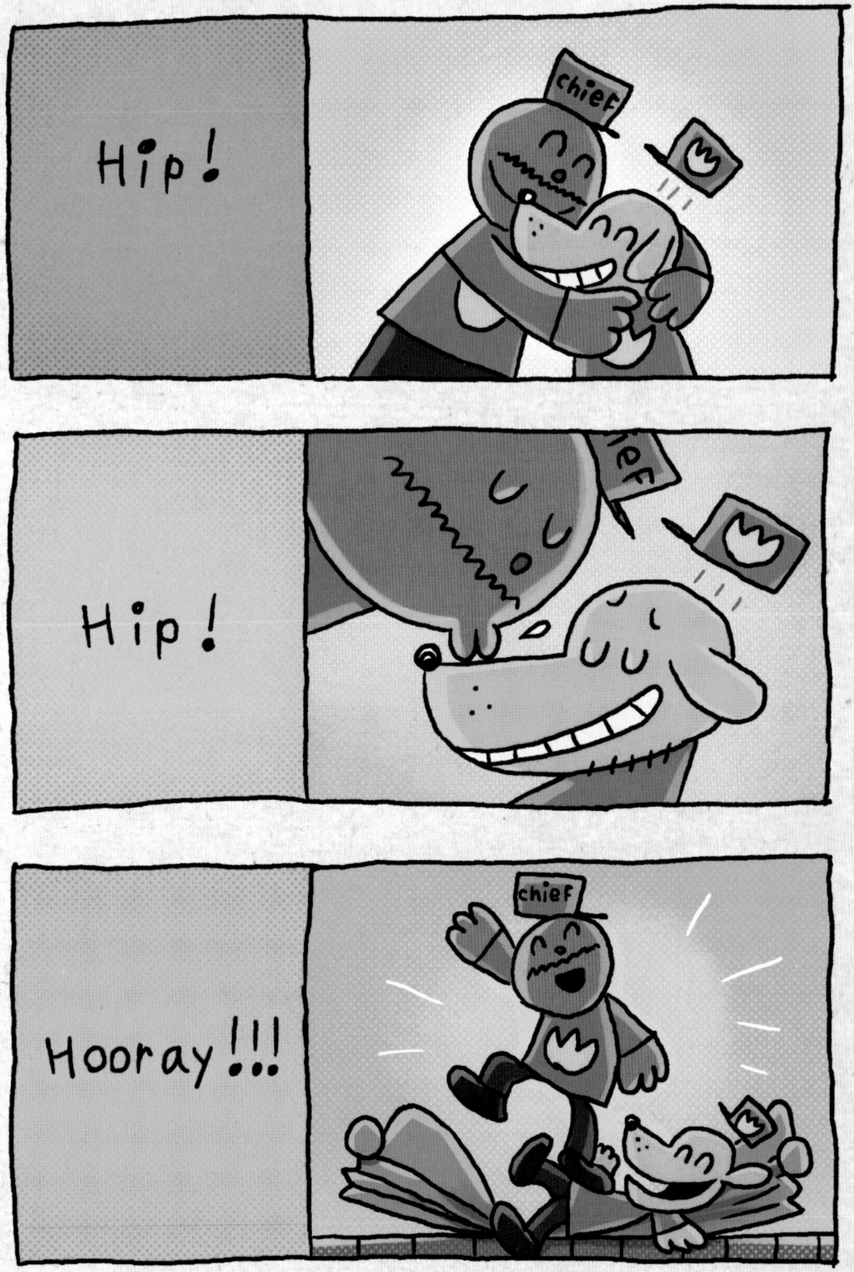
Hip!
chief
Hip!
Hooray!!!
chief

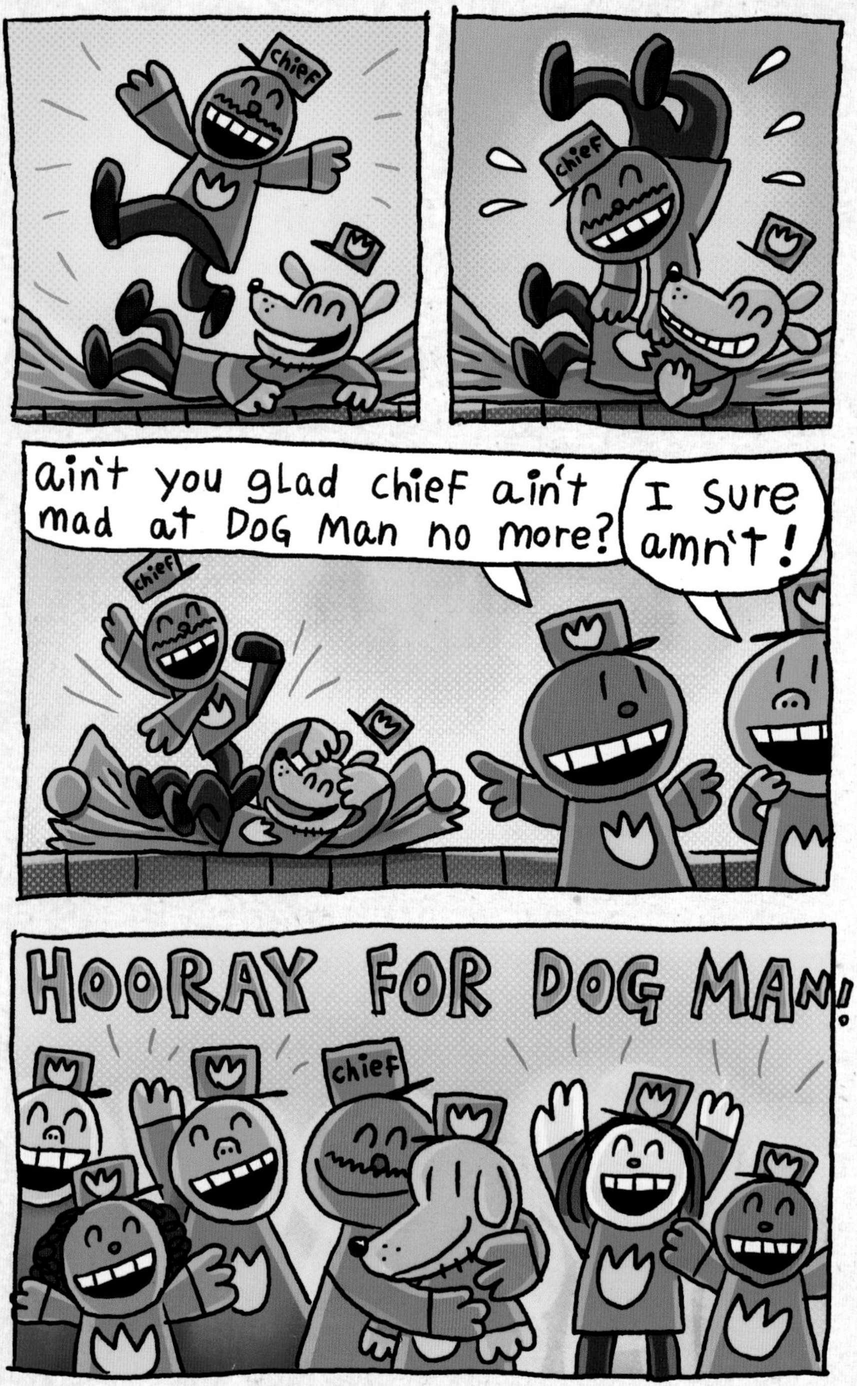
ain't you glad chief ain't mad at DOG MAN no more?
I sure amn't!
HOORAY FOR DOG MAN!

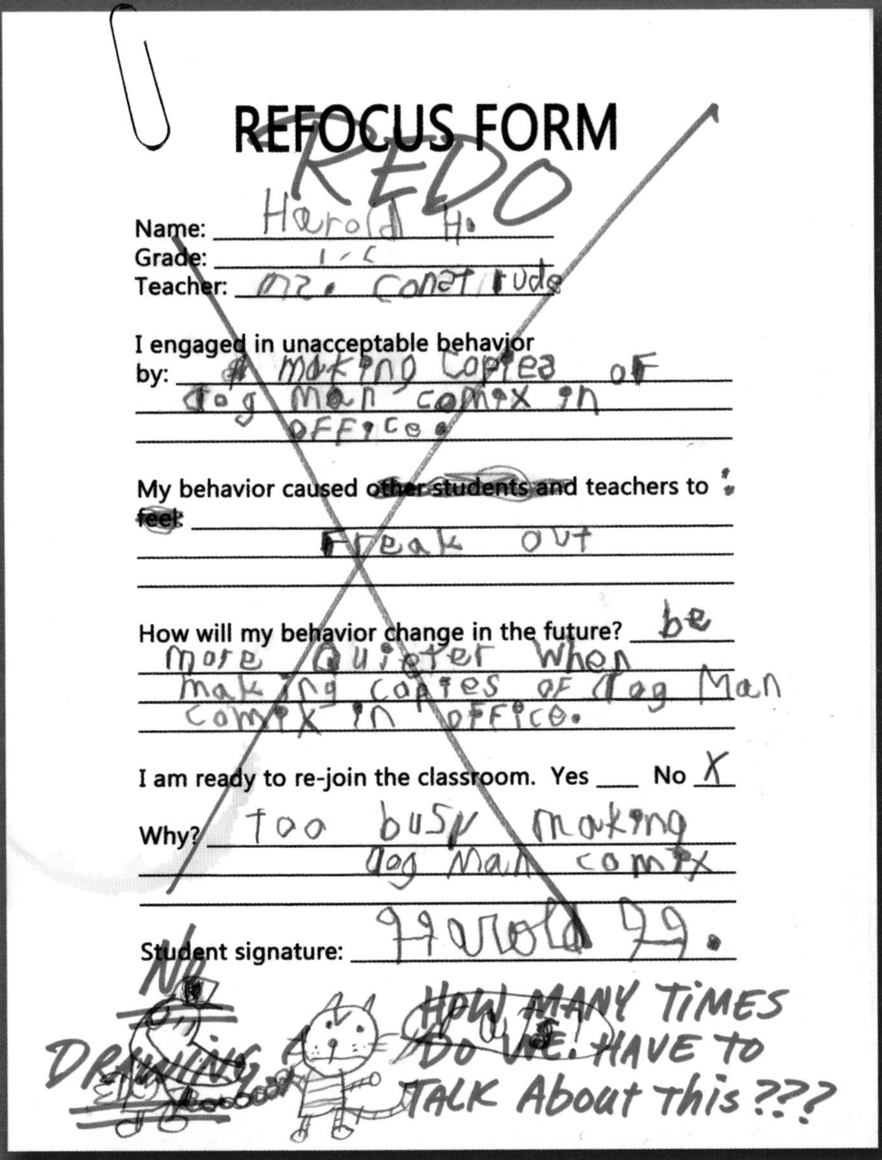

REFOCUS FORM

REDO

Name: Harold H.

Grade: 1st

Teacher: Ms. Construde

I engaged in unacceptable behavior by: making copies of dog man comix in office.

My behavior caused ~~other students and~~ teachers to: ~~feel:~~ Freak out

How will my behavior change in the future? be more quieter when making copies of dog man comix in office.

I am ready to re-join the classroom. Yes ___ No X

Why? too busy making dog man comix

Student signature: Harold H.

NO DRAWING

HOW MANY TIMES DO WE HAVE TO TALK ABOUT THIS???

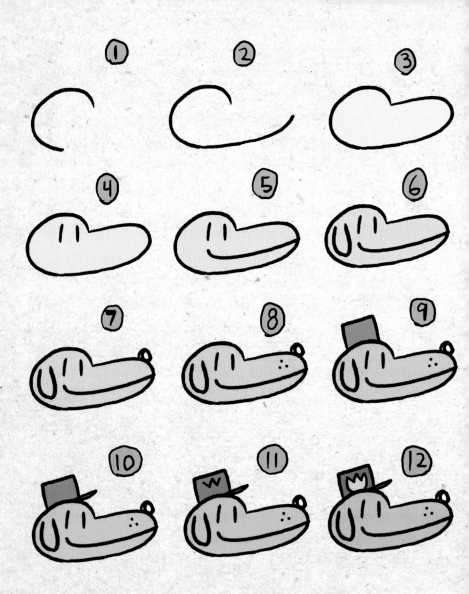

BE EXPRESSive!!!

Happy   Happier   Supa Happy

Worried   Sad   Determined

ascared   Angry   sleepy

HOW 2 DRAW

2

PETEY

in 24 Ridiculously easy steps.

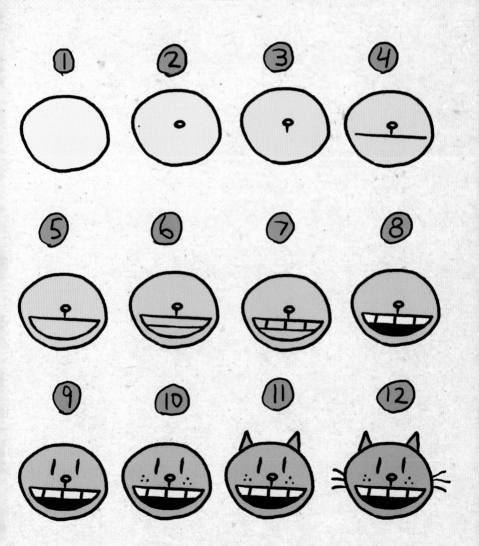

BE EXPRESSIVE

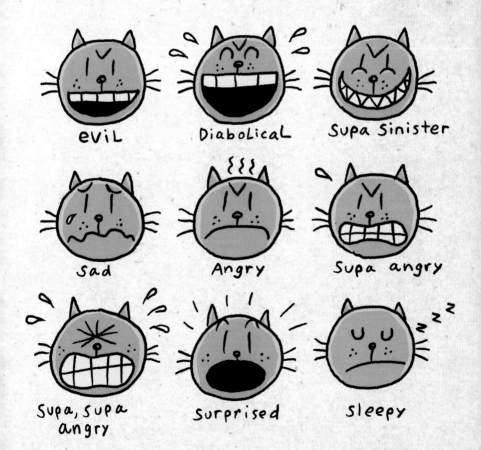

evil

Diabolical

Supa Sinister

Sad

Angry

Supa angry

Supa, Supa angry

Surprised

Sleepy

HOW 2 DRAW PHiLLY

iN 24 RidicuLousLy easy STeps!

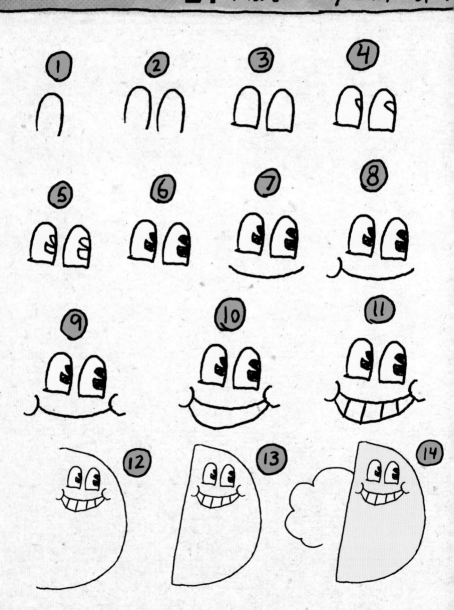

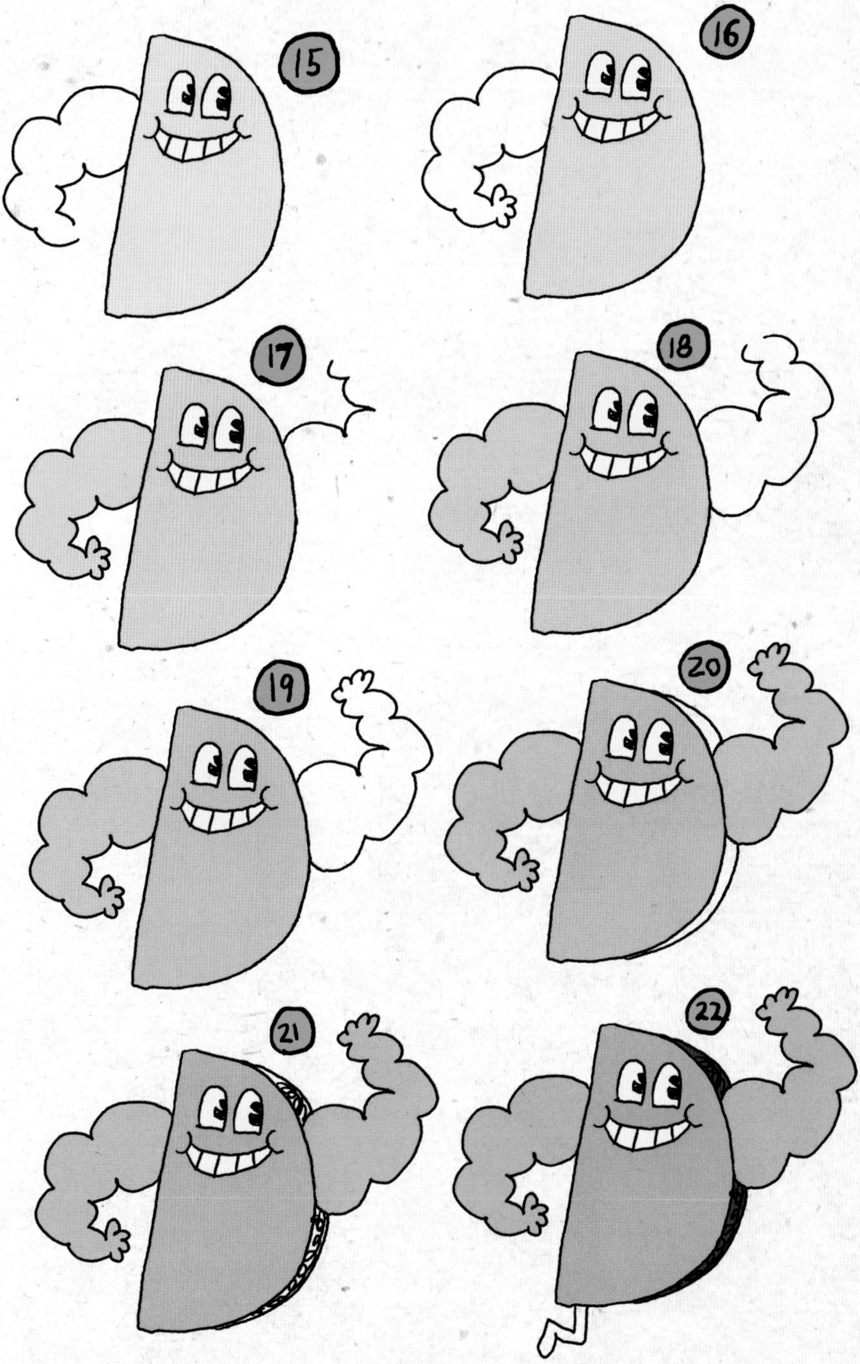
15
16
17
18
19
20
21
22

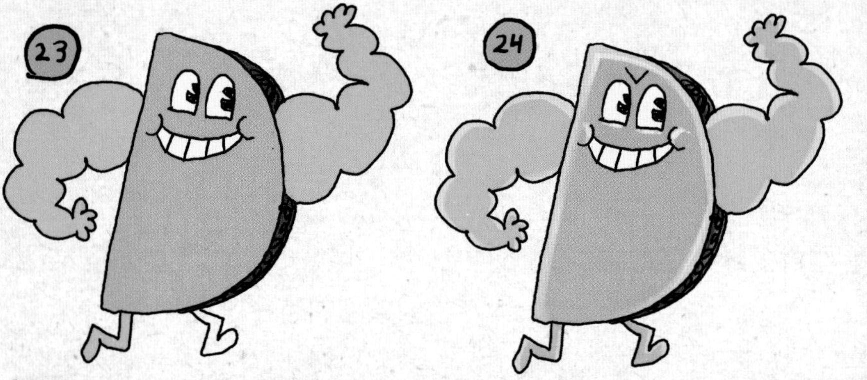
23
24

BE EXPRESSIVE!!!

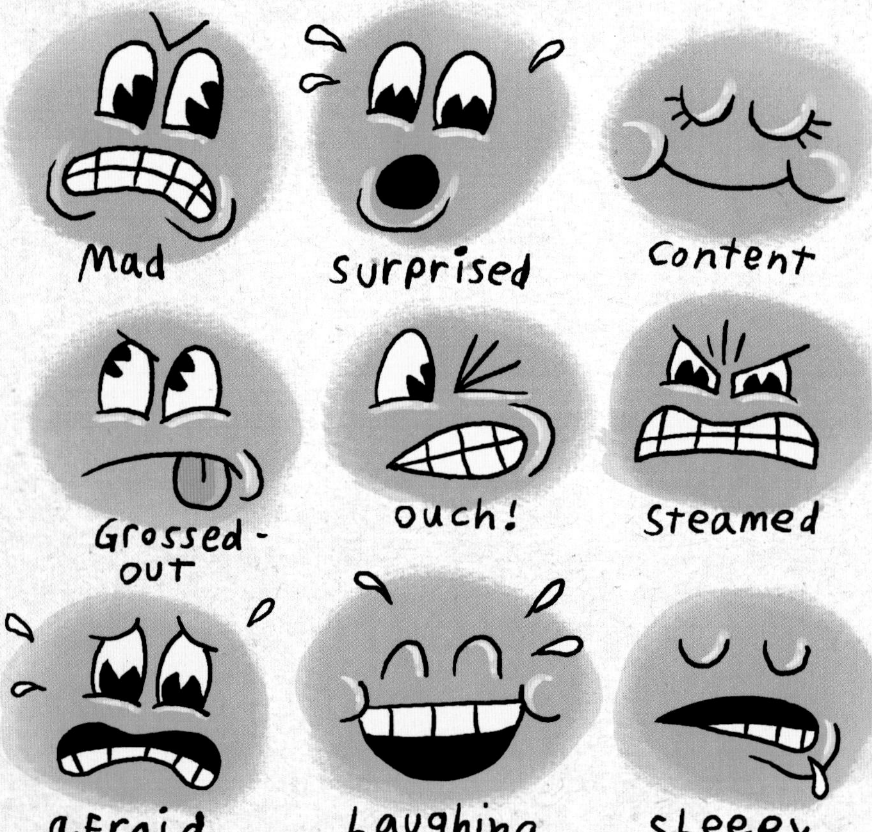
Mad
surprised
content
Grossed-out
ouch!
steamed
afraid
Laughing
sLeepy

HOW 2 DRAW INVISIBLE PETEY
in 8 easy steps.

① ② ③ ④

⑤ ⑥ ⑦ ⑧

BE EXPRESSIVE!!!

Happy   angry   sad   oBsequious

231

ABOUT THE
AUTHOR-ILLUSTRATOR

When Dav Pilkey was a kid, he was diagnosed with ADHD and dyslexia. Dav was so disruptive in class that his teachers made him sit out in the hallway every day. Luckily, Dav loved to draw and make up stories. He spent his time in the hallway creating his own original comic books — the very first adventures of Dog Man and Captain Underpants.

In college, Dav met a teacher who encouraged him to illustrate and write. He won a national competition in 1986 and the prize was the publication of his first book, WORLD WAR WON. He made many other books before being awarded the 1998 California Young Reader Medal for DOG BREATH, which was published in 1994, and in 1997 he won the Caldecott Honor for THE PAPERBOY.

THE ADVENTURES OF SUPER DIAPER BABY, published in 2002, was the first complete graphic novel spin-off from the Captain Underpants series and appeared at #6 on the USA Today bestseller list for all books, both adult and children's, and was also a New York Times bestseller. It was followed by THE ADVENTURES OF OOK AND GLUK: KUNG FU CAVEMEN FROM THE FUTURE and SUPER DIAPER BABY 2: THE INVASION OF THE POTTY SNATCHERS, both USA Today bestsellers. The unconventional style of these graphic novels is intended to encourage uninhibited creativity in kids.

His stories are semi-autobiographical and explore universal themes that celebrate friendship, tolerance, and the triumph of the good-hearted.

Dav loves to kayak in the Pacific Northwest with his wife.

Learn more at Pilkey.com.

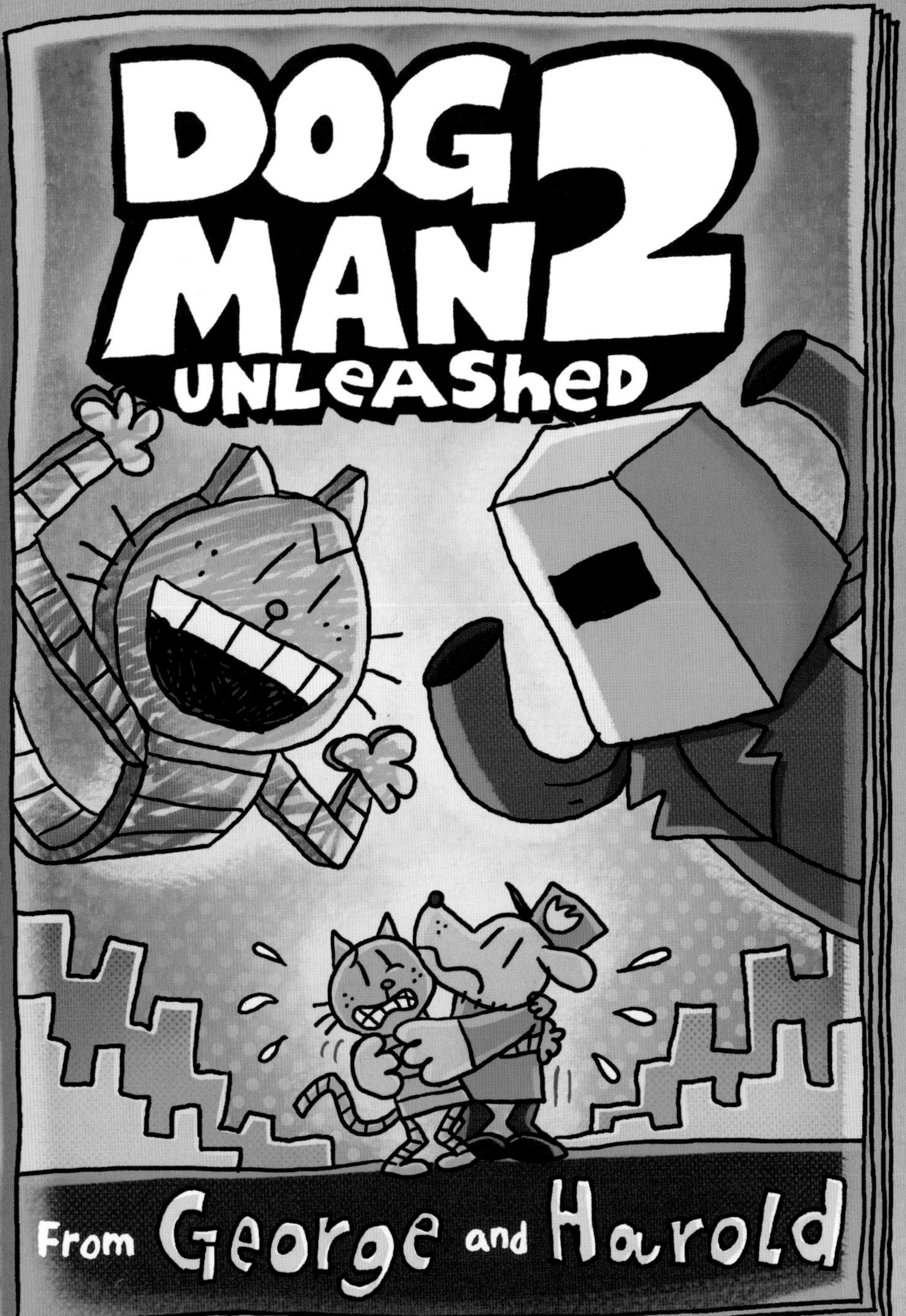
DOG MAN 2
UNLEASHED
From George and Harold

CALLING ALL CARS!

A Brand-New DOG Man noveL is COMING SOON!

In a Time of darkness and despair...

when strange new viLLains arise...

...and sinister scoundrels poison the minds of the meek...

We Love You, Petey!

Yeah!

Hubba-Hubba!

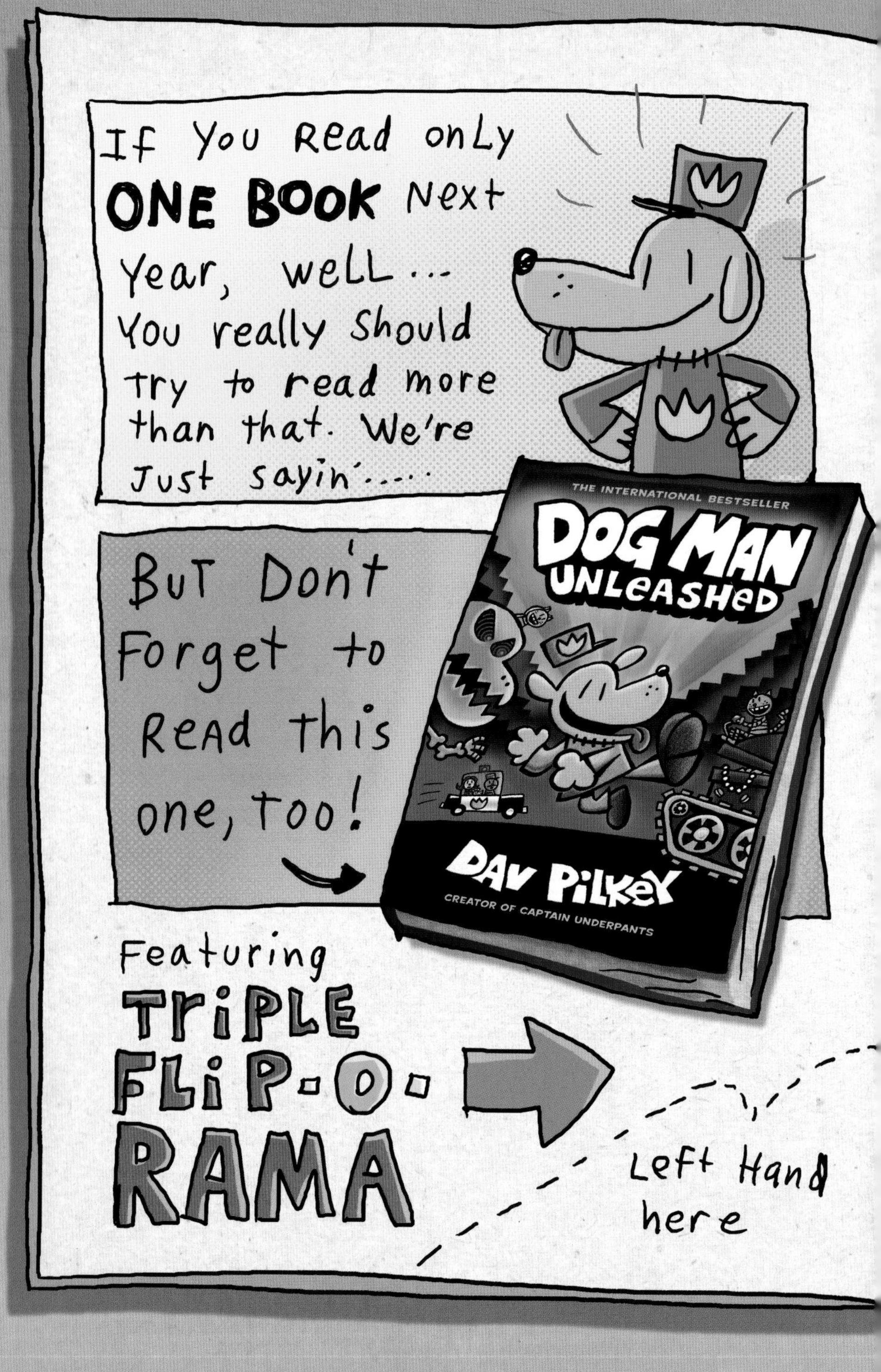
If You Read onLy ONE BOOK Next Year, weLL... You really Should try to read more than that. We're Just sayin'.....
THE INTERNATIONAL BESTSELLER
DOG MAN UNLEASHED
DAV PILKEY
CREATOR OF CAPTAIN UNDERPANTS
But Don't Forget to Read this one, too!
Featuring TRIPLE FLIP-O-RAMA
Left Hand here

You'll HOWL with Laughter.

You'll scratch with suspense!

You'll scoot your butt on the carpet with JOY!

Right THUMB here

You'll HOWL with Laughter.

OOOOO! OOOOO!

You'll Scratch with Suspense!

You'll Scoot your butt on the carpet with JOY!

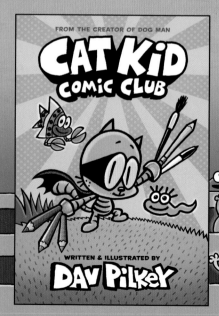